A
FLICKERING
LIGHT

A NOVEL

JANE
KIRKPATRICK

DOUBLEDAY LARGE PRINT HOME LIBRARY EDITION

WATERBROOK
PRESS

This Large Print Edition, prepared especially for Doubleday Large Print Home Library, contains the complete, unabridged text of the original Publisher's Edition.

A FLICKERING LIGHT
PUBLISHED BY WATERBROOK PRESS
12265 Oracle Boulevard, Suite 200
Colorado Springs, Colorado 80921

Scripture quotations or paraphrases are taken from the following versions: King James Version and the Holy Bible, New International Version®. NIV®. Copyright © 1973, 1978, 1984 by International Bible Society. Used by permission of Zondervan Publishing House. All rights reserved.

This book is a work of historical fiction based closely on real people and real events. Details that cannot be historically verified are purely products of the author's imagination.

Copyright © 2009 by Jane Kirkpatrick

All rights reserved. No part of this book may be reproduced or transmitted in any form or by any means, electronic or mechanical, including photocopying and recording, or by any information storage and retrieval system, without permission in writing from the publisher.

Published in the United States by WaterBrook Multnomah, an imprint of The Doubleday Publishing Group, a division of Random House Inc., New York.

WATERBROOK and its deer colophon are registered trademarks of Random House Inc.

ISBN 978-1-60751-849-5

Printed in the United States of America

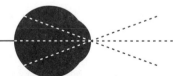

This Large Print Book carries the
Seal of Approval of N.A.V.H.

To the descendants of Jessie Ann.

CAST OF CHARACTERS

Jessie Ann Gaebele — a photographer's apprentice

Lillian Ida Gaebele — a seamstress and older sister to Jessie

Selma Selena Gaebele — a singer and younger sister to Jessie

Roy William Gaebele — a budding musician and younger brother to Jessie, nicknamed "Frog"

William and Ida Gaebele — parents of Jessie and owners of a drayage in Winona, Minnesota

August Schoepp	Ida Gaebele's younger brother
*Voe Kopp	friend of Jessie's
*Jerome Kopp	Voe's brother
Frederick John "FJ" Bauer	owner of Bauer Studio
Jessie Otis Bauer	wife of FJ and professional photo retoucher
Russell, Donald (deceased), Winifred, and Robert	children of FJ and Jessie Bauer
Mrs. Otis and Eva	Jessie Bauer's mother and sister
Luise	FJ's younger sister
*Daniel Henderson	friend of Voe

Herman Reinke	FJ's North Dakota ranch partner
Nic Steffes	owner of Winona Cycle Livery and Dealer
Lottie Fort	milliner in Winona
Ralph Carleton	a Winona evangelist
Mayo brothers	physicians in Rochester, Minnesota
Miss Jones	a speech and language specialist
Mrs. Johnson	owner of a photographic studio in Milwaukee, Wisconsin
Henry and Mary Harms	Harms family

Marie Harms	Milwaukee host for Jessie Gaebele

* Characters identified with asterisks are created from the author's imagination. The female photographers identified in the text are actual historical figures.

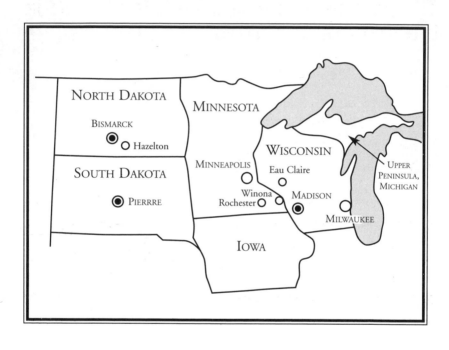

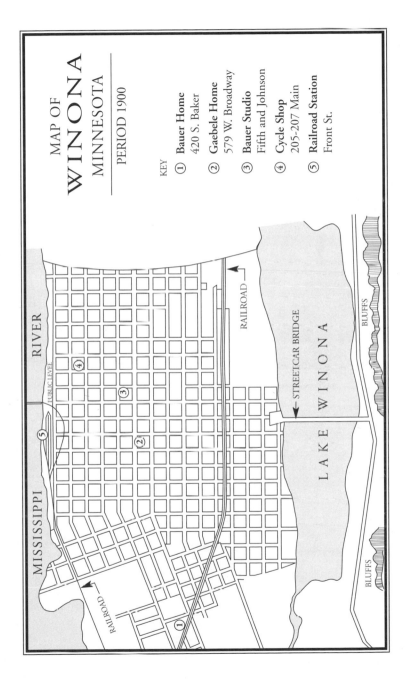

MAP OF
WINONA
MINNESOTA

PERIOD 1900

KEY

① **Bauer Home**
420 S. Baker

② **Gaebele Home**
579 W. Broadway

③ **Bauer Studio**
Fifth and Johnson

④ **Cycle Shop**
205-207 Main

⑤ **Railroad Station**
Front St.

MISSISSIPPI   RIVER

PUBLIC LEVEL

RAILROAD

RAILROAD

STREETCAR BRIDGE

LAKE WINONA

BLUFFS

BLUFFS

BLUFFS

BLUFFS

Faith, hope and love are the three eternities.
To look up and not down, that is Faith;
to look forward and not back, that is Hope;
and then to look out and not in, that is Love.

—REVEREND EDWARD EVERETT HALE, *Woman's
Home Companion,* July 1907

The Truth must dazzle gradually
Or every man be blind—

—EMILY DICKINSON,
"Tell all the Truth but tell it slant"

Then you will know the truth,
and the truth will set you free.

—JOHN 8:32, NIV

Love . . . consists in . . . that two solitudes
protect and border and salute each other.

—RAINER MARIA RILKE,
Letters to a Young Poet

Subjects

In my favorite portrait of myself, I am wearing an opaque eyelet dress, layered, with the scalloped edges of the hemline barely whispering across the studio floor. The dress could have been worn for a christening, though its lavish detail would have stolen something from an event where the child ought to be the focus. The child, wearing a long, flowing white dress that could be handed down to brother and sister for each successive important day, that's what matters at a christening. The child is what people should gaze upon at such an event, not a mother or aunt or friend wearing a too-elegant eyelet dress.

It could be a wedding dress, but of course, it wasn't.

I find so few photographs of myself that I wish to share with others, but in this one I appear taller than my five feet two inches, as I've chosen a hat with ostrich plumes swept up in the back and high over my head. The plumes shade my eyes with dried berries that flow out onto the hat's white brim in a cornucopia of fruit. My hair, the color of oiled leather, is coiled up beneath the brim. (My little brother, Roy, says I have hair the color of the cow pies dotting the pasture on our grandparents' farm, but that's the nature of little brothers born in the new century, or at least was Roy's creative nature before the . . . event.) The milliner did splendid work, and the white of the felted hat brim brings the eye to the dress, which is what I wanted. The beauty of the dress is the real subject of the photograph.

My mother called it my "kept-woman dress." It was no such thing, and it pained me to hear her say it. In time I came to know full well that I'd received favor, undeserved and accepted unwisely. But there are always misunderstandings in families, always sacrifices worthy of making too, no matter how strained they may seem at the time.

I'd seen the dress in Choate's window as I walked bundled up against

Minnesota's blistering river winds. The dress spoke of spring and newness, something I longed for. I vowed to buy it. And so I did, saving twenty-five cents a week for six months before bringing it home one fine summer day. Of course, I'd asked the clerk to set it aside for me and put fifty cents down so they knew I was serious, that I'd keep my commitment.

In this photograph, I posed myself at the edge of a bench made to look like marble. Its molding can't be identified as something specific but suggests lush relief and gives interest to the eye, though not enough to take away from the true subject. Morning light radiates through the studio windows.

I'd painted a board white and set it just beyond the arc of the exposure so that the morning rays reflected against it and poured soft beams back onto the dress, keeping the area to my right in shadow. It seemed fitting with so much of my life a chase of shadow and light. Behind me I used the scenic drop of dark woods reflecting against a full moon shining. My face seems almost backlit by that sphere, a feature I hadn't anticipated. It fascinates me that I can set up a subject, think I have everything perfectly arranged, and then only afterward see things I had not noticed, little things, like spots of light that highlight the tips of my size-three black high-button boots or a moon giving unexpected brightness. It seems I turn reflective after the fact, surprised by what was always there that I failed to see.

I had wanted the soft natural light to raise the detail of the eyelet dress and the overskirt and emphasize the hours of work that must have gone into making it, to shade gently on my shoulders and maybe, just maybe, to bring into focus—something one might notice after prolonged viewing—the rings I'm wearing, or the necklace.

I leaned slightly forward, no easy task given the whalebone corset that fit as close to me as soap to skin. I clasped my hands at my knees. At the last minute, I also decided not to look at the camera but to gaze away, toward something I couldn't quite name but knew I wanted. I did not smile. There are times to smile and times to cry and times to be serene. I see sadness in my eyes.

Voe opened the shutter, exposed the film, then closed it, using my 3A Graflex. I developed the photograph myself.

I never intended to show the image to him.

But he saw it there among the other exposures of funeral flowers and family portraits made on New Year's Day. A child had jiggled on her father's lap, so that photograph was wasted, but I hated throwing the picture out because I did appreciate the family composition. The prints lay on the table outside the developing room, some of the edges beginning to curl because I'd wanted to save costs and didn't use the more expensive paper.

He wasn't supposed to be there, recovering from his illnesses and everything else.

His mustache twitched as his long fingers moved the photographs aside, then stalled at the one of me. He lifted it, adjusted his glasses, then lowered

*the print to catch my eyes. I couldn't
tell if his smile was wistful or contained
a certain sense of pride . . . for his part
in my having produced such a precious
photograph or my part in being willing
to have myself as the subject. I didn't
ask. Instead I pulled the picture from
his fingers, careful not to touch him,
and directed his attention elsewhere.*

*I could do that and discovered nearly
too late that I often had to.*

ONE

Doing the Right Thing

Against the morning darkness, Jessie Ann Gaebele quietly lit the stubby candle. Its feeble light flickered in the mirror while she dressed. She pulled her stockings on, donned her chemise, debated about a corset, decided against it. She'd make too much noise getting it hooked. No one was likely to see her this morning anyway, and she'd be back before her mother even knew she'd left the house without it. She could move faster without a "Grecian Bend," as ladies magazines called the posture forced by the stays and bustle. She guessed some thought it an attractive look for a girl in 1907, emphasizing a small waist and a rounded derrière. Jessie claimed both but had little time for either that morning, and timing mattered if she was to succeed. If Jessie didn't catch the moment, it wouldn't be for lack of trying.

She spilled the dark linen skirt over her petticoat, letting it settle on her slender frame. She inhaled the lavender her sister Selma insisted be added when they made their own soap, something they did more often now since they'd moved to Winona, Minnesota. Selma was prone to sensuous scents; sensuous music too, her husky voice holding people hostage when she sang.

Jessie looked at her sleeping sisters. The candlelight cast shadows on the tousled hair of Selma, her younger sister, and on the nightcap that Lilly, her older sister, always wore. ("It will keep you from catching vapors in the night," Lilly claimed.) Jessie pulled on the white shirtwaist. Even in sleep they reflected who they were when awake: Selma, dreamy and romantic; Lilly, organized and right. Always right. Jessie slept somewhere between them, literally. In life she guessed she had a bit of both of those girls' practices in her. Selma would approve of Jessie's morning goal for its dreamy adventure; Lilly wouldn't. But Jessie'd organized it as Lilly would, leaving little to chance. She'd walked the route, knew the obstacles. She anticipated what she'd find when she got there. If she could make it on time.

Luckily there were only five buttons down the back of her blouse, close to the high neck. She considered waking Selma to help her button them but decided against it. Selma would want the details and wake up Lilly, who would question her judgment. Jessie would not lie. Lilly would point out how ridiculous she was being, rising early and setting out for such foolishness when she had an important appointment in the day ahead. "*That* should be your emphasis," Lilly would say. She spoke as though *she* were Jessie's mother. Oh, she meant well; older sisters did. That's what her mother told her. But still, Jessie was tired of having every person in the family older than she considered wiser and worldlier too.

So Jessie reached back and buttoned the blouse herself, then centered a beaded-buckle belt on her tiny fifteen-year-old waist. *Hat or no hat?* Going out in public without her hat would be too casual. Someone just might question what she was doing or, worse, remember and tell her mother. She could get by without the corset, but she'd best wear the hat.

She tossed a shawl around her shoulders, grabbed her shoes, then dropped one by mistake. She held her breath, hoping no one would wake. She blew out the candle and waited.

"Jessie?"

"Go back to sleep, Selma."

"What are you up to?"

Jessie moved to her sister's side of the bed and whispered, "Don't wake Lilly, all right? It's a secret. Can you keep a secret?" Her sister nodded. "I'm going on an adventure."

"Can I come too?"

"Not this time. But I'll tell you all about it after you get home from school. Just don't tell, please? If Mama asks, just say you don't know. Because you don't."

"Is it about a beau?"

"You read too many of those stories in *Woman's Home Companion.* No boys. Nothing like that."

"I better tell Mama." She pushed the quilt back onto the empty space where Jessie had slept. "She won't like you going off by yourself in the night."

"No!" Jessie looked at Lilly to see if her loud whisper had awakened her. "It's nothing. I'll be back before breakfast."

"All right. But you'll tell me everything?"

"Everything necessary," Jessie said.

Her sister settled back under the quilt, and Jessie picked up her shoe. She'd nearly crippled her adventure before it even started! She tiptoed past Roy's room with special quietness, careful of the oak floor that creaked at a certain place near the head of the stairs. Roy had hearing like their mother's. That woman could tell when any of them squabbled in the bedroom over a hairpiece even when she was outside in the yard, hanging up clothes on the far side of the house while the wind blew! Sadness bordered Jessie's thoughts of her little brother like a photographic frame. Jessie slipped past his room, past her parents' door, out onto the porch with the swing, and sighed relief.

Outside, Jessie inhaled the morning. Late March and the promise of an early spring. Not long before flowers would poke their heads up through the crusty Minnesota ground. She heard a steamship whistle bawling its presence at Winona's docks along the Mississippi. The shawl would be enough to ward off the cold once she started walking, and the promised sun would warm her up when she stood still. Within an hour, dawn would offer up its gift but would wait for only a few seconds for Jessie to receive it. After that, the shapes she wanted to capture would change, and soon the snow would be gone, the city would stop the burning, and she'd have to wait another year. She had little time to spare. She couldn't be late today.

On the porch steps, she pulled on her high-button shoes over scratchy wool socks, then grabbed the heavy leather bag from behind the porch latticework, where she'd placed it the night before. Her uncle August Schoepp had given her the bag and its precious cargo just last year, she supposed in memory of their time at the St. Louis World's Fair. It was her treasure. She drew the strap over her shoulder, centered the weight on her right hip, then set off, holding the bag out to prevent the bruises it often left behind. The corset might have been a help to support her back against the bag, but it was too late to think of that now.

She set a fast pace on Broadway, liking the feel of the new concrete's solidness pounding up through her slender legs. She crossed the street, kept walking. Pigeons flew from the rooftop of the Winona Hotel. Pancakes of dirty snow exposed themselves in the shaded window wells. The clank of railroad cars connecting and departing at the repair yards broke the morning calm. Against the gas streetlights, fingers of elm and maple branches rose before her. There'd be buds on them before long, and the maple sap would drip like dark honey down the trunks, making a rich contrast of brown on black.

She turned the corner, walked several more blocks, then at the lamplight flickering in the bicycle shop's window, Jessie grinned. Mr. Steffes had remembered. He was not a founder of the city, but he'd been around to see many of its changes while running his cycle livery and dealership and doing repair work on the side.

A bicycle leaned against the framed wall. Maybe he meant for her to just take it. It would certainly save time. But he might have left it for someone else. She'd better go in and check.

Jessie stepped inside, the small bell above the door announcing her arrival. She scanned the room. "Mr. Steffes? I'm here. Is the bicycle outside the one you meant for me to take?" The silence felt heavy. The shop smelled of sawdust, the kind brushed onto the wooden floors to soak up grease and oil. It was awfully cluttered. And still. "Mr. Steffes?" Jessie swallowed. "Remember? I left you a nickel for the use of the bicycle this morning. I said I'd come early." She stumbled over a bucket filled with rags. Maybe she could earn the five cents back by offering to clean up this place.

That thought made her cringe. Her mother would not be pleased to know she'd spent a nickel of her own hard-earned dollars from the book bindery on something frivolous like a bicycle rental, especially because she'd recently been released from the bindery. There was little money to spare with her father's illness, which the doctors couldn't name or fix. He had so much pain that they'd had to leave their Wisconsin dairy farm near Cream and move across the Mississippi into Winona, where the girls could find employment and they could be closer to the doctors. Her father eventually worked in the dray business and drove a team to make deliveries, but they all worried over him, her mother and brother and sisters, fearing he might have one of his episodes and suffer excruciating stomachaches that couldn't be stopped without laudanum and rest.

Prickles of uncertainty clustered at

her temples. This morning's ride was important too, important for Jessie. If somehow her mother found out she'd spent the money, she'd just have to convince her that it was for a worthy cause—though how she'd do that she wasn't sure. When she tried to explain this recent pull on her, this desire that came over her, the words came out as flat as a knife and not nearly as sharp.

She'd deal with that later. Jessie pushed her spectacles up on her nose, set her shoulders, and took a forward step, moving past the shadow ghosts of bicycles and what appeared to be one of those new ringer washers in need of repair. Her skirt caught on a bicycle seat. When she straightened, she saw a sliver of light, a thin string that marked the bottom of a back room door. Had it just come on? "Mr. Steffes, I don't mean to bother you, but it's Jessie Gaebele and I was hoping I could just—"

She heard a groan, then what sounded like scuffling followed by a thump.

She readied herself for someone to come charging through the door. When that didn't happen, she listened to her throbbing heart, swallowed, then pushed the door open to face this complication of her day.

>─┼─◆─○─◆─┼─<

F. J. Bauer yanked at the heavy drapes, the purple velveteen loosening splinters of dust to shimmer in the sunlight. He preferred white lace-hemmed sheer covers for the windows, but Mrs. Bauer suffered from headaches, and the light, well, the light could touch them off. She wasn't in the room now though, so he relished the dawn's washing in. He listened for the train that clicked the tracks beside his home; he could set his watch by it. He placed the ties to hold back the drapes. As he turned, he adjusted his spectacles and scanned the latest books he'd purchased, encased behind glass. He'd treat himself to reading when he returned home that evening if he wasn't too tired.

A sound down the hall moved him toward the nursery in their house at 420 South Baker Street. He'd built a new photographic studio on the corner of

Fifth and Johnson in 1895, and it was one of the finest. Everyone told him that. A two-story white clapboard structure with a studio room that captured natural light. He'd wanted to build family quarters into the studio, but Mrs. Bauer had objected. Work should be separate from family, she'd said, though how a man was to do that he didn't really understand. He did this work *for* his family. The home they lived in was comfortable but nothing as fancy as what his friend Watkins had built; but then, FJ lacked that man's resources to both solicit and promote. He shook his head. Confound that Watkins for marrying into good fortune!

FJ's wife, Jessie Anzina Otis Bauer, whom he called Mrs. Bauer at her insistence, sometimes worked with him in the studio, mostly retouching photographs. He had thought she'd be good with customer complaints, something his impatience aggravated. She was a comely woman with intense blue eyes that gave her a nearly romanesque beauty, though her slender frame belied anything robust. He had hoped she'd help with developing photographs too. But the chemicals frightened her, she said, and the flash lights she pronounced "dangerous," the flamed powder exploding before the shutter closed. She preferred the quiet isolation of the dark retouching room, erasing the wrinkles of an autocrat who wished to look younger than his years, or using a brush stroke to add sparkle to a mother's tired eyes. After he built the new studio, she'd urged him to set up a retouching room in the house so she never had to come to the studio at all, but so far he'd resisted that. After all, wasn't she the one who wanted work separated from family?

What he had liked best about his old studio was its closeness to his children. He could hear the boys' laughter and petty arguments as Russell and Donald made noises with their wooden horses. A pang of memory shot through him at the thought of his boys, but he set it aside. He passed the water closet door. He'd have to get it fixed and felt a little shameful for having lost his temper when Mrs. Bauer locked the door and wouldn't come out when he asked. Instead, approaching the nursery now, he focused on the comforting chattering sounds that came from two-year-old Winifred. She'd be suckling at her mother's breast.

He hesitated at the nursery door. He wanted to run his hand over his only daughter's silky hair, tie a bow into her curls himself, exchange a few words now that Winnie had begun talking a streak. But Mrs. Bauer preferred that such intimacies as nursing or diaper changing be accomplished without his presence. Mrs. Bauer also wished to wean the girl, but it was FJ who'd convinced her to wait a bit longer. "What could be better for a child's health than her mother's milk?" he'd told her. He recalled the conversation.

Mrs. Bauer had raised her eyebrow in warning. "Russell," she said. They were at the table, and their eight-year-old ate his egg while they spoke.

"Yes ma'am?"

"She was speaking *of* you, not *to* you, Son," FJ told him, then persisted. "Cow's milk will do when they're older, but if you can give the child life's fluid from your own body, you ought to. At least until she's three. *Bitte.*" Russell had giggled; FJ's wife had blushed, then turned to him with narrowed eyes, his pleading in German falling on deaf ears, or so he'd thought.

He was all for scientific advancements, and the pasteurized milk developed by Halsey nearly twelve years previous probably added to the nutrition of the liquid. At least that's what some proposed. But it wasn't in wide use, and there could be problems. Chemicals did cause problems. He was well aware of that, having endured his first attack of mercury poisoning the year Donald was born.

Brought back to the present by that terrible memory, that deep crevasse of yearning that sucked his breath away, he gasped, seeking to fill the loss. He wondered if Mrs. Bauer thought of Donald while she suckled Winnie. Maybe that was why she wished to stop. He hadn't considered that before. It would be three years this October.

On impulse, he opened the nursery

door. A child's quilt lay over his daughter's head and his wife's breast as the child nursed in the muted room. A small lamp reflected Mrs. Bauer's eyes, which opened with a start.

"What are you doing?" she demanded.

At her words, Winnie pulled the nine-patch from her head and sat up. Mrs. Bauer grabbed at the wool and pulled it over herself. "Papa!" His daughter lifted her arms to him. The gesture warmed him. She would give up mother's milk to have him hold her.

Mrs. Bauer pulled her daughter's arms down. "Papa has to go to work," she said. She still clutched the cloth over her shoulder and breast, covering herself. "Don't you." It was not a question.

"I wanted to say good morning. To you both," he said.

"You wanted to please yourself," she said, though under her breath.

Was she right? Was such a wish so terrible? He decided against defending. "I'm sorry I intruded," he said. "I was thoughtless."

"Yes. You were."

He backed out as Mrs. Bauer pushed Winnie back to nurse, pulling the cloth over them both. But Winnie resisted. "Papa!" She yanked the quilt and wailed.

"See what you started?"

He closed the door, stood outside it. Winnie cried, calling for him, screaming. He didn't know whether to go in and rescue his wife from his daughter's temper or the other way around. Either way, there'd be a fury to pay when he returned home. He lifted his hand to the glass doorknob, then heard her say to him through the closed door, "I'll take care of this, Mr. Bauer. No need for you to fret or disrupt your busy day." Her sarcasm melted over him like icy snow and left him just as cold.

He walked on down the carpeted stairs to the kitchen, turned on the gaslight, and fixed himself hot coffee and toast with marmalade, working to put the incident behind him. While he ate, he scanned the *Republican-Herald* for his ad. They'd gotten it correct this time. He wiped up the crumbs from the daisy-dotted oilcloth and cupped them in his palm, dumped them into the wastebasket. He surveyed the plate rail, each item tidy in its place. No clutter in this kitchen. He heard no more cries from upstairs. She'd settled Winnie down. He donned his bowler, buttoned his coat, lifted his cane, and stepped outside. His morning had begun.

As he walked, he could smell smoke from the fires set at the base of the bluffs, burning shrubs away. The flames moved up the face in a kind of dance, back and forth in a mesmerizing amber weave. If he were closer, he'd hear the licking and spitting as they hit patches of snow and were doused at the top of the ridge. It was a rite of spring to see the fires light up the night, a tradition on the bluffs, which rose nearly six hundred feet above Lake Winona. The predictability of seasonal displays calmed him.

He reviewed his day ahead. Several portrait sittings were scheduled. He thought of the clients as he walked toward his studio. He enjoyed that part of his work most, the staging and cajoling people into a level of comfort so they could be captured on film. People read his *Republican-Herald* ads, saved their money, got the family "attired," arrived, and then turned all shy or nervous about having scheduled themselves for something they suddenly defined as frivolous or self-indulgent. The Germans, his own people, were the worst, not wanting to "waste" money and yet loving the results once he got them past their frugality and focused them on family.

It was up to him to give them reasons to sit before a stranger, staring at a lens that would capture this moment in time. He wondered if they thought the photograph would somehow hold them hostage, so they could never be different from what the photograph revealed. He assured them they could be and insisted that photographs are just a slice of their life meant to stir the memory, not to carve the image into eternal stone. "Years from now, when the children are grown, you'll be so pleased you took this time. The same money put into your house or into your horse won't have memories nearly as fond as what this photograph will bring. And this return comes with a fine wooden frame and nothing you have to clean up after." They'd laugh, then, and settle down.

They didn't know about the creativity needed to use light or to pose a subject or to decide how long to expose the film. Even the backdrop he chose put its mark on the photograph. Things not really there could be made to seem so. A woman's hard-worn years carved against her face could be softened; a man's natural scowl could be lessened with the right angle. Every child had beauty with the right light, the right pose. These were tricks of the trade: the use of sunlight and setting mixed with time.

Sometimes the photographs could also reveal qualities in people and in relationships that he wouldn't even notice until after the film was developed. How far apart a wife and child stood from the husband and father. The way a father's hand reached out to a child with a bit of grime still beneath his fingernails; the surprising evidence of a mother's presence. Once he'd photographed a toddler barely able to stand, and so the mother had squatted behind the studio chair, seeming to hide while stabilizing the child for the duration of the exposure. When he pulled the photograph from the developing solutions, he'd seen her shadow, just a hint of her being there behind the girl. It said so much about a parent's wish to give protection and strength to a child without always being seen.

Protection. The German poet Rilke had described love as two solitudes come together to protect, border, and salute each other. He'd loved Donald that way; he had. He'd bordered Donald, saluted his son's efforts. He just hadn't protected him.

He put the memories away, and at Fifth Street he walked up the steps and turned the key to his studio door, coming in the front the way his clients did. He paused for a moment to look at the photographic display in the bay window. The year that Donald was born, the gold medal he'd won for his portrait work had been stolen right out of the lobby. The police never found it, and they'd made him think it was his own fault for posting such a valuable piece right where others could see it. But confound it, what was the point of receiving recognition if one couldn't show it off just a little?

His other awards—announced on paper and framed—helped adorn some of the portrait work, the eyes of the subjects gazing out at him. It was good work he did. He could be proud of it even if his judgment resulted in the gold medal's loss. A businessman had to announce his accolades. They engendered confidence in clients. Burying the praise in a safe? What would be the point in that?

Inside, he hung his hat on the oak rack at the end of the mirrored bench, straightened his tie, then walked to the appointment ledger on the desk in the reception room.

He hoped the first appointment, set for nine, would be on time. The light made all the difference.

He adjusted his glasses, checked his schedule book, and frowned. At ten, he had appointments with two women who might become camera assistants. A flash of annoyance crossed over his mind. Mrs. Bauer had made those arrangements. She ought to have known it wasn't the best time of day for an interview, not when the sunlight was so necessary for his work. Interviews should be late afternoon. He tapped with his pencil. He'd have to pull the heavy drape up against the glare and then lower it for the portrait sitting at eleven. He had another scheduled at one, another at two, then planned to work in the developing room until closing. Well, perhaps Mrs. Bauer felt the harsh light of late morning wouldn't be good for a sitting but would work fine to decide if two ladies ought to be hired to assist him.

He didn't want to hire any help. His former assistant, Risser, had taken over the studio while FJ spent an extended time in North Dakota; then that arrangement soured. FJ had returned to find things deteriorated. A fire had damaged the reception room and destroyed many of the valuable glass plates in his Grove collection, from which he had numerous requests for prints. It was a terrible loss, though fortunately he'd stored the Charles Tenney collection plates at home, and some of the Grove plates in the middle of the sets of negatives were salvageable. FJ took back the studio, and Risser went on to become competition, opening his own studio just blocks away. FJ had trained the man for four years, though he'd say he had come with skills. Risser claimed his brother had a photographic business in St. Louis where he'd apprenticed, but FJ always wondered if he hadn't just been some itinerant tramp photographer anyway. Risser had left him faster than a grease splat could ruin a man's good shirt.

Perhaps Mrs. Bauer thought women would be less likely to leave once trained. But he'd lost other women he'd trained when they moved on to be assistants elsewhere. He settled on hoping for washer girls who wanted jobs with a little less scrubbing involved. Maybe this time he'd have more mature women rather than those with starry eyes for photography. The latter could be more annoying than helpful.

He bristled remembering the *Republican-Herald*'s story that urged "young women possessed of a well-ordered and dependable camera, an artistic taste, a deft hand, and a wide acquaintance" to increase their dress allowances by creating "society booklets" for their friends. They offered no competition to him. His objection was to the idea that the mere possession of a camera could turn someone into a professional, a creative artist. What nonsense. The photographic business was about so much more than that.

What he'd advertised for was someone he could train who could take over the studio when the poisoning hit again. Someone reliable, someone who could learn to develop, to take pictures, yes, and schedule portraits, but mostly to work the chemicals. He intended to photograph as he could. It was just the chemicals that destroyed. Mrs. Bauer could have done it if she chose to; she'd had minimal exposure through the years and wouldn't be at risk the way he was, though he'd told her not to hold the chemical-laden brushes in her mouth while she made a pencil correction on the film. No telling what such chemicals might do. If she were here, the children could be with him through the day too. It would be a family affair. He supposed that was the other reason the interviews annoyed him. Mrs. Bauer could but wouldn't. Mrs. Bauer had her ways.

Mrs. Bauer's father had been a traveling photographer, and she "knew the business," as she often told him. Or she'd poke at him with, "If Papa were here, he'd say . . . ," or, "If Papa were still alive, he'd want you to . . ." Not-so-subtle reminders that it was Mrs. Bauer's father who had gotten FJ started in the business and that, at his death in 1894, it was her father's estate that had allowed the studio to be built.

Now that he thought of it, it was probably a marvel that she'd listened to him about not weaning Winifred. She so seldom did follow his advice.

He stepped into the office, seeking a cigar. Mrs. Bauer didn't like him to smoke, and he didn't. He chewed them instead. He opened the small tobacco box, pulled a cigar from it, and bit into the end, letting the thin paper caress his tongue, the tart taste of the tobacco re-freshing. He looked at the ledger again. Mrs. Bauer had written in her fine hand *Jessie Gaebele, Voe Kopp* on the ap-pointment book. He chewed the tiny fla-vorful flecks. Good German names. Jes-sie Gaebele. He ought to be able to remember that one at least, Jessie be-ing his wife's first name too.

He heard the bell in the reception room. His clients were here. He inhaled, put aside the cigar. He hoped the young women he'd be interviewing afterward would be on time. Tramp photographers often weren't timely, always stopping to shoot a bird or some lake scene. He was a studio portrait maker, and he prided himself on punctuality and pro-fessionalism.

Studio work and an artist's eye re-quired discipline and timing and paying attention to the light. Always, one must pay attention to the light.

>─┼─◆─⊙─◆─┼─<

Mr. Steffes had a gash on his head as wide as Jessie's eyeglass lens, which she pushed back on her nose as she bent to him, perspiration working against her. "Mr. Steffes, what's happened? Please wake up, please!" Her heart pounded and her hands fluttered over him, wondering where to touch him to offer help. His eyes were closed, and she looked around for a clean rag to wipe his forehead of the blood, keep it from settling in the pool of his eyes. Head wounds bled fiercely. Her father had fallen once and struck his head. But though a bucket of blood had spilled around him, making them all rush and worry, there'd only been a tiny gash when the bleeding stopped. She wouldn't assume the worst.

No clean rags anywhere. She lifted her skirt and with her teeth tore a section from her white petticoat, then pressed the cloth against his head, wiping gently but hoping to keep his eyes clear. She rolled him to his side because that had seemed to help with her father's pain. She wished he'd moan again or say something, anything. She'd have to leave him to go get help. The other businesses wouldn't be open yet, but she could ride the bicycle to the hospital and tell them that Mr. Steffes had fallen. Jessie could let them rush to him while she rode off to finish her task.

Abandon him? She'd never do that.

She looked through the dirty window. There was still the right light, the dawn just now opening its eyes over the city. That moment between the darkness and when morning pulled itself up into the face of the sky made for the finest exposures.

She looked at Mr. Steffes and silenced the dawn of her desire. There'd be no photography this morning. Lake Winona would shake itself of night without her setting up her camera to capture the flames flickering and dancing their way up the slopes to Bluffside Park, burning out in a puff of snowmelt at the top. There'd be another day. Next year, she supposed. The annual bluff burn was nearly finished. She took a deep breath. She knew the right thing to do here, and she would do it.

She scanned the room, looking for some way to put pressure on the wound, to halt the bleeding while she went for help. She already had blood on her white shirtwaist sleeves, but that didn't matter. She stood up, hands on her narrow waist, thinking. She felt her belt. She removed it, lifted his head, hooked the buckle over the cloth, and buckled it. It would have to do. She pushed against her knees, stood, rushed toward the door.

A groan and then, "Miss . . . Gaebele?"

She turned back. "Oh, Mr. Steffes, I'm so glad you're awake. You've hit your head."

"Someone hit it for me," he said. He pushed to get himself to sitting, wobbled. She offered assistance. He reached to feel his face, then felt the cloth against his head, fingered the beads on the buckle.

"I didn't see anyone here," Jessie

said. "Nor see anyone leave. I think . . . that is, I think you fell."

"The floor tripped me up?" he questioned. He tried to turn his head and moaned again. "There're the culprits," he said. He pointed to an anvil that he must have stumbled over and the sharp corner of a bench that had broken his fall. "Them's what did it." He nodded toward the bench, an act that caused him to gasp again. "Came up behind me, I'd say." He tried to smile at her then.

"Are you well enough for me to leave you to go get help?"

He started to nod, stopped himself. "Take the bicycle—oh, you needed it this morning." He looked up at her with tears in his eyes. "I've ruined your adventure. I have no phone. Your mother, your clothes, all spackled with blood. What will she say?"

His words dipped and dived, flying like bats.

"Oh, she'll find words," Jessie told him as she straightened her hat. "Don't you worry about that. Just sit still now, promise?"

She hated to leave him, but she had to. She noted the camera bag where she'd set it when she made her way through the cluttered shop, then stepped onto the bicycle, wishing she had a pair of those special women's trousers lady bicyclists in the magazines wore, and pedaled off.

The doctor's residence was closer than the hospital, so she went there and told him what had happened. He said he'd join her shortly as he pulled his breakfast napkin from beneath his chin. Jessie returned, riding over the boarded streetcar tracks, raced in to Mr. Steffes, then kept up a steady stream of conversation with the shop owner, one of his eyes seeming to float away from the center. He looked like he might doze. She buttressed him with pillows from his narrow cot, kept him sitting upright. His Thomas clock struck nine just as the doctor arrived. She waited for instructions, but when none came, she accepted the belt the doctor handed her as she told him what she knew and described what ministrations she'd performed.

The doctor told her she'd done the right things, handling the "blood without fainting," as she backed her way toward the door. But Mr. Steffes kept saying how grateful he was and how fortunate that she had been coming so early and how he might not have lived without her, a fact he exaggerated. Jessie figured he'd later realize that he wouldn't have been there so early nor stumbled in the dim light if she hadn't wanted to rent the bicycle at that hour. She waited for what she thought to be a proper time, then asked if it would be all right if she left. It wasn't just the appointment edging her toward the door; it was the accident and her part in it.

"Do you want me to call your parents?" the doctor asked. "About the blood on your blouse?"

She looked down. "No, that's all right."

"You run along then, Miss Gaebele," the doctor said.

"Do what the doctor tells you," she told the bicycle shop owner. And with that she reached for her shawl, pushed up her spectacles, grabbed her camera bag, and backed out the door.

The sun felt warm now, and the big clock on the courthouse clanged the three-quarter hour. She turned backward, holding her hand to her hat to stare at the clock. Nine forty-five? Where had the time gone? She'd have to prepare a double explanation now because she didn't have time to make it home before her interview, and she'd barely make Mr. Bauer's studio. She'd have to do the interview without her corset and with bloodstains on her blouse. What businessman would hire someone so disheveled?

She walked her fast pace toward Johnson Street, where she was to meet her friend Voe Kopp, all the while wondering if she didn't need a little bit more each of Lilly's organizational bent and Selma's capacity to adapt if she was to accomplish her dreams. She prepared an explanation for the bloody sleeves, an account she hoped would meet her mother's muster and the critical eyes of F. J. Bauer, the photographer. The loudest voice she heard as she raced along was Lilly's: "How could you risk losing a necessary job the whole family needs for something as frivolous as a photograph?" Jessie didn't have an answer for that.

Two

A Hesitating Heart

There were times in Jessie Gaebele's young life when she hadn't thought about having a career, but those times were long ago. At thirteen, she'd been employed by the Jones and Kroeger Printing Office for two dollars a week. She had been hired to bind books, but she fell in love with the pictures. Eleven girls worked there. Once a girl had stolen Jessie's wages from her coat pocket. The lights had gone out—they often flickered, but this time the windowless room turned black—and when they came on again, the money was gone. Jessie knew who took it. The girl was the only one who'd been in the coat closet during the blackout. Jessie'd been so angry she told the girl, "The money will burn in your pocket, and wherever you work you'll be fired."

She'd told her employer, but it couldn't be proved. At Jessie's next paycheck, though, Mr. Kroeger gave Jessie the additional wages along with her current earnings. And the girl was fired, at least from the bindery. Jessie supposed she should have held her tongue, as such loathsome words weren't exactly Christian, as her mother would later tell her. Then earlier this winter, Jessie cried when Mr. Kroeger told her she needn't come back the next day, and only felt a little better when he told her a man with children to support had asked for work, and the owner decided to give him the job. A man's job mattered more, her mother reminded Jessie when she arrived home, and Jessie guessed she agreed. Lilly said maybe she'd been a poor performer and that's why she'd been let go, but her mother hushed Lilly. Jessie had to find employment. And then there'd been this perfect opening, so maybe the worst thing—losing her job—could be converted into a good thing. When the Bauer job advertised, her mother said there were angels looking out for her. *They must have been sleeping earlier at the bicycle shop,* Jessie thought as she rushed along.

Work was what Jessie did. Even before they moved to Winona, while living on the farm there'd been chores to do—important tasks, such as taking the cows the three miles to the water each day, then herding them back up the bluff to the barn without the benefit of a dog. In the winter, before walking down the valley to the village of Cream and school, the girls cracked pond ice so the cows could drink. They wore thin leather shoes, and the drifts were deep with no trails except what their feet pressed. Her sandwiches often froze by the time they arrived at the still-chilly one-room school.

Today, as Jessie walked toward the impending interview, the cool breeze forcing her to pull her shawl more tightly around her, she remembered arriving at her school late one chilly winter day because of the snow and cold. She and Tillie, her seatmate, were always getting in trouble for chattering, and on that day the one-armed schoolteacher, Mr. Buchmuller, Tillie's uncle, had arrived late too, so the school still felt as cold as the woodshed. While he hated gum-chewing, he hated whispering more, and when he turned from lighting the fire, he heard the *pst-pst* sound and thought it was Tillie and Jessie. It hadn't been, but the burdens of life fall unfairly, Jessie soon learned. To punish the girls, he sent them to the boys' side of the room and made them each share a seat with a boy for the day.

She'd been furious at the injustice, made to sit by smelly boys. But the boys had made her laugh, and she and Tillie winked at each other, and Jessie decided to enjoy her day as the room heated up and filled with the scent of drying-out woolen stockings. The burdens may fall unfairly, but one could always turn a misery into something good. Well, almost always.

She'd liked living at the upper end of the valley in Cream. Moving to the city had made them all sad, her especially, to leave behind the refuge she found in the woods among the sumacs and shallow limestone caves. At least in Winona she could look out their second-story bedroom and see Sugar Loaf. Her father called it by its old name, Wapasha's Cap. The land formation reminded Jessie of a cone of candy like the one she'd had at the St. Louis World's Fair. She'd let her eyes scan the treetops and the spires of St. Mary's Academy that poked their way into the green. On Sundays after church they sometimes drove the buggy up to Bluffside Park, where one could look out over the world and even see Wisconsin in the form of bluffs on the other side of the Mississippi River. The world was full of pictures, and they were best observed from heights.

A blast of wind struck her, and she shivered despite her hurrying pace. This job as a photographer's assistant would offer a warm place to work in winter. The pay would be adequate, she was certain, and there'd be excitement, new things happening each day. Best of all, she'd be learning about what she'd come to love. At a photographer's studio she'd be viewing photographs as part of her job instead of having to sneak looks while she bound the books they illustrated.

She felt a stiffness as she pulled her shawl closer. The bloody sleeves would add nothing to her interview success. She had to face facts. Mr. Steffes's plight had been the more important, and if the opportunity arose, she'd tell Mr. Bauer what had made her late and why she wasn't dressed at her perfect best. She hoped he'd understand. At least she hadn't fainted at the sight of Mr. Steffes's blood. Maybe she could get a job at the Winona Hospital.

"Jessie, you goose! You nearly walked me over." Voe stumbled in front of her like an apparition escaping from the studio wall. "I almost went in without you. It's time, right now! What kept you?" Her eyes caught the sleeves. "Are you all right? Where'd the blood come from?"

"It's not my blood," Jessie said. "Mr. Steffes had an accident at his shop, and I was able to help him but—"

"The bicycle man? What were you doing there?"

"It's a story," Jessie said. "I'll probably have to tell it to Mr. Bauer, to explain my appearance, so I don't think I'll take time now."

"You look like dog-tossed food."

"Is my wave piece centered at least? I can't imagine Mr. Bauer taking me seriously if the curls have been pulled to the side." Jessie patted at her hair.

"Your hat's on straight. But . . . the blood. I can't take my eyes from it."

Jessie stared at her sleeves. The stains ran the length of her forearm and onto the curl of cuffs at her wrist. The shawl wouldn't cover it. She sighed. "There's just one thing to do then." She set the camera bag below the bay display window. With her teeth she tore at the sleeve, ripping the cloth so it ended at the elbow's bend. Her right arm was perfectly fine but there was nothing to be done but rip it as well. "May as well be balanced."

She'd heard Voe's gasp at the first tear, and her mouth was still open at the second. Jessie plucked at the threads, stuffed the torn pieces into her bag, and straightened her small shoulders as she hiked the bag up and over her head, the strap forming half an X across her chest. "I'm ready."

The torn sleeves were just one more thing she'd have to explain to her mother.

>─┼─♦>─○─<♦─┼─<

F. J. Bauer checked his watch. His clients had taken more time than usual to settle themselves in for the sitting. They were a young couple, recently moved from the East and wanting to re-assure their families back in Manhattan that they hadn't dropped off the face of the earth in this wild northwest country of sawmills and flour mills, steamboats and trains. But they'd bickered between themselves, made comments to him about angles and such, and he was about to suggest they reschedule when they were more certain of what they wanted to convey when they suddenly sat, stared into the camera, and said they were ready indeed. They had just gone out the back way when he looked at his watch. He clipped the clock casing shut as the bell rang. Well, at least his interviewees were prompt. This was encouraging. He opened the door expecting to see two young women, perhaps even wives, seeking work to supplement their husbands' meager pay.

Why, they're just girls, he thought. *Children.* One so small she was not much taller than his Russell. He frowned. She carried a camera case that nearly outweighed her. Just the thing he'd hoped to avoid: a camera girl, someone who thought she knew photography. She also happened to have a sparkle of strength in her eyes that suggested she'd not be easily trained.

It was not what he'd hoped for, but then, life never was.

The one was much too small. She probably couldn't manage his large cameras. But if she could learn developing, if she had an eye for such, well, maybe she could perform. If she'd take direction. She reminded him of his wife years before: warm eyes, full lips that turned up slightly as though she was always ready to smile.

The other girl was husky. She'd carry cameras without trouble. But she had dull eyes. FJ always looked at the eyes. The taller of the two would be slow, he ventured, but dutiful. The small one's gray eyes with flecks of gold and blue held a snap to them. Too bold perhaps, wearing her bare arms exposed beneath a shawl and looking at him with curiosity, he thought. Her eyes looked as though a laugh might bubble through them. So young.

He'd been young too when he began. At thirteen he was apprenticed in carpentry, and by age sixteen immigrated to America from Kirchheim, Germany, arriving with the clothes on his back, a fifty-cent piece in his watch pocket, and a straw hat, the rest having been lost when the ship was disabled and the trunks lost at sea. The wind took his hat at the dock in New York.

A great-uncle who waited for him in Buffalo promised five dollars a day—top wages indeed in 1882—working at his icebox-building factory next door to his great-uncle's tannery. FJ had hated the smells and, worse, his having to dress

3 5569 00006358 4

for dinner and listen to people chatter on around him in English, of which he understood not a word. He didn't know then that his great-uncle Jacob Scholl-kopf had founded Niagara Falls Power Company, a bank, breweries, and other businesses he might have worked into. The constant pressure of his having to "perform" for his great-uncle, plus the pressure from workers who suggested he didn't earn his wages but was granted into them, made him leave the safety and promise of his family.

He found another job building furni-ture and worked to pay back his pas-sage costs. He taught himself English, then joined the National Guard by changing his name from Gottlieb Frie-drich Bauer to Frederick John Bauer and making himself a few years older. He'd made his way in America, but sometimes he missed what other boys were able to do: play ball in the streets, learn to ice skate, go on hayrides. His life was always about work.

Now here before him were young girls likely bound on the same path as he had been: working, working. It was too bad.

He wanted more for his own children, wanted them to have privilege, not so they assumed it was their right, but so they'd have a childhood, a time of joy and laughter, even if he hadn't had much of that himself.

Well, he'd see what these young ladies had to say. He'd discover whether they'd be the type to leave when challenges arrived or stay until the job was finished.

><+>-O-<+><

Jessie decided that Mr. Bauer asked dull questions, though she tried to answer them politely while her eyes scanned the reception room. They were seated on a dark horsehair couch, and Mr. Bauer sat in a wingback chair, a notepad on his lap. He occasionally looked up over round eyeglasses. He wanted to know where they had worked before, if they had. Would their employer give them references? How much schooling had they completed?

She supposed those were important questions, but wasn't it more critical to know how much photographic experience they might have, whether they knew when something was supposed to be upside down and when it wasn't?

They answered, told him they were fifteen and sixteen years old, had good references, and Jessie had graduated from the eighth grade from Madison School on Sanborn. Voe did not finish school but had gone to work early, she said, cooking and cleaning for others. He even asked what hours they'd be available. Jessie thought that a silly question. Their parents would fill their hours if they didn't have employment, so any hours working at the studio would be better than scrubbing floors and rubbing knuckles raw on washboards.

But then it got interesting.

"Do you understand that I'll pay you five dollars a week?"

"Those are fine wages," Jessie said. "Thank you." She sat back, her feet barely reaching the carpeted floor. Five dollars was better than she'd hoped for.

He held up a finger. "But only after you've attended classes with me for six months."

"You won't pay us while we're working?" Voe asked.

"It's fortunate that I'm not asking you to pay me," he said, "for the experience and expertise you'll be receiving. There are new laws afoot that will require certification in order to become a photographer. One will have to demonstrate that one can handle the chemicals and the flash-light work. None of this amateur risk of explosions, people burning their eyebrows off, and such."

Voe giggled.

He frowned, then continued. "Such episodes have led to fires in studios, so it is not a laughing matter."

Voe lowered her eyes.

"Though I use the flash less than most photographers in the city. If all works out well, you'll have a good wage. More than double your book bindery." He turned to Jessie now. "If what you told me was truthful."

"Of course it was truthful," she defended. She wasn't sure she wanted to work for this man, who suggested that amateurs were dangerous or that he couldn't trust what they said. Still, this job would get her closer to her dream than she'd ever been before. She'd *have* to take photographs now. It would be part of her . . . profession. She'd be able to devote the time to it, and neither Lilly nor her mother would be able to complain that she daydreamed or wasted her days.

"I wonder," he said, "about your camera experience." He nodded toward Jessie's leather bag sitting like a patient dog at her feet.

"Jessie has lots," Voe said. "You'll have to teach me harder, I guess. Maybe I'll have to stay after school. I'm used to that." Voe had long eyelashes, and she fluttered them at Mr. Bauer. She fanned her face with her long fingers, her white cuticles flashing like snowflakes against the dark drape pulled back to allow the sun through the tall window. *Why, Voe's being flirtatious,* Jessie thought.

Mr. Bauer scowled when he turned to Jessie. "Are you one of those camera girls producing social booklets?"

He spoke with a challenge, reminding her of Papa when she disobeyed. "No. I mean, yes, I have a camera so I guess I'm a camera girl, but no, I haven't ever tried to make a book of photographs. Except in the bindery," she added. "Where I was required to."

"So what do you do with that camera? What is it?"

"I just take . . . pictures. Of the park or the lake or snow melting. This morning I'd hoped to get a picture just at dawn of the burn racing up the bluff. I've been watching at night from my window, and I love the flicker of lights. They dance as the flame weaves back and forth, and then there's this explosion at the top, where fire hits snow and *poof,* the fire is out. I wanted to capture that, just when the light was perfect. But I was interrupted." She sighed, then brightened. "It's a Kodak," she said. "Would you like to see it? It's the preloaded one, from 1888. It takes a hundred round photographs, two inches in diameter. I have to send the entire camera back for developing, and I have to save my money for that."

Mr. Bauer grunted, but he didn't shift his eyes to look at the ceiling the way some did when she enthused about her camera.

She knew she ought to stop talking, but she wanted him to know how much she loved photography. "I saw Jessie Tarbox Beals at the St. Louis World's Fair, the Lewis and Clark Exposition that President Roosevelt dedicated," she babbled, "in 1904."

"I know when it was," he said.

Jessie nodded, enthusiasm wrapped in memory propelling her forward. "I saw her standing on a twenty-foot ladder to shoot. I'd never seen a woman doing that before. My uncle August was with me, and we watched what she took and how she moved around the crowd, and she seemed to be everywhere. I heard she took a picture of Mr. Roosevelt and his son. My uncle took me up on Mr. Ferris's observation wheel. I wished I had the camera to take a picture from that height! We saw the Gerhard sisters' exhibit on Olive Street too. They took portraits from the Pike and anthropology exhibits and used natural light. The people, those from the Philippines and other exotic places, looked so . . .

friendly," Jessie continued. "They could have been a person living next door who dressed differently, that was all. It was wonderful, and I'd give anything if I'd had pictures of what I saw there. To hang on to."

"You're quite the reporter yourself," he said, and this time she heard laughter in his tone. She felt her face grow hot. "Mrs. Beals is quite well known for her newsworthy photographs, as are the Gerhard sisters. Do you anticipate taking pictures of fires and dray accidents too, as Mrs. Beals has?"

"No. I only meant to tell you—"

"Of your experience. Very good." He looked annoyed again. "And what would you hope to do once you've had my training? Leave me to run your own studio, if not to take photos of accidents and such?"

"I could," she said, "but that wouldn't be my plan. I want to stay near my family. I'd like to see if I have the eye to capture beauty in landscapes or people. It's a way of . . . expression," Jessie added. She looked down. The room felt hot. She couldn't explain how she felt, not really. She was saying too much. "Besides, the last time I looked, Winona had seven photography studios in addition to this one. I doubt it could handle yet another. You don't have to worry about me."

"Especially one owned by a woman," Voe added.

"I might like to travel," Jessie said, brightening. "To faraway places. Taking pictures of the people and the rivers and lakes and maybe even mountains— that's what I want to do. For the memory of them, though. Not to compete in business."

Mr. Bauer appeared to study his notes. Jessie wanted to jump into the silence but knew that quiet was a gift that ought to be respected. She gazed around the reception room, noticed books as well as photographs. She imagined herself greeting people, then watching this man work and learning from him. She'd always been a good student if the teaching wasn't all from books.

"Miss Gaebele—is my pronunciation correct?"

"It's pronounced *Gay-bell.* With emphasis on the front."

"Miss Gaebele, then." He continued on with her nod. "And Miss . . . pronounced *cup,* I presume? Yes. Well then, you girls understand that there are hazards to this profession not found in any other, beyond the flash-light issues. Those you can learn to avoid with discipline and routine. But there's the sickness, the jaundice, mercury poisoning. I have already had it. In 1901. It took me six months to recover. The second time, in 1904, I entrusted this studio to Mr. Risser and hoped to heal at my farm in North Dakota. But I needed to return." He pulled at his mustache, ran his hands through his black-as-ink hair. He didn't elaborate. "It's said that each time the sickness comes, the recovery takes longer. I've been exposed my whole life, though. You ought not to dwell on the possibility of your becoming ill. If we rotate the chemical work, none of us will. But others might worry for you. So I wanted you to be aware."

"What's it like?" Voe asked. "The sickness."

"The skin becomes spotted, and the stomach wants to divorce the body," he said. "One's mind is good though forgetful, but the body weakens."

"I wouldn't like that," Voe said. She shivered.

Jessie turned to Voe. "He's only had the sickness twice, and he's been a photographer for . . ." She looked up at him.

"Since 1894. Twice, in my forty years of living."

"That's twice in thirteen years of being a photographer. I don't think we'll have anything to worry about, Voe."

Voe shrugged.

Jessie calculated further. Mr. Bauer was just two years younger than her father. Working for the photographer could be like working for Papa, who'd be a kind employer.

Mr. Bauer stood then, erect as a military man, dapper with his starched collar and cuffs. His thick mustache covered his upper lip. His nose was narrow and appeared to have never been broken. She might call him handsome in a prim sort of way. But she thought she saw sadness in this man's brown eyes too.

"Miss Gaebele, you will need to pay attention," he said, "if you're to acquire the necessary skills to pass the certification test."

Jessie lowered her eyes. It wasn't polite to stare and worse not to know what your employer might have just said.

"I don't plan to take a test," Voe said. "I did enough of that in school. Can I still be in your employ?"

"You have to listen and learn. It's not required that you take the exam, but I'll want a certified person to run the studio should I become ill again, and if Miss Gaebele doesn't take the test or pass it, then I'll be looking for new employees. And you, Miss Gaebele? Are you one to avoid an examination?"

"Oh, never. How else could I discover what I didn't think I could do?"

He appeared to like her answer, for she thought she saw light come into his eyes behind his lenses, tiny as a pinprick. He adjusted his dark tie.

"Very well, then. One last thing. While you are in training, I do not want you to photograph on your own. I will ask that you leave your Kodak behind when you come here. In fact, I suggest that you leave it here in this studio until I feel you have acquired the necessary discipline. You've likely learned bad habits that I'll need to change if you're to be a useful assistant. I'll decide the subjects and the settings of photographs that I might allow you to take. At first, you will not be photographing at all. You'll be learning how to schedule appointments, develop and make prints. If you're very good, very observant, perhaps you could be taught retouching. If you wish to work a little extra. It could earn you more money, though much of that work my wife, Mrs. Bauer, does. As she has time. Are these conditions acceptable?"

"I'll need to ask my ma if I can work for six months without pay," Voe said. She crossed her arms over her chest.

Jessie had heard what he said about not taking photographs, but she couldn't believe it. What a waste not to allow them to do the very thing he was hiring them to do! "What a waste of . . . pluck!" Jessie blurted.

"You'll have to unlearn bad habits." He looked at Jessie. "And, Miss Kopp, you'll likely have some habits in need of work as well."

Did she want to give up what she loved doing for even a short time in order to achieve what she wished for? Maybe she should just walk out the door now. But she didn't.

"Tell her it's like . . . going to the Winona Normal School," Jessie advised. She spoke firmly, belying the pounding of her own heart. *No photographs for six months?* It would be like giving up food. But then maybe such a sacrifice was what she deserved. She'd had it too easy. Now things were about to change.

"Very good," FJ said. He pointed his pencil at Jessie. "Because it is. And I'm not charging you any tuition the way Winona Normal would. You'll come out with skills that might lead you to a profession nearly as valued as teaching. At least you could assist your families until you marry."

Voe giggled again. "Jessie's married to that camera."

"Looks like she'll be getting a divorce

then," Mr. Bauer said. "If she's in my employ."

"I'll tell my ma," Voe said. "But I bet she'll be just as miffed as Jessie's ma when she sees her bloody blouse sleeves shortened as they are." She pointed to Jessie's bare arms.

"Are you injured?" Mr. Bauer said, confused.

"Nonsense," Jessie said.

But he stepped toward her as though to lift her arm to examine it, then stopped.

"It's . . . camera related," Jessie told him. "A gamble of the profession, one might say. But nothing to worry over. Thank you for your interest though. That's very kind."

"Very well," Mr. Bauer said. "You're willing to accept my terms?" He stepped back, became professional again.

She'd only had the camera a year, but it had become as much a part of her as her corset. She'd gotten by without *it* this morning; she supposed she could get by without the camera too, but it wouldn't be as easy. It would be like gazing into a window, wishing for a fancy dress hanging there right in front of her, but unreachable.

She'd have to keep her word once she gave it. It wouldn't be forever. She'd learn new skills, prove herself to Mr. Bauer, and before he ever imagined, she'd be back taking photographs. That would be her goal.

"Agreed," she said. She picked up the camera case as though it were a precious child and handed it over to him. He nodded, then set it beside his chair. Jessie stared at it. Had she made a terrible mistake?

"You begin on Monday at eight in the morning. We'll start with a tour of the facility. Today, you may leave by the front door, but in the future, please use the back entrance. That's where employees enter."

Both girls offered him gloved hands, then left. Jessie considered what she'd just agreed to. Lilly would say it was one of the requirements of employment, and small sacrifice at that. Selma would tell her she'd just given up a piece of her heart. Neither sister would be totally correct. Jessie was in the middle: a *small* sacrifice did not quite describe the act. And while she hadn't given up a piece of her heart, she'd surely made it hesitate by leaving her camera behind.

THREE

Expectations

Mrs. Bauer—it was how she thought of herself—drifted through the house, feeling wispy and unfinished, dragging her palm across newly dusted tabletops, lifting the fern fronds to tease her fingertips. Winnie napped and Mrs. Bauer had tasks to do, as any mother did. It was time to reorganize the closets. It was a task she felt she must accomplish at least monthly. But a great emptiness veiled her today, a fog she couldn't brush away. She had no energy, not even to argue with Mr. Bauer about weaning Winnie, a subject he'd inappropriately brought up some weeks before. Any residue of strength she might have had he'd robbed from her this morning by his intrusion. It was no concern of his, or ought not to be, this detail of child rearing. Weaning was within the purview of women, of mothers and grandmothers, not husbands and fathers. He still had so much to learn.

When her father had brought Mr. Bauer home following one of his photographic meetings, Jessie Otis, then a mere sixteen-year-old girl, had found him dashing and charming. He could make her laugh. He had a sweet smile and eyes as calm as Lake Winona on a still summer day. She could sink into those eyes. He was "going places" her father had told her. He had "property," small cottages in Winona and a photographic studio in St. Charles a few miles away. He was a quick study, her father said, would learn photography in a snap.

They married on February 17, 1891, just a few months shy of her eighteenth birthday, and before long he bought out Grover Studio in Winona along with its enormous set of glass plate negatives, which her father said would make Mr.

Bauer good money, all those pictures of landscapes that people wanted. Mr. Bauer had turned a good number of them into postcards once the postal service permitted both the address and a message to be written on the same side, leaving the opposite side for photographs. Some people still sent leather postcards, but Mr. Bauer was sure that would stop soon enough, though sometimes his "vision of the future" didn't ring true. He said it was the timing of things that allowed an idea to become a practice one could pursue toward perfection. But sometimes timing took away a vision too. Donald had been taken from her by an inexplicable moment of tragically bad timing. She pressed her hand to her heart. Donald's memories wore heavily.

Like a tablecloth unfurled, she lowered herself onto the divan with its claw feet and oak arms she could grip, her linen skirt settling over her knees. She liked the cool of the wood. It gave her strength, which she desperately needed to accomplish her tasks. But today the carved wood offered her no force. She aimlessly turned pages of a book, not remembering anything she'd read. She was vaguely conscious of birds outside the window chattering. Or was it neighborhood boys playing? Russell had come home from school, donned his playing knickers, and headed out the back door, barely stopping to give her a peck on her cool cheek. That was just as well. She didn't like displays of affection, even from an eight-year-old.

Paper cut her finger and she stood, sucking on it, aware of the salty taste. At least she could notice it. She sighed and went to the cupboard where her husband kept his salve. His mixture did actually soothe. It was too bad that J. R. Watkins sold a product much like it. Watkins's business had taken off when he moved it to Winona in 1885. Once, in a flash of argument, her husband had hinted that Watkins and he worked on a salve formula together, but Mrs. Bauer really doubted that. She wasn't sure why. Her husband was a truthful man. As far as she knew. Still, they remained acquainted with the Watkins family, her husband having taken the great man's photograph, which the company placed on a postcard and used for promotion. The Bauers didn't exactly socialize with them, nor with the lumber people like the Lairds and Nortons. They weren't in that class. But they'd attended the funeral of Mary Ellen, JR's wife, when she passed in April 1904. It was the same year as Donald's accident. She gasped a stuttered breath. She hated it when everything she thought of in a day seemed to come back to sweet Donald and the great emptiness of his death.

She looked for cleanser to clean the wound. Her husband was always a step behind other businessmen who prospered. Oh, they had a comfortable life, but he'd made investments in the salve, kept detailed ledgers, but nothing really came of the orders. A few were shipped, mostly to North Dakota and Seattle, where Watkins's products weren't so easily acquired. Mr. Bauer had seen military duty in the West and remembered the prairies, liked them, left behind the salve with some friends there, south of Bismarck. He received a few orders after that.

He'd left so much more behind in North Dakota.

Everyone had urged them to have another child as soon as they could after Donald's death. Again, people intruding upon the intimacies of a marriage, making such suggestions. People had no idea of the strain.

Well, perhaps they did. At least the relatives knew she'd gone home to live with her mother when her father died in 1895 and stayed longer than was socially acceptable. She hadn't cared. Her mother needed looking after, or at least she told herself that. Her sister and her brother, Orrin, were of no help even though they lived in the same town. Or had Orrin moved on by then? She couldn't remember. She came back to Winona but returned to her mother's again in the fall of 1900. Mr. Bauer had begged her to come back, to bring Russell, just a baby then. He'd been talking about investing in cropland in North Dakota, and she had put her foot down. As if such an investment made sense. They'd argued; she took Russell and went home to her mother's.

But Mr. Bauer charmed her with his easy, persistent smile. He told her of the government's plan to permit homestead claims to be proved up. He'd get a partner, someone to stay there to do the work. They'd share the crop profits. And he could even set up a photographic studio in nearby Hazelton, make it seasonal so it would pay. And then she could travel, take her mother and Russell and visit relatives wherever they'd like. There'd be resources. *Resources.* He spoke about money as though it was something to be consumed rather than saved for times of trial. She'd had plenty of trials.

She'd listened and returned to him. Nine months later, Donald was born, in late 1901. Dear, dear Donald with his light hair and sweet smile. She sighed. The paper-cut pain was almost desirable, distracting her thoughts of Donald. She pressed her finger, forcing blood she let drip over the dry sink. She watched it drop by drop, then decided to ease her discomfort with the salve, wrap the small throb in her handkerchief. Later she'd have to put extra bluing in the water to remove the stain. Scrub it hard.

Mrs. Bauer drifted back into the parlor and picked up the picture her husband had taken of the three of them, her and Russell and Donald. She evaluated herself. It wasn't one of her best photographs. She looked harsh, half her face in shadow. She'd retouched it, hoping to bring out the natural fullness and a small lift to her single-strand lips, barely wider than a yarn thread. She'd held the brush in her mouth to keep it moist while she perused the detail on the plate. Russell stood behind her, his hand gently on her neck, so protective. Only Donald smiled, and now he was gone. She ran her fingers across the cool glass that covered Donald's face.

She heard the door slam. Russell shouted, "Did you see me, Mother? I hit the ball further than anyone."

"Farther than," she corrected.

"They said I was too young to play with them, but I hit the ball fur . . . farther than even I thought I could."

"That's good. You ought to stay in now, wash up for supper. Your father will be home soon." She looked at the kitchen clock, annoyance spearing her lethargy. He should already be here. He'd probably stopped off at one of his lodges. No telling when he'd be home now.

She thought she saw a flash of anger cross Russell's eyes. Mrs. Bauer shared his sentiments, though for very different reasons. She simply could not count on her husband to be home at any given time. It was a small thing to expect, and yet he wouldn't comply. "We'll eat without him," she said. "Wash up." She grabbed at the cupboard door, jerked plates out, slammed them on the table.

Feeling angry was better than feeling nothing.

Chaos greeted Jessie once she reached Broadway Street and home. Her stomach growled to be fed, but her mother had other plans.

"I've had your father looking all over town. You had an interview this morning," her mother said. "You left the house in the dead of night. Roy told us, though it took him a while." Her little brother waved and grinned as he sat at the table, but then he almost always did grin. He burped then, a belch that sounded like a bull-frog's croak and had earned him the nickname of Frog, at least from Jessie. "Roy," her mother chastened.

"I left early morning," Jessie corrected.

"You didn't eat any breakfast and went off on your own without permission." Her mother looked at the clock. "Nearly noon. What have you been doing? Never mind. You've missed your interview. I thought it was something you might even enjoy. Where have your thoughts gone these days! Do you know how rare it is to find work that waltzes with one's interest?"

"Waltzes, Mama?" This from Selma. "I didn't think we were allowed to dance."

"Hush, child," her mother said. She wiped imaginary dirt onto her white apron in that way she had when she was annoyed, crossed her arms over her broad chest. Ida Gaebele was a force to be reckoned with, and this morning that force was a full tornado.

"I didn't miss the interview, Mama. I got the job," Jessie said. "Voe and I were both hired."

"You told Voe about the opening? Clara Deacon would have been so much the better companion for you than Voe. I didn't know that girl cared much about photography or anything associated with a trade like that."

"Voe's a good girl, Mama. I don't know why you don't like her. Besides, Mr. Bauer wasn't really looking for a camera girl."

"But the ad said—"

"He wants someone blank as a school slate."

"I see why Voe would qualify, then," Lilly said. She'd come home for lunch from her work in the glove factory.

"Hush now. It isn't nice to speak ill of others."

"But Mr. Bauer was willing to take me on anyway," Jessie continued. "We start on Monday."

"That's good, then, I suppose," her mother said. "Though your disappearing

this morning is still to be explained."
Jessie looked over at Selma. She hadn't
said anything about seeing Jessie leave.
She'd kept the secret, but Roy with his
tuned-in ears had heard her and told
their parents anyway.

"What on earth happened to your
sleeves? Did the man put you to work
today? He'll have to pay for repairs or
provide a clothing allowance."

"There was an . . . incident. Early this
morning," Jessie said. She reached for a
dry slice of toast on the oven's warming
shelf. "Mr. Steffes of the bicycle shop
was injured, and I helped him." Jessie
sat down and picked at the crumbs that
dropped onto the checkered oilcloth
spread over the table. "I got blood on
my sleeves, so I tore them off as I didn't
have time to come home to change, and
I knew you wouldn't have wanted me to
embarrass myself with stained clothing,
or be late for the interview, either."

"And what was so important that you
had to leave this house without breakfast and without telling anyone where
you were going *and* before you were
properly attired for your interview?" Her

mother squinted. "You're not wearing a corset."

"A photograph, Mama. I wanted to take this picture—"

"I might have known," Lilly said. "What sort of photograph would lure you to the cycle shop?"

"I was only . . . I heard him fall and I had to help him and get the doctor, so I missed the photograph anyway and then hurried along to Mr. Bauer's. I had my priorities right, Mama."

"Is Mr. Steffes all right?" Lilly asked as she removed pins and hung her small hat on the rack.

"I guess so. He was in good hands when I left."

Jessie filled in the details, embellishing just a bit for Roy's benefit. He liked stories. With Mr. Steffes "in good hands," her mother became practical. "Did he let you use the bicycle to make your appointment?"

"I didn't even ask. He was . . . scattered in his thinking, Mama. From his injury. Like when Papa fell that last time before we moved."

"Well, he might have loaned you the

bicycle since you'd taken the time to help him."

Jessie decided to wait to tell about her rental. Perhaps she wouldn't even have to. "His shop could use some cleaning. I thought I'd see if he might like a cleaning girl after I work at Mr. Bauer's studio. Maybe a couple of afternoons a week."

Her mother nodded agreement. Then her eye caught that shirtwaist again. "Well, let's get them sewn back on, those sleeves."

Jessie lowered her eyes. "I left them at Mr. Bauer's studio."

"You tore your blouse at your new employer's? But I thought—"

"I tore them before the interview, Mama, and didn't have anywhere to put them, so I put them in the camera bag. I'll get them back on Monday."

"You forgot your camera?" Selma asked.

Jessie took a deep breath. "Mr. Bauer doesn't like 'amateur camera girls,' as he calls them. So I had to agree to . . . that is, to leave my camera there and not use it for six months. Until I'm certified." She cleared her throat. "When he'll start paying me five dollars a week."

"F-f-five d-d-dollars. Is th-th-that goo—?"

"Yes, it's very good, Roy," his mother finished for him. Jessie ached each time her nearly six-year-old brother spoke, his words like a taffy pull stretching out and out but without any sweetness. She didn't like it when others cut him off and finished things for him either. It just made him lower his eyes and speak less. She'd heard about a hospital in far-away Seattle that treated young children like Roy. She wondered if she might somehow get him there. But Seattle was even farther away than Rochester, which had a fine hospital, but even that would take money they just didn't have. "Hush now while I get these details."

"It's more than twice what I made at the bindery," Jessie told Roy. "After paying Mama and Papa for my room and board, there'll be enough left for me to buy you a whistle if you'd like, from my first earnings." He nodded. "You'll just have to wait a bit. Because it's an apprenticeship, and I won't be paid for . . . six months."

She knew the family needed what she could earn, and she hoped her mother wouldn't just dismiss the Bauer Studio job because of the long delay in payment. This was such a grand chance, as her mother had already noted, to do something she loved.

"Six months. That makes no sense. I'm not sure we can afford—"

"Mr. Bauer will be training us, as though we were at the normal school. When we're finished, I'll take a test and be certified, and then I could work for any photographer in the city. I could even go to other cities." She didn't add, *And maybe one day have my own studio.* Women didn't own many businesses in Minnesota, not photographic ones. You had to go to big cities like Chicago or St. Louis to see professional women photographers, and she suspected her mother would never approve of her going to places like that. She wouldn't approve of such a dream. It wasn't practical in the least.

"He also said if I wanted to work extra, he'd give me special training in re-touching," Jessie continued. "I'll have a profession, Mama. Just as if I'd gone on to high school and normal school."

"But six months . . . What could take so long to learn?"

"Chemicals." She made her voice light. "He said sometimes photographers get mercury poisoning and then have to be away from their studios for months at a time. He wants us to learn all the business so we can operate his studio, handle the books, take money, make prints, and such, even when he isn't there to tell us how to do it. It's a very responsible opportunity. There'll be laws passed requiring such certification, Mama. That's what he said, and this way I'll learn correct procedures. It's more schooling. You and Papa always said schooling is important."

Her mother said nothing, then, "Yes, it is." Jessie sensed resignation. She thought her mother might not have heard her words about the mercury. "But six months without pay. I think we'd best discuss this when your father comes home, Jessie. Meanwhile, you go change your shirt. Those ragged sleeves look like a dog chewed the edges."

"Lilly, will you help me sew them back on?"

"If you ever get them returned. Your new employer is a strange one, if you ask me," Lilly said.

"I don't remember that I did," Jessie said. She smiled. She'd gotten through her mother's and older sister's objections. She just had her father's to deal with now.

⊱┈⟡┈◯┈⟡┈⊰

Lilly, with her perfectly coiffed hair despite a day's work as a seamstress and packager at Stott and Son, sat across from Jessie at the supper table. Selma adjusted her spectacles and slipped into the chair beside Lilly. Both Selma and Jessie had eyes that required correction with lenses; no one else in the family did. Roy fussed with the oilcloth, and Jessie put her hands over his to stop the fluttering movements. He looked up at her, surprise in his eyes. Sometimes Jessie wondered if he was aware of things he did. She wished she could give those hands something productive to do, but right now she prepared herself for the questioning she knew would come. She only hoped she could carry her arguments through to acceptance.

A parent sat at either end of the dining room table, and her father blessed the food. This was followed by the passing of potatoes and opinions about Jessie's active day.

"I've already decided," Jessie defended when Lilly told her she was being taken advantage of. Lilly's comment had surprised her, as she'd thought Lilly would say it was just part of the working world to be apprenticed out without pay. Lilly presented herself as so much wiser all the time. "It's a fair trade," Jessie continued. "No different than going to school, but I won't have to pay for the apprenticeship. Because that's really what it is."

"It's forced labor," Lilly said. "We're forming a club at work where we can talk about things that the women workers all have in common, and one of them is how we're treated at our employment."

"Stott's a good employer," Jessie's father said. He was a tall man with a full head of hair that had just begun to gray. Jessie thought him handsome. He must have weighed thirty pounds more than Mr. Bauer did. He had wide, short fingers, and Mr. Bauer had long musician's fingers. Her father's bushy eyebrows lifted as he spoke to Lilly, passing the potatoes as he did. "That's a good job, Daughter. One not to trifle with."

"I know that, Papa," Lilly said. "But they'd never ask us to work for six months without pay."

"I'd like to have him take my picture sometime," Selma said. The big bow she wore at the back of her head dwarfed her pale face, made her look younger than her eleven years.

"I'll photograph you after I've had my training," Jessie said.

"It just isn't fair," Lilly insisted, her arched eyebrows perfectly plucked.

"Your sister could be right, Jessie," her father said. He combed his thick mustache with his fingers. Lilly beamed as she leaned back into her chair. "Six months is a long time without pay. Most apprenticeships at least provide room and board while their workers are learning."

Jessie couldn't explain it, but somehow the sacrifice of no earnings and no photograph taking felt, well, warranted. It would make her success have more meaning.

"But it's a professional apprenticeship, not just learning a simple skill, Papa. That takes time. Some of the photographers in town charge for such classes. And girls aren't even allowed to take them."

Her father nodded. "Well, now, let's take a look at it. Every opportunity arrives in a carpetbag. Sometimes there are rocks in that bag and sometimes gold nuggets. We all have to decide how to convert whatever we've got into whatever we want."

"I-I-I w-w-want—"

"What? What do you want, Son?" Jessie's mother interrupted. "More potatoes? Rolls? Eat your greens."

Roy shook his head. "I-I-I w-w-want . . ." He swallowed. "I-I-I w-w-want g-g-gold."

Jessie's father tousled his hair. "Don't we all, Son."

Jessie smiled at Roy. She'd love to give him treasures.

"Jessie will just have to see if she has gold or if she'll have to lug some rocks before she can fill that bag with what she wants." Her father smiled at his middle daughter. "I think it's a fine opportunity."

"She won't be able to contribute," Lilly complained. "And I'll bear the results of that, I suppose."

"You're older. You're working. You can afford it," Jessie said.

"Jessie, don't be sassy," her mother said.

"I don't know why you always take her side," Lilly said.

"She didn't," Jessie said.

Jessie's father frowned. She'd been too quick to snap at Lilly. Why had she been so impulsive when she was so close to achieving what she wanted?

Forks poked at sausages. The clock ticked.

"It's how we spread the load in this family," her father said at last. "Each does her part, Lilly, as she can. And we help each other. My parents helped me; we can do likewise." His voice held a wistful tone, and Jessie wondered what dream he might have planted that never came to bloom. "You're of fine help and support to us, Lilly. And we need that and appreciate it. Very much."

"And what part will Jessie be doing? If she's working all day for nothing, at something she even *likes* to do, and then doesn't contribute—"

"I hope to get an evening cleaning job," Jessie said. "And I can help Mama more with the laundry. Or I can rake the leaves this fall. So you won't have to, Lilly. I know the dust bothers your cough."

"Well. That would be a start," her older sister said. The dust from the elm and maple leaves always left Lilly fighting a cold once the cool weather came.

"And you'll speak to Mr. Steffes since she was so helpful to him this morning," her mother told her father. Did her mother give some sort of signal to her father? Jessie couldn't always tell what their raised eyebrows or the set of their jaws might be saying.

"I heard about that. And what were you doing there at that hour of the day?"

"Seeing about . . . employment," Jessie said, and hoped the slant of truth would slip the subject on to something else.

But it didn't.

"Employment? Strange to be applying at Steffes's when you had the interview with the photographer," her father said.

Jessie sighed. She may as well tell the whole truth because it always came up to catch her anyway. "I'd rented a bicycle, Papa. So I could ride out past Lake Winona to take a picture of the bluff fires right at dawn. It was going to be so lovely. But then Mr. Steffes fell and I had to get the doctor, and then I got all bloody, and then there was the interview and—"

"You rented a bicycle?" Lilly slammed her fork down. "Papa, why does she have money for such things as that?"

"I didn't actually rent it," Jessie said. "So I'm sure I can get the money back."

"I'm singing on Sunday, aren't I, Mama?" Selma asked. "Irene and me?"

"Irene and I," her mother corrected. "It was announced in the paper already. Yes. Hush now."

"Don't let her change the subject," Lilly complained. "Jessie's always getting by with things, and Selma helps her."

"I don't get by with anything," Jessie said. "I do my part and I'll do even more in the next six months. I won't even have the pleasure of using my camera to take my mind off the drudgery."

"If I couldn't sing for six months, I don't know what I'd do." Selma sighed. "Life would be just . . . devastating." She put the back of her hand against her forehead, reminding Jessie of a woman on a theater advertisement looking dramatic, lying back in some swain's arms. Lilly rolled her eyes, and Jessie's mother appeared to wiggle her mouth to control a smile.

"I'll speak to Nic Steffes about your working, but you'll have to ask for your nickel back, Jessie. And"—to Lilly, her father said—"she'll be without her camera companion, so there is a sacrifice she's making too. We'll see if absence makes the heart grow fonder."

"Or if out of sight, out of mind," her mother answered.

"Just so her body isn't out of duty," Lilly said. "I've got some dresses in need of a soaking that she can help me with on Saturday."

"Whenever you wish to begin, Sister," Jessie said cheerfully. She'd gotten through the supper without committing to anything worse than red washboard knuckles.

>─┼◆>─O─<◆┼─<

An early moon rose as FJ walked the streets from his Knights of Pythias lodge meeting to the steps of his South Baker Street home. He always liked the way the trees etched themselves against the moonlight, sharp as a scissors' cut. Sometimes there'd be a cloud wisping across the Winona sky and the moonlight would reflect upon it, giving depth to the cloud and illuminating something more than what the eye first encountered. For a moment he'd feel, well, comforted. He didn't think of himself as a religious man, though he faithfully took his wife and family to the Second Congregational Church each Sunday. Religion was like a basket to him, a container for rituals and routines, filled to the brim with practices that had lost their luster and left little room for enlightenment. He attended more for the children and for Mrs. Bauer than for any kind of comfort he expected to find there. He appreciated the intellectual stimulation of the minister's words and often sparred with him after the service, drawing upon details gleaned from his own library of classics written by Dante, Shakespeare, and Descartes. Second Congregational seated some of the city's finest. Attendance was something one just did, and he didn't expect any moments of satisfying spiritual feeding within those walls.

But at moments like this—an encounter with something familiar, trees against moon, light against clouds—he'd find his spirits lifted to a place not bordered by faith or reason so much as by unexpected beauty. Awe, some might say. It was only a moonlit tree on a lovely night, but it gave him comfort. He felt almost sad when he entered the house and the moon with its iron-grate design disappeared.

Inside, he called out to let Mrs. Bauer know he was home. His mind went to his children. He'd talk with them about their days, read a story to each, then say good night. Then he'd scan the paper while Mrs. Bauer reheated his dinner. He hoped she was over the disruption of the morning. He wasn't sure whether to apologize again or to let it be. He'd wait to see what her mood was. Hopefully, they'd have a civil conversation about each other's day, hers with stories of the children or what sewing she might have done, whether the garbage had been transported as scheduled or whether he needed to order ice. He'd have to tell her that while he didn't appreciate her having used a portrait time to schedule interviews, he thought he'd found what he needed in the two young women: the one being spirited and bright, and the other being teachable and loyal. Good qualities all if he could help them master the skills he wanted. The time he invested would be worth it if the girls could assume the duties should the sickness overtake him again. And if not, they could double the output of prints and speed up development, earning him happier customers. If only he could stay well.

He'd had bouts with rheumatic fever since he'd been in the army, and perhaps those episodes had weakened him, made him more susceptible to the mercury poisonings. But then most of the men he knew who made their living as photographers had at least one bout with the poisons—unless they spread the work around, and that's exactly what he intended to do. If he never needed the girls to run the studio, well then, after a few years he could perhaps help them find employment with other photographers, where men did need trained assistants.

His easy mood cautioned as he placed his hat on the round table beside the door and felt the silence slice like the calm before a storm. Silence sparred with concern. Too quiet. It wasn't even eight o'clock. Surely Russell was still up, and he'd asked Mrs. Bauer not to put Winnie to bed before eight so he could play with the child for a time.

Not again, he thought as he turned back to look at the moon. It was up above the trees, so bright it created a shadow of the house framed against the lawn. So peaceful everything looked. Nothing to match the turmoil in his gut.

FJ paced his way through the house, his mind racing to the first evening when he'd returned home to an empty house. Eighteen ninety-four. They'd been married for three turbulent years. Oh, not shouting and such, not on his part; he was never one for that. Mrs. Bauer made her voice heard though. She was young and he'd given her ample time, or so he'd thought back then. Time to adjust to marriage. Time to visit her mother, every day if she wanted. He'd moved her mother to Winona from Ellsworth in fact. He'd encouraged her to come to the studio, to learn the busi-

ness with him. He'd pushed for more intimacy. She'd resisted. She was still
young, he knew, but he wanted a family,
wanted children laughing and scamper-
ing around the house. What was the
point of working so hard if not to have
children to share the fruits of the labor
and, more, to leave it to?

Then one fine summer evening he'd
come home to emptiness. She'd left
him, moved her dresses and chemises
and jewelry and cold creams into her
mother's house. When he finally worked
through the ups and downs of worrying
over something having happened to her,
it was the next morning. He walked to
her mother's house, where she met him
at the door and told him her mother
needed her now, what with her father's
death and her sister Eva's being newly
married and not able to help her mother.
"She can't be alone."

But her mother had often been alone
while her husband traveled for his photographic business. Ernestine Otis was
a capable if not eccentric woman who
distinguished herself in Winona commerce by never carrying a purse. In-

stead she wore layers of petticoats into which she'd sewn pockets, and whenever she purchased items—pieces of material for quilts she started but never finished—she'd have to paw through yards of fabric in order to find the pockets that had coins in them. She didn't need her daughter with her, but FJ needed his wife with him. It was where a wife belonged, beside her husband.

Eventually he'd gotten his mother-in-law to agree, but not his own wife.

He'd bought flowers and started her on bottled mineral water, to no avail; he spent long hours at his lodge because the house felt as empty as an overdrawn well.

What finally brought her back after nearly six months was beyond him. He'd begun to think she would never return, and then one night he came home and there she was, sitting at the table, his dinner warming in the Monarch oven. That he didn't know why she'd returned meant he couldn't prevent what might make her leave again.

She did not wish to speak of why she left or why she'd come back, but she'd been more ready to be intimate with him. The matter of children had taken nearly four more years of gentle persuasion, but in 1899 Russell was born.

She'd gone home again the next year but returned in less than six months, and he told himself that perhaps she needed that respite to be with her mother, learning how to tend a newborn. Two years later, Donald arrived. She announced that there'd be no more children and moved into her own bedroom. Only one time had she let him in and then only because he cajoled her, convinced her for a night that marriage meant a working through of problems, shared tenderness, not an escape where only one person achieved happiness. Not that he thought her happy, but neither was he. After that single evening together she'd seemed contented, and he thought perhaps he'd made a way through her resistance.

But then Donald had . . . There'd been the accident, far away in North Dakota, and he'd had to come home to tell her, the worst journey of his life. Friends had pressed them to have more children right away. None knew that she was already with child.

FJ had hoped they could help support each other through this wilderness place, but they had not. She claimed illness from the childbearing, wanted to be left alone. He buried his grief in his work.

Winifred arrived four months later, and with Russell, they became the children that partially filled his emptiness. He wasn't sure about Mrs. Bauer's.

As he entered the kitchen this March evening, he did not smell a warming meal, no boiled potatoes or roast beef. He thought of other reasons why there might be no dinner. It was toward the end of the month and the household budget might be a little low. He'd have to check, but there was surely enough for a chicken. If there wasn't, it was Mrs. Bauer's duty to inform him so his children and their parents could eat sufficiently.

She might not feel well. Her headaches might have consumed her evening. He looked for a note. She had agreed that if she ever left him again, she'd leave a note. There was none. A single lamp burned in the kitchen, casting shadows on the curtains. He walked through to the dining room.

"Mrs. Bauer? What's keeping you?"

He made his way through the still house, took the steps two at a time to the second floor and the bedrooms, then opened Russell's door. He felt his heart pounding—from the stair climb, he hoped, nothing more. The boy was asleep. It was early, but at least he was there; well, breathing evenly as FJ pulled the blanket over the boy's shoulder and heard his own heartbeat slow. He found Winnie sleeping quietly in her crib in the nursery, and he caressed her hair, something he'd wanted to do that morning. His knock on Mrs. Bauer's door brought no response. He opened it slowly, never quite sure what he'd find. The door creaked. She wasn't there. The oval mirror of her dresser reflected his own frantic look.

He returned downstairs, calling through the house, not so loud that the children would be awakened or alarmed. She had to be there somewhere! She'd never leave the children by themselves.

They rarely used the parlor. The drapes there kept the room cool in summer and cold in the winter. It would be cold this evening. A pump organ filled up one entire wall of the small and heavily furnished room, and sometimes Mrs. Bauer played it to soothe her nerves. But he heard no music now. His eyes adjusted to the darkness. No moonlight penetrated here. He started to open the drapes to let the moonlight in when he was startled by her words.

"You finally join your family," Mrs. Bauer said.

"What are you doing sitting here in the darkness?" The words came out sharper than intended, but she'd frightened him, sitting there faded into the mahogany chair beside the door. She'd begun with accusation. He'd defended. "A small light surely won't hurt your head."

"Not that it matters to you," she said. "If it did, you'd be home at a reasonable hour, have time with your children as you were so anxious to this morning.

Winnie's been coughing. These March winds stir her and make her ill."

"She appears to be sleeping soundly," he said.

"You would check on the children first."

"I would have greeted you first, you know that. I couldn't find you, and you failed to answer when I called. Please, don't argue. I'm sorry you've had a difficult day with the children. My own day has been . . . informative, if you'd care to hear of it."

"Thrice told? I imagine you've told the story to your lodge men. You certainly don't need to lower yourself to repeat it to your ignorant wife."

"Ignorant?" She'd never referred to herself that way before. "Nonsense. Join me in the kitchen, and I'll tell you about the girls you had me interview. We have eggs in the house, yes? I'll fix us some scrambled if you've not had any dinner."

"I'm very tired, Mr. Bauer. Now that you've lowered yourself by coming home, I believe I'll go to bed. And, yes.

There are eggs. It's good you know how to scramble them."

"Why do you do this, Jessie?" He corrected himself when she cleared her throat. "Mrs. Bauer. You're far from ignorant. I'd be pleased to share my day with you. And I don't think of coming home as something I don't want to do."

"Yet you're never here in a timely manner."

"One time this month have I stopped at the lodge. One time, confound it! I never know what sort of reception I'll receive when I do come home. I'm always welcome there," he said, immediately wishing he hadn't.

"That's it, isn't it? I make your life miserable. I never do it right. How can you even bear to look at me?"

Her voice rose in that strident way it had, like a wave at sea growing and growing. If he didn't interrupt it, she'd escalate and go on for hours. She had in the past and he didn't want that, not now. He was tired too.

"You're right, Mrs. Bauer. You're absolutely correct." He folded his hands as though in prayer. Maybe he did pray. "I should have come immediately home. I worked late, but that's no excuse, leaving you here with the children. I'll fix tea for you if you'd like."

"I've had enough tea to float the Boston flotilla. Yes. I do know a little history," she said. "I know *our* history good and well. Shall I repeat it to you? What you did?"

There'd be nothing he could do now. Every flutter of an eyelash, every lift of his eyebrow, even a tug on his mustache would carry with it messages he hadn't put there. He made his face like stone.

She rose from the chair. He waited for her to come closer to assault him with her words. He'd stand his ground. He had to. But instead she slipped like a shadow through the door, leaving him and the room as dry as a photographic plate.

FOUR

Candlelight Eyes

There is satisfaction in reaching for what one wants, even if attainment escapes one's grasp. It was the thought on Jessie's mind when she woke from a sound sleep the first morning of her new job. She washed in the cool water in the bowl, dressed, and found Roy waiting for her in the kitchen. He was her champion, the one who saluted her adventures.

She pressed against his cowlick and said, "I'll take word pictures over the next few months since I won't have my camera."

Roy rubbed sleep from his eyes.

"Wh-wh-what h-h-happened to your c-c-camera?"

"Mr. Bauer is keeping it until I learn new habits," she said. "I'll get it back, and when I do, the next pictures I take will be more professional. You wait and see. I never did like to do the practice exercises that Kodak recommended. I just liked to shoot and see what I got. Now that's probably all I'll be doing, practicing." Still, each day she'd learn something new; each encounter at the studio would be one she'd try to re-member and "picture" in her eye to share with Roy even if she didn't have the camera to assist her.

"Wh-wh-what's p-p-professional?"

She thought, then said, "Someone with a certificate saying they are, I guess. That they're authorized to do a thing. That they both have the skill and then take the risk of using it. You have to do both to be authorized and profes-sional."

"Y-y-you don't need a c-c-certifi-tifi-cate."

Jessie brushed the blunt cut of his hair back from his eyes. "Thanks for that," she told him. She'd sacrifice for Roy. That thought would help her fill the empty days without her camera.

Mr. Bauer began the morning instructions with a tour of the studio's reception room, pointing out his awards in portrait work and telling them he'd won a gold medal from the National Photographic Association. "But it was stolen in '01. The thief was probably one of my customers who saw the gold and totally ignored the great emotional treasure the award held for me."

"Probably shouldn't have stuck it out there in the open," Voe offered.

Mr. Bauer had a pained look. "I've heard that somewhere else," he said but didn't elaborate.

The room was lighted from the top with skylights. Jessie could look up and see the tips of branches from the towering elms, though not enough to lessen the light's effect. The room felt comfortable without being too elegant and would put most people at ease with its dark greens and muted reds. Too rich and people would likely protest the costs of their portraits; too simple and they'd wonder if the photographer had the skill or experience to expose the richness they hoped to see in the finished product. Jessie noted that this business was a balance.

"I like that one," Jessie said, pointing to a portrait of two men dressed as though they lived in biblical times.

"It's always best not to just announce that you like or don't like something," Mr. Bauer instructed, "but rather to say what you like about it or don't. How it makes you feel, for example."

Jessie hadn't thought much about putting feelings into words, let alone trying to figure out how the portrait affected her emotions. He urged her on, lifting his hand to the picture hanging on the wall. "Go ahead," he said. "Tell me what you see there."

"I see strength in their faces," she said. "The lines from their eyes are deep, as though they've weathered much. They look humble too. The man looking down is almost in prayer, and the other's eyes are looking upward."

"The light makes their bald heads stand out," Voe said.

"But the light also complements the one man's staff," Jessie said. "It makes the whole picture look . . . warm. I like the way their beards appear soft too. Fluffy. And their cloaks are rich, but I don't feel poorly looking at them. I feel . . . safe," Jessie decided. "Safe and warm. It's a fine photograph, Mr. Bauer."

"It is," he said. "I didn't take it, however. It's from the Knaffl brothers out of Tennessee. You can see the name there." He pointed to the small signature. "It's become quite a famous plate and is as close to a painting as anything I've ever seen done with a camera. It was actually inspired by a painting called 'Frieze of the Prophets' by John Sargent."

"Should you show off someone else's work in your reception room?" Voe again. "Won't it lead your customers to believe their work is yours?"

"He has his work here too," Jessie defended. She'd moved around the room, looking for the little signature on each piece that told who the photographer was.

"But you thought that one was his," Voe said.

That was true before she knew to look for signatures, but before she could respond, Mr. Bauer said, "I think it's good to have before me, every day, the work of a master, someone I can emulate, to remind me of the possibilities in this . . . art. Yes. I think of this as an art and not just a commercial venture, though I can assure you that the Knaffl brothers have elevated commercial photography to a new level. It's been said of that plate that if it had been arranged as an original piece and not as a copy of the painting, we would have a first example of creative art in photography. Such is one of the things I'm striving for. Creative art in studio photography."

"Was it all done at once?" Jessie asked. Mr. Bauer frowned. "I mean, did the brothers do things to the background of the picture afterward? Or was it developed just the way it looks?"

Mr. Bauer's eyes lit up like candlelight. "Very observant, Miss Gaebele. Very good question. I suspect that the lighting effect was created in the developing process with dodging." Jessie frowned. "It's a way of using one's hand to limit light to certain sections on the plate, to cause an effect you want. It's not only what the eye sees that makes a fine photographer but also the accoutrements, the way a subject is arranged, what surrounds it, what the shadows can do. And then of course what the workman creates in the darkroom. But it all begins with the artist's eye."

"Workmen," Voe said. "I don't think of photographers as workmen, not like draymen or lumbermen. I've seen painters at carnivals, and they have just as much fun as the ones they're painting. That's what artists are, just fun people. Like Gypsies."

"You're just saying that because you were named for a Gypsy," Jessie told her, laughing.

"Now, girls, we photographers are workmen. It is a labor to create these pieces, but it is good labor. There is great joy within it. Your carnival painters know that's in part why people stop by to be painted—for the adventure, if you will. That doesn't minimize the artistry.

There's nothing wrong with finding joy in work," he said. "No one wants to have their photograph made by a drudge," he added.

"What's a drudge?" Voe asked.

"It comes from the German word for *slave*," Mr. Bauer told her. "I don't consider myself a slave to my work, though my wife might at times." He straightened his tie at his narrow neck, pulled at his collar. "I consider my work an opportunity, and that's why I keep that picture on my wall. There are opportunities everywhere in a workman's day. That's a lesson for you young women to remember rather than quibbling over Gypsies."

He moved the girls on, then, into the studio proper. One large room comprised the operating room, as Mr. Bauer called the place where subjects sat and had their photographs made. The room did not have a skylight, just a small circular window set quite high in one wall. On the opposite side of the room, a large bank of windows provided natural light, starting partway up the white wall and ending nearly at the ceiling. Leaded glass formed elongated diamond shapes from top to bottom. Jessie caught a look at herself in a round mirror on a stand off to the side. She pushed back loose strands of hair that had slipped from her bun.

Chairs of various kinds graced the hardwood floors, some with but one arm, others made of white wicker. Curtains hung on rods beside small reflector screens that could be moved into position to add softness to the subject. Jessie tried to memorize each item while Mr. Bauer showed them where he kept the back drapes and rolls of carpet that could be spread out on the floor. In a side room he stored small benches and tables with a pot of dried flowers, vases, pillows, even books with different textures.

"Props," he told them, "to add interest or to set the viewer's eye to a certain aspect of the subject." Jessie's mind began to swim with the details she would need to keep track of. This was nothing like pointing her Kodak at a flower and clicking, wondering what she'd get once the film was developed.

In the center of the vast room stood

the camera, a large, square apparatus draped with a black cloth. It was the true focus. Mr. Bauer had arranged it on a cabinet with a brass wheel on the outside, and Jessie realized instantly that by turning the wheel he'd be able to move the camera up and down. Wheels at the bottom of the cabinet made it possible to move in on the subject. With it, he could take a full stance, a half shot, and even a full facial view without the person ever having to change position. He'd have more options for printing and surely a better chance of framing a pose in a way that would please the customer.

They walked through the printing room next, full of frames the size of trunks and brass ones small enough to hold in one's palm. Cardboard mats of various shapes and colors showed cuts made by a sharp knife, and they were kept in a drawer built into the wall for such use. "It's never finished until it's in the perfect frame," Mr. Bauer told them as he opened a door to a small room with another door on the opposite side.

"The mysterious darkroom," Voe said

in a ghostly voice as Mr. Bauer pulled the first door shut behind them. "It's pretty small."

The space the three of them stood in was close enough that Jessie touched Voe's back with her fingertips, and she could sense Mr. Bauer just a foot or so behind her. She thought she smelled cigars on Mr. Bauer's coat, though the scent wasn't quite as strong as real smoke. Every scent seemed heightened in this little space.

He punched the light and the room turned dark. "Hey," Voe said. "I don't see how you can get any work done in such a little darkroom."

"Please open the other door, Miss Kopp, if you would."

Voe did, and chemical scents assaulted Jessie's nose as her eyes adjusted to the orange glow of the room. Shelves lined the sides, holding bottles and tins in the windowless room. A single faucet hung over a sink at the side, and the remainder of the room consisted of high wooden benches. Jessie assumed these were drying benches where prints could be laid after their chemical baths.

"We were in the protection room, Miss Voe," Mr. Bauer explained, "not the darkroom. This is where the developing occurs. We keep the protection room so that no light comes in from the outside should someone forget that negatives are being worked on and ruin them with the exposure of light. Not all studios have such little entryways," he told them, "but they will have some other way of telling a person not to enter under any circumstances. Signs or a gas bulb lit up just for that purpose. It could be very costly if one entered when one should not. When entering I recommend you always turn down the light as I did before opening the door into the darkroom."

He assured them they'd be spending plenty of time in this room, but for now the tour continued to a room that was little more than a closet with a small light on a table. Artists' pads of paints sat on the desk beside brushes.

"The retouching room," he told them. "And occasionally people wish to have their pictures colored. It's something we do here. But it requires extra training. If you want to earn additional money after the training period, this would be an area of skill you could acquire. I came in early to do a little work here myself."

Then he took them into what Jessie considered the business area, where they were to become familiar with the ledger book, entering prints and their prices, noting whether someone had paid or not, setting up appointments when people called the studio number. Most of this business work was accomplished in a small room off the reception area so the girls would be able to hear when someone entered but the records would be kept private. Jessie remained attentive. Money was important in her family: getting it, keeping it, and using it so a family could have security. Obviously Mr. Bauer had similar values.

That first morning, she and Voe paid close attention to Mr. Bauer's instructions, and while he rarely praised them, neither did he deride them. He answered questions thoroughly and in ways that Jessie could understand.

When she didn't, she waited for Voe to ask again, as Voe often needed to hear an instruction more than once in order to fully take it in. If she asked a question Jessie thought she knew the answer to, Jessie used those occasions to test herself on her knowledge, pleased when she could have answered the question with the same terms Mr. Bauer chose.

A portrait of an attractive woman and two small boys hung in the office room, right where the eye could see it when looking out toward the reception room. Mr. Bauer didn't talk about that picture though his name was on it, and so Jessie didn't ask and neither did Voe, whose attention had been drawn to a piece of pottery sitting on a table.

"This is pretty," she said, picking it up.

Mr. Bauer took it carefully from her. "It is. I acquired it while in North Dakota, from a Chippewa Indian there. I admired it and she gave it to me. Quite generous, considering . . ."

"Considering what?" Voe asked.

"Let's just say it's a precious piece, one that Mrs. Bauer prefers I keep here instead of at our home. I rather like the designs."

"They're like the window diamonds in your studio," Jessie said.

Mr. Bauer turned to her, said nothing, but he had that candlelight in his eye again.

"It'll take some time," he told them both as he set the pot back down on the table, "but you'll want to ask the right questions when people come in or when they call about a sitting in order to make it easier to be ready for their session. There's a great deal of preparation that goes into making an award-winning photograph," Mr. Bauer said.

"Who gives out such awards?" Jessie asked. "Like your gold medal that was stolen?"

"The National Photographic Association. I attend their events regularly in Chicago or Philadelphia, Minneapolis, wherever they're held. It means travel but it's a worthy expense, for it's there where one discovers new ideas and where work can be showcased for new commercial use."

"I like to travel," Jessie said. "With my camera."

"We don't take our cameras," Mr. Bauer cautioned. "Unless we're offering classes. We go there to learn new techniques, to meet old friends, make new ones."

"They probably don't let women go there anyway," Voe told her.

"Ah, but they do. There are several female photographers besides your Jessie Tarbox Beals you encountered at the world's fair, Miss Gaebele." He turned to Jessie. "Mary Carnell of Philadelphia takes mostly children's photographs. Miss Belle Johnson of Monroe City, Missouri, loves to photograph felines. Kittens," he told Voe as her mouth opened to ask. "I suspect she does much more, but those were the ones she submitted at the last congress. Quite impressive. And of course, Frances Johnston. She's made quite a name for herself as a garden and architectural photographer. Her self-portrait, done nearly ten years ago now, has become quite famous."

"How come?" Voe asked.

Mr. Bauer's face took on a sour look,

and Jessie wondered if he wished he hadn't brought the subject up. He cleared his throat. "Not that I'm condoning this, you understand. But it is a public photograph now." He tugged at his mustache. "Well. It's taken in her studio. She's wearing a skirt and shirtwaist. She's sitting in front of her fireplace."

"Sounds dull to me," Voe said, gazing at her fingernails.

"Well, it shows her . . . petticoat, while her legs are crossed at the knee instead of at the proper ankle, and we can see her striped stockings right up to that knee."

"Oh," Voe said, looking interested now.

"She holds a beer stein in one hand and a cigarette in the other, and she's wearing a boyish hat. The portrait has done nothing to advance the cause of women photographers. In my opinion."

Jessie wondered where she could see this self-portrait but decided to wait until later to pursue that.

"My mother would never let me pose like that," Voe said.

"I bet she isn't married," Jessie said.

"My mother is so," Voe said.

"I was talking about Mrs. Johnston," Jessie told her.

"She is unmarried," Mr. Bauer confirmed. "As a 'bachelor girl,' she spent months on a battleship with several hundred sailors taking photographs, traveled to greet Dewey when he returned from the Philippines, and her agent got those military photographs sold for nearly a thousand dollars." He gained volume while he spoke, and Jessie thought he sounded irritated by the woman's successes. His words clipped out short and were peppered with passion. Or maybe he didn't like her commenting on the woman's marital status. Maybe he didn't like his employees commenting at all.

"No one telling her she couldn't, I suppose," Voe said.

"You're right, Miss Kopp. A married woman with the responsibilities of hearth and home would find it difficult to do such things."

"But think of the freedom," Jessie said. It was one thing for a woman to attend a fair, but to travel the world, to meet interesting people, to earn money doing what she loved and spend it as she saw fit—for family, for alms, for pleasure—that was truly privilege. "She can wander anywhere she wants and no one will question it so long as she carries a camera. What a grand life for a woman." This first day on the job was proving to have insights she had never imagined.

Jessie discounted the possibility that her words were responsible for blowing out that candlelight in Mr. Bauer's eyes.

FIVE

Seeking Safety

Spring passed like a summer storm, heightened with activity followed by tedious lulls. Jessie rarely had time for anything but work. Mr. Steffes had accepted her suggestion that she clean his shop at least three times a week. Her mother was happy she'd gotten her nickel back and earned more to boot. On those days, Jessie still had extra laundry, as her aprons were always covered with grime. She even turned down an invitation from Lilly to join friends at Latsch Beach along the river to see if the water was warm enough to swim in. "I'm just too tired," she told her sister and welcomed instead a nap on the screened porch where the girls slept during the summer months.

This photography was serious business that required constant attention. She made mistakes, mixed chemicals incorrectly, wasn't as patient with clients as Mr. Bauer wanted. She read books and his journals with discussions of apertures and such that might be beyond her, though she told not a soul of her fears. In her dreams she wasn't a fine female photographer traveling to exotic places. Instead she stood on a ladder in precarious climes, often slipping just before she reached the top rung. She'd wake up with a heart-pounding start.

September would be the time when she'd begin earning money and, she hoped, pass her certification test. Her plan was to stop working for Mr. Steffes after that. She'd convince Selma to take the three days after school. He'd recovered slowly from his fall, and having someone clean up made his life easier. It wasn't difficult work, just messy, but Mama might not want her youngest girl working alone at Mr. Steffes's shop late in the day. She'd overheard a concerned conversation between her parents about Selma's daydreaming related to her "hobby," as they called Selma's singing. At least, she thought the conversation was about Selma. An after-school job might address Selma's apparent distractions.

Still, the bicycle wheels in the shop fascinated Jessie. She'd never paid much attention to mechanical things, but now that she spent those evenings attempting to clean and order Mr. Steffes's shop, she found that the shapes and surfaces intrigued her. Jessie liked the way the spokes cast shadows on a grease tub behind the wheel, causing the steel pail to take on stripes. A closeup, taken with a camera, would make people wonder what it really was, what subject the photographer had meant to take, and cause a conversation. She could set the camera so it looked up and through the spokes and maybe move the tub behind it and just focus a small portion of the photograph on those spokes. It would be unusual. What she saw wasn't like any photograph she'd ever seen, but then each photographer saw something different. That's what Mr. Bauer told her. That's what gave one a voice, or in this case, an eye.

She longed for her camera though. She felt like a rib had been cut from her side, leaving her lopsided. She needed it to keep her balance, something she hadn't been aware of until the gift of the camera had graced her days. She made a few sketches of interesting objects but didn't have the same satisfaction as when she took a photograph and then later, upon printing, got to see the image as though for the first time. She wouldn't actually take pictures, even if she had the camera, since she'd made the promise, but she could practice framing images. She used her hands to make a circle to isolate the image in her mind.

It had become an annoyance and a wasteful requirement that she leave the camera with Mr. Bauer, who had even put it away somewhere so she wouldn't be tempted to use it. At least he'd given her the torn sleeves before he hid it. She hadn't even been able to finish the roll on the Kodak and send it back, not that she had the money to get the film developed anyway, at least not right now. Her uncle August had paid for the previous rolls. Once she had money, the Eastman Company would send the camera and new film to her so she could take another hundred prints. But Mr. Bauer had been specific, and his instructions were otherwise easy to understand. It was only another month before she'd have the camera back.

The stillness of Mr. Steffes's shop captured her too. Dust mites would shiver through arcs of light shining in from the small but clean windows. Once Mr. Steffes left for the day, she had the place to herself, and she found she liked to work in silence, just the brush of her broom against the floor or the rumble of a passing dray penetrating the walls of the shop. The streetcar didn't come this far, and with the shops closed, there was little reason for a horse to *clop-clop* its way along the street, but sometimes there were late deliveries. A rodent might poke its head from its hole and make a scraping sound or two, but Jessie had managed to silence those noises after a time by putting wire mesh over the holes and suggesting to Mr. Steffes that he place poison in dishes to kill the rats.

She'd become accustomed to the smells too: from grease and old stained rags, the brush of dirt that she swept out the door each day, especially after a downpour, when mud clung to the rubber tires of bicycles loaned and returned. She usually opened the two small windows while she worked, to air the place out, and she did that now. The sultry August evening air dampened her cheeks, but she was more interested in the way the wood weathered on the windowsill, creating streaks of paint and texture that would make an interesting design photographed and developed from a dry glass plate.

"Why is it," she asked herself out loud, "that when I'm not supposed to take a photograph, I find them everywhere?" She hummed as she worked, grateful that no one looked over her shoulder, that daydreaming wouldn't cause anyone trouble. Here was a place to let her mind rest from all the details of the studio, of trying to please Mr. Bauer, of worries about Roy and her father's health. Somehow this physical effort served as a good complement to the work of her mind.

Jessie made sure the doors were locked after Mr. Steffes left. She didn't want to invite trouble. First, though, she had wrestled with two bicycles leaned up against the front of the shop and brought them in through the narrow door. Mr. Steffes hadn't asked her to do anything other than clean, but she had suggested he find a better way to account for his bicycles, as he was prone to leave them outdoors and check them in the next day. That didn't make good business sense to Jessie, so she rolled the cycles in and lined them up in the iron stalls she'd gotten him to forge. At the very least she thought he ought to build some racks for the outside where the bicycles could be chained and locked so people would have to come in before using them. Jessie suspected that any number of bicycles found their way into the hands of men who used them, returned them, and never did pay despite the name on the shop as a livery.

"Oh, it all works out," Mr. Steffes told her. "If a man has need of wheels but lacks the funds to pay, he will in time. Besides, eventually they purchase and I'll have their business making repairs. They tell others who rent, then buy, and so it goes, one day to the next."

It seemed a precarious way to run a business, but then she was just a girl and didn't understand commerce—despite heeding Mr. Bauer or watching her father or listening to her grandparents or even quizzing her uncle August about this and that. Still, if people had a reason to come inside, they might consider purchasing a bicycle and not just renting.

Mr. Steffes never took out an ad in the *Republican-Herald* or the *Winona Independent,* the latter being a morning paper that might serve his clients well. Well, she was pleased it was part of her job at the Bauer Studio to find out what she could about managing a business, the way people paid, how they got post-cards printed, what the costs of ads were, how money came and went. That reminded her of another question she wanted to ask Mr. Bauer.

"Don't you ever stop working?" Voe shouted at the locked door. "You're in there, aren't you, Jessie?"

Jessie wiped the tools Mr. Steffes had used during the day, then lined them up on the wooden bench. She unlocked the door. Voe appeared as she often did, as a star just showing up in the night. "I'm just keeping my agreements. Don't you think this would make an interesting photograph?" Jessie asked. "See how the size diminishes with each pair of pliers? I could fan them out and—"

"You do see things in the strangest ways," Voe said. She tucked a strand of her blond hair back into the circle of braids at her ears. She wore a straw hat with a flat top and looked ready for fun, her double chin jiggling as she laughed and suggesting she was heavier than she really was. "I stopped by to see if you'd come to the beach with us."

"Who's 'us' and for what?" Jessie

asked. She picked up the broom and began to sweep as Voe chattered.

"Just a few of us chums. We're going to the lake and putting canoes in."

Jessie did like the water.

"I'd have to go home and talk to my parents first. They always like to know where I am."

"Don't they let you do anything without asking? Some girls our age are already married."

"Not in my family," Jessie said. "No dancing, no drinking, no smoking, no card playing, no—"

"But there's no rule against canoeing, is there? Or sitting at the beach and watching the rest of us?"

"I imagine they'd let me do that," Jessie said. "But I really don't know if I want to."

Jessie's parents would likely let her go with her chums. But today, digging a bit in the garden or reading to Roy seemed preferable to the chatterings that would happen at the lake.

"My brother's going to be there," Voe said in a singsong voice. "He's kind of sweet on you, you know. He asked me specific if you'd come."

"I get pretty tired by the time I'm through here," Jessie said.

"How long will your parents make you do this? Seems a tough punishment just because you left the house early one morning, especially when you got the job at Mr. Bauer's and everything."

"It's because we're not getting paid," Jessie said. "I need to help at home. Just like you do."

"Not this time. My ma liked your argument that it was a free education, and she said if I could get myself a trade, it would be worth having me studying and not tiring myself with extra work for six months."

"I don't really mind the work. I get to see lots of picture possibilities," she said.

"In bicycle wheels and tools?" Voe laughed as she said it, careful not to allow her light summer dress to flounce toward the dirty wheels. "You're odd, Jessie." It was, though, one of the things Jessie liked about her friend. She saw the world straight on, while Jessie could supply the slants.

"I'm an odd duck who makes a noisy quack," Jessie said. "So why would your brother care whether I joined you or not?"

"He likes a challenge. He's going to own his own farm one day, you'll see. Come along. I'll go back and tell your ma that you'd like to join us."

"No!" Jessie was certain her mother wouldn't appreciate Voe's speaking for her. "I'll finish up here and then come down to the beach if I can, but only for a little while."

Voe shrugged and headed off.

Jessie locked the door behind her, then worked a little longer, cleaning up the cast-iron sink Mr. Steffes neglected. Now she really did need a bath! She closed up and fast-walked toward home. Selma said she walked like a shore bird, taking quick-quick steps. But Selma had long legs, and Jessie had to take three to her one to keep up, even though Selma was four years younger.

On the way home she decided that

she wouldn't ask to go to the lake at all. Jerome Kopp wasn't someone whose interests she wanted to encourage. He'd once noted that her name had different meanings and told her that *jessy* meant to give someone the "worst licking of their life." "Give them jessy!" he'd shouted when two boys at school were fighting. She was aghast that her name could be used like that!

The truth was, none of the boys at school nor the brothers of the girls she'd worked with at Kroeger's had interested her in the least. They acted silly in the presence of girls, pushing one another and bragging. Lilly's beaus were gentlemen, but Lilly kept finding things wrong with each suitor who came her way. "I have high standards," Lilly told her mother when her mother suggested that some young man's interest ought to be encouraged instead of pushed away.

"Such high standards might keep you under our roof for longer than you'd like," her mother had told her. Lilly didn't let such words distress her, not even when they came from her mother, though Jessie thought she'd made those comments after a boy of particular interest stopped calling. Lilly seemed sad after that, and then she'd gotten, well, irritable, a state she was constantly in, it seemed to Jessie.

Jessie took a petal from Lilly's vibrant flower. She had high standards too, and Jerome Kopp didn't match them, not that she'd speak such truth to his sister. Instead, she'd go home, rinse her hair with henna to bring out the shine, and take a sponge bath. The air was so humid. Then she'd read to Roy or, better, let him take his time to say whatever he wanted without anyone else's interrupting.

A low roll of thunder caused her to look up. Swirling dark globs of cloud promised a downpour. At least it might cut the sticky heat. She turned the corner where she could see her home and nearly groaned when the porch came into view. There stood Voe and Jerome, along with several others of the "collection," as her father referred to Jessie's chums. They sat on the porch steps while Lilly and Selma rocked on the swing. Her parents leaned at the porch balustrades. Roy sat off to the side.

She sighed.

"There she is!" Voe said. "Hurry up now. Your ma says you can come with us. We're going to play Old Mother Wobble Gobble, so bring lots of hair ribbons and handkerchiefs."

"Not too many," Jerome said. "I'm going to give you jess—" He stopped himself. "I mean I'm hoping to get me a cherry in that game."

Clara, one of the girls in the crowd, laughed. "There'll be no kissing, Mrs. Gaebele. Jerome's just a big tease." Ma had frowned with Jerome's boast, and Jessie didn't think Clara's words had reassured her. Good, maybe they'd forbid her to go. But they said nothing.

"It'll take me a while to get ready," Jessie stalled. "Why don't you go on ahead? I'd hate to hold you up."

"We don't mind," Voe said. "Do we, Jerome?"

Jerome was as husky as her little brother was thin. But he was a muscled husky, formed from farm work. A big, blond German boy. "I don't mind waiting, Jess. I enjoy talking to Mr. Gaebele here about dairying and such. I don't hardly ever get to see you at church, you're out of there so fast."

At the mention of church, Jessie's mother's shoulders relaxed. Jessie thought him wise; he knew how to butter up her father and her mother all in one breath. "You attend the Youth Alliance?" Mrs. Gaebele asked.

"Sometimes. Lots of us do," he said.

Jessie just wanted to be left alone. She sent her father a pleading look. But tonight he was blind.

"Run along now, Jessie," her father told her. "You've worked hard enough for one day."

"I'll help you heat the bath water," Selma told her. Jessie blushed. Lilly just shook her head. Jessie wasn't going to get her way tonight; even she could see that.

><+>•O•<+>•<

One of the nice things about a Minnesota summer afternoon, FJ thought as he walked home, was that it lasted so long. Mosquitoes came out, yes, and one had to keep the children from being bitten, but it was possible to work a little late, stop at the lodge, and still be home in time to toss a ball to Russell. The boy was tall and slender with soulful eyes like his mother. He was a fine lad to spend time with.

Thunder turned FJ's eyes skyward. Dark clouds clustered like grapes to the south. A downpour might wash out his hopes to toss that ball with Russell, but they could use the rain.

He swung his walking stick, a habit he'd acquired when he first suffered from pneumonia while with the Seventh Cavalry, Troop G. They'd been sent to the frontier, and the regiment was known for having replaced Custer. Later he was stationed at Fort Keogh in Montana. He had frequent bouts of fever there, and his bones ached terribly when riding, so by the time his unit arrived in Fort Meade, South Dakota, he was worn down and ill and had to spend eight weeks in the hospital. Pneumonia and then rheumatic fever, they called it. He called it deathly ill. He used a cane as he recovered, and the walking stick

had become a part of his uniform, re-
placing the sword that now hung in the
library at home. At his commander's
recommendation, he left the infantry
and joined the hospital corps at Fort Riley, Kansas. He had the pleasure of exercising Custer's old horse, which had
been brought to Fort Riley to live out his
old age. But once again the illness
struck. This time they sent him to Fort
Snelling outside Minneapolis, for the cli-
mate. He improved there, taking part in
various company expeditions as part of
the hospital corps. FJ participated in
"police actions" rather than heavy fighting, which suited him fine. He had no
taste for killing. The last Indian action
he'd seen was against the Milaca Indians in Minnesota.

He shook his head of the memory.
The campaign had required the hospital
corps to follow, and what he witnessed
there left such a sour taste in his mouth
that he left the army soon after. Had he
stayed but one year more he could have
been commissioned as a physician.

Mrs. Bauer sometimes reminded him
of that decision as being a poor one,

that he could be a doctor now instead of a photographer. But she hadn't been there. She didn't know.

His cane clicked against the stones, and he became aware of the sudden quiet. No bird sounds, no rustle of leaves. His skin prickled. He felt the wind change suddenly, coming not out of the southwest but from the north, and yet the trees blew as though the southwest wind still pushed them, swirling the branches like eggs whipped in a bowl. Birds flitted away in large flocks, silent, which seemed odd. So odd, FJ looked up again.

Black and greenish clouds hung terribly low from the sky. He must have been daydreaming, because he hadn't realized that the temperature had dropped. He felt a chill in the air and rain started falling, the wind pelting the drops against his face and clothes. He was several blocks from home on South Baker Street. It would be best to turn back to the studio and wait until the storm passed, so he lifted his cane and headed back toward Johnson Street as the wind pulled at his hat. He slammed his hand onto his head, holding the bowler in place. Wind filled up his coat sleeves like balloons. Tree branches broke and twisted as they fell to the ground. He felt off center and looked down to see the sidewalk lift slightly. Roots belonging to trees several yards away cracked the surface at his feet like ice breaking on a spring lake. Like a long breath, the trees lifted up, held, then exhaled back into their roots. He nearly stumbled on an uneven surface. Lightning flashed. He caught himself, jumped away from the breakage, and watched a tree fall in slow motion toward a house. He gasped. More lightning, heightened wind, and then before him he saw a gaggle of young people.

They swung baskets and twirled around, laughing and letting the wind push them about. *They don't realize the severity of the storm!* FJ recognized his employees. Yes, Miss Kopp's height made her stand out, and Miss Gaebele's small form appeared locked between her friends. He heard shouts as the rain began to pelt them. Dust and dirt like tiny pinpricks bit his face, and he could see them rub at their eyes and turn their backs to brace against the fury. Miss Gaebele stumbled and fell. It took all his own strength to not be bowled over.

Now leaves and sticks and broken branches swirled like a circling horse, and wonder of wonders, he actually had to lean into the wind just to stay upright. With his cane he motioned to the group to turn back and shouted, "To my studio!" He pulled his hat down over his ears and held his coat tight around him, pushing his way toward them, motioning with his cane.

"Take cover! My studio!" Old maple seeds winged their way up from the street and swung at their cheeks. Miss Gaebele was so small she could easily be lifted by the force of this wind. "You know the way, Miss Kopp!"

"It's on Fifth and Johnson," she shouted to the others and turned them all like a herd of frightened calves.

They started to run then. The boys with them raced after Miss Kopp, charging toward the studio, leaving Miss Gaebele and another young woman exposed to the elements, barely able to stand. Hanging his cane over his arm, FJ reached them and took each girl by the elbow, and together they pushed up the street against the wind, leaves and dirt a nightmare around them. A terrible cracking sound forced the woman to hold her ears, and as one, they stopped and turned to see a giant oak pulled from its roots crash across the street where they'd just met up.

"Quickly, quickly! Hang on to the porch banisters," he shouted when they reached the studio. He patted his vest for his key, found it, opened the door, and let the now sopping-wet crowd into the reception room.

The largest young man with them pushed against the door and slammed it shut. "Into the darkroom," FJ told them. The girls led the way through the double doors and into the interior of the studio. The day was as night, and Miss Gaebele pushed the lights on using the button on the wall.

"Wouldn't we be safer in the basement?" the young man asked.

"What kind of storm is this?" one of the others asked.

His answer was drowned out by the sound of a train, and the house shuddered like a runaway wagon on a hard-rutted road.

➤-┤◄➤-O-◄➤-┤◄

Jessie shook. She'd never liked storms. The root cellar was the place they'd gathered whenever the storm clouds stalked the valley near Cream. They kept extra water there and jerked venison, which enabled them to stay a few days if they needed to. Her father would make light of things, have them tell stories, say prayers, but his reassurances were never quite enough to relieve Jessie of her fears. This storm had come up so quickly, and she'd felt near panic at watching the others run off without her and Clara. The wind had swirled and pressed against her, and she thought she might be lifted and tossed aside.

She'd never been with people other than her family during a storm; she hoped her parents and sisters and Roy were safe, hoped she was safe here.

Were the others as frightened as she was? She looked at their wet, dripping faces. A loud pop sounded and the room went black.

"The electric lights have gone out. Not to worry," Mr. Bauer reassured them.

"Jumping Jehoshaphat, you'd think the trains couldn't run in a wind like this," Jerome Kopp said. Jessie thought his voice was higher pitched than usual, and it lacked the cocky tone.

"That sound isn't a train," Mr. Bauer said. "More likely a tornado. And the lights . . . I suspect a tree has just taken out the lines."

"Tornado! My pa says Winona doesn't get them. Must be just a strong wind," Jerome argued. "Tornado. Pawh!"

Jessie wondered if they ought to have tried for the basement, but they were here now. She huddled close to Voe, swiped rain from her face. No one spoke for a time, listening to the wind. Her ears hurt. She swallowed and thought about Lilly and Roy and Selma, about her parents. They had to be safe.

After a time, they heard no more

sounds but their own breaths. "I'd like to get out where there's light," Voe said.

"Is it safe?" Jessie asked. Her teeth chattered.

Mr. Bauer patted her shoulder. "Why, you're cold," he said. "And shivering. Well, of course. You all must be. Cold and wet. Let me step out and see if the studio still stands. I'll start a fire in the fireplace so you can dry out before going on your way to let your parents know you're all right. I'm sure the phone lines will be down."

"My pa won't be that worried about us," Jerome said. "He knows I can take care of me and my sister. I can take care of you too, missy," he said, groping for Jessie's shoulder. His fingers got caught in her bun, and she slapped at him, glaring, though she supposed he couldn't see her in the dark. She stiffened.

When Mr. Bauer opened the door and let the natural light into the room, Jerome was still shaking his hand as though he'd touched something hot.

Jessie turned toward Mr. Bauer. "I am cold. But I need to go home to see if everything is all right."

"Let's all get out of here," Jerome said. He'd made himself the leader. "No sense waiting for a fire to dry us out. Let's see what damage has been done." He said it with a gleeful curiosity in his voice that saddened Jessie. A wind such as this could have easily harmed a great many people. She hoped her family had taken refuge in the basement.

Mr. Bauer went out into the reception room and called to them. "The worst is passed. Lots of puddles. Nearly a stream washing down that street, so be careful as you go. Watch for roots that have been lifted up; the trees could be unstable."

The group stepped gingerly down the steps, gazing at the changed world. They pushed aside broken and blown branches, their green leaves clinging to them the way a deer leaves bits of hair against a fence: evidence of damage. Voe turned around slowly.

"All the trees are naked," Jessie said. "There's hardly a leaf left on them. It looks almost like . . . winter." *We should take some pictures,* Jessie thought, the idea bringing a level of calm to her.

"We should photograph this," she said aloud to Mr. Bauer, who had walked to the far side of the yard and looked up, to see if there was damage to the roof, Jessie supposed.

"What? I'm sorry, I didn't hear you."

Jessie hurried beside him now. The others had headed out, and she'd motioned to them that she'd catch up. "We ought to take photographs. For the paper." His look said he must think her unfeeling. She should be worried about her family, not trying to take pictures of disasters.

"The *Republican-Herald* rarely uses photographs, even half tones. Just those cartoons and drawn ads. It's too expensive to make the lithographs of them."

"It was just a thought. I mean, look at the trees, all bare. That's something you won't likely see again anytime soon."

"Why would you want to photograph something so sad?" Mr. Bauer said. He stared at her.

"People remember tragedy," Jessie said. "They take photographs of infants in their grave clothes. You said that yourself."

He looked pained when she said that. "Yes, yes, but people must grieve." He turned away and began gathering branches to clear a path back to the studio. He picked up pieces of the plaster fountain, dropped them onto the pile of branches.

Jessie looked around. What had been there before—trees full of foliage, dahlias in late summer bloom, gardens with fountains sprouting—it was all changed now. The town would be mourning too, and they might want to remember what they'd survived. "People will be grieving here too," she said, "and maybe a photograph could help."

"It's not a healing art, Miss Gaebele." He said it like her father might, teaching, warning her. "I wouldn't try to make it into one. You'd best hurry along and catch your friends, check on your family. I'll lock up and go home to see if everything is all right at South Baker."

"You live on South Baker?" she said. "You have to walk within a few blocks of our house on Broadway to get there. If it's all right, I mean, if you don't mind, I'll wait for you to lock up, and we can walk out together."

"Yes. Of course. I can walk you to your door and reassure your parents."

She was surprised at the relief she felt knowing he would be with her when she found out if her own family was all right. They moved without words through the cluttered path. The twister had cut a swath through the city, and they could see just the edge of it. The wind had caused roofs to be peeled of their shingles. Broken glass lay everywhere. People stood in small clusters, telling stories of what had just happened to them. They'd had a close call. Everyone still whole knew it, and there was a kind of grateful surprise in their faces at having escaped.

A gray and white mourning butterfly flitted past them as though it knew what people would begin doing now, putting the pieces back together. Maybe photographs didn't have a place in the midst of raw grief.

At home, Selma and Lilly competed with each other to tell their story of racing to the basement and described how bottles of preserves fell off the shelves and how loud the rumble and rage of the wind had been. "I-I-I w-w-was s-s-scared," Roy got out before their mother interrupted to thank Mr. Bauer for escorting Jessie home. She sent Jessie in to change her wet clothes while Mr. Bauer described to Jessie's father what they'd seen.

The Gaebele house had lost some shingles from the roof, and an oak tree had fallen so close to the house that when Jessie looked out the window, all she could see was green, but otherwise they were fine. Jessie hoped Mr. Bauer would find the same good news when he got home too. She frowned. She hadn't told him thank you or good-bye.

In the morning, the paper reported that the tornado was one of three reported in the region, the first to touch down in Winona in the past fifty years. Two storm fronts, one from the southwest and the other from the northwest, had converged right over the city, and damage would have been worse if not for the bluffs on either side of the river to counter the storm's fury. At least that's what the old-timers all said. They reported its being one of the few tornadoes in their collective memory, and Jessie knew it would feed the mill workers' talks for weeks.

No deaths were reported in Winona proper, but considerable damage had befallen the many trees that lined Winona's streets and the houses that the trees chose to fall on. Several days later the paper did report the discovery of a missing woman's arm, identified by the ring still on a finger. The authorities returned it to the grieving husband, widowed in a nearby town by the twister. Three cars of the Green Bay and Western Railroad had been blown off the tracks. Local pastors preached that the storm was the wrath of God against those who turned a deaf ear to His ways and refused to heed the temperance movement.

No photographs appeared to record the amazing storm, but several days later Jessie saw postcards for sale with a picture of the grain storage down by the railroad tracks. The roof had spilled in on itself, and boards were driven into the side of the wooden structure along with pieces of iron that must have been lying nearby.

People did want to memorialize tragedy with pictures. *Mr. Bauer could have made some money,* Jessie thought.

But what Jessie wanted to remember most about the day couldn't be photographed. After finding her family safe, she most treasured an awareness of Mr. Bauer's kindness, his protection of her when the others ran off. And then there was that gentle touch. Men offered all kinds of help to a woman in distress. Jerome, though, abandoned her and Clara in the storm's rising fury, then groped her when the storm passed. Fortunately he'd only gotten his hands caught in her hair combs. He'd misjudged her height in the darkness or he would have gotten his face well slapped.

Mr. Bauer's touch was tender on her arm as he guided her and Clara to safety in his studio. His touch reassured; it was a listening touch that heard she was shivering and cold. He'd acted protective in the way he patted her shoulder and when he said he would see her safely home. His actions had so reminded her of her father's caring ways that she'd nearly cried then with relief. Her fear had passed, swept away by the safety of her family and this good man.

As he'd swung his cane toward his own home, Jessie watched from her upstairs window. In the future, that's what she'd look for in any serious suitor. Kindness and compassion, sturdiness in a storm. These were the qualities that truly marked a man.

SIX

Doors of Opportunity

It might have been the unseasonable cold or the early rains, maybe the soaking he'd taken on the day of the storm, or maybe just the change in routines brought by autumn's prelude, but in mid-September, FJ came down with what the doctors said was pneumonia. His skin turned a vapid yellow color, and they added jaundice and told Mrs. Bauer that he would need to be kept down until he recovered. She was to feed him meals of greens.

Mrs. Bauer had been through this before. As a patient, her husband made few demands on her other than to assist him to the water closet and to help him settle himself when she brought the tray of food. In some ways, it was easier having him ill: he was home; she knew where he was. The boys—she started the thought, then amended it—Russell could spend time sitting on his bed and sharing his stories. He had done that that the last time FJ became so ill, and the two had seemed to grow closer to each other. Mrs. Bauer felt, well, almost excluded as she stood at the door watching the two of them, and yet she appreciated that FJ engaged the child without her having to entertain. She had other things to do.

Winnie needed tending. And while the child might bring her white Steiff bear in to her father to play, pointing out its little brown nose and rubbing the soft fur, while she might carry on little girl conversations with her father and tell him what the bear was thinking, FJ tired easily. Mrs. Bauer still needed to occupy Winnie and continue to tend to household duties as well.

And then there was the studio.

"I believe," FJ said haltingly, "the girls can keep it going." Mrs. Bauer had expressed concern after one of the doctor's weekly visits. FJ coughed and she handed him a cloth to spit in, then took it carefully from him and put it in the antiseptic wicker basket beside the bed.

"They're quite young, and you've had only these six months to train them," she reminded him. Her fingers fluttered at her collar. *I need to wash my hands.*

"True." He coughed, got it under control. "But you could go there. Offer assistance to them." She hadn't responded. "Phone messages as needed," he'd finished before another coughing bout began. "I'll be well. Soon. With your good care."

He'd coughed then so hard that he held his stomach, and she realized how little he really understood his own illness or the impact it had on her. On the family. He didn't realize how weakened he'd become, how susceptible, working long hours, spending time at the lodge or stopping at the YMCA, which he also considered "part of the commerce." He'd catch some bug there and go down. She'd have to carry the load now, never knowing if he really would get better and certainly not when. The last bout of coughs ended with him falling exhausted back onto the bed. She noticed a yellow scum on the linen. She'd have to change the pillow slip. Again.

They could afford help at the studio, but not here in their own home. At least she assumed as much, though she'd never come right out and asked him for a live-in girl to help with the children. Still, he should have noticed. Especially now. Maybe she'd use this opportunity to broach the subject. A live-in girl would not only help her but would raise their status among members of their set. All the other successful businesspeople had hired girls, one of the Irish ones maybe, or those sturdy Norwegians. But there was the money . . .

She took the tea tray from his room and walked to the kitchen, hating that she was irritated with him, especially when he was so ill. *What kind of a wife am I that I'm annoyed at an ailing man?*

Winnie napped, thank goodness; Russell, still in school. She could indulge herself. She sank onto the kitchen chair and let her mind go into that wasteland of the future. Her breath came faster. Her fingers began to tingle. *Now I'm getting ill?* Her mind raced toward the vast cavern of uncertainty that formed like a must around his illnesses.

When FJ was well, he was predictable and reliable. She knew in her heart that his veterans meetings and the chamber time helped the business and therefore the family. But these illnesses. She felt another flash of anger directed toward her husband. He minimized her concerns. He always had, patting her on her head and telling her she could handle things, that all would be well. It might not all be well. They'd had financial strain in the past because he overextended their risk. That ranch, for one.

She dropped a cup and watched it shatter on the linoleum flooring. She must not think of that ranch.

She bent to pick up the broken china. Why had he been out in that August storm in the first place? That's what had caused this. He could take the streetcar for most of the way. He just never liked to use it except to take them all to church. He had to walk nearly fifteen blocks to the studio, a journey he said was good for his heart, but not when the weather could turn as it had. Wind blowing every which way.

She'd been terrified at home alone with Winnie, screaming at the way the pressure hurt her head. Winnie patted her arm, saying, "Mama, sick? Mama, sick?" She tried to stop her own shouting, knew that was her role, but her head pounded.

Russell rushed in then, and he took Winnie and urged her and Mrs. Bauer to go to the basement. "Until Papa gets here," he said. "The storm won't hurt us there." They huddled for what seemed days, but it was only an hour. The day darkened as though night, and the thunder was right above them, rolling like dozens of croquet balls being cracked by the mallet right next to her head.

FJ finally came home and told her of his rescue of some young people, of turning back to the studio and waiting out the storm with them. But his coat was dampened clear to his undershirt, and he was chilled even standing in front of the fire. He'd gone to the studio the rest of the week, seemed to do well through the month, but this morning, after attending Second Congregational, he'd collapsed in the water closet and called out to her in a croaking voice. She'd seen then the yellow in his eyes and the cast to his skin, and heard the rasping cough. She'd heard it the night before but hadn't wanted to admit it.

At least there'd been no damage to their studio or their home from the storm, just some tree branches spread like pickup sticks around the yard. Russell picked up what he could. FJ got someone with a saw to take care of the larger branches. They'd have wood for the winter to supplement the coal. A garden statue had taken a tumble, but it was plaster. They'd find another. Overall, the cut of the twister had bypassed South Baker Street, and she was grateful. But now there was this storm: his illness. Again.

She heard her husband cough though she was way down here in the kitchen. She put her hands to her ears, pressed until she felt the pain. "Perhaps the storm didn't bypass us at all," she said out loud. *Do something. Don't sit here and think.*

She stood to wash the few dishes and put them into the cupboard. FJ was ill. It was the way it was. She'd have to go down to the studio and meet these girls. She probably should have done it before, but she hadn't wanted to. Her place was in the home, and that was work enough for her. More than enough. FJ had no idea.

At least the doctor was optimistic, and they'd been through this before. Perhaps these girls were bright and quick studies and could carry on the business. It was just a matter of time, and he'd be well. That's what she'd tell herself. She'd take Winnie to her mother's and go to the studio tomorrow. She'd have to take the streetcar. FJ had said that a motorcar was being readied for sale, but it wouldn't likely be anything they could afford, nor would he teach her how to drive it anyway. Not that she'd want to learn. If he hadn't built the studio so far from the house, this wouldn't be a problem. Where did he keep the key? There was so much she'd have to remember.

>⟶⟨⟶⟩⟶O⟶⟨⟶⟩⟶⟨

"What do you suppose has happened?" Voe asked. The girls stood outside the studio on a Monday morning. Mr. Bauer was always there before them, fixing hot water for tea or coffee for himself. They'd talk about the day, and then he'd begin instructing as the girls trailed him like little ducks. By now, each girl did a portion on her own, including entering figures into the ledger or ordering supplies for the developing room. Jessie enjoyed setting up the operating room for the scheduled sittings. But they'd taken few portraits as yet, and their apprenticeship would be over this next week.

Since the storm, Jessie had seen Mr. Bauer walking down Broadway past their house. It wasn't much out of his way, she guessed, and it was a good reminder for her to finish up her morning toilet and head out to work.

"Come to think of it, he didn't walk

past our house this morning," Jessie said.

"Does he usually? You never said that."

Jessie shrugged. "Only since the storm, when he realized how close we live to the studio. It's not much out of his way, and remember he said that walking is good for his heart."

Voe made a face at Jessie.

"What?" Jessie asked her.

"Oh, just that he took both you and Clara by the arm during that storm, and my ma's etiquette book says right in it that no man should offer his arm to a lady who is not his mother, sister, aunt, or wife. And there he was, touching you both."

"Only to help us. I'd like to see an etiquette book that objects to offering assistance. Your brother sure didn't. Besides, you were so far ahead, how could you see that?"

"I turned around to see if you were all right. And Jerome was making sure we got there."

"A wind like that could lift me up like a kite and drop me in the middle of some cow pasture or on a rooftop. I was glad he took my elbow to help keep my feet on the ground."

Voe looked at her. "I guess you are sort of puny."

Jessie laughed.

"This is the morning when we're supposed to start getting paid," Voe said. "Right?"

"No, it isn't. We won't get paid until the end of next week."

"If he doesn't show up to train us, he ought to pay us. After all, we're working for free so we can have a trade."

"We still have to pass the test," she said.

"*You* have to pass the test. I agreed to work and learn and be paid ever after, even if I never took the test. You're the one that's good at tests."

"One of us has to be certified in order to run the business. That's what he said. But neither of us is going to be running the business any time soon, so let's not get all flummoxed over it."

"What kind of a word is that?"

"I saw it in one of Mr. Bauer's books. He has novels and everything on the bookshelves. Some of them are in German, which I learned to read. But others are in English. He said I could take them home if I wanted."

"Reading's work for me," Voe said. "I like to play card games and dance. Oh, sorry. I know you're not allowed to do either."

"It isn't anything I miss," Jessie told her. She pushed her spectacles up on her nose. "Not when I have a camera. When I get my camera back," she added.

They sat on the back steps looking out over the yard. Leaves and branches lay there. The men Mr. Bauer hired to clean it up hadn't made it to their yard yet. Jessie stood, removed her jacket, and hung it on the railing, then began gathering up the branches, making a pile.

"We aren't being paid to do lawn work," Voe said.

"We aren't being paid, remember?"

"Oh, right. Well, you'll get all dirty."

"It's better than sitting and waiting. Besides, we get a benefit of looking out at a lovely lawn, and we can't see it with all these branches in the way. Those flowers need weeding too. They look so naked without their blooms that at least we can keep the weeds down for them." She peered closer at one of the peonies. "I think there's a new bud. Imagine, this late in the year."

"Storms confuse everything," Voe said. "So do prairie fires. We had a fire at our farm once, and it burned the orchard, and the next January the trees had blossoms on them. It was the strangest thing. Oh!" Voe startled as the back door opened from the inside. "Who are you?"

"I'm Russell Bauer," the boy told her. "I'm eight years old, and I'm old enough to come here all by myself and to be here. My mama said so."

"Well, good for you," Voe told him. "Do you know where your pa is?" Voe looked behind him to see if Mr. Bauer had followed him in. "He's the one we're waiting on."

"He's home. Sick, ma'am. My mama sent me here to tell you that you should go home today. Come back tomorrow and open up. Here's the key."

"Don't give it to me," Voe said. She backed away from it as though he held a snake. She nearly walked backward off the porch.

"I'll take it," Jessie said as she approached. She brushed her hands on her skirt and took the key, putting it into her pocket. "Did your mama want us to contact the appointments your father had scheduled for today, to let them know not to come?"

"She didn't say," he said. "Ma'am."

He was a handsome child, lithe, with serious brown eyes. Jessie recognized him as one of the two boys in the picture hanging in the office area. He wore his hair smooth with a part to the side just as in that picture. He'd said he was eight, making him a few years older than Roy. He leaned slightly forward as though he was accustomed to looking down at someone, being attentive. *His little brother must be the other boy in the photograph.*

"I'll take care of this," Jessie said, patting her pocket. "You tell your mama thank you for her confidence in us. We'll be here in the morning. Maybe your papa will be better by then."

"I don't think so," Russell said. Jessie watched his eyes tear and his lower lip quiver.

Jessie thought of her own father and his illnesses, how he'd sometimes writhe on the floor, holding his side. Nothing frightened her more than seeing him in pain, watching her mother try to help and not being able to, all of them feeling helpless. Her stomach started to hurt just thinking about it.

Jessie used soft words to calm him, the way she did when Roy clung to her. "If he's seen the doctor"—Jessie waited for Russell's nod before she continued—"then he's in good hands."

"Is it the mercury poisoning?" Voe said.

"Poisoning?" Russell turned to her. He looked alarmed.

"He told us he sometimes became ill, for a time, from doing photographic things," Jessie told him. "She just wondered if that was what had caused his illness now."

"Mama says it's the jaundice and 'monia." He struggled over the last word. "She didn't say nothing about poison. Didn't say anything," he corrected himself.

"Pneumonia," Jessie said.

"New-monia. I don't know what happened to the old one, but with this one he coughs and looks a funny color and has to stay in bed."

Jessie encouraged, "I bet you help him by talking to him and assisting your mother when this happens." Russell nodded. "Meanwhile, we're here to assist with photographic things. And you're there at home to be with him. So he won't have any worries and he can put all his energy into getting well."

He wore a forced smile and wiped at his eyes with his fingertips. "I pray for him," he said.

"Good. We can do that too."

"I better get back," Russell said. He didn't make any move to leave, though.

"Would you like us to walk back with you?" Jessie asked. He seemed so young to have come so far.

"Nope. I mean, no ma'am. I can do this on my own. My mama said I could."

"Looks like you'll have to wait to see where Mr. B. lives," Voe whispered to her.

Jessie ignored her. To Russell, Jessie said, "You be careful now. Your mama will be looking for you, so you go right back."

As Russell headed off down the street, walking beneath the leafless trees, Jessie said, "That was an odd thing to say."

"What?

"About my wanting to see where Mr. B. lives. Why would I care about that?"

Voe shrugged. "I was just being . . . attentive," she said. She beamed as though she'd used a fascinating word to good avail.

"You attended to nonsense," Jessie told her. "Let's go inside and see what you can be attentive to in there."

"We're supposed to come back and work tomorrow."

"It's poor business not to let people know there's been a change. They'll be very upset if they arrive and no one is here to take their pictures."

"Well, I've been given the day off," Voe said. "I'm going to the beach. I'll see you tomorrow." And with that, she headed off down the street, nearly over-taking Russell before turning a corner and disappearing.

Jessie shook her head and headed in-side to look at the appointment book. Two sittings were scheduled. A single portrait, one woman; and a family with a child. She picked up the phone to make the cancellations, held it to her ear for a moment waiting for the operator to come on and ask for the exchange. Then she put the receiver down. Her heart started to pound.

Do I dare?

What would be the harm of waiting for them to arrive, telling them of Mr. Bauer's illness, and asking if they'd prefer to reschedule? But since she couldn't tell them when he'd be better, she'd offer this alternative: perhaps they might like to have her do the sitting, as she was Mr. Bauer's apprentice. After all, they were already here and ready. Why not? If they didn't like the photo- graph, they wouldn't have to pay. That was Mr. Bauer's policy, and it could cer- tainly be hers. On his behalf, of course. It was just good business sense to offer. Mr. Bauer wouldn't want her to do any- thing less.

⊱—⊹⊱—◦—⟨⊹—⊰—⟨

The rest of the morning, Jessie tidied up, then set the camera just the way Mr. Bauer would have. She'd watched him often enough, hadn't she? She felt an- ticipation, a tiny prickle of fear too, but didn't one always feel a little fearful when trying something new? She'd just do her best. Jessie piled her hair up high to give her added height and dignity. She brought out a long scarf and some books for possible props.

The woman arrived at the studio on time. Jessie was glad she'd redone her hair even if the earth-colored wisps worked their way out around her ears. Lilly's dark hair had natural waves and was thick as Grandma's gravy, and it al- ways looked tidy and shop-girl smart.

Jessie hoped she looked as confident as Lilly always did.

This woman, about Lilly's age, held herself stately as Jessie told her, "Mr. Bauer has taken ill and won't be able to do your sitting today." The woman's shoulders dropped, and she actually looked relieved. Jessie wondered if she might be just as nervous as Jessie was.

"Oh. Well. How unfortunate. I can come back another time." She started toward the door.

"I can reschedule you," Jessie said. "Or I could do the sitting." The woman hesitated. "I've been asked to run the studio while he's ill." That was partly true. "Of course, if you don't like the results, the policy will apply that you needn't pay."

"Well . . ."

"There are other studios in town. Polonia's has a good reputation, though I can tell you from experience that Mr. Bauer is one of the best. He's won awards and gold medals for his portrait work, and he's a fine instructor, so I believe I've gained much from my association with him."

"Does Polonia's have a female photographer?"

"I doubt that," Jessie said. Here was
the opening. "There aren't many of us
around, though I did see some feminine
work exhibited in *Camera World,* in the
magazine that just came, so there are a
few more women venturing into this
artistic field. Would you like to look at it,
to see if the subject was handled as you
might like? Women do have a different
eye for these things, I think."

"I would. If you don't mind."

Jessie located the issue she had de-
voured whenever it first arrived. Mr.
Bauer maintained the membership,
hoping to have some of his work published in it, though the editor, Mr. Stei-
gliez, was said to be *very* selective.

Together the two women turned the
magazine pages, and Mildred Simmons,
the client, pointed to a style or two she
liked. "I have a large nose, you may
have noticed," she said, putting her
hand to her face. "And I don't think I'm
particularly . . . pretty. This woman"—
she pointed—"she isn't really attractive

either, but the portrait makes her seem so. I'd like that."

Jessie'd had time to look at her client, to watch her, and she risked now saying what she thought were Mildred's fine features. "You have beautiful hair, Miss Simmons—"

"Please, call me Mildred. I hate the formalities, don't you?"

"I'm Jessie Gaebele, Jessie. Beautiful hair and lovely skin, as white as cream and without a blemish." The woman put her fingers to her face. "And a fine, elegant neck. I think we can emphasize those qualities with the right lighting. And I would not have you look directly into the lens but rather gaze down, perhaps to the side, so we can capture that elegance without sacrificing softness."

Mildred's face blushed. "You could do that? It's an indulgence, this portrait. I've become engaged, and I want to my fiancé to have a portrait to put into his satchel when he travels, to carry with him."

"Let's see what we can do." Jessie led her into the operating room as though she'd done this sort of thing a hundred times.

>-+-<>-O-<+-+-<

What Jessie told her mother later about the episode was how quickly the time went. "I was glad the sittings were scheduled two hours apart because the first took much longer than I thought it would. I had to help put the client at ease and then identify her photographic strengths and then find words that would help her share my views, assuming I was correct in my assessment. And with Miss Simmons I apparently was. Once she seemed to trust me, it was really fun, Mama."

Jessie sat at the table, eating one of her mother's ginger cookies, glad this wasn't one of the days she had to go to Mr. Steffes's to work. "I made her laugh, and her whole face changed. I had her look at a book and sit by the window, and then in front of the dark screen with no reflecting light at all, and the window light fell just onto her hair and high-lighted the side of her face." Jessie spoke to her mother's back as her

mother rolled a piecrust at the dough-
boy. "When I developed the dry plates,
the pictures turned out as I thought they
would! What I imagined in my mind I
could actually make appear on the print!
It was magic, Mama. Maybe that's what
the Kodak ads mean when they say
where the camera is, there is 'Witchery
of Kodakery.' "

"Hush now, the way you talk," her
mother said, swinging around. She
pointed with her rolling pin. "No magic
and witches in this house."

"Sorry, Mama. But truly, it was one of
the best afternoons I've ever had."
She'd leave out the witch talk when de-
scribing the absolute joy that came from
creating something she thought beautiful and that pleased another. "I even
fixed tea for her afterward." Jessie had
read that back East, the women photographers held afternoon teas in their studios to help people feel comfortable and
to advertise the quality of their operating
rooms. She took another ginger-cookie
bite. "The family with the child that was
scheduled did decide to wait until Mr.
Bauer is better, but that worked out well

too because I had more time to develop Mildred's plates without feeling rushed. Oh, Mama, it was just the best time!"

Her mother spoke into her piecrust. "I always pray you'll have a good day, though I'll add words tonight about this witchery nonsense." She placed the flat dough into the rectangular pan. They'd be having deep-dish apple pie tonight from the looks of it, using up the rest of the dried fruit to get ready for this year's crop. If there'd be any, considering the storm. "What's Mr. Bauer's illness anyway?" her mother asked.

"Pneumonia. At least that's what his son Russell told us. He came to the studio all by himself. He said he's eight years old."

"The Bauers had another boy, about Roy's age, I think. And a little girl? The boy was killed a few years ago. It was in the paper. Some strange accident with a horse."

"An accident? He lost a son? How awful." Jessie thought how close Roy had come to a similar fate. "How sad for them." She swallowed, enthusiasm for her day disappearing from lightness into weight.

"There's a portrait hanging in Mr. Bauer's office of a woman and two boys. Russell was one. The other must have been that little brother. And his mother. I guess we'll meet her tomorrow. She's going to come down and 'show us how to do things.' "

"I thought that's what you were being trained for all this time."

"It hasn't been quite six months. Mr. Bauer may not think we're ready. But I think we are. When I show him the prints of what I did today, I think he'll be pleased."

Her mother didn't say anything for a time. Jessie sat thoughtful. "Are you so sure of that? He asked you not to take any photographs while you were in training."

"I didn't do anything bad, Mama. I didn't!" Jessie's heartbeat matched the thumping of her mother's rolling pin.

"Just taking pictures when he asked you not to."

"This was different. It was *his* camera," Jessie said. "I promised not to use *my* camera."

"Jessie, slanting the truth is still a lie."

"It was to maintain *his* business," Jessie defended. Her mother's words shamed her. "Besides, I'm nearly finished with the training. How could he object to that?"

SEVEN

Reflected Light

Jessie awaited Mrs. Bauer's visit by arriving early and cleaning the studio. She wiped the leather chairs with turpentine into which she'd dropped lemon juice. In the kitchen, she scrubbed the sink's tea stains with borax and salt until the white shone bright. Back in the reception room, she noticed fly spots on the oak armrests, on the windowsills too, so she mixed milk with warm water to wipe them down. All the while she thought about Mrs. Bauer. Would this woman want to make great changes in the way they'd been doing things? Was she a skilled photographer like her husband and father? Would she resent these two young girls who spent their days with her husband or be grateful that the studio was in good hands?

When the first hour passed and Mrs. Bauer still hadn't arrived, Jessie nearly went off with Voe, who once again thought they should just close up shop and leave. Instead, Jessie sent Voe to inventory the developing chemicals to see what they might need to order, while Jessie checked the schedule. There were two more sittings arranged for this day, and she decided she'd handle them the same way she'd managed yesterday's appointments. At least until someone told her not to. Her mother's warnings she set aside.

Mrs. Bauer arrived shortly before the lunch hour. She kept a stern look, narrowing her otherwise full lips into a line made straight by her clamped jaws. Little warmth flowed through her deep brown eyes, which Jessie thought were a most striking feature. When people looked angry, Jessie wondered if they might actually be frightened; she wondered that now. Mrs. Bauer's full cheeks each had a patch of red smudged on them. Jessie thought it was rouge, but the woman had completed a vigorous walk if she'd come all the way from South Baker Street. That probably explained it. Despite her stern look, she was a truly beautiful woman who held an equally beautiful child tightly by her hand.

Mrs. Bauer did not introduce the child to Jessie or Voe, but she would be Winifred, whom Mr. Bauer had spoken of so often. The child had her mother's olive skin with dark eyes, but hers sparkled with curiosity. Jessie assumed the child had visited the studio on weekends with her father, but she moved around the reception room as though seeing things for the first time.

"What's this?" she asked her mother, who tried to talk with the girls. "What's that?" she'd ask, picking up a large feather fan sometimes used in the operating room. Jessie'd put it in the Indian vase in the reception area as a flourish of color.

Mrs. Bauer answered Winifred with short, clipped responses, and Jessie noted that the color on Mrs. Bauer's cheeks grew deeper with the child's frequent requests for attention.

"If it would be all right with you, Mrs. Bauer, Voe could take Miss Bauer—Winifred's her name, right?—to the kitchen area. I brought some of my mother's cookies in. We could talk here, and I'd be sure to let Voe know what we discussed. Is that all right with you, Voe? I mean, Miss Kopp?"

"That's the bird's chirp as far as I'm concerned," Voe said, reaching for Winifred's hand. "I was hungry for some of your ma's cookies after I made up the order."

Mrs. Bauer sighed, tiredness settling on her face. "That would be helpful. I don't intend to spend the entire day here. I've left Russell at home with his father, but I don't want to put that burden on him for longer than necessary. I'm sure Winifred will appreciate a cookie. Go along with Miss . . . Kopp," she said, checking to see if she'd gotten Voe's name right. "Miss Gaebele and I will talk and come get you in a moment."

It pleased Jessie that Mrs. Bauer

knew her name. Perhaps Mr. Bauer had discussed Jessie's work here. Or maybe he'd complained about his one head-strong assistant.

"I have no idea how long we might have need of you girls to run things," Mrs. Bauer said. She sat on the edge of the reception room divan, knees tight together, hands folded on them. She looked ready to take flight. "The last time Mr. Bauer became so ill, we had someone run the studio and we spent the following year in North Dakota. But we . . . There were . . ." She took a deep breath. "But Mr. Risser left us to buy his own studio, and so we returned to Winona once again. Of course, we had never sold the house. We fully intended to come back. My mother lives here now. That was the mercury poisoning. But he's had pneumonia before too. The doctor seems to think that's what this is."

"I'm sorry to hear he's so ill," Jessie said. "My father has bouts of illnesses too. We all worry over him and pray for his recovery, but it is a hard time for my mother."

Mrs. Bauer turned her full gaze at Jessie. "Indeed. Few people understand the strains of illness unless they've experienced its effects on the family. Thank you for acknowledging that."

Mrs. Bauer sat silently, then pulled at the fingers of her gloves. "Let's look at the schedule." Jessie handed her the appointment book. "These will have to be cancelled, I imagine," Mrs. Bauer said. "I doubt you've had time to do the portrait work or the developing that would maintain the reputation of the studio."

"I did have a little experience in camera work before I came here," Jessie said. She swallowed. She didn't want to make herself sound more skilled than she was. "My uncle August purchased a camera for me after the St. Louis World's Fair, and I enjoyed myself immensely taking shots. That's not studio portrait work, but I did come with a little understanding . . . enriched by Mr. Bauer's instructions, of course. He's explained everything he's doing in portrait work. Of course, we did develop many, many plates."

"Most of your efforts should be to fulfill requests for prints from plates already made. There's still strong interest in the Tenney collection and the few surviving Grove plates, is there not? We were so fortunate not to lose them all in the fire in '04." Her mind appeared to go somewhere distant with the mention of the year.

"A number of postcard sales come from those prints," Jessie agreed.

"They do. People like to send prints to family, especially over the holidays." Mrs. Bauer was back and all business again.

"He'll want to run the ads again for Christmas, won't he?"

Mrs. Bauer seemed confused, or perhaps she hadn't considered the loss of revenue if they couldn't do portraits at that time of year. Christmas, Mr. Bauer had told Jessie, made or broke their yearly finances. "I'll have to ask him. Or perhaps you can confer with him by phone when he's feeling a little better." She began to fidget with her gloves, moving them back and forth between her hands. "I can continue to do touch-up work. Maybe at home, though we're not set up well for it. But of course, there won't be much need for that if no sittings are scheduled."

Jessie cleared her throat. "I did keep a sitting yesterday," she said. "The client said she wouldn't mind having a woman take her picture, though I told her I was only an apprentice. I thought—that is, I was only trying to be helpful."

Mrs. Bauer stiffened. "And did you develop the plates already? There's a level of skill required for both, you know."

"I do understand," Jessie said. "I have developed them. I'll get the prints if you'd like."

"Yes, I would."

Jessie's heart pounded while she made her way to the developing room and took the prints from the hangers where they'd dried. She didn't bring them all. She'd already calculated that if the Bauers were upset at her for having used the plates, she could replace them. They cost $3.60 a dozen. She'd have to work extra days at Mr. Steffes's to make it up.

Winifred's laughter drifted from the kitchen. Jessie thought then that Voe would be good with children in the operating room. It wasn't Jessie's strong suit, especially if she had to manage the camera and lighting and everything else. She and Voe could do this together. In fact, they'd need the two of them to really make it work if there were family portraits scheduled.

Mrs. Bauer stared at the prints Jessie handed her. The clock ticked as Mrs. Bauer looked back and forth between them. Jessie hoped she wasn't about to be fired and wondered what kind of failure it meant that someone could get dismissed before she was even paid. She couldn't stand the silence. "I can pay for the plates if you think the photographs aren't worthy of the studio. And the chemicals. I work another job and it might take me a while, but I can repay everything. I didn't mean to do anything but to help out. I realize I have much to learn."

"I know Mildred Simmons," Mrs. Bauer said. "She attends Second Congregational, and this photograph"—she looked up at Jessie—"makes her look more beautiful than she really is. Has she seen these?"

"Not yet. I haven't called her back. I know I was being bold, but I really thought if I could do it well, it would help your studio overall. I don't want to do anything to hurt it. Mr. Bauer's been so kind, such a good instructor, that I took the risk."

"These are quite good," Mrs. Bauer said. "Quite good. I like the way you've captured Mildred's sweetness. People seem to pass right over her as though she isn't worthy of note, but that isn't how I see her. This photograph is how I see her."

Mrs. Bauer appeared to smile. At least the corners of her tight lips lifted. Jessie beamed. She thought she'd found an ally in those eyes.

>-!-◆-○-◆-!-<

"Who took these?" FJ demanded. His head pounded and he gasped for breath. He tightened his fist, frustrated.

"One of your shop girls." Mrs. Bauer fluffed up the pillows behind his head,

her eyes moving toward the chewed cigar on the nightstand. "That can't make
you well," she said. She picked up the
cigar and tossed it in the wastebasket.

FJ grunted. "Few vices left." He
coughed and decided he didn't have a
very strong argument for cigars at the
moment. He looked back at the prints.
"Mildred Simmons. Doesn't reflect her,"
he said. "She'll hate them."

"Do you think so? Both Miss Gaebele
and I thought they showed off Mildred's
best features. She really is soft and gentle. And her nose, well, you hardly notice
it in the photograph. Instead you see
this thoughtful-looking woman with gor-
geous hair and translucent skin."

"You two thought it looked good?"

"Yes. Miss . . . Kopp entertained Winifred. I suspect the girl is good at the
more tedious work. But Miss Gaebele
has an eye, wouldn't you say?"

"Don't like them," he said. He tossed
the prints onto the covers. "Mildred's
not that lovely."

"But you're the one who says portraits capture the heart of the person.
Now see, she's done that and you don't

like it. Well, I like it. And Mildred is bound to. The girl must have gotten her relaxed and comfortable, the very things required. I think she should continue to do the sittings, at least until you go back."

"What about the Johnsons? They were scheduled for yesterday." He coughed.

"They decided to wait for you. But if we tell people that Miss Gaebele is your assistant, I think they'll proceed. Of course they can always have the choice, but we need the revenue, Mr. Bauer. You know that."

"I told both of them to leave the camera work alone. Until their training was complete."

"It was really complete, Fred," his wife said. She rarely used his first name, didn't even know that it was his middle name, that he was born Gottlieb Friedrich Bauer and that he'd taken Fred and added John when he came to America, dropping that totally German name. She only used Fred when she wanted something.

"Christmas is coming," Mrs. Bauer

continued. "You've always said it's our busiest time. I don't think we can afford to let those appointments go. You should have let them take portraits by now. Were you extending their training? Longer training didn't help when you had the other two assistants, Miss Schulz and Miss Phalen."

"No. They went off to work for Risser," he said.

"Well, you don't want to lose these girls. Let them do the work."

"I'll be well before Christmas," he said. "And I have prepared them. They did it all except expose the film and manage the flash powder."

"You see? They learned. At least Miss Gaebele did."

She was right. "Will you do the re-touching that's needed?"

"If necessary," she said, though she bristled. "I imagine you haven't had time to train them on that. Or on tinting."

He shook his head.

"I'll do my part with the retouching. You do your part, FJ, by not being so disparaging of them that they up and quit. Otherwise you might have to call

Herman Reinke and tell him that the partnership of the ranch is done for and just sell that . . . place."

This discussion had made him weak. He wondered if perhaps he wasn't also dealing with the mercury effects, the numbing of his fingers, the overall weakness. Add that to his raspy breathing. She was probably right about the cigars. But wrong about selling the ranch.

"As long as we're paying them, we may as well get the work out of them we can," Mrs. Bauer insisted.

A coughing seizure took him over. "All right," he said finally. She held a cup of water up to his mouth for him to drink. "Let the girl take the sittings. But I want . . . to see the prints. Before the clients. And you'll retouch."

"Agreed," Mrs. Bauer said.

At least he'd gotten his wife to participate again. He'd have to deal with Miss Gaebele's bold moves later.

>-⊹>-O-⊰-⊰

"What's she like to deal with?" Lilly asked.

"Who?"

"Mrs. Bauer. She's been your boss these last few months."

"She's all right," Jessie told her. They were dressing for the Christmas program, in which Selma and Irene Fleischer would be singing a duet. Selma had been prepared and bundled up and had left with her father an hour earlier to rehearse yet one more time at Immanuel Evangelical. Selma didn't need it, but Irene insisted. "Mrs. Bauer is a little snippy at times and reminds me of Mama with her directions, but she doesn't stay at the studio for very long. Since the colder weather, I carry the prints to their house. I worried about her sending Russell back and forth to do it. He's such a somber boy. Takes his work seriously."

"She came into Stott's today and bought several pairs of gloves. Christmas presents, I imagine. It would be nice to just go into some store and buy whatever you wanted, wouldn't it? I noticed that Gillespie's and McMahon's had all their shoes on sale. I'd sure like to have gotten some high-button shoes."

"I'd like a pair of their warm boots," Jessie said. "The snow's already up to my knees, and when I shovel the walk, I can barely toss the snow over the top of the bank. Bunches keep falling back down onto my shoe tops, and then I have to dry them out. But I can't keep them off because it wouldn't be seemly to take someone's portrait in stocking feet."

"You're shoveling the walk there? That man has you doing everything. At least you're finally getting paid." She stuck a long hatpin into the felt, fluffing the ostrich feathers with her hands. "They must really like you."

"Aren't you going to wear your fur hat?" Jessie asked. "It's cold out there."

Lilly looked at Jessie in the mirror. "I suppose you're right about that," she said and removed the long hatpin. She put it in the porcelain holder on their shared dresser, fluffed the feathers once more, then lifted the hat from her head and put it back into its cardboard box. "I miss spring." Lilly sighed. "You'll have to take my portrait one time. When the weather warms."

Jessie nodded. She decided not to tell Lilly about Mr. Bauer's less-than-enthusiastic response to her portrait work. She couldn't understand it, really. She'd taken the test and passed it fine. She'd been able to convince nearly all of the scheduled portrait appointments to allow her to do the work, and no one, not a single person, had decided not to take at least one finished and framed print. Several clients had purchased four and five. She'd gotten new customers that way, when satisfied people told others about the studio.

A younger clientele expressed willingness to spend for portraits, and she'd even scheduled a couple of Norwegian loggers for a sitting next week. They were spending the holidays with family in Winona. Lumbermen, Mr. Steffes told her, had lots of money to spend and usually spent it on "women and liquor." Mr. Steffes had relatives in Wisconsin's Chippewa woods. He claimed to know all there was to know about loggers and immigrants. When she'd told him of her new appointment, Mr. Steffes said, "Get ready for the strong scent of toe jam because those Norwegian loggers don't like to wash their feet in the cold weather. Even if they don't take their boots off, you'll be introduced to their toes. It's why they have those big smorgasbords with all the rich smells. To cover up their own." He'd grinned, showing off a hole where a tooth should have been.

Jessie smiled with him. "I think it's the Swedish who have smorgasbords," she'd told him.

Now, standing at the bedroom mirror, Jessie said, "Yes, I'm finally getting paid. It's a good wage and good working conditions."

"Except for shoveling snow. Well, at least you have your camera back."

Jessie didn't correct her sister. She hadn't wanted to tell her of that snag and have to listen to her lecture about how Mr. Bauer took advantage of her. She hurried out the door, shouting over her shoulder, "I'll see about helping Mama get Roy going. Uncle August and Grandpa and Grandma will be here any minute. We don't want to be late for Selma's concert."

Jessie did wonder what sort of argument might have gone on with the Bauers when she broached the subject of their payment and getting her camera back. Mrs. Bauer looked this way and that, as though she hadn't known about the details of either.

But when Jessie brought the photographs to the Bauer home for Mr. Bauer to assess, Mrs. Bauer had met her in the foyer and handed her paychecks for her and Voe, their first in six months. She told Jessie that Mr. Bauer expected her to take the test and that he would discuss the camera issue with her later.

"Later?" Jessie had said. "But it's my camera."

"He says you did not keep your agreement with him."

"But I've run the studio for him. For you. Why would he object to my having my little camera back? I've taken no photographs on my own. That's what I agreed to. They've all been for the studio."

"Mr. Bauer has his ways," Mrs. Bauer told her. "That's all I know. You'll have to work it out with him."

The Bauer foyer was a place she'd gone to twice a week since then. Jessie would sit on the hat bench and wait for Mrs. Bauer to confer with Mr. Bauer. Sometimes Winifred joined her, and the time would go faster then as the child chatted about her bear or told her stories of imaginary friends. At least, Jessie assumed they were imaginary with names like Hestia (whom Jessie knew was the Greek goddess of hearth and home) and Hera (known to be jealous but also the protector of marriage). Mr. Bauer was likely reading the classics to Winifred, as these were things he spoke about sometimes at the studio when they worked in the darkroom or waited for clients. He probably had a few leather-bound books in the case that told such stories too.

Mostly Jessie sat alone in the Bauer foyer, where a fire warmed the open room. She could hear muffled conversations between the two. After a time, Mrs. Bauer would come down the stairs and convey Mr. Bauer's concerns about her work. There were always complaints, and a part of Jessie wondered if she

ought to continue the portrait appointments since Mr. Bauer was apparently
so upset with her skill. But Mrs. Bauer
insisted she proceed, and the clients
liked the results. Jessie had made the
commitment to run the studio, and
she'd keep it, at least until he was well,
even if he hadn't kept his word to return
her camera.

She'd looked for her Kodak, wondering where he might have put it. It wasn't
in the operating area. Well, of course, he
wouldn't want his customers seeing
something so amateurish. It wasn't upstairs in the attic portion, or downstairs.
It wasn't anywhere in the studio that she
could find. She even had Voe looking for
it on the high shelves that Jessie
couldn't reach without standing on a
ladder, and even then there were cubby-
holes she never could see far enough
back into. Her shortness was an annoyance. So was not getting that camera
back.

She had to put those thoughts aside
now as she hustled Roy along so they
could attend the Christmas concert.
She arrived in the kitchen just as her un-

cle August stomped the snow from his boots. "How's my little camera girl?" he said as he swung Jessie around the room.

"Neatly dressed and ready to go . . . until you came along," she teased. He set her down and she straightened her hat, held her muff with one hand.

"Well, pickle my fingers then," he said. "Here." He handed her a small box not much larger than her palm. "For my favorite niece. An early Christmas present. To go with your camera."

"You spoil the child," her mother said, but her tone was kind. Jessie suspected that her mother's next-to-youngest brother was a favorite of her own. His ears stuck out from his head and looked like loose flaps on a man's winter cap.

"May I open it now?" she asked.

"We really should be going," Lilly said, joining them.

"Are Grandma and Grandpa out there waiting?"

August nodded his head.

"I'd better hold off then. It's cold, and they don't need to be in it longer on my account."

"Oh, go ahead," August urged. "They've got hot bricks under their feet and a buffalo robe to wrap them."

Jessie removed her gloves, tore off the string, but carefully folded the paper for later use. Inside the box were two little silver spoons embossed with *St. Louis World's Fair.* "These are just precious," Jessie said. "Little salt spoons." She showed them around.

"I've saved a few trinkets from St. Louis. I'll dribble them to you now and then," he said. "For your trousseau." He winked at her.

"If my girls ever marry," their mother said. She pointed her finger at Lilly, who scowled.

"I do wonder what boy would want a scamp like Jessie," August said.

"One with good sense," Jessie said. "I could support him better than your suspenders."

He faked pain.

She helped settle Roy down as he put his coat on. "Boys are silly and thoughtless. Not you, Roy. I'll wait for a gentleman."

"You have to be wary of older men," August teased.

"I don't think years necessarily add wisdom. They could just count up years of dementia. You're seventeen years older than I am. Are you demented?" She grinned as she said it, as his face again showed mock pain.

"L-l-let's go!" Roy ran out the door, followed by the rest of the family.

Within minutes they were driving through the night on a sleigh pulled by her grandparents' big team, the *ping pingle ping* of the bells jangling in rhythm to the horses' hoofs. Later, the older people and August would spend the night, the girls giving up their bed for their grandparents and August bunking in with Roy. Jessie and her sisters would curl up in quilts on the parlor floor before the little stove, and there'd be a huge breakfast in the morning with bacon from the farm and eggs and the cinnamon rolls her grandmother Schoepp had spent days making. Jessie loved her grandparents, and it always pleased her to be able to say that she'd grown up "just down the road" from their farm. Jessie'd even been born in their home.

At the other end of the valley lived her other set of grandparents, as slender and small as her Schoepp parents were large and looming. Her mother's parents had settled early in the Cream valley, claiming the flat, rich farmland fed by a year-round stream. They'd come into Winona the following morning after attending a service at the Herold Church up on the bluff. She couldn't imagine a better life than to have so many relatives so close, and getting along with one another too. Family was what mattered. She looked at Roy as they sped along the wintry streets, and tears threatened to freeze on her cheeks.

Inside the newly rebuilt church on the corner of King and South Baker, Jessie was hit with the smell of kerosene lamps swinging from overhead wires. At the two stoves, people had placed their bricks to reheat them. They'd be bundled in blankets later to keep everyone's feet warm on the ride home. Evergreens and red bunting decorated the sanctuary. Dozens of tiny candles lit the branches of a tree that rose to the ceiling. Men stood next to the evergreen ready to replace any candles that burned too close to the greenery, but Jessie always imagined they guarded the presents that would be given out to all the children. She was too old for those gifts now, but she remembered the joy of receiving treasures at the Herold Church when she was little. A china-faced doll with leather arms still sat on the dresser. The Gem Roller Organ, ten years old now, had been a Christmas gift. Putting the rolls in and listening to the hymns play was still a special feature of the Gaebeles' Christmas morning.

Selma and Irene sang like angels in the concert, her sister's alto voice melting over them like pure maple syrup. The choir followed, then a piano solo that made Jessie wish she could play such music. She could plink out tunes so long as she remembered the melody. Something happened to her hands, which seemed to move without her when she sat on that round stool in front of the keys. If she looked at her hands while she played, she'd get stumped, but if she just let the music flow through her, she could sometimes play trills and chords and sound like someone who had practiced for years.

This experience was somewhat like faith, she decided: if you tried to think about it too much, you'd stumble, but if you just trusted and kept going, there'd always be the next note to come. Sometimes Jessie went with Selma to the sanctuary for her rehearsals and she'd play after the real accompanist left. But she'd never dream of playing in public. Besides, she had another life now, one she'd always dreamed of having—capturing beauty through photographic art.

Jessie looked around at all the different faces shining in the lights. A wood stove burned hot in the back, but she could still see the breath of those sitting near the front. Just a little breath, and the girls all kept their hands inside their muffs. These faces: every one of them could be a portrait, Jessie thought.

Jessie's mind wandered as the room filled with worshipers. Part of what she'd liked about running the studio with Voe these past weeks were the adventures she could look forward to each day, the new clients, the freedom to experiment in the darkroom, and the independence to eat lunch when they were hungry and not just when Mr. Bauer said to. They'd done well for the studio, or so she thought. She'd written ad copy that was published each week. Appointments were scheduled. Collections came in soon after she sent out the statements, and she made bank deposits just as Mrs. Bauer had told her to.

Mrs. Bauer was cordial, and even when she shared bad news with Jessie about how her husband didn't like certain aspects of the photographs she'd taken, Jessie found her easy to work with. Jessie took the criticism as lessons she still needed to learn and didn't carry away bad feelings either about Mrs. Bauer or her own work. Mr. Bauer was expected back after the first of the year, and a part of Jessie wasn't really looking forward to it. She might be limited to the darkroom again or, worse, relegated just to office work, working the typing machine and answering calls.

There was the matter of the camera they'd have to work out, not to mention the rash of critical comments. She'd made notes. She wanted to learn. It wouldn't be a pleasant discussion with him, but a necessary one.

The Gaebele children sat on either side of their parents on the long pew. During a change up front, when the choir left and another soloist stepped up on the stage, Jessie leaned forward, scanning to see if she knew anyone on the other side of the relatives' pew. Uncle August winked at her and she waved. Her mother frowned. Jessie turned and looked back. Her eye caught Winifred's. The child wiggled her fingers in greeting. Jessie waved her gloved hand in reply. The child had a good memory.

She saw Mrs. Bauer and Russell too, though neither noticed her. Then she saw Mr. Bauer. He looked so thin! He'd always been slender, but now he barely had skin enough to cover his bones. He'd lost some of his hair. The woman seated beside him moved, and her hat now kept Jessie from seeing any more of the Bauer-filled pew.

Here she'd been thinking poorly of him, almost wishing he wouldn't return because it was going to interfere with her enjoyment of her profession. She hoped to catch his eye and nod hello but didn't. She turned back when her mother tapped her knee and motioned for her to pay attention. The pastor had begun.

He spoke of light and what it meant to the world when Light flooded the darkness of men's souls. Jessie turned her attention to the front. This was a divergent sort of sermon for him, as he often spent time on darkness and sin. "Light is directional, telling us which way to go when there's a storm. The lantern swings to move us right or left to safety," the pastor said. He had a thick German accent, and Jessie had to focus on each word. She could understand a little German, though she didn't speak it. She believed that God's light offered guidance, but she still struggled with why things happened to innocents like her brother. Well, she knew in part. She worried about why she didn't always do what she knew she should.

"Light is warm. Those of you sitting far from the stove tonight might question that, way up here where the heat doesn't reach." The pastor was being cheerful, Jessie thought. Tonight many people who weren't members attended to enjoy the fine musical numbers. Perhaps he hoped to lure them back for another time with his gentler words. Jessie wondered if he'd hold the usual altar call at the end of this service. Selma went up every week to reaffirm her faith. Jessie had done it once, and that was enough.

"Light can not be pushed or rushed. It is either there or not, and no matter how quickly we want a sunrise after a dark, dark night, light takes its own time. It is the absence of light that we notice. That's what darkness is, especially to men's souls, an absence of Light." He paused, and for a moment Jessie thought he might go into that familiar theme of darkness. She fidgeted. She deserved to be reminded of all the wrongs she'd committed. But he continued with his voice light and joyous. He held a candle, which he now lit.

"Light can go out," he said. "But even after it does, there is an afterimage, isn't there? You look at this candle I hold. Stare closely now." Then he blew it out. "Now close your eyes, those of you with them still open. Close them and what do you see?" Jesse did this. "Do you still see the candle? Yes? That is the Lord's light in our hearts, burning there. Even when we make mistakes in our dark hours. Even though He has gone away from our sight, even when the light goes out—as the lives of those we love do— we can know that that life lives on as an afterimage in the hearts of those who re- main behind. Remember that as I invite you forward tonight. Remember that and be drawn into a new place in your hearts and out of the darkness of men. Amen."

Jessie hoped he also meant women could have the darkness drawn from their hearts, then felt a little guilty to have thought that. It wouldn't be an idea of which her mother would approve.

In the shuffle of gathering up hymnals

for the final selection they'd all join in singing, Jessie turned back. As she did, the woman with the large hat who had kept her from seeing Mr. Bauer bent to retrieve her song book, and when she did, Jessie watched Mr. Bauer wipe his eyes. *Tears?* Perhaps the talk of the afterimage brought his deceased child's life burning into his eyes.

Jessie lowered her eyes and turned them to the front. It wasn't her place to intrude on another family's pain. She watched as Selma once again rose, not to sing but to go forward. "Come along, Jessie," she urged. Jessie shook her head. Some things didn't need to be repeated.

EIGHT

The Eye Behind the Camera

Cold sunlight bathed the operating room windows on the day Mr. Bauer returned to his studio. Jessie dreaded this meeting, uncertain of her future given his criticisms of her work. Should she even bring it up or wait for him to? If he didn't, she'd always wonder about it, carry with her the confusion of whether she held a warped view of her ability or if she truly needed much more training.

Jessie pushed at her spectacles. Her nose perspired even in the cool room. Mr. Bauer sat with her and Voe, who crossed her ankles and chewed gum as they perused the ledgers, the appointments, the prints requested and provided, those paid for and those still pending.

"Would you not chew your gum, Miss Kopp? It's highly unprofessional and not very complimentary of your face." Voe complied, putting the glob into a tissue that must have wrapped up one of her Christmas presents. Mr. Bauer appeared ready to begin their day, when Jessie cleared her throat and said she wanted to speak with him about the photographs he'd criticized. Voe excused herself.

"Don't go," Jessie said. "I mean, you might learn something from what Mr. Bauer didn't like about the ones we set up," Jessie said.

"I did what you told me to do," Voe said. "So you can tell me later if you want to change it for next time. I'm going to make some tea. Would you like some, Mr. B.?"

Voe called him Mr. B. with Jessie, but she'd never called him that in his presence.

"Mr. Bauer," Jessie hissed at her.

"Mr. Bauer." Voe curtsied.

Instead of being upset by the familiarity, he smiled at Voe. "Mr. B. is just fine. I think of myself as FJ," he told them. "A good short version. No reason you can't have a short version of your own. As a matter of fact, I wonder if it would be acceptable for me to call you by your given names, Voe, Jessie. When others are about, of course not. We'll keep it professional. But when it's just we three, I believe we can be a little less formal, don't you think?"

"Suits me swell, Mr. B.," Voe said.

"I'd like that, Mr. Bauer," Jessie said. "Mr. B." She tried it on, felt her face grow warm with the unfamiliarity of it spoken in front of him.

"Or FJ if you prefer. Now then, let's get back to your concerns about the prints. You have a list there, I see."

"Yes." She looked pleadingly at Voe, who waved a palm of encouragement as she left to make tea. "Mrs. Bauer told me what you didn't like about them," Jessie said. "I tried to use your comments to improve the next sittings, but I never seemed to get it right. The clients were happy, though."

He frowned. "I'm confused. Aside

from the first print of Mildred Simmons, the one that I felt you had no authority to take, I had very little to say about your work. For an amateur, I thought you performed adequately." He coughed. "Maybe you misunderstood Mrs. Bauer."

"She was very specific about what she said you didn't like. Look here." She showed him a print. "The background was too dark. That's the note I took. But I wanted it that way, to put more contrast to the faces of the children. And here." Jessie pointed to another picture. "Here you said that I had a poor angle, that it made the woman look harsh. But the photo actually softens her. And I thought that the line of the window behind her moved the eye to that side of her soft face. Here you said it was out of balance, but see, the book is in the lower right quadrant and the vase with flowers is at the upper right. They offset each other, just as you taught me."

He lifted several of the prints, put them down, picked them back up, squinted and pushed his glasses up. "I don't remember saying those things," he said. "I might have been delirious with the fever. I'll have to ask Mrs. Bauer."

"So you do like them?"

"Oh, there are improvements to be made, but you're quite inexperienced. That you've managed to have so many happy customers is reassuring. You've made it quite clear what the subject of the photograph is, and that's very important. No diffusing. Clarity. But Mrs. Bauer's telling you the problems like that—some of her comments don't make any sense. You must have misunderstood her."

She risked another issue. "Am I wrong about your not wanting to return my camera to me either?" She pushed her spectacles up on her nose, crossed her arms over her narrow chest.

"Why, it's at the house. I never intended to keep it. I was sure I told Mrs. Bauer to return it to you when you began being paid. She did pay you?"

"We've been paid. But I've been hunting for that camera and wondered why you wouldn't give it back to me."

"I wonder why I didn't either," he said. "Confound it! This is very strange."

Perhaps it was Mrs. Bauer who didn't like her work. Or maybe he was delirious when he made the remarks.

"I'll speak with Mrs. Bauer. I believe I'll do that now and return your camera to you as well." He rose to leave, and Jessie could see by his quick movements, jerking his coat from the tree, pressing his hat on tightly, that he was upset. "Yes. I'll see if Mrs. Bauer can shed some light on this little mystery." He wrapped a wool scarf around his neck. He started out, then turned around. He lifted her hand and patted it, held it for just a moment. "Thank you for the hard work you did while I was ill. I'm so sorry about this confusion." He looked into her eyes, and Jessie felt gratitude from him that warmed.

He removed his hand, aware that he had perhaps violated a border. He picked up one of the prints Jessie said he hadn't liked. He seemed momentarily confused again, tapped it against his hand.

"I'll bring your camera back in the morning. It was wrong of me to have separated you from it. You do have quite a talent, Miss Gaebele. I'm sorry if I conveyed anything less."

⊱━━◆━━○━━◆━━⊰

He had given them gloves for Christmas and said they were from the Bauer family. Voe's were a black pair with tiny stitches, and Jessie's gloves were the color of cream. They were both leather, and Jessie wondered if Lilly would be able to tell if she had sewn these particular gloves from Stott's. It would be hard to create things that couldn't be recognized as your own, Jessie thought. She'd have to be more understanding of Lilly's irritations, knowing that she lacked tasks that fed her uniqueness.

To herself, Jessie acknowledged her disappointment with the gloves. She'd wanted FJ to see her as distinctive, separate from Voe. Oh, she knew they both worked for him, had been hired at the same time and all that, but Jessie had done more work and meant to make photography her career. Voe would be the first to admit that it was "just a trade" for her and one she was happy to leave behind each day when they closed the studio door.

Not Jessie. Once she'd gotten her camera back, it was as though she'd been starving for months and at last could eat and be satisfied. She finished up the roll, taking shots outside of all sorts of things that some might think frivolous. She took a picture of the Chicago and Northwestern Railway Station and managed to get a buggy in the foreground with its unusual painted white wheels standing out against the maroon-colored body. A train was in the station the day she took the shot. A yellow passenger car followed the coal tender car. She'd always liked the rail station because of its red brick and a roofline that reminded her of old European mansions. She fully intended to tint the photograph once it was developed, and she made notes to remind herself of the oil colors she'd need: yellow ochre for the passenger car, lamp black for the train, crimson lake and hemp black would color the maroon buggy, and for the blue gray roof she'd

use a little prussian blue and crimson
lake to create a weak purple tone.

St. Stanislaus Church and School
was another photograph she hoped
would turn out well. The turrets and
domes of the massive building that took
up an entire block in Winona were often
photographed from the front, but Jessie
wanted one taken at the corner. Whenever she walked past that Gothic-look-
ing building, she thought she was in
Russia or maybe Germany, places she'd
likely never visit, and yet the architec-
ture had been transplanted right here to
their little town of Winona. She took
photographs of mallards skimming Vs
across the water at Levee Park, and
when the snow began to melt, she shot
interesting views of its changing
shapes. But her favorite, one she hoped
would turn out, was of the drive to
Sugar Loaf, the natural wonder that
people on the steamboats always
looked for to tell them they were nearly
home. A storm brewed on the day she
took that picture, and she made notes
so that if she decided to color it for a
postcard, she'd get the hues just right.

She also photographed Winifred with her little camera. It was the last picture on the Kodak roll. FJ had brought Winnie in for a birthday portrait.

"And when is your birthday, Winnie?" The child looked at her father.

"February 12."

"Mine too!" Jessie said before catching herself.

"Is it?" FJ said. "We should take a photograph of you too, then, Jessie. You can give it to your mother for a present."

"I'd like that," she told him. "But first Winnie's."

"Yes. Winnie's." He posed Winnie with just a gold necklace against her bare skin. She had her little shirt off. It was cool in the studio, and Jessie put a cloak around her until he was ready with reflectors and lighting and just the angle he wanted. "I'll develop it with a kind of mist around her shoulders," he told them. "And I don't want any color except her skin tone and the delicate chain. I want those eyes and that wonderful mouth of hers to be the focus."

Winnie fidgeted until he said, "Hold

your breath now," and she did, looking up with her beautiful eyes, posing. "Breathe now, Papa?" she asked after a few seconds.

"Yes, *Liebchen,*" he told her, using the German word for *sweetheart.*

"I sit for Papa," Winnie told Jessie. "Do you like to sit for Papa too?"

Jessie felt herself blushing, though she didn't know why. "I like to help your papa take beautiful pictures of his best girl," she said. "And now I'll take one of you too, all right?"

She nodded. "I'm Papa's best girl."

"That you are, *Liebchen.*" The child beamed and posed still again even though her father hadn't asked her to.

Jessie took her shot, then helped the almost-three-year-old Winnie put her dress back on over her chemise. The child chattered, and Jessie listened and laughed with her.

"Want some chocolate?" Voe asked, and when Winnie nodded, Voe took the child to the kitchen. "Now let's get your photograph," FJ said.

"Mine?" She hesitated. He had yet to explain the confusion between Mrs.

Bauer and himself with regard to Jessie's photographs. She wasn't sure why, but she sensed a tension between the two, and somehow her photographs had become a part of that. She wondered if Mrs. Bauer would approve of his wasting time and dry plates on portraits of a shop girl.

"It really isn't necessary, FJ," Jessie said.

"Now, it isn't every day that a young girl turns sixteen," he said. "Your beaus will enjoy having a likeness of you."

"My mother or my uncle might, but there are no beaus for me."

"That'll change," he said. "Sooner than you think. This'll only take a moment. You know how to sit."

She did sit down, fussed with her hair, settled this way and that on the side chair. She felt suddenly exposed in front of the camera with him behind it, as though he could see something through the lens that she didn't intend to reveal. She wondered now if others felt that way when she stood behind the camera. It concerned her that she was doing something frivolous when she should be

working, and even though her employer
was saying it was fine, she felt uncomfortable. She stood.

"I'd really rather do a sitting, if we
must, when I've had time to prepare
my hair," she said. "And to choose a
blouse that compliments me more. Who
needs a working-girl photograph?" She
laughed, feeling awkward. "If we're going to do this, I'd like to look . . . taller, at
the very least."

He came out from behind the camera
and smiled with his entire face. "I'm not
sure I can make you taller, but a gentleman defers to a lady's need for a fresh
toilet. You prepare tomorrow, and we'll
do the sitting then. I should get Winnie
on home anyway. Mrs. Bauer will worry."

"Speaking of Mrs. Bauer," Jessie
said. "I wondered if you . . . Did you
have an opportunity to discuss with her
the concerns about my photographs?"
She sometimes waited so long to bring
up an issue that by the time she did, the
trouble had faded itself out.

"I did," he said. He'd turned his back
to her and fussed with the camera
wheel, raising it to prepare for the family

he'd be photographing tomorrow. "And I must say I am no more clarified in my thinking than I was before. She insists that I made the comments and was quite upset that I should retract what I said and put the blame on her. That's what she called it, 'the blame.' "

"I didn't think you were being unkind. I just didn't understand what you meant about them, how I could improve them next time," Jessie said.

"I tried to tell her that, but she—" He stopped himself. "I'm sorry. You've no need to be embroiled in our petty marital disputes," he said. "I found the photographs to be not grand but satisfactory as I looked at them without fever. I regret that Mrs. Bauer felt compelled to share with you her delusions. *My* delusions," he corrected. "Can we let it go at that?"

"Certainly." She still wondered what wasn't so grand about them. "I hope that if you have judgments about my photographs, should I be allowed to take some independent of you in the future, you'll share any thoughts you have. To make them better."

"Agreed," he said. "Your asking is a sign of a professional mind. One never improves his art without curiosity and risk."

He went to the kitchen to retrieve Winnie, and on the way back through he stopped at the desk where Jessie bent over a ledger. "I didn't mean to make you uncomfortable, suggesting a birthday portrait for you. Sometimes I do things meant to be kind that turn out otherwise. I wouldn't want that to be the case, with you especially. I'm very fond of you, Miss Gaebele. I hope you know that."

He pressed his hat upon his head. Winnie rushed to kiss Jessie's cheek as Jessie knelt to her, and then the two were gone, leaving Jessie with a wondering ache in her heart.

>-!-<>--O--<>-!-<

"Don't be ridiculous," FJ told his wife. "She's simply a young woman who works for me. Nothing else. How do you get yourself into thinking these things?"

Mrs. Bauer had greeted him at the door several days later, fire in her eyes.

"Winifred said you were fond of Miss Gaebele and making a birthday portrait of her, that you said it right in front of the child."

"That alone should tell you there's nothing to worry about. Of course I said it in front of the child. Both of them are children. Miss Gaebele is turning sixteen on the same day Winnie turns three. They're children. Minnesota doesn't recognize a girl as a woman until she turns eighteen, remember? Where is your mind going?"

"I was a child when you married me." He turned away. "And those other shop girls you employed—"

"Who deserted me, if you remember."

"You tried to make me out to be the bad person about those pictures," she said.

Her eyes had that blaze to them that could mean hours of her ranting with nothing to stop it. The more he attempted to be reasonable, gentle, or sweet, the more her voice raised, and before long she would bring in "the history lesson" as he called it, reminders of all the low and thoughtless things he'd done through their nearly seventeen years of marriage.

"Jessie. Mrs. Bauer. Calm yourself. The children are here. There's no need for your upset."

"No need? You express fondness for some young girl. It's probably not the first time. Maybe that's why Miss Schulz and Miss Phalen left. How do I know that isn't what you do when you're off at your conventions? After all I do to raise your children, to prepare your meals, to take care of you when you're ill, and this is how you repay me?" She tore off her apron and rolled it into a ball. "Fix your own supper, Mr. Bauer. Perhaps you should get used to it."

She ran up the stairs, the argument ending with the slam of her door.

Winnie shook. He put his arm on her shoulder. "It's nothing you did, *Liebchen.* Mama's had a hard day. We'll let her rest. Let's find Russell, and the three of us will fix something to eat. Maybe I'll try my hand at a little éclair. Would you like that? Hmm? You will help me stir the eggs." Winnie nodded, but her lower lip pooched out. He tickled his fingers beneath her chin, and she smiled. "Good. Now where's Russell? Is he in his room? You go get him. That's a good girl. We'll let Mama rest, and we'll do this together."

The child ran off, and he slumped into the kitchen chair. There had never been a partnership between him and Mrs. Bauer, never the reality of two people moving on the same path toward common hopes. The most precious things he had in his life were his children, and Mrs. Bauer had given him those. Yet nothing he did could assure her that he was faithful, reliable, dependable. Even if he came home every night without going to the lodge or to the Masonic temple, where his comrades all gathered, even if he neglected those possible commercial referrals so necessary in his business, and came here every day exactly by six o'clock, he would still have to face the uncertainty: perhaps silence, or more likely, unexplained rage. If she was even here. She'd gone home twice to her mother, and he fully expected her to do that again. He just didn't know when or why.

Her behavior had worsened with Donald's death, and he held himself accountable for that. Everyone said it was an accident, but he'd kept the boy standing between his knees. Donald would be alive today if he hadn't done that, and so he'd carry the weight of his poor decision to his grave. The horse was a favorite of Mrs. Bauer's too. Tame. Well trained. He shook his head. They'd all been in this malaise for nearly four years now.

Maybe Mrs. Bauer was right. Miss Gaebele did bring lightness to his days. She did make him feel as though he had something to offer by allowing him to help her develop skills. Even so, he thought of her as a child, which she was. Nothing more. And he didn't know why he should deprive himself of pleasure in doing things for people who seemed to appreciate it, unlike his wife. He could do nothing to please her, or at least that was how it had come to seem.

"Papa?" Russell entered the room. "Is Mama all right?"

"She'll be fine, Son. We'll fix some supper and offer her some, but she may

refuse it. We grownups have had a mis-
understanding, but it isn't about you.
You mustn't worry. Wash up now," he
said, standing. He picked up the apron
and put it over his head, tying the sash
around his waist. Russell started to
smile. "What? You think a man can't
wear an apron? I know how to do a few
things around here. Time you learned
too. Here's an apron for you as well." He
pulled one from the linen closet, tidy as
his tackle box. Winnie giggled. "I'm giving you dish cleanup duty," he told his
son. "And you, missy, you're the chief
egg swamper."

Winnie grabbed his legs and hugged
him. Russell groaned, but it was a groan
of joy. FJ touched his daughter's soft
curls, smiled at his son. At least he
could still give pleasure to his children.

>-+◆>-○-◆+-<

Jessie did bring in a pleated silk blouse,
her Sunday best, and a string of pearls
she "borrowed" from her mother under
the guise that she wanted to try a new
prop. She intended to weave them into
her hair. He didn't mention the portrait.

Jessie swallowed her disappointment, to shy to bring it up. At the end of the day, she took the blouse and pearls home.

>─!─◆>─O─<◆─!─<

Jessie Gaebele turned sixteen in 1908 at a party her parents planned that included Voe, Clara Giese (who had run through the storm with her), and Jerome, who always seemed to be around when food was served. Voe had brought him along uninvited. Lilly told her if she didn't want Jerome around she'd have to be blunt. "That's how I dealt with Sam," she said. Sam was one of Lilly's beaus, and Jessie had liked him. But Lilly said he was fond of "brew," and she'd never marry a man with that kind of palate.

Jessie's uncle August appeared, as did several other friends of her parents', and of course her sisters and brother, Roy. Sweet, gentle, damaged Roy.

After the cake, while people took turns on the White Mountain Ice Cream Freezer handle, Jessie opened gifts. Mr. Steffes gave her a certificate "good for a bicycle ride once a week." Her uncle added another treasure from the world's fair, a rose glass cup with her name etched into the red. "Did you do all this during the fair?" Jessie asked him.

"I must have," he said, and he winked.

Lilly had sewn a new blouse for her, and Selma gave her a fragrant lily of the valley plant she'd nurtured from seed that would bloom in the spring. Her parents gave her a subscription to the monthly *Woman's Home Companion.* Lilly scoffed at that.

"That magazine has articles by radical women. Like Charlotte Perkins Gilman," Lilly said. "She advocates the woman of a house pay for household help so she can work outside, both contributing to the household coffers and helping the economy by giving some poor wretch a job cooking and cleaning."

"I wasn't aware of that," her mother said, frowning. "But the editor is Reverend Edward Everett Hale. He always offers the most encouraging things to think about. I've bought an issue now and then. I think it will help all you girls think of womanly things."

" 'Faith is looking up, hope is looking forward, and love is looking outward instead of inward,' " Jessie quoted. "I remember seeing that in one of the issues you bought, Mama. I'll like looking at them. A photographer has to keep up with the times, Lilly."

Her sister scoffed again.

"I like the stories they publish," Selma said. "And the dress patterns. Won't you like looking at those, Lilly?"

Voe gave Jessie a card she'd made with little pieces of dried flowers glued to make the shape of a Kodak. Inside she'd placed some coins.

"But you worked hard for this money, Voe. I'm sure you have things you'd like to buy."

"I never would have kept that job while Mr. B. was ill if it hadn't been for you organizing and directing. So it's a little bit I set aside for your present and then figured you'd know better what to do with it."

"I'll get my prints developed," she

said, hugging Voe. "Thank you so much."

"That was very thoughtful of you, Voe," Jessie's mother said.

Roy raised his hand and pointed before they heard the knock at the door. Selma opened it, and there stood FJ.

"Mr. Bauer," Jessie gasped. "Are you lost?"

"On my way home."

"He works very hard," Jessie told everyone. "I should have been working this Tuesday, so thank you for giving me a day off to have my party."

"Invite the man in," her father said. There'd been an ice storm, and as Jessie motioned for him to enter, she looked at the trees outside. The ice pelted one side of the tree trunks, making them look nearly white in the late afternoon, while the backs of the trunks were bare and black. She wished she could rush out and take a photograph of this checkered contrast.

"It's Jessie's birthday," Selma told Mr. Bauer. "That's why we're having a party."

"My daughter's birthday is today as

well, so it was easy to remember Miss Gaebele's special day. I just wanted to drop something off for her." His spectacles had steamed in the warm room, and he looked over them as he handed Jessie the package, which felt damp to her hands but not cold. He must have carried it close to his person.

She hesitated, feeling awkward opening the gift in front of everyone. She didn't know why. She'd opened everyone else's present with a dozen eyes looking on.

"Go on," Selma urged. "What is it?"

It was something in silver with *St. Louis World's Fair 1904* engraved on it. She lifted a small case out of the paper wrapping. It fit in the palm of her hand and opened on a single hinge. Inside could rest three or four small photographs.

"I knew you were fond of world's fair items," he said. "You said your uncle had gotten you things."

"That I did," August said, and he thrust his hand out and introduced himself. "But I didn't see anything like a photographic case to purchase."

Jessie turned the small case over in her hands. She couldn't remember receiving a present that spoke so well to what she loved, except for Uncle August's gift of the Kodak, of course. But this . . . this was spare and splendid.

"Well, what do you say?" her mother urged.

"C-c-cat's got her t-t-tongue," Roy said and grinned widely.

Jessie brushed the hair from Roy's eyes, found words.

"I'm . . . It's . . . beautiful, Mr. Bauer," Jessie said. "Thank you. I didn't warrant, that is, I don't deserve—"

"Let me hold it," Selma said, and Jessie passed the case around, grateful to be rescued from her stuttering words.

"Hey, there's a photo inside," Jerome Kopp said when the case got to him. "Wanna take it out, Jess?"

She'd seen the back of a photo when she'd opened it but hadn't wanted to turn it face out in front of everyone. She wanted to keep some small part of this present as just hers, though she didn't know why.

"No, just let it be," she told him.

"Ah, come on." Jerome lifted it and looked. "Swell," he said before turning it around and holding it up for everyone to look at.

No one else said anything for a moment.

Finally, Jessie asked, "When . . . when did you take it?"

"When you were helping get Winifred—that's my daughter—ready for her portrait. It's a profile, and I could take out the background easily enough. I thought it a good likeness."

"Your glasses are where they're supposed to be," Selma said, "instead of sliding down on your nose."

Jessie said nothing, afraid that any words would give away what her heart was telling her. She waited for the photograph to be handed back to her, waited until each had looked at it and commented then on "how pretty it was" and "what a good likeness" and all that nonsense.

It wasn't a good likeness at all.

The girl in that photograph had flyaway hair, and she hadn't worn her earrings, which any self-respecting woman would have for a portrait sitting. But worst of all, it wasn't like her because the girl—no, the woman—in that photograph was beautiful. She'd been made so by the eye behind the lens.

She closed the case around the picture and realized people were saying farewells and that Mr. Bauer was backing his way to the door, appreciating their hospitality for allowing the intrusion. She nodded to him, thanked him again, she thought, and then he was out the door. She remembered just as he moved down the steps. "Tell Winnie happy birthday for me!"

"That I'll do," he said. He tipped his hat in the waning afternoon, hooked his cane over his arm, and stepped away.

"Well, that was a fine present and a nice surprise for a girl's sixteenth year," her father said.

"The old man has taste," Jerome said.

Voe punched him in the shoulder. "Not that you'd know about that."

"I know what I know," he said. The look he gave Jessie seemed to peer inside her, accuse her. She looked away

only to see Lilly holding the same penetrating gaze.

><>O<><

"You'd better be careful," Lilly said as
the girls undressed that evening.

"I'm always careful," Jessie said.

"You know what I'm talking about."

"What?" Selma asked. "Tell me because I sure don't know."

"It's none of anyone's business," Jessie said. "Besides, it's your imagination.
Mr. Bauer is a kind man who wants to
see me succeed as a photographer,
that's all. He likes to instruct. He likes to
encourage. A silver photographic case
is a thoughtful gift, more generous than
he ought to have indulged in, but I did
run the studio while he was ill and
through the Christmas season too."

"He remembered your birthday!" Lilly
hissed.

"It's the same day as his daughter's.
You're making too much of this, Lilly."

Jessie removed her dress shields and
placed them on the dresser for airing.
They were damp.

"Is there something wrong with Jessie

getting a present from the Bauers?"
Selma asked.

"No. There's nothing wrong with it,"
Jessie said. "Lilly sees goblins stalking
where there are only good wishes roam-
ing about."

"I'm not talking about the photographic case," Lilly said. "It's the photograph in it that worries me."

It concerned Jessie too, but she
couldn't let Lilly or Selma know that.
"He's just like Uncle August to me," Jessie said. "Those older men like to amuse
themselves by delighting young girls.
That's all this is. I bet he remembers
Voe's birthday too and gives her something equally as special."

"It won't have that kind of a photograph in it," Lilly said. "I can assure you
of that."

"It was a candid shot. Something he
did . . . spontaneously." She pulled her
nightdress over her head, let it slide
down her narrow hips, the heat from her
body filling the flannel. She tied the ribbon at the neckline, then began taking
the combs out of her hair. "His child was

the subject of the sitting. She's such a sweet little girl."

"Let me brush your hair, Jessie," Selma said, and Jessie sat on the bed while her sister knelt on the log cabin quilt behind her. She hoped the conversation about the photograph was over. She wished she had her own room right now so she could consider the jumble of feelings that tossed around inside her.

"Jessie, you know what I'm talking about. The eye behind that camera"— Lilly hesitated, looked into the round mirror to catch Jessie's eyes—*"feels deeply about the subject."* She mouthed the words so Selma wouldn't hear them.

"The camera was set for his daughter, so of course that makes sense," Jessie said, making her voice light. She looked away then. "That's enough, Selma. I'm really tired." She slid beneath the layers of quilts and buried her face into the down pillow, not wanting to deal any further with the confusion of Lilly's observations and the clutter of her own thoughts. She was sixteen years old and feeling strange. Maybe she was coming down with something. Yes. That was probably it. She closed her eyes and prayed for sleep while dreams skipped across her mind like stones across a distant lake.

The Pose

*Posing someone seeking a portrait
means creating the proper setting for
them. The setting, after all, is a party to
the pretense. Posing is attentive to detail. I'm reminded of the gospel story of
the fishermen complaining that they'd
not caught sufficient fish and being told
to return and fish deeper. Return and
go deeper. They were seeking fish, but
going deeper forced them to reflect on
things, to bring up wisdom and not just
what they thought they'd gone after.
Going deeper changed their pose.*

 *The photograph posed here is of two
of my friends, Voe on the right, and
Clara. I loved the new moon and
placed the girls to look as though they
balanced each other. It was quite a
contraption, that new moon, and became popular in the studio, giving a
portrait an almost spontaneous look,
though I'd purposefully arranged every
detail of their hats and hands. I handed*

Clara my beaded purse to lay on her knees. I set the feathers on their hats just so. Voe's hat was made of plaster bananas. I smoothed the wrinkles on their skirts with sliced cucumber, rubbed a cloth along the points of Clara's shoes to make them shine. Nothing was as it had been when they'd walked in; it was all posed. Sometimes what seems to be the most casual is really quite predetermined.

You'll note as well that Clara, on the left, swings her feet. She's above the floor, while you can't see Voe's legs, covered by the moon. I could have put them both on one side, but I liked the offsetting quality of their positions. They weren't in the same place even though their bodies might appear so. But they sat tuned to each other, though they looked toward the camera. Initially I had them looking at each other, but they laughed too much and could not hold the pose. So I placed their hands just so and had them look at me, forget they sat with a friend, and make the lens their pal.

In a studio pose, one looks for the

very best way of making the subjects look more like themselves than they might really be. There is a quality of pretense, a facade that people carry around on their person. They don't really want the real, known-only-to-a-few person to come through to everyone they meet. It would unravel their souls to let everyone see who they are, really. Souls seek safety and find it in silences. It's a kind of feigning, and when I posed FJ's clients, I helped him with the pretense on more levels than one.

The position of the hands, for example, can suggest power, or supplication, or frustration. I've posed an old man's hand vertical on his knee but in a fist because it allowed him to hold it still long enough to add the seconds needed to expose the film. He liked the result, said it made him look "regal," as though he held a staff. His daughter didn't like it though. She said it made him look hard, and he wasn't. But you see, he liked that it suggested a view of himself he wanted and now could affirm even if he didn't feel regal most of the time.

Which props one puts into the picture can also change the pose. Is the woman looking at a book so we see only a profile? Perhaps she's holding a hat loosely at her side, suggesting casualness. Many women like that look, though in interaction with others we rarely let ourselves look unplanned, casual. We're always seeking ways to appear natural, relaxed, and happy when in fact so many of us aren't. Even worrying about what others think of us can be time consuming, and yet we do it, even when having our portraits made. Perhaps more than ever when we're having our portraits made. I'm quite critical of pictures of me. Perhaps it's human nature to want to be received in the good light that we see ourselves in. We experience disappointment when we aren't so accepted. There is a kind of nakedness (a word my mother would gasp at) in having a photograph made. A risk, too, that someone will see through our pose into our very souls. I've heard there are people in the world who do not ever pose for photographs for fear it will do something to their souls. They avoid mirrors for the same reason, and reflections of themselves in water.

The birthday gift from FJ was a mirror that told everyone, even before my own acknowledgment, that I was on the brink of stepping into a deeper place. I could feign friendship. I could feign professionalism. I was merely a student learning all I could—that's all I was. I told myself and others any number of things that from afar made perfect sense. FJ and I worked closely together. We shared business conversations. Some weeks we spent more time with each other at the studio than we spent awake with our families. But these things happened among colleagues in the working world, didn't they? One must learn limits, borders, boundaries. What did the German poet Rilke write? That love meant to "protect and border and salute." It was the border we needed to address. Or I did. I didn't even know for certain he felt anything for me. Except for that present and the portrait inside.

I reasoned that what was happening

to us had happened before women ever left the home to work. Consider the pose between a finely dressed female and a bank teller, for example. Or sometimes looks might pass between a pastor and his organist and be understood as longing that moves no further than one's eyes. The borders are protected, but someone else watching might misunderstand, might not recognize the pose as one subject to limits. I'd read of such things, though I'd never seen it.

For FJ and me there was no need to say anything. As long as we didn't, I felt safe, could tell myself I just wasn't interested in younger boys, not interested in tying my life to a man of any age, for that matter. I didn't deserve such an alliance anyway. I couldn't find within me the right to such joy meant to last a lifetime. I wanted to cultivate my passion for photography, and doors had opened to allow it. Each of us had been created for such uniqueness, hadn't we? Created that way, yes; deserving of it? No. I carried fear within me, of what I wasn't certain. I had un-

wittingly protected my heart all the while I worked with Mr. Bauer. Then he gave me that gift, and it caused me to go deeper but not yet to face the fear that I wasn't worthy of that artistic passion, wasn't worthy of the joy.

Afterward, posing as disinterested parties in a photographic studio could go on no longer. How to proceed became the issue. Maybe if I had simply held the thought but not put feet to it, maybe all would have passed over without entanglement or trial. Quite frankly, I didn't know what FJ understood about what he'd done in giving me the case and the photograph inside. Men can sometimes be quite dense about such things, not realizing the nuances read by others, those little details that can make or break a scene.

When the shot's been taken, there is extricating to be done, even with a solo portrait. The props are removed from the subjects, feet now placed so they can stand. There is the moment of discomfort as the subjects walk away from the background and the bench they've sat upon and step back into the real world. The fantasy is gone. A kind of loss is felt. The photographer lightens the moment, says something to suggest that it went well, that they'll be pleased with the results, and then they leave, no longer in a portrait pose but taking on another that helps them manage in the world.

When I finished the shot with my friends, they chattered to each other and coordinated in order for each to step off that new moon structure safely and go their merry way. As with a teetertotter that children play on, one simply cannot walk away from that kind of pose without consulting the other first, or great pain ensues. Yes, it's best to work things out step by step when extracting from a pose, if one can.

It was a lesson I would learn the hardest way.

NINE

Adapting

FJ enjoyed the laughter of his daughter on her birthday. Winnie's giggling always warmed his heart. He tried to put behind him financial concerns. They'd made it through the bank foreclosures of 1907, and fortunately the Winona Bank, where he held his accounts, remained solvent. But he'd decided to put money into stocks just before the financial panic, and those investments proved useless. He chided himself. He was forever climbing aboard wagons that raced over precipices he hadn't seen. His forecasting might as well have been formed in a fog. Congress had appointed a committee to establish a better monetary policy, but he had little hope that anything would come of it. The illustrated ad in the paper had it right: large corporations held the hammer while consumers and small businessmen were the nails.

He'd probably have to cut expenses. He certainly didn't want to deprive his children of anything. And Mrs. Bauer always needed more household money. He didn't want to say no to that. It would lead to argument. No, it was better to let things at home go on and to make expense cuts at work.

He could cancel the subscription to *Camera World,* much as he liked taking it and the girls enjoyed reading it. At least Jessie did. The *World* taught him that the Lumière brothers, French chemists, had developed a process for color photography. Maybe tinting would fade away. They already manufactured photographic materials and had invented some kind of moving-picture camera. Now color. Should he invest in that? He would have to learn of these things through the conventions if he cancelled the subscription, but even convention going must be curtailed.

The lawsuit he'd brought against the Dakota farmer who had let his stubble burn get out of hand had gone nowhere. He'd lost five thousand dollars' worth of timber as well as the house, outbuildings, and his cattle. He was insured but not against all losses. Maybe he'd still get something out of the neighbor, but he doubted it.

He supposed he ought not to have indulged in the silver photo case for Jessie. But he'd seen it in the store, and the price had been reasonable as it was nearly four years old. It was appropriate for her, loving photography as she did. He hoped it would turn her head toward portraiture work. It concerned him that she was interested in the landscape side of photography rather than the studio side. The international argument about whether photography was art had waged for years. Large numbers of photographers considered themselves Photo-Secessionists. They saw themselves as "amateurs" who didn't want to associate with professionally trained

portrait photographers and held separate gallery exhibitions. FJ believed a
professional photographer could be
artistic, but he also knew that making a
great photograph required technical and
scientific skills. Miss Gaebele would
have considered herself a Secessionist,
he imagined, and that was unfortunate.
She had potential, but not if she persisted in taking artful landscape shots
rather than cementing her skills in the
studio first. She liked the splash of a finished photograph but seemed to abhor
the daily rigors necessary to build up
her understanding of this art.

He tried to read the afternoon paper
as he awaited the birthday cake and
candles so they could sing to Winnie.
He wondered if the Gaebeles sang for
Jessie. A twinge of discomfort fell on
him. Probably it was the cost of the gift,
given their financial concerns, that took
away a bit of the joy of the giving. Or
maybe it was the way in which Jessie
had reacted to the photograph. He
wasn't sure she liked it. The others
seemed stunned by it. He thought it a
fine likeness, but it hadn't warranted

near amazement. Or perhaps he'd misread their looks. That young Jerome appeared to admire the picture of Miss
Gaebele. The responses of the others,
including Jessie, didn't make any sense
to him.

Maybe it was just the age difference
between himself and the young people.
The Kopp boy didn't look too worldly,
and Jessie was a young girl and perhaps didn't appreciate the quality of that
unposed portrait. Or that it had been
taken by a true professional. Maybe he
was a little annoyed that she hadn't
seen the skill in it nor her own natural
beauty as a model. He sighed. He would
have to let the girls go before too long
unless something changed. They were
hard workers, and he thoroughly enjoyed the conversations with Jessie
about how she would compose a photograph or sell more postcard pictures.
Commercial success was about finding
new clients or cutting expenses—it was
as simple as that—and Jessie was always considering new ways.

Maybe he could sell more of his
salve. He hadn't quite perfected the

formula, but it was still a product worth what he charged and much less than what Watkins charged for his. That man had practically made his liniments and laxatives household necessities, just like the almanac Watkins published each year with its calendars and weather predictions and recipes and songs printed in both German and English. It was nothing more than a fat advertisement sold as a medical book. Right on the front it announced: "The J. R. Watkins Medical Company." FJ knew about medical things, and these . . . concoctions weren't medicine. But it worked for Watkins. The man was a millionaire right here in Winona, having married into that King family's great wealth. He'd made his products a requirement for everyday life. If only photographs were. Or his salve was.

He watched his daughter and son laughing together. If he could find a way to convince people that having a photograph made was a part of a family's need, part of their history, a way to treasure and remember, that might free up more people to spend money on his im-

ages. He was so grateful he had photographs of Donald. They kept the boy
alive to him.

He'd given Winnie the little picture
he'd made of her. She'd spent a minute
staring and said, "Oh, Papa, I pretty,"
which made his heart sing. Then she'd
set it on the round end table, already
forgotten, and pulled open her mother's
gift, a pair of ice skates.

"That's a surprise," he said. Mrs.
Bauer was always so nervous about the
children getting hurt, and she didn't
skate. Neither did he. She hadn't discussed it with him. She must have paid
for them from the household accounts.
He'd have to speak with her about that.
But on the other hand, he too had spent
funds without consultation, though not
on the gloves they'd given both the
shop girls at Christmas. Those gifts he
and Mrs. Bauer had agreed on.

"Russell thought it would be fun for
the two of them," Mrs. Bauer said of the
skates. "He can take her sometimes
when I have my headaches and just
need quiet. You're not always here to
help."

FJ took the words like stones and put them in the bag labeled *Disappointing Husband and Poor Father.* The bag never filled, just became heavier and heavier.

"That's good of you to offer, Russell. Perhaps we can take the streetcar to the lake this weekend. Would you like that?"

"Then we can all go," Russell said. "Can't we, Mama?"

"If I'm feeling up to it," Mrs. Bauer said. "I have so many headaches in this cold, cold weather. I understand why some people make their way to Tampa. It's too bad we can't." *Another stone.* "It might benefit your own health, Mr. Bauer."

"It might," he said. "So would going to North Dakota. The air there is as pure as a saint's tears."

"It's also colder than the ice house in winter and wouldn't do a thing for my headaches." She massaged her temples.

"You're right, as always," he said.

"I did see an advertisement in the *Watkins Almanac* for their Vegetable Anodyne Liniment," Mrs. Bauer continued.

"It's meant for back pain but it might be of use on my neck and reduce my headaches. I wonder if you might pick some up for me, Mr. Bauer?"

"Anything that might help, dear," he said. He straightened the paper but couldn't concentrate on what he was reading. Something about child labor laws. It was important, he knew. He folded the paper. She never wanted to try *his* ointment. Many of those who used it deemed it worthy, but Mrs. Bauer wasn't one of them. She knew he didn't wish to further Watkins's successes.

Maybe he could bring in more income by asking Jessie to put her innovative mind into salve promotion. The idea lightened his mood. He would make cuts in expenditures—perhaps go without his cigars or maybe the German edition paper. He could always read it at the German library. If he could increase sales of either the photographic work or the salve, he could keep the girls on. At least one. The girls needed money too. It was an act of charity to make sure they continued to have employment.

Look at those poor children in the article, working at nine years of age in the
coal mines or the garment districts of
New York. Yes, he was doing his part to
assist with child labor, offering a safe
place to work and fair wages. A man
had to do what he could, and FJ would.

>-•->-○-<•-•-<

It was spring when the Kodak photographs were finally developed with the
help of Voe's gift and some of Jessie's
savings. It felt like Christmas all over
again, opening up the envelope to see
each round print and being reminded of
the day she'd taken that shot. She was
especially proud of the photograph of
the oak trees made while lying on the
ground and looking up through the
leaves. She'd forgotten she even took it.

"Why t-t-trees?" Roy asked. They sat
in the living room where the gaslights
flooded the small table. A cream cro-
cheted doily acted as matting for each
of the small photographs.

"I don't know. I guess because they're
so sturdy and strong and beautiful. I like
the way the branches are etched

against the sky. See how perfect the leaves look? You can't see their flaws, the little worm holes in the leaf, or how the edges curl up sometimes. Even with this little camera you can capture the perfection of a natural thing like a tree. Now if I had a big camera, with dry plates, one where I could develop the prints myself, then I could take really beautiful pictures."

"Th-these are b-b-beautiful," Roy said.

"I'm glad you like them. I bet the trees are different in every country, aren't they, Roy?" She knew he loved to read the traveling books she brought him from the library. He nodded. "Someday we'll travel to other places and see those trees. Does that sound like fun?"

"Don't build his hopes up," her mother said. She sat crocheting.

"I-I-I f-f-fixed this f-f-for you." Roy handed Jessie the photographic case. Sometime during the past few months of opening and closing it, Jessie had lost the little screw that worked the hinge. She'd later found it stuck between the floorboards of her bedroom but couldn't put it back in. Roy had asked to borrow the case that morning "to h-h-hold it."

"How did you do that?" Jessie asked him.

"W-w-with your h-h-hatpin," he said, beaming.

"I never thought of that. Of course, I couldn't have seen it anyway, not even with these eyeglasses, because it's so tiny. I'm glad you could. That took lots of patience too, didn't it, Mama?"

Her mother didn't look up. "I suppose."

Jessie felt it her duty to get her mother to notice Roy's strengths and not just the things he had difficulty doing. "I'll put one of these photos in the case," she told Roy. "You choose."

"I l-l-like th-that one." He pointed to the one FJ had taken. Her mother raised an eyebrow.

"Choose another one," Jessie said.

"T-t-take one of m-m-me," Roy said.

"You mustn't be self-interested," their mother cautioned. "It's bad enough that Jessie is so captivated by her own image. I don't mind the tree photos, but the one of you, well, that concerns me."

"It's nothing, Mama," Jessie said. "It was a practice shot, taken at the spur of the moment, and he would otherwise have thrown it away." Her mother's lips pursed. Jessie snapped the photo case shut. "We'll take one of you reading your book," Jessie told Roy. But her mother's words had poked her present joy.

>⊷⊹⊷○⊷⊹⊷<

By early summer, Jessie had a little more money now, what with working two jobs, so she could get the prints developed more quickly and was able to save for a better camera. She'd told Mr. Steffes she would leave once she got her camera back, but he had begged her to remain. "Some of the lads I might employ don't have nearly the drive you do. Maybe cut the days back to just one?" he said. And so she had.

Lilly was miffed that Jessie had pin money when Lilly didn't. But Jessie gave all her studio wages to her mother, and the family decision was to allow Jessie to use Mr. Steffes's payment for less needful things, like developing her Kodak shots more quickly. She hoped that one day she'd earn enough to have her own place to live, though she'd always contribute to the family's needs. To Roy's.

Jessie photographed a group of girls being baptized at Latsch Beach shortly after it was opened. In addition to the girls as subjects, she was conscious of the background, the men in suits and the women dressed in their best white dresses standing on the shoreline. She'd gone into the water herself and taken the photograph, looking back with the girls in the foreground. One girl stood at an angle to the camera, one with her finger in her ear, shaking water loose. A couple of others had their arms close around themselves, chilled in the spring water. All looked bedraggled in their navy sailor dresses with white trim, yet they all had smiles on their faces, which was as it should be at a baptism, Jessie thought. Just looking at the photograph brought back the memory of the day. That was the power of art, she decided, to take a person back—and inward too, to intersect life with expectation.

She had been baptized as an infant. But other faiths urged adult baptism. Most of the girls in the photograph were probably Selma's age or younger, which didn't seem very adult to Jessie, but every faith offered something different, and that seemed all right with her.

But the baptism photograph upset her mother. Jessie showed it to her in the kitchen with Lilly and Selma standing around. "What were you doing there in the water at such a sacred time? How am I to explain to our friends that it was my daughter dressed in her bathing dress out there taking a photograph?"

"I think you explained it well," Jessie said. She laughed.

"Hush now. Are you being wise with me, young lady?"

Her scolding startled Jessie. "No. I meant you had explained it well. I just went into the water in my bathing dress and took the picture."

"But why?"

"It was a special occasion. That's when people take photographs," she argued. "The girls have all asked for prints. I intend to take a picture of the picture, in Mr. Bauer's studio, so that I can print copies myself. I'll be able to make a little more that way to put into my savings."

"And aren't you fortunate that you get to have savings," Lilly said. She washed her hands with that new Ivory soap, and the scent tickled Jessie's nose. She sneezed.

"I want to buy one of those Directorie dresses, from Paris. *Sheaths,* I think they call them." She winked at Selma.

Her mother gasped. "I saw a drawing of one in the paper. Police had to rescue the poor woman in Chicago who wore one. No petticoats, the material cleaved to her body. She might just as well have been . . ."

"Not naked," Jessie finished for her. "The material merely emphasized the beauty of the human form. She wore a Merry Widow hat too, Mama," Jessie said. "And some said she had on fishnet stockings, whatever those are."

"Save your money for the poor people who survived that Japanese steamer that sank, or for the poor immigrants whose fathers are in the north woods while they survive here without kith or kin to help them. You'll not wear such a thing in my house."

"I'll dress at Voe's then," Jessie said. Her mother shook her finger at her. "I'm teasing you, Mama. It's way too much money anyway, but I do like to look at them. The design makes the models look so tall."

"I could hardly focus on their height with every other curve in their anatomy out there for all to see."

"What I'm saving for, Lilly, is my own real camera, that I can take out of the studio and make plates from. Until then, I'm only an amateur photographer, not a professional one. I want variation in my subjects. It's not satisfying to reproduce print after print that looks like it could have been done in any studio."

"The picture Mr. Bauer took of you wasn't just some cookie-cutter portrait. I'd never seen anything like that one before," Lilly said.

Jessie sent a look to silence Lilly, nodded toward her mother, then redi-

rected the subject. "Amateurs see photographs as art more than as a scientific
rendition. I read that in an article, and it
made sense to me. I don't always know
how to talk to Mr. Bauer about how I
want to make photographs, and while I
work for him I feel required to make the
studio shots the way he wants them.
But on my own, when I carry my own little camera, well, I see living people doing things. Action."

She pointed to the photograph of the
baptism, and Lilly followed her hand to
the print. "Look at their smiles," Jessie
continued. "And how bold the one girl
stands with her hands on her hips, staring right at me. Only one girl is dressed
in white. She's an outsider."

"Or was late for the planning meeting," Lilly said.

"See how she stepped back so all I
got of her was her face and the white
bow in her hair? You have to look
closely to see her dress hidden behind
all the other girls. They all look so . . .
alive, so happy, which is what should
happen in a baptism, shouldn't it?"

"I suppose so," her mother agreed.

"And the people on the shore, they're cheering them on. They likely brought the girls, and when I have this picture made for them and purchased for five cents, they'll always have a memory of that day."

"So amateurs make photographs for memories," Lilly said. "And profession- als make photographs for income. Am- ateurs expect people to spend a lot of money on something you can keep in your mind."

"But my mind gets filled up. Doesn't yours? And if I can make a picture, as a painter does, then all that matters of that time will be preserved. You know I can't draw very well. I can't sing like Selma. You have to help me sew, Lilly. This is what I do." She pointed to the photograph.

"You sound like a preacher trying to convince people," Lilly said. "Or your- self. Or maybe Mr. Bauer. Will he let you make prints of these?"

"I'll have to pay, of course, for the plates and paper, but I'll get that back when I sell the prints. I'll go to the girls' homes, Mama. Several already told me their mothers want the pictures."

Jessie's mother shook her head. "In such times, with banks unsettled, a new president being elected and all, I can't imagine families spending money on such frivolity just so you can buy a camera."

"I've been reading about women photographers, Mama. There are a lot of them. One even lives way out in Washington. She raises her children, she teaches, she paints, and she makes art photographs that are beautiful. They move people. That's what I want to do too, but I'm practical. I'll hold down however many jobs I must in order to do what I want."

"You'll have to hold several," Lilly said. "But how you'll ever get enough money saved to make your living doing what you love, well, that's just a dream. Women's dreams rarely come true."

"Mine will. I want to do this on my own, and I'll not let anyone stand in my way."

"Is someone standing in your way? I

wonder who that might be. You or someone else?"

Jessie picked up her print. It was becoming annoying, but she couldn't always answer Lilly's probing questions.

———✦——○——✦———

The truth was, FJ had not liked her baptism picture. He found fault with the setting—girls standing in water up to their ankles—and with the way she'd cut one girl off at the side while having plenty of room at the other end. "You didn't frame it well," he added. "You should see what you want to take right through the lens and have it centered."

"I like it off center," she said. They were in the kitchen area of the studio, and Jessie had fixed tea for him and Voe. They sat at the table before the morning duties began. At least when they met like this he treated the girls as though they were . . . adults, able to articulate what they wanted and to negotiate.

"See," Jessie continued, "I have the trees to the left and the bathhouse to the right to set the composition."

Mr. Bauer continued to shake his head. "I think it best if you don't show me these . . . works. They're disturbing, not properly posed."

Jessie sat up straight. "I was about to ask if I might make prints from them, in your darkroom, by taking photos of the photos."

Mr. Bauer stared at her. "I think not."

"I'd find a way to pay for the plates and the chemicals. I'm not asking to do this for free." Purchasing the solutions would take money from her camera fund, but if she couldn't make copies of the image, she'd fail on her first order of real business: the requests for the baptism prints.

"You're nearly out of some solutions, Mr. B.," Voe offered. "I've been keeping track. Jessie asked me to do that, right, Jessie?"

Jessie nodded.

"What if I worked through my lunch hour," she said, "and you taught me retouching? You said you could teach us, Mr. Bauer. Remember, Voe?"

"I'm not interested in learning retouching," Voe said, throwing her hands up in protest. "Sitting in a dark little room making pinpricks in eyes of people who closed them during the picture, or taking out a spot that showed up on a woman's face, huh-uh. I don't think it would be good for your eyes either, Jessie. You don't see all that well now!"

"I see fine," she protested. She turned to Mr. Bauer. "If I took on some retouching, you could decrease the time it takes for prints to be returned to the clients. You'd make more money, get more framed prints sold. Maybe even sell a few more postcards to Mr. Cutler's company."

Mr. Bauer flinched. Jessie wished she could take back mentioning Mr. Cutler. He published a great many postcards, but he was also a photographer in his own right. Mr. Bauer had occasionally made comments about him as "the competition," saying the man's story that he'd braved fourteen rattlesnakes to take a photo of the famous rock formation Indian Head was a marketing ploy. Jessie didn't want to bring up anything that could divert the conversation.

He pulled at his mustache, a sign that

he was giving a subject serious consideration.

"If I teach you during the lunch hour, you wouldn't get paid for that time, you understand that?" Jessie nodded. "I'll train you in exchange for the print expense. You'd have to make the prints after hours, when all the other work was completed for the day. I wouldn't want the Bauer Studio imprint on them. You can understand why."

"Anything," Jessie told him.

"Well then, we have an arrangement," he said. He put out his hand to her, to shake it as though she were a true businessman or, at the very least, a businesswoman.

On the way home, she realized she'd have to stop working for Mr. Steffes totally if she was going to work late making prints. Maybe Selma would like the Steffes job. Jessie would just have to charge a little more for the prints in order to make up for the lost wages, but she'd be earning money doing what she loved instead of sweeping up grease globs and dust. Selma wanted a job. It would all work out in the end. She looked forward, not back. Wasn't that exactly what Reverend Edward Everett Hale had said in that magazine that one should do?

>–+–◆–○–◆–+–<

"Your sister isn't interested in such work. You have a job to do, and it's good work at Mr. Steffes's," Jessie's mother said.

"Yes, I am, Mama," Selma countered. They sat around the round, oak dining table they'd brought with them from the farm. As Selma talked, she picked at a wide grain in the top of the table. "Jessie says it's easy work even if it is a little dirty."

"You just turned twelve," their mother reminded her. "None of my girls has gone to work before she was thirteen. If you leave that job, Jessie, you won't have the pocket money for your photos and such. You'd better think twice about giving it up. I think it's been good for you to have two jobs. You're much more . . . directed, more reliable."

"Learning retouching will help my career. And it'll help the studio so Mr. Bauer will keep us employed."

"He'll never let you go," Lilly said. She reached for the vinegar jug.

Jessie ignored her and hoped her mother was too distracted to notice the remark.

"Is the studio having financial problems?" her father asked. He pointed to the green beans that steamed in the middle of the table, and Roy lifted the bowl and passed them to him.

"Everyone is having financial problems," their mother answered.

"Once the election's over it'll settle down," Jessie's father told her.

"Please let me help," Selma said.

Lilly said, "She could help save for Roy's trip to—"

"Hush now," Jessie's mother interrupted her.

"What trip?" Jessie asked.

"I know all about it. I know all about it," Selma sang.

"Wh-wh-what trip?" Roy asked.

"We'll discuss it later." Her mother glared at Lilly and put her finger to Selma's mouth, indicating she should keep something a secret, then began dishing up the boiled tongue. "Selma may work for Mr. Steffes."

"Wh-wh-where am I g-g-going?"

Her mother shushed Roy as she had Selma, and the room became silent, with only the *click* of spoons against the china and the quiet slurp of soup.

Jessie hated beef tongue, didn't like her tongue touching the little bumps. She put her fork down. She'd been left out of a family plan. Her stomach hurt. What was it they were saving for? And why had no one told her? Or Roy?

TEN

Retouching

Mrs. Bauer had been nominated to be president of the newly formed Second Congregational Ladies Aid Society, and they had a good many projects to attend to this year. They hoped to raise money for the poor at events held at least once a month. Weekly women gathered to knot comforters to be sent by Christmas to the poor of Minneapolis. She assumed there were no poor in Winona, or the reverend would have suggested keeping their comforters here at home. Growing up in Ellsworth, Wisconsin, she'd seen plenty of poor people, but since marrying Mr. Bauer, she hadn't been exposed to such things and assumed it was because of Winona's affluence as a river, flour, and lumber city.

This year, at her suggestion, the Ladies Aid Society planned to serve meals at the election sites to raise funds for the needy. They'd also hold luncheons, the profits sent to the Frontier Missionary work in Oregon, which served the Indians there. Organizing these projects would take its toll on Jessie Otis Bauer. She was not a strong woman, after all.

Grandmother Otis had let it be known that while she loved seeing Winnie and Russell, she did not wish to entertain them while Mrs. Bauer attended to her society events. Russell, of course, could entertain himself in the summer months while the women met, but Winnie would need watching throughout the year.

She conferred with Mr. Bauer about this issue, deciding to press him for assistance as he had pressed her to allow herself to be nominated.

"That's a wonderful thing!" he'd told her when she said her name had been placed in nomination. "Think of the referrals you can recommend."

"It's to do good works, Mr. Bauer," she said. He'd actually come home at a reasonable hour and sat in the kitchen while she prepared their supper. It did seem that he was making an effort to be more conscious of her needs.

"Nevertheless, it will allow you to represent the studio in new venues. Without your having to say a thing, people might think of a portrait for themselves when they look at you, knowing you're married to a photographer. It could help the holiday trade."

"I'm not going to have a cabinet portrait sitting beside me," she snapped. "Even if I am elected. And I'm certainly not going to promote the studio from my president's chair, assuming that I become the president."

He shook his head. "No. But you'd be surprised. When people see a musician on the stage, enjoy the sounds he makes, and feel comforted, they leave and consider music lessons for their children. They associate certain experiences with future actions. You can't underestimate the value this might have for the studio."

She felt annoyed that he had turned a potential triumph of her own into something commercial and related to him. "You don't find it possible that my name was placed because I have the ability to lead?"

He smiled. "I spoke to Mildred Simmons at the concert. The first thing she said was how much she appreciated the fine portrait our studio had provided and that you'd done such fine work in retouching. I suggested to her that you were quite talented in many ways. And that you might be a good president for the society. She paused only a moment before saying, 'We need new interests.' So you see, I might have had something to do with your rise."

Mrs. Bauer knew she should have been pleased that he'd recommended her, but there was something about it that seemed to diminish her own capacity to be noticed.

"If I am elected," she told her husband, "I will need help with the children while I'm at the meetings and events. I assume you'll be available?"

"Confound it, Mrs. Bauer! I don't see how."

She felt her face grow warm with indignation, which he must have noticed, for he told her, "Well, you can bring Winnie down to the studio, of course. Or I'll take her with me in the morning on those days if you'd like. She seems to like the time there. And the shop girls."

"Your Miss Gaebele will need to take over the retouching too," she said. She left no negotiation in her voice. This was something she would indeed control.

"I knew that was coming," he said.

"Well, don't expect me to be able to wipe away the blemishes of your clients and still be out there doing the things that will bring you more clients. Don't ask me to do something and then take away my ability to do it just because you don't want to do your part. I've had more than enough of that from you!"

She watched him. He swallowed hard. If he remained calm, she might stay calm, but if he began to disagree with her, gave her fuel for the fire she could feel rising within her, it would end up as one of the explosions. He had so much control over her! She hated the uproars, felt awful when they were over, but she seemed to have no control over them, not really. He never learned how to stop them! Fire burned in the back of her neck. She'd heard her own voice grow strident and found herself praying, actually praying, that she wouldn't explode this time, that she'd remember what she had done and said later, when it was all over. She inhaled, muttered her prayers for calm.

"Will you help me or won't you?" She was aware of the edge still in her voice.

"Of course I will. Miss Gaebele can do the retouching, just as you said. She wants to learn the skill anyway in exchange for the use of the studio, to do some work of her own. It's a good exchange. I'll bring Winnie. Miss Kopp can watch her when we're otherwise engaged."

She felt her heart race but took deep

breaths. Sometimes that helped soothe the fire inside her. She put her spoon down, watched her hand shake. She sat. Fixing supper could wait.

"Fine. Then I'll let my name stand."

"Good. Excellent. You really will do good things for the community, Mrs. Bauer. I'm quite sure you will."

They had held the election a few days later, and she won! It was the oddest feeling to be asked to chair the society. She wasn't sure women had the ability to be in charge of things, though she'd read in the paper that just this past Sunday, the wife of Winona's Baptist minister had taken the pulpit to speak while he was out of town. That would never happen in the Congregational Church! Fortunately, she'd never be asked to stand up in front of the congregation. She'd be a "behind the scenes" leader. She'd learned that phrase in an article discussing the people who worked silently behind the president. After all, that's what she'd always done as Mr. Bauer's wife, worked behind the scenes. It hadn't brought her happiness, but maybe doing good things at the society would.

>─┼─◄≻─○─◄≻─┼─◄

There was something both artful and complete about enhancing a print. Jessie fully intended to compose photographs that didn't need retouching, but sometimes the camera emphasized detracting qualities that the naked eye wouldn't notice in the setup. Because a photograph was the capture of a moment in time, a viewer could dwell on such features and find the flaws in the subject. In everyday living, with people in action, their faces shifting like kneaded dough as they spoke, one really didn't notice little blemishes or a nose out of proportion to a face. Retouching often improved reality.

Jessie liked retouching; what she didn't like was Voe's teasing, something new of late. "He likes you, Mr. B. does," she claimed.

"He likes you too."

"His eyes light up like fireflies when you enter the room. I see it."

Like Selma, Voe always read the romance stories in *Woman's Home Companion* first and would tell Jessie about the dreamy men, the hopelessly contrived meetings of young lovers, and the great tragedies of forbidden love.

"You see things that aren't there," Jessie said. "Not all relations between working men and women are preludes to a composition for violins."

"Huh?" Voe said.

"Never mind," Jessie said.

"I just think Mr. B. holds you special."

Voe was starting to sound like Lilly. Jessie didn't think she was being naive. She'd had time to put his portrait of her in perspective and didn't let herself dwell on the deeper feelings that might be there behind the lens. Mr. Bauer was an older man, not unlike her uncle August, who liked to look after people, give them special gifts at times because the joy that resulted was mutual. Mr. Bauer was a gentle father, and while she'd rarely seen him with his wife, there were certainly no stories bandied about that he was anything but a faithful husband. He'd employed women assistants before, and they'd gone on to work for other photographers. Chances were that he'd given them special gifts on their birthdays too, especially if they shared the day with one of Mr. Bauer's children.

The darkroom did put them close together, though Voe was almost always there too. But in the retouching room they'd been alone, and he'd had to stand close to instruct her, lean over her shoulder so that she could sometimes feel his breath raise the tender hair on her neck. Once or twice she felt his vest against her summer shirtwaist, smelled the cologne he wore. She was glad Voe didn't bring up the portrait he'd taken of her, and more grateful Voe didn't know of the most recent intimate incident that had left perspiration on her upper lip in addition to her nose.

"If you can draw the eyes open," he had said, leaning over her back, pointing, "the clients really do want their baby's portrait as though the child were still alive."

The baby, about a year old, had died of a fever, cause unknown, and the older siblings had convinced their distraught parents that they needed a likeness made, a photograph of Baby George. Jessie had not gone out to help shoot that photograph. Mr. B. rarely did portrait sittings outside his studio, saying such work reminded him of tramp photography. Clients weren't often happy with the results, giving a bad name to professional photographers like himself. Jessie suspected he didn't like to do it because he couldn't control the lighting or the setting either. But he had done this one, and he'd done it alone "as respectfully as I could," he said later.

Mr. B. started her instruction by telling her the history of certain practices. But she stopped him and told him she'd read a book about it.

"What such book?" he asked. "You can't get all your knowledge from books, Jessie." He turned on the small lamp and directed the light to the plates they worked on.

"James Ryder's book," she said. "It's all about his life and work and how he introduced retouching to this country way back in the 1800s. He wrote about this curious thing some photographers did to get that softer look. They'd stretch a piece of catgut from the lens board of the camera to the floor, and during the exposing time, they'd pluck it, like playing a viola." She twisted in her chair to look at him as he stood behind her, his hands on the back of her chair. "It gave just the slightest movement, which softened the sharp edges of those precise German lenses. Did you know about that?" He'd grunted agreement, redirected her to turn back to the print. "Sometimes they'd leave a little space between the plate and the paper too. That made a kind of fluffy look to the photograph." She turned back.

"What's the name of this book?"

"*Voigtländer and I: In Pursuit of Shadow Catching.* Nineteen aught two. They serialized part of it in *Photo-Beacon.*" She turned around again. "Voigtländer is the name of a German camera lens."

"I'm well aware of that. Let's work on this print now, Jessie."

"I read of it in one of your old issues and then found the book in the library across the street, not the German library. Lots of photographers objected, I guess, and didn't think it was authentic to remove moles and such from people's faces."

"Every art form has to go through struggle until it is shaped into newness," he said. "That's why there will always be this argument between the mechanics of photography and its artistry. Even the size of photograph we use now certainly wasn't the norm. Early prints were more like your small Kodak ones, and those who made albums had to adjust to the larger size just as the plate makers and photographers did."

"But it was all for the good in the end," Jessie said. She turned back. "Which brush do I begin with?" He leaned over and retrieved one. She'd never worked on this kind of print before. She smelled that cigar smell again as he leaned over her. "Very industrious, Miss Gaebele, teaching yourself." When he used the more formal address, Jessie wondered if she'd offended him. But his voice addressed her as less of a student now and more as a colleague. She turned to smile at his compliment, became aware of his mouth, the narrow lips, his mustache trimmed to perfection. He told her how much easier it was to work on the negative than how it had been done in the old days, with black inks, crayons, and oil spread across the paper prints in order to help the retouching pencil do its magic. "Mrs. Bauer holds the brush in her mouth between strokes, to keep it moist. I've wondered if that's safe," he mused. "But she's never gotten ill. We begin," he said, "by imagining what we want to see at the end of our work, what we want the print to say if it could talk."

She turned back. Something he had said annoyed her, and she just wanted him to instruct her now so she'd get the skill and be able to do this sort of thing on her own, without his hovering over her. He pointed and they began work to retouch this precious child on a negative. It was a hot May day, and they did

the work at a table area of the darkroom, with frangible light and no orange
glow. They had to hover over the plate,
both of them closely focused on the
child's face. Jessie wanted the face to
appear alive so the family would have
their son back, if only in their hearts.

With pencil in hand, Jessie worked on
the closed eyelids, creating life where
there was only death. She forgot her annoyance with FJ as she worked and instead held the task as sacred. For this
family, her efforts would bring the child
to them as a lively, warm, and loving being and perhaps erase some of the sadness of their loss. Her art was healing,
unlike what FJ had once said.

They didn't need to retouch the
child's smile, as it was one of serenity
and peace.

"Thin the eyelid," he directed. "An infant doesn't have much skin there." As
they progressed in this fragile work, he
became more clipped and short in his
instructions despite his soft voice. Jessie wondered if he thought of his deceased son. Maybe he was grateful he'd

taken photographs of Donald while the boy lived.

Jessie did as she was told, her head bent. She occasionally reached up to tuck a loose strand back into her hair roll, wishing she'd used a different comb to keep her hair in place. She pushed at her glasses.

"Make the iris smaller, I should think," he said. "You don't want it to look like the child is a stone gargoyle. Less iris will be better."

Jessie added more white around the iris but then, without really any reasoning to support her choice, she took away a tiny bit of blackness from the side of the iris, leaving it almost white.

He exhaled.

"So it will look like a reflection," she defended. "Which a real eye does in a photograph."

He leaned in but still didn't speak, and so she turned to see if he objected. Their faces were nearly as close together as paper to glass plate. Tobacco scent lingered on his breath. He no longer looked at the negative but instead stared at her.

She could see the light reflected in his eyes, just a tiny candlelight of white. It was as though he stared into her soul, and she remembered what Lilly had said about the photograph being taken by a special kind of eye.

She moved back slightly, her heart beating in a wild way she didn't understand.

He straightened too. "Such a little thing," he said. He reached out as though to touch her but then turned and picked up the negative, the edges of the glass held tight against the palms of his hands. He coughed, turned away from her. "The eyes make the child alive. In this one small moment of time, his parents will have him back almost as if the photograph had been taken while he lived." He put the picture back down. She thought his hands shook a little. He pressed his fingers to her shoulder. They felt warm and brought a fluttering as though a hummingbird had settled in her chest.

"I've done all right then?"

He patted her shoulder then the way a man does his dog and stepped back.

"You'll do just fine without me, Miss Gaebele," he said. "Just fine."

◦━◦━◦━◦━◦

FJ held the newspaper but didn't read it. Instead he considered what had occurred—innocently enough, but it had happened nonetheless. He needed to limit the time he might have alone with Jessie. Miss Gaebele. Or he'd have to let her go. He'd come to this conclusion on the way home and affirmed it while pretending to read his evening paper. His children talked in muffled tones to their mother in the kitchen as he only partially digested news of the election and Taft's chances. The girl had done nothing to encourage him, but there was about her a kind of vibrancy that flowed from her, whether she was teasing with Voe about their weekend activities or chattering with his children. She carried a light that drew him to her, a fire that could burn. He could imagine her at the Minnesota State Fair, where her uncle apparently reined supreme with her, taking her to carnivals and whatnot. The girls spoke with vigor about the hayrides following their Youth Alliance gatherings at the church Jessie attended. He wasn't sure why, but his eye seemed to catch her name in the *Republican-Herald* column listing those participating in such events. Jessie and her sisters would be there along with Voe and several young men. Well, that was as it should be.

Why he bothered to read such drivel was beyond him, though occasionally efforts of his wife's Ladies Aid activities would be listed there as well. He made it a point to mention this to his wife, to salute her worthy work.

Mrs. Bauer appeared to enjoy the adulation of her successes. She'd been much more predictable of late, more open to his affection. Not adoring enough for his kisses by any means, certainly not passionate, but not resistive of his touching her shoulder or giving her a peck on the cheek. Perhaps success at that level had given her confidence, and he was grateful.

So why had he felt whatever it was he *had* felt with Miss Gaebele? Perhaps it was just a simple longing to have his efforts appreciated. Miss Gaebele did that, made him feel as though his work had merit.

It might be better if he let both girls go. Salve sales had not picked up, and while they'd surely retouch more prints with Miss Gaebele's quick study, and he wasn't having to pay her for instruction time, expenses continued to rise. Keeping up with the technology of his profession was expensive. He needed the girls' help but not at the expense of his own, well, desires.

Desires. That was much too intense a word to use for that momentary emotion he'd felt in the retouching room. Jessie was a lovely young girl who had done something quite remarkable in the retouching of that baby's photograph. He'd been thinking of Donald, feeling terribly guilty all over again, and aching for the family who had lovingly dressed the baby in his christening gown, embroidered and tatted to perfection. The oldest son—there looked to be ten or more children at the house when he arrived to photograph the infant—had taken the baby from his mother's arms

and asked where FJ wanted to pose the
boy for the photograph. FJ had picked
up a velveteen pillow and then motioned
toward a table near the window. The
child looked as though he were sleeping. FJ had swallowed back tears.

He supposed he was thinking of all
that when he'd stood too close to Miss
Gaebele in the retouching area. The way
she'd brought those eyes alive . . .

It wasn't desire he was feeling. How
could it be? He was a father and husband and must be, yes, twenty-six
years her senior. No, it was . . . compassion, empathy. He simply wanted to
help the girl refine her raw talent. And
she had it, there was no doubt about
that, even though she seemed to move
it in directions he didn't think were worthy of a great portrait photographer. But
what she'd done with the eyes of that
child . . . he shivered with the thought
of it.

That's all it was. He had recognized
great talent and been moved by it. The
subject had been a deceased infant,
and they'd had just a brief moment of

physical closeness. These things happened in such snug work space where men and women stood shoulder to shoulder, so to speak, to accomplish a thing.

It couldn't occur again though. If it did, he'd let the girls go despite the strain it would cause him.

He coughed, a brackish bark of a cough. *Not again.*

Or maybe he could keep just one employee. He hated thinking of rehiring and retraining, especially when he might become ill again at any time. Besides, how would he explain their dismissal to his wife? He'd have to think this through.

>─+◆─○─◆+─<

Her husband had not approached her for more than a platonic touch in some time. Tonight, Mrs. Bauer found that to be a comfortable state as she prepared their evening meal. She had the kitchen window open to the twilight, a breeze fluttering the printed curtain. He never mentioned having another child, and she was grateful for that. Winnie had been already along when Donald was killed or she never would have wanted to carry a child while she grieved another. But Winnie was a dear, and Russell had certainly brought joy to her life. When she watched some of the younger mothers with their babies during the society meetings, she almost felt a longing for a baby again. But she'd be thirty-four in June and she wasn't a strong woman, so carrying a child might be difficult.

She listened to the children behind her, looking at the latest *Woman's Home Companion.* Or rather, Russell looked at it, giggling at various times. She ought to take it from him. She'd forgotten that they advertised Peetz corsets right there with drawings that looked almost life-like. Winnie grabbed it from him and tried to cut a picture with the scissors she'd commandeered from Mrs. Bauer's sewing box.

"Not the magazine, Winifred. Mama wants to read the prize-winning letter." The Vellum Paper Company had offered a prize for the best letter written on their stationery, and the magazine had printed it. Mrs. Bauer wanted to read it to improve her own letter-writing capabilities for her society work. "Let's put that away," she told Winnie, though she didn't reach for it.

"I'm cutting," Winnie told her mother.

"It's for Strawberry Bombs." Russell pointed at the recipe next to the letter.

Mrs. Bauer looked where he pointed. "It will be that time of year soon," she told him. "Why don't you let Russell cut it, Winnie? I'll save it, and we'll have a bomb at the first fruits of summer, all right?"

"Not just any fruits," Russell said. "Strawberries."

"Where are there strawberries?" Her husband had entered the room. He smiled at the children. He always smiled at them first. Russell told them what they were up to. He had his hand on Russell's shoulder. Her husband liked to touch. She wished she were more comfortable with that. "I'll cut it out for you, Mrs. Bauer, if you'd like."

She nodded and turned back to the

preserved beans she'd opened. She'd be pleased when the garden began producing. They'd eaten all the canned peas and peaches. Mrs. Bauer preserved for her family and for her mother, whose hands hurt her so much. It hadn't stopped Mrs. Otis from buying up cloth pieces, but it had kept her from making quilts with them. Her mother's house was stacked with piles of colorful cloth, a riot of chaos that Mrs. Bauer could barely stand. Yet when her garden produced, her own kitchen looked as though vegetables and fruits had exploded, with so many stems and jars scattered about the room. There was no place even to sit at the table as she worked long into the night, unable to stop and start again in the morning. She could keep it up for days, it seemed, and then she fell exhausted into bed.

"Your name is in the paper," her husband said. "For the money raised at your last event. I forget the name of that project."

"The chicken potpie dinner," she reminded him. She reached for a match to light the stove.

"So it is," he said. "You've done good things for Winona, Mrs. Bauer. I'm proud to say"—he kissed her at the back of her neck—"that I know you."

She stiffened. Yet it warmed her to think that he'd read about her and that he'd commented and given her praise. She even felt her face grow hot with the double meaning he might have intended with the biblical phrase "to know." "I should hope you know me," she said. She turned to him and smiled.

He looked startled, said, "There's always room to know you better." He had a different look in his eye now and stayed close to her, putting his arms around her waist and tugging her to him.

"Not in front of the children," she whispered. She felt confined by his arms and backed her way out of them. He always went too far.

"I'll take that as a direction for later activity, when the children are fast asleep?" he asked.

"You might," she said. Why had she said that? She relaxed when he stepped back.

"I'll await a knock on my door," he said and smiled.

Now she knew she blushed. She wondered what she'd do.

⊰—⋅⟡⋅—⊙—⟡⋅—⊱

Jessie overheard her parents, their voices rising through the floor vent into the girls' room. She'd come up the back stairs to find a ribbon to tie her hair off her neck as they played Pom-Pom Pull Away in their backyard. Roy loved the game, which involved little more than him trying to touch the girls running past him. When they were "caught," they'd belong to his team. Her hair had jostled loose, and she'd told them she'd be back in a minute.

"She does seem less dreamy eyed," her mother said, and Jessie assumed she spoke of Selma as she pawed through the hanky drawer for the ribbon. "I was worried if she left Steffes's job she'd lose heart." Yes, they must be talking about Selma, but what would she lose heart about, and was Selma thinking of quitting? She hadn't said anything to Jessie. She kept listening, wondering if they'd talk more about Roy's trip.

"August's camera really brought her through," her father said. "I wasn't sure she'd ever forgive herself before that."

"It's never easy, such a thing," her mother agreed. "I'll be forever grateful to him, finding the perfect diversion. I didn't want to lose both of them."

"August was the messenger of our prayers," her father said.

"Well, it's nice to see her blooming."

Jessie sat down on the bed, shaking. She was who she'd always been, and they didn't know it. She didn't deserve their prayers.

***

Jessie handed Mr. B. the mail, putting the brochure on top. "This looks like fun," she told him. It was August, and Mr. B. made known his plan to attend the National Photographic Association's congress in St. Paul scheduled for the following month. The brochure listed expected exhibits, classes, and potential contacts. "I'll bet there are all kinds of interesting classes to take there."

"One of the necessities of owning a professional studio is attending these events," he told her. "Tramps don't need to worry as much about the demands of their clients, who expect impromptu sittings to have their flaws." He read the material, turned it over in his hand. Jessie went about her work but turned when he said, "You're too young and inexperienced to gain any benefits."

The words hit her like a snowball to her heart. She hadn't been contriving to go. She was an employee, nothing more. She knew that. But he'd responded to her as though she was indirectly asking for something, trying to wrangle him to spend money to send her. Or worse, to take her along with him. Her mother wouldn't approve of either.

"I . . . I know that, Mr. Bauer. I just meant it must be fun to do in addition to—"

"The only playing I allow myself is taking time on my way home to visit my younger sister, Luise, in Wisconsin."

She'd done something to upset him, but she didn't know what. Ever since their encounter in the retouching area, he'd been distant with her, had returned to calling her Miss Gaebele. She'd only wanted him to enjoy the congress, but he behaved as though she were a manipulating child.

><+>-O-<+>-<

FJ stared at the flier for the congress. It was best that he crush any of Miss Gaebele's inappropriate expectations before they took bloom. He was a married man with a family. What had happened in that instant in the retouching room a few months back had occurred without guile of any sort on either part. But young girls had a tendency to fantasize. He'd left a farmer's employ before joining the army because the man's daughter had misunderstood his kindness. Women were drawn to those novels that suggested love was the divine ideal and could be found despite the realities of life. He was a faithful husband, and he loved his wife. He did. Jessie, Miss Gaebele, was young and naive. She was quite beguiling with those eyes that seemed to change color from brown to gray as she told of some spirited story. Young. That's what she was. He was the adult who needed to set the borders, and that he would do.

ELEVEN

The Fruit of the River

Dreams of pale skin and flowers bursting like fireworks filled Jessie's nights that fall. She often awoke hot, her heart pounding. She'd sink back into her pillows in the predawn darkness and listen to the branches scraping the window or stare at the pressed-tin ceiling, waiting for her heart to slow. The dreams carried longing stitched into a backing of guilt. Yet she'd done nothing wrong. She had let her emotions reach out but had not let them grasp anything firmer than sand.

The night before, she and Lilly lay awake for a time after Selma's soft breaths began to soothe the night.

"You're so fortunate, Jessie," Lilly told her in one of her rare reflective moods. "You're doing what you want and moving toward something good in your life. Why would you risk it all for . . . a fantasy?"

"I've got my slippers on the floor," she defended. "An instructor who feels at ease with his students teaches better, that's all."

Lilly rolled over and put her palm across Jessie's hands, which were folded on her stomach as she stared at the ceiling, and gripped her fingers tight. "Jessie," she whispered. "You're telling yourself stories that only you can believe. If you mess up this chance to have a real life, you'll disappoint us all."

Again.

"Uncle August gave you that camera. You're so lucky!"

Yet she daydreamed when she ought not to. Maybe she couldn't accept that she was as special as Uncle August claimed. Maybe she felt guilty being treated differently. "Maybe I don't deserve a joyful life," Jessie said. "You remember what happened. Maybe none of us does."

"That's not so, Jess. 'Desire realized is sweet to the soul,' that's what the proverb says. Didn't you memorize that one? Having a desire is a good thing. We shouldn't counter that just because we have regrets. We're not supposed to stay locked in fear that we'll mess up again."

"We always mess up," Jessie said.

"Not if our hopes come from the right place and not from our own, well, lusts."

Jessie felt her face grow hot. "I'm not lusting." She picked up her sister's hand and removed it from her. "Go to sleep."

Even while she protested to Lilly, Jessie wondered if she was lying to herself about the lust. Not about her not deserving joy though. Joy, she knew, was nothing she should claim. She had caused harm those years ago, irrevocable harm, because she'd been tending to her own wishes. To cope, she'd escaped into a photographic garden she shouldn't have entered. Now she faced the possibility that this good place might become something she could never let go of. Her mouth felt dry as summer sand. She needed a drink of water.

She rose and turned on the gaslight, poured water from the stoneware pitcher into a glass. A moth flitted in through the window. It fluttered at the light. *Foolish thing.* If not for the glass globe, it would burn itself up, yet it flailed at the glass. Why would it do that, destroy itself?

She stared at the moth, disgusted. She'd let Lilly and Voe make more of the relationship with Mr. Bauer than what was there. What they imagined was forbidden. He was a married man, so much older than she was, and she wouldn't act on her . . . daydreams. Couldn't. Not that he was the least bit interested. There were limits there, borders. Her family and her faith must be the globe that kept her from certain fire.

So why do I put at risk what I say I want? If her parents suspected her affections, she'd be banned from the studio. Her father might even have words with Mr. Bauer, humiliating her further. Maybe she'd end up working for the rest of her life, as Lilly did, at something she could never fall in love with.

Falling in love. It was safer to fall in love with someone unattainable than to risk letting her heart be known by a Jerome, perhaps, or even by someone she had yet to meet, someone who might truly see into who she was. Thinking of Mr. Bauer, older and kinder like her father, and the gentle way he treated her, maybe that protected her from . . . something. But why did she resist caring for a young beau? And why would she risk this artistic passion of hers, the dream of a career, by entertaining something forbidden?

She cupped her hand over the moth as it fell exhausted to the carpet. Jessie lifted it to the window and set it outside on the sill, then turned the lamp out. She didn't want to know if the moth was dead. She imagined the cool of the morning reviving it.

>–▸–◦–◂–◅

Jessie walked a fast pace to work through the October cool. She'd never tell Lilly, but her sister's words had brought her daydreams into focus. She had a vocation she enjoyed. Unlike Lilly, who worked in the glove factory, Jessie spent her days feeling full, almost as though it was spring every day. She knew this was rare indeed, especially for a girl who didn't cotton to conformity. Yet Lilly's confrontation had spurred her. She'd decided to remove herself from the threat.

At her mother's insistence, Jessie had memorized scripture. She'd hated the tedium of learning by rote, but her mother insisted she could then draw on encouraging words no matter her circumstances or location. She hated to admit it, but her mother had been right, and now a verse from Ezekiel came unbidden to her as she walked fast-paced along the route to work. "And by the river upon the bank thereof, on this side and on that side, shall grow all trees for meat, whose leaf shall not fade, neither shall the fruit thereof be consumed: it shall bring forth new fruit according to his months, because their waters they issued out of the sanctuary: and the fruit thereof shall be for meat, and the leaf thereof for medicine."

Some of her favorite verses had water in them. But this morning, it was trees, and those in front of her caught Jessie's eye. She watched red and yellow leaves drift to the ground. The bur oaks and red oaks hung on to their treasures the longest. Maybe she was like them, clinging tightly yet knowing they would eventually be torn from their branches. She'd have to rake them all this year since last year the tornado had stripped the trees and she hadn't needed to keep her commitment to Lilly. Lilly had reminded her of that at supper the night before.

Jessie's eye went to the sounds of chickens in the backyard pens. They were beginning to molt, and their feathers lay like large snowflakes on the pecked ground, signaling a hard winter. A wind gust picked up and tore at the pale gold leaves of the birch tree, one of the first to turn. Those chalky, peeling trunks always looked so exposed. Her eyes turned toward the sounds in the trees, where a flock of blackbirds gathered, a sign of the coming winter. A sun spot on the lawn highlighted squirrels chattering at their pile of nuts, which they worked over and then rushed off to bury. Jessie smiled. They scurried to their task just as she did.

The verse said to her that there would always be a way to survive, that there would always be provision, though not necessarily as one expected. Like the squirrels, she'd have to scramble. Healing was possible—hadn't her father been better since they'd moved off the farm? There'd be ways to recover from pain; that's what the medicinal leaves of the scriptural trees represented. She hoped she could count on such promises even though Roy hadn't been healed.

Just this past week Roy had told her why he didn't play with the children in their neighborhood anymore. "Th-th-they m-m-make fun of m-m-me."

"They tease you?" He'd nodded. She held him, wishing she could take his hurt away. It was she who'd given it to him; she was the one deserving of pain.

"You just tell them they'll have to deal

with me," she told him. "Tell them your sister is bigger than they are and she'll set them straight."

"I-I-I c-c-can't say all th-th-that." He burped his famous deep frog sound.

"I know, Frog," Jessie'd said. She felt the tears come. She blinked them back. "And some of those kids are as big as me, aren't they? I'll ask Papa to drive you to school."

"P-P-Papa does."

So it wasn't in the morning the bullies got to him.

"Remember the story of David and Goliath?"

He nodded.

"Well, I don't want you throwing stones, but I want you to remember that the first thing David did was thank the Lord for his success even before he lifted his stones. You just act like you're going to walk right through their words, because you will. Let them bounce off you like popped corn."

He grinned at the image.

"And when you get home, you can tell me about it, okay? I'll come right home from work. I'll help you forget those mean old chums."

"P-p-popped corn w-w-words." He pretended to pop a kernel into his mouth and burped his frog burp again. She wanted to stay and play with him, but her feet shuffled uneasily beneath the table. Regret stuck in her throat; her glasses were smudged from wiping at her eyes.

She needed to look for healing trees on the bank, for Roy and for herself, expecting they would reappear because the waters flowed from "the sanctuary." All the creative joy and sustenance and healing flowed from that sanctuary. She had to remember that, find ways to spend more time in that place of refuge instead of in the field of risk.

As strange as it was, the verse spoke to her of photography too, of how her eye and her art could bring healing to others through what they saw in a picture. She could find encouragement in art, put salve on her wounds. But Roy was another matter.

That they hadn't included her in the family plan to take him to the new clinic in Rochester saddened her. Despite what they said, she knew why she'd been excluded. She was fully capable of contributing, and she would. Her mother had said that Jessie would've gotten Roy all excited if she had known. They feared she'd have told Roy, yet it was Lilly who let the peanuts roll out of that bag. No one was certain anything could help his stuttering, and they didn't want his hopes raised. "Besides," her mother had said, "it will take some time before the money will be available to make the trip and the stay required for the evaluation."

So her working for months without pay had been a sacrifice for Roy as well as for her. He hadn't deserved that.

Once she'd been allowed in on the plan, Jessie insisted on adding to the savings, knowing that her plan to purchase her own Graflex camera could be put on hold. She would do the right thing.

It was also the right thing to quit working for the Bauer Studio and find employment that would allow her to develop her interests on her own too. She

felt a little disloyal going to work for another photographer, but another studio
would hire her without thinking of her as
someone in need of instruction. They
might pay her more as a certified photographer. She could hold her own, she
felt, in all aspects. She could have gone
to that photographic congress if she'd
had the money, if she'd wanted to,
though her mother might have intervened. She still had things to learn, she
knew. She would have to learn by trial
and error, by reading the photographic
magazines, and without Mr. B. leaning
over her. Yes, getting out, that's what
her dreams had taught her.

Or perhaps it was that moth that had
warned her.

As she approached the studio, her
stomach tightened and she took a deep
breath. After the incident in the retouching room, some of the easy comfort
she'd felt with him had vanished. She
nearly always felt mixed up, sometimes
wanting Voe to be with her whenever
Mr. B. was around and sometimes wishing Voe would be sent to the train station to pick up more dry plates and

chemicals so Jessie would have time with him alone.

That was the troubling thought that Lilly's warning highlighted. These things probably happened at other establishments where people spent more time with fellow workers than with their own family members. But she'd been around her father's friends, knew some of the church elders, and they were fine, upright men too; her heart never pounded so when they were around.

She'd never been aware of any feelings for any of the young men at the Youth Alliance who went on the sleigh rides and certainly not for Voe's brother, Jerome. The only feelings she had for him were like those that cropped up with spiders in the root cellar: they came with the territory, but she didn't have to like them.

She needed to get on that river and float away, not just because of thoughts about Mr. Bauer but because of opinions about his wife as well. She thought Mrs. Bauer ought to be more helpful to her husband's work. She could have done the retouching as she had before, and Jessie never would have had the opportunity to spend so much time alone in the retouching room with Mr. B. Mrs. Bauer rarely came by the studio. She didn't honor the hard work he was doing to support his family. Mr. B. brought the children more frequently than he had before, and while Jessie loved having them around, it couldn't have been easy for him. He'd said once when she ventured to comment on how often Winnie was coming by that "Mrs. Bauer has been ill of late." Yet she saw in the paper that she was busy being social, planning events for good causes, yes, but nevertheless away from her family. Wasn't a wife's first duty to her husband and children? When Mr. B. came in looking more tired than usual, a part of Jessie wanted to just prop him up, make tea for him, and look after him the way her mother did her father.

That thought had bothered her the most. Thoughts alone might not be sinful, but left unchecked they could lead to actions that were.

He had a wife. Jessie was not her, nor did she have any intention of being so.

He might have a loveless marriage. She'd heard of those. Lilly even used that reality as a reason why she'd likely never marry herself. "Love fades," she'd told Jessie after she stopped seeing a particular beau. Mr. Bauer had the children, and Jessie had no doubt of his love for them and theirs for him. What went on between a husband and wife was none of her affair. That was the thought she had to bolster.

Whatever had gone on before was water under the bridge, and she was on that water now, moving away. She'd find a job that paid more, and then she could help with Roy's trip to the Mayo brothers' hospital as well as save small amounts for her camera. This was what a career woman did: assess the situation, choose the best path, and take it, trusting that resources would arrive and putting unwarranted feelings behind her.

Jessie had decided to tell Voe today that she would be looking for other work, but she'd wait to tell Mr. B. until she was hired elsewhere. She looked for the good things in this choice as she walked. No more teasing from Voe and no more questions from Lilly. Even Selma's romantic swoons wouldn't apply to Jessie anymore. Most of all, Jessie would have no more pounding heart when it ought to be quiet.

><ⵙ◆ⵙ—O—ⵙ◆ⵙ<

Winnie looked sleepy as Jessie opened the kitchen door in the studio. Mr. B. had prepared cocoa for his daughter; the can sat on the counter with its Walter Baker label pointing toward her. With a silver spoon, the child scooped up Egg-O-See cereal, milk dripping from the soggy mass. The box lay tipped over, and cereal flakes like those molted chicken feathers lay scattered all over the table.

"Jessie!" Winnie said, dropping the spoon as she ran to hug her.

"Oops, let's get that spoon back in the bowl," Jessie said as she walked the child back to the table. "Maybe we can put some of these flakes back in the box."

"I sorry," Winnie said, trembling.

"Don't cry," Jessie told her. "I need to get my coat and hat off."

"Didn't mean to spill." Winnie's eyes blinked away tears.

"It'll clean up faster than if we had a cat to lick it," Jessie reassured.

"I like cats," Winnie said, settling back on the chair. "They make Mama cough."

Voe entered and stomped her feet to warm them. "It's only October, and I'm already an ice block," she complained. "Ooh, Walter Baker cocoa. Do you think Mr. B. would mind if I fixed myself some?"

Jessie checked the temperature of Winnie's cocoa. "Where is your papa, Winnie?"

"There." She pointed to the other room.

"It's kind of odd that he'd leave her here by herself," Jessie said.

"I eat alone lots of times," Winnie told her. Jessie raised one eyebrow. "Well, I do."

"You're just three years old."

"Three and one half," Winnie corrected, holding up pudgy fingers.

"Heat up Winnie's cocoa when you fix your own," Jessie said to Voe. "Hers has cooled off. She must have been here for some time."

Jessie made her way through the office area and into the reception room, where a fire burned to take off the chill. It could use another log. She added one, then removed her hat, hung up her suit jacket. She put her reticule in the desk behind the door, smoothed her linen skirt. She turned toward the studio operating room. Mr. B. wasn't there, nor did she see any sign of his having been there yet this morning. The shades were drawn, and he usually opened them first. She moved toward the developing room. *He must have forgotten the time,* Jessie thought.

She opened the door into the small room where they'd stayed during the storm, careful to close it behind her tightly. In the darkness, she knocked on the inner door. "Mr. Bauer? Are you in there? We were just wondering." She didn't hear any sounds. She knocked again. "Mr. Bauer?"

As she opened the door, her eyes adjusted to the orange filter he used over the light in order to see while he developed. She scanned the room, seeking him, finding him near the solution tubs.

"Are you all right?" she spoke as she approached. He looked up, surprised, as though he'd never heard her knock or enter. "We were wondering. Winnie was alone in the kitchen and—"

"Winnie. Alone." He frowned. "Oh. My. I got carried away." He rubbed his temples. "I think I've discovered something, Jessie," he said. "And if I'm right, it could revolutionize photography."

He asked her to step back out into the operating room, wiping his hands of the solutions he'd been working with. He asked her to sit. "I have a special request," he told her. "I'd like you to pose, Miss Gaebele, for a portrait that I intend to develop with two images on it, with both appearing as clear as Sugar Loaf against a morning sky."

"Is that possible?" Jessie asked. "The images always come out blurry when there's more than one on the plate."

"I believe I've found a way. I've been working at it. At night, after you and Voe leave. Early in the morning, when I first arrive. And if I have succeeded, it will be the first of its kind, and I can take it to the congress next year."

"I guess if you take my portrait, I'll get to go too," she said. She made the comment light, but she experienced a tingle of excitement at the idea of having her portrait seen by professional photographers.

"Miss Gaebele . . . I, no, it wouldn't be seemly, I—"

"Oh, I was only teasing, Mr. Bauer." Jessie had flustered him. She felt emboldened by that and by the possibility of being a model for such an experiment. "Would I be paid for the posing?" She'd heard that artists' models were paid extra. "This is nothing . . . lewd. Nothing—"

"Certainly not." He dismissed her with a brush of his hand. "I'd like you to wear just what you have on. A lovely blouse with lace collar is perfect. No, don't worry about your hair," he added when Jessie touched the high bob on her head. "And yes, I will pay you extra. I can hardly consider this request a part of your normal duties."

Several thoughts raced through Jessie's mind. She wondered if she should ask her mother if it would be acceptable to pose for a portrait that might be seen by many and used perhaps for advertising the studio's business. Maybe there was some sort of contract she ought to sign. She didn't want to be naive as a businesswoman. Her parents might object to her doing it without a written understanding, especially if the pose was too exposing, not that she'd allow a provocative shot. Was it acceptable to have others ogle a young woman's image? Mr. B. would never suggest that, though she'd heard of photographers' models who did at least partially disrobe. Now that she thought of it, she'd never seen a portrait of a woman alone in a studio's window, even with a tailored collar tight at her neck.

She thought of Lilly's look on her birthday as she stared at the candid shot he'd made of Jessie. She swallowed. It wasn't as though she'd gone to a dance or visited unannounced without wearing her gloves or carrying her calling card. But photographs could tell more than the subject wanted them to. She didn't want anything untoward revealed. This would be an opportunity, then, to show others that the camera described their relationship as simply employer photographing employee. What could be the harm in it? It was unlikely that anyone she knew would ever see the photograph anyway—she wasn't a model for a corset or anything like that. Even if he proved successful in making a double exposure on the same plate when, to date, no one else had, any notoriety would be in the camera world. If Mr. B. wanted to use the result for promotion, she could talk to him then about a contract and tell her family. Why, they might even be pleased with the extra funds available to put toward Roy's trip.

A tiny twinge of hesitation preceded her commitment, but she was, after all, her own person, fully capable of making a decision related to her career, wasn't she? And she'd planned to quit working for him without consulting her mother. So she guessed she could continue for a short time more without a conference too.

"I'd be pleased," she said, "to advance your artistry."

Mr. B. posed her on a plain bench and asked her to please fold her hands in her lap. Behind the camera he fidgeted, rolled it closer, measured distances. Then he came to her and lifted her hands just so. His were warm, and she felt small calluses on them as though he'd worked with tools, which surprised her. He was always so prim, so nattily dressed. Maybe he liked gardening.

He adjusted the lace on her blouse. Jessie blinked. This was why women preferred female assistants, she thought, to handle this kind of special posing. He didn't touch her, just the lace, but Jessie was aware of his closeness. He removed her glasses. She felt awkward and exposed.

He knelt to line up the hem of her dress the way he wanted it. He was beginning to bald, she noticed. As he bent, she could look directly on the small circle of his bare pate. His ears were small, not like her uncle August's. Mr. B. squatted before her now, pushed his glasses up on his nose, then adjusted her hands once again. It seemed to Jessie that he held her hands just a bit longer than he needed to. She pulled away first.

He patted her hands then, pushed up on his knees to stand, and looked at her. Her heart began that pounding again. *Hesitate, hesitate.*

"Keep that serene look," he told her. "It will take some time to expose the film. Then I'll have to change the camera angle just slightly. But if you can remain in the exact position, it will be best. Can you do that? Not move even when I am moving here?"

Jessie nodded. As he walked away from her, her heart beat normally. It was nothing. He was merely posing her as he did all his clients, gently touching to present their hands just so. She inhaled and set her face as he worked with the camera. She was certainly not a romantic like Selma. She didn't see hidden motive in every movement. Nor was she a logician like her sister Lilly, weighing every little emotion against the logic of it all. But as she watched him move the wheel to raise and lower the camera, to set things, she knew that today was not the day to plan to resign from the studio, not when there was something as exciting as a double exposure and her small part to play in it. Quitting the studio would have to wait.

>–◆>–०–‹◆–‹

The Bauer Studio kept busy through the fall with new requests for prints and portraits. Jessie kept her thoughts of Mr. Bauer in check, made sure to keep herself at distances from him. As Lilly had pronounced one evening as she discussed her own beau troubles, emotions could be kept in check with a little willpower.

Still, she looked forward to coming to work. She enjoyed the banter with Voe and with Mr. B. She found the clients fascinating too. She knew that in high school people studied biology and something called anatomy, which addressed the way bones and organs are covered with skin. She found herself noting the angle of a man's chin or the distance between a woman's upper lip and her nose and even the varying depth of that small indentation between the two.

She commented on that once when they developed a portrait of an older woman who had a decided groove above her lip, and Mr. B. told her a German tale of how angels made those indentations to help children forget all that had happened to them before they were born.

"The angel touches them as his last act before the child arrives on this earth, and then all they can remember after that is heaven's light, the illumination we move toward as we try to find our own way." It was a treasured story.

Jessie thought she could be under the spell of photography for her entire life. When she finished reading the latest issues of *Camera World* at the library, she imagined herself not just having a special camera to call her own but owning a studio, holding afternoon teas the way the women photographers in New York did. She'd travel, take her photographic equipment to the top of Sugar Loaf, or even risk the excursion trains out West. There were trains direct from

Winona to Seattle now. Jessie's aunt lived in Seattle. She could get in touch with her and stay for a time, shooting photographs, making her way in that booming city that people spoke of as though it was wild and untamed. Jessie scoffed at that. It couldn't be all that wild. They had a children's hospital there.

Why, if the Mayo brothers couldn't help Roy, she'd suggest they all go to Seattle to see if doctors there could. She imagined them traveling to Pikes Peak on the way. She'd seen pictures taken from the top of the mountain and wondered how they did that, photographing and developing so people had a special remembrance before they ever headed back home. She smiled to herself. Mr. B. would call that "mountaintop tramp photography" with all the variables Pikes Peak could introduce.

She did understand some of his concern about tramping after he'd told her that Mrs. Bauer's father had done it. "He called himself an itinerant photographer, but it's the same thing," Mr. B. explained. "Just as with those flash-light clubs, it minimizes the true professionalism of photography."

She didn't tell Mr. B., but she wished she could go to one of the camera flashlight events the photographer Van Vranken offered twice a month at the YMCA. She'd like to learn more about the powder and setting it afire. It wasn't as progressive as the process used in Mr. B.'s studio, but it did allow amateurs to advance their skills. And Mr. Bauer used it on overcast days, when natural lighting wasn't enough. She'd watched him prepare the powder, and he spoke as he worked of what he was doing, but he never allowed her to do it herself. She was still an amateur in his eyes, even though she'd passed the professional certification test.

It didn't matter. Women were not permitted in such classes.

She'd once suggested to Mr. B. that he offer a course to include girls, but he said that "would ruin my reputation." She wasn't sure if it was the classes for amateurs or the involvement of girls that would do that. If the congress liked his work next year, why, perhaps he'd offer developing classes to professionals and she could be his assistant at least. She chastened herself. She would leave once she knew of the double exposure's acceptance.

She was fortunate to have a career at all. Lilly glowed when she sewed. She could look at a pattern in a magazine and replicate it. She'd made Gair's Supporters for all of them, and their shirt-waists stayed put all day with the belt hooks holding both the blouse material and the skirts. Jessie had suggested that Lilly take special orders, but more and more fashionable women were buying from the catalogs and wearing ready-made dresses like those advertised in *Woman's Home Companion.* Even so, Jessie convinced Lilly to let her make up little cards that could be left at the library or the post office. Just that day, Jessie had secured permission from Mr. Bauer to leave the cards where portrait clients could pick them up.

"No pushing them at people," he told her.

"Never fear," Jessie told him. She

smiled and placed them in a little card holder her father had made.

Voe looked at the cards. "I should do something like this to hand to my beaus," she teased. "So they can always ring me up."

"You could. When I worked at Kroeger's, we made up all sorts of interesting calling card designs and just added people's names to them in the lettering they liked."

Jessie had gone on to tell a funny story about a woman's name being mixed up on the card, and while she listened to Mr. Bauer's and Voe's laughter, she felt rich, content. She was a professional woman able to assist her sister, her brother, her family, and keep her emotions in check in her workaday world.

"Maybe Mrs. Bauer would be interested in one of Lilly's gowns," Jessie said. "Lilly's really very good at what she does."

He held the small card in his hand. Jessie had drawn a swooping *L* that nearly bordered the card and then put Lilly's name and added *Fine Stitching as*

YOU Like It. "I emphasized the *you*," Jessie told them, "because people like to know they're in control."

"You're quite right, Miss Gaebele." Jessie thought he agreed with her understanding of how clients liked to decide how to sit for their portraits, but he proved her wrong. "My wife does have need of some change in clothing right now."

"Winter's coming. Can Lilly make coats too?" Voe asked.

"Not so much for the weather," Mr. Bauer corrected. "But she is . . . that is . . . we are expecting another child in March. I'm sure she could benefit from, ah, dresses with expanded waistlines."

⋙⋯◇⋯⋘

Jessie left work early and walked across the street to the library. It was one of the few places where she could be alone, quiet, and no one would bother her so long as she had a book open in front of her. When she felt low, she also liked to take the streetcar to the end of the line and walk back. Seeing other people, places, helped remind her of Ezekiel's river and took the blues away. At the library, she often didn't read what was before her but used the book as a prop to separate her from anyone else in the room while she thought.

She kept a list of new words that she used to expand her vocabulary and carried it with her. Those who had gone on to high school always sounded so much wiser, and Jessie decided that was due to the words they chose. *Complect* was her latest word. It meant "to join by twisting or weaving." She thought it the perfect word to describe her current life. Another definition for the word described her feelings about what Mr. Bauer had shared earlier that day. *Complect* also meant "intertwined."

She had no idea why the news of Mrs. Bauer's being with child made her sad. It was ridiculous. They could have as many children as they wished! They were married and, apparently, happily so. She had nothing to say about such things. They were good parents, looking after their children, loving and caring for them. They'd had a child die. Perhaps this was a way through the pain of that, to choose to have another. It was none of her affair.

Her face felt hot as she thought of what must have transpired to bring about this new life. *March,* he'd said. That meant the child was conceived . . . shortly after their encounter in the re-touching room, before the posing for the double exposure. She should have left the studio when she first told herself she would. Why hadn't she? She was as hopeless a romantic as Selma, and that was the truth! She took the photo case from her reticule and rubbed her hands across the embossing that read *St. Louis World's Fair 1904.* She should give the case back, cut any connections to the Bauers. She opened it and looked at the portrait. He had made her appear beautiful, desirable even, in that picture. But maybe it wasn't the eye behind the lens that made her look so attractive. Maybe she was a lovely woman despite her large nose, the glasses, her wispy hair that never stayed where it was sup-posed to. She ought not to think like that! Acknowledging one's own attractiveness was sinful, wasn't it? Maybe she was being punished for such thoughts, for having had such a blessed life. No, she was being punished because of Roy, her Frog. She wasn't supposed to have joy at another's expense. There would always be something to pull the rug from under her happy, dancing feet. She just needed to stop dancing. Dancing wasn't allowed.

She looked at the photo again. No, she didn't normally look so splendid. It was the camera, not her.

She put the photograph away. If he had created an image that made others gasp in awe, it was just because he was good at what he did. It had nothing to do with whether he held her in a special place in his heart and had revealed it from behind the lens.

Special place in his heart! She scoffed, out loud apparently, as several people turned to her with frowns on their faces. The librarian put her finger to her lips.

Jessie felt tears burn behind her eyes. She picked up her reticule, pulled her cape around her shoulders, and de-

cided: she was upset because it was totally inappropriate for Mr. Bauer to have
even shared such marital intimacies
with his employees. What went on between a man and his wife had nothing to
do with her. He should keep such information to himself. All he had to say was
that he'd give Lilly's sewing card to his
wife. He didn't have to share. At least
she had time to prepare her response
when Lilly crowed to her that Mrs. Bauer
was expecting a child. *If* Mrs. Bauer
contacted Lilly. She probably would. Mr.
B. was the kind of man who would see
the referral as a way to help a young girl,
Lilly in this instance, make her way in
the world. And Mr. Bauer was the kind
of husband who might even make the
order himself, to surprise his wife.

She'd stop calling him Mr. B. That
was much too familiar. He was her employer, nothing else. Maybe even tell
him so if the occasion arose. Otherwise
she'd simply go back to being his assistant, no different than Voe. "Miss Gaebele" would be the more appropriate
address from now on. She would set the

tone. She had a career to plan for, and that's just what she'd do now instead of daydreaming about an older man's finding her intriguing. She would set the boundaries. Her eye caught the title of a fat book as she left the library: *Major Greek Goddesses.* It made her think of Hera, protector of marriage but also a woman with envy in her eyes.

With Hera on her mind, she left the library. The light was still on at the studio. He was working late. Jessie considered going there to tell him that she wanted a more formal relationship with him, that she'd be calling him Mr. Bauer from now on. And she'd be seeking other work. She started across the street, waiting for the bustle of autos and buggies and delivery wagons. They moved slowly as though on a river. She hesitated, turned away.

She headed home instead, prepared to tell Lilly that she just might have found a customer for her Fine Stitching as YOU Like It business. But she wouldn't say any more than that. Jessie had let herself be waylaid. She had wanted to be noticed, to be someone

special by being in that double exposure.

More than what she'd wanted had actually been exposed.

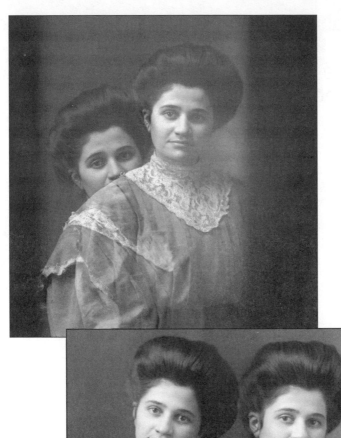

Exposure

The purpose is to allow light onto the film and therefore unveil something that would be otherwise hidden; that's what an exposure really is. It takes time, of course, and I still thrill at the way an image appears as though from dreams to reveal itself on paper. A double exposure was quite rare in those days, and I didn't think FJ would have the ability to accomplish what he set out to do. Not that he wasn't a skilled artisan; he was. But his hands also moved with jerks I attributed to his impatience. I noticed it sometimes when he straightened a gentleman's hair with his comb or when he adjusted a woman's ribbon. That was when I would ask if I could assist in helping pose the subjects. He would agree. At any rate, the ultimate judge of a successful double exposure is keeping both images scissor-cut clear, and this is difficult to do if the photographer shows a nervous twitch.

Clarity is always what a photographer strives for. Well, that and a photograph that sings out from within in some inde-scribable way. Photographs that make one take in a breath while being drawn into the image. It is what I want in my life too, those moments of sharp breathing, perfect clarity, fully drawn in.

One could not do a self-portrait as a double exposure. Given the time it took to expose the plate, the subject would have to sit extremely still, not moving while the camera moved. So it took two people. Even after I had left the studio, I felt I'd be willing to assist him as a model, but then other things did inter-vene.

I wanted this to work for him. His dis-couragement after losing his foothold when he'd been so ill kept a kind of daze over him, I thought. A successful double exposure could bring him confi-dence, if not a little fame. He'd have to work long hours trying different things in the darkroom, but in there he acted most at home. Oh, he was charming with the clients, but I could tell he got annoyed too, wanting them to just sit as I posed them for him or to accept the feather prop I handed them. His photographs of children, especially of his own, were notable for capturing gentleness, though he was noticeably tired after sittings with young children. Their natural exuberance made them squiggle and squirm, and the day could be a disaster if he couldn't get them settled. People wouldn't purchase an exposure that wasn't clear. That was always the challenge.

Clarity was all I'd ever wanted in a photograph of myself. Clarity, but not enough to expose certain feelings or intentions that would only add complications to my days.

The first exposure he showed me was quite remarkable. My arms were combined almost, my facial expression only slightly different. But the second one, with one image behind the other, made me pause. What stood behind me? What was it I saw out there in the world that I resisted or reached out for? How had I come to so expose myself?

TWELVE

Double Exposure

FJ phoned in late to tell the girls that he was going to the hospital with his wife and to carry on without him. It was March 19, 1909. Miss Gaebele had answered. While he waited at the hospital for news of the birth, he thought about her cool voice on the phone when she told him she hoped all would go well. Something had changed in her. "We'll handle things fine here," she'd said. He was probably imagining it, but the girl had been less vibrant of late. Not sullen exactly. Distant when he gave instructions about how to always return the chemicals to their usual slots so that they wouldn't get confused and perhaps cause physical harm; less enthusiastic when he admonished her to use the lower voltage light bulb in the printer so as not to "burn" the negative she made from the plate. He missed her light delight, as he thought of it, which had characterized the studio the year before.

He had not given her a present for her seventeenth birthday. Perhaps that had offended her. But no, the coolness had happened much earlier than that.

He was hoping that the news he planned to share—that the congress had accepted his double exposure for the July exhibit—would please her. There'd be an article in the paper, and such publicity would only help his business. All in all, he felt quite contented. Russell and Winnie were staying for a few days with their grandmother. He'd be heading to North Dakota to oversee the planting next month. The fall flax crop sale had exceeded expectations and lifted pressure from the studio operations. He'd recommended less wheat, and that had been a good decision, even though Reinke had resented the flax success. Best of all, he had a child about to be delivered, and he was certain that his wife's troubled times would be over now.

She had been often sick and in bed, her emotions up and down like the roads up the bluffs and back. Sometimes her feet swelled and she couldn't walk. Those days he'd remained at home to assist. He was grateful he hadn't let either of the girls go, as the business continued without interruption despite his wife's special needs. But now that would be over, and he was glad of it. The baby would arrive without difficulty. His wife had never had trouble delivering. Tonight he'd give out cigars to his cronies at the lodge. At least he hoped he would.

He took a cup of coffee the nurse brought to him.

"While you wait, sir."

His hands shook.

"I'm sure everything will be fine, sir," the nurse said.

"If it's a boy, we'll name him Robert," he told the nurse.

"That's a fine name," she said and left him alone.

He hoped everything would go all right for his wife, for them, for this child. They hadn't yet picked a girl's name. Maybe Joan, a name related to Jessie, named for her mother.

Jessie. So interesting that he had two Jessies in his life: a wife whom he loved and an employee who somehow had found a place in his heart. He cared about the young woman and her future. That was all it was, and he hoped she understood that. Maybe that was why she'd seemed cool of late, had even asked to be called Miss Gaebele again, even when it was just the two of them working in the developing room. He'd honored that, of course. But it did take away a little of the informality of being at the studio.

Perhaps the double exposure would bring some of that back. He could only hope. Maybe he should consider taking her to the congress meeting in St. Paul this year, to show off his model. He'd have to think about that.

For now he would concentrate on his

wife and bringing this infant into the world and keeping the baby safe, ever so safe.

⊱┈◈┈○┈◈┈⊰

Jessie's pursuit of employment at other studios had gained her nothing except sore feet. Polonia's was too small and Mr. Polonia did all his own work, he told her, had no need for assistants. She tried to be discreet, not wanting the news to get back to Mr. Bauer, but her mother heard it from a woman at church who had seen Jessie going into Van Vranken's studio.

"Were you delivering something?" her mother asked. "I didn't think studios worked together like that."

"No. Yes. No. All right, Mama. I'm looking for additional work so I can contribute to Roy's trip and maybe one day be out on my own."

"Why didn't you say so? Ralph Carleton is looking for a full-time assistant. Your father could approach him for you."

"The evangelist? Oh no, Mama. I want to stay with photography."

"You could have a worse employer," her mother said. "His influence might do you good."

"It probably would," Jessie said. "But I was hoping to advance my art too."

"Your art. Is that the only thing that drives you?"

"No, Mama."

She was certain she told her mother the truth.

———————

President William Howard Taft was scheduled to visit the Winona Normal School. When Jessie learned of it—her father mentioned the proposed visit was in the paper—she urged Mr. Bauer to take a camera and get a picture of the president.

"It's much too difficult to catch a face decently while the subject is moving. It's hard enough in the studio. Think of it as taking photographs of kittens," he said. "Or young children. I haven't yet taken one of Robert because it's not reasonable to ask a child to sit so still. Maybe when he's six months old." Jessie remembered the stillness of the infant who had died. "But a president can be as energetic as an infant or a cat," Mr. Bauer continued. "Very likely he will be either getting into his car or getting out. He won't be standing around waiting for a photographer. Those around him won't allow the citizens to come too close either, Miss Gaebele. It would be a blurred shot at best."

"But you could try. You did a double exposure, and that was a challenge. This could be a nice feather in your cap."

"You think so."

"I do," Jessie said. "He's going to be at the normal school. And there's a parade later as well. Why not try to take a parade picture too?"

"No parades. I'm not interested in that. Too—"

"Trampish," Jessie finished for him. He nodded once in agreement. "It's not tramping," she continued. "You've said yourself that much of the quality a client wants comes from the developing, the retouching. You can do magic in the darkroom."

He lifted his eyebrows. "Can I, Jessie?"

He looked at her in an odd way, she thought. *Flirtatiously?* There'd been none of that after she'd asked him to refer to her as Miss Gaebele. He'd acted surprised, but she told him that sometimes she called him Mr. B. when she was at home, and her family seemed to think that too informal. She had decided not to call him that anymore and would like it if he'd remember to use her surname as well. He had complied. He forgot sometimes, but then he'd had much on his mind with a new baby at home.

"Outdoor photographs don't suit me," he continued.

"I hope I never grow too old to try a few new things," she said.

He harrumphed and turned away.

She would take it herself then. But the next day he changed his mind. "You're right, Miss Gaebele. I can try something new. I'll see what I can do with my camera on my shoulder, though I must tell you, it reminds me of tramp photographers. I have worked to keep them from piercing real photographers with their sharp talks about giving people high quality when they know they can't. Their failure sets a bad name for those of us who could succeed."

"You'll need an assistant," Jessie said.

"I'll need both of you. One to carry the plates and one to help with the camera setup. It's probably insane to try such a thing, but at least the weather is cooperating."

They left early and set up the camera near the normal school, hoping they'd anticipated the place where he'd come out of or get into his car. It felt like a picnic almost while they waited. The camera made them look official.

The big man, Taft, came out of the school earlier than expected. He stood, shading his eyes, viewing the crowd. Jessie and Voe scurried after Mr. Bauer, who fast-walked with his cane and carried the stand while Jessie rushed behind him with the camera. They paused at the president's touring car.

"Over here, Mr. President!" Jessie shouted.

She handed Mr. Bauer the camera,

and he quickly put the plate inside as Jessie jumped up and down. The crowd began to move toward the president, but she kept calling, and he looked toward her as he came around to enter the vehicle. He stopped, posed, his large belly arching before him.

Mr. Bauer got the picture of President Taft as he stood up in the presidential car. It was not a double exposure by any means. Instead it was a portrait captured outside, with Mr. Bauer making the best of elements he couldn't control. It was a very good likeness, Jessie thought. Very good indeed.

The picture was written about in the paper. Actually, Jessie wrote the article for the *Republican-Herald.* She'd been very careful with her grammar and asked Mr. Bauer to look it over. He tugged at his mustache as he read, made several suggestions, then nodded his approval. His smile warmed her to her toes. She submitted a print of the picture as well. The local newspapers still resisted using photographs, but it didn't matter. The article saluted Mr.

Bauer's work, and the portrait was in the glass-encased window of the Bauer Studio gallery now. Any number of people stopped by to see it. Mr. Bauer planned to take it to the congress in July.

Jessie sent the article to the president in Washington DC. By return mail, the White House requested prints. Jessie howled when she saw the letter's return address, and she opened the mail as she always did, singing out to Voe, who helped pose a couple in the operating room as Mr. Bauer directed.

"You see, you weren't too old to try something new," Jessie said, bursting into the room. "The president of the United States of America wants *your* work. Your cabinet card will sit in the White House!"

"What's that?"

"I'm sorry," Jessie apologized to the couple holding their pose. "Mr. Bauer's picture of President Taft has been requested by the White House. You're being photographed by a man who photographed the president!"

The couple beamed. So did Mr. Bauer. She could make things happen. There was art in that.

⊱┈⊷⟩┈○┈⟨⊷┈⊰

In September, two events surprised Jessie. Mr. Bauer's double exposure was written up in the St. Paul paper in an article submitted by someone attending the congress. Later the Winona papers ran it too. The exposure was touted as a unique contribution to the photographic field. His model, of course, was not mentioned, but Mr. Bauer had done something innovative. Perhaps there'd be increased interest in his techniques and Jessie would be a part of whatever exciting changes might come from that. She could imagine people choosing a double-exposed portrait to be framed or that others might come to learn how he'd posed and developed the print. She had helped him in the darkroom, had washed the plates and worked the solutions as he tried over and over to make sure that the double exposure was clear and that each of the two images of her appeared as he wished.

He'd used the smaller glass plate, but it was still a dramatic photograph, and she was pleased for him and pleased for herself.

"You're a fine model, Jessie," he told her.

She beamed at his praise but made sure she never stood close enough that he could pat her back or that she could smell the scent of baby powder on his shirts.

The second surprise came the following day, when Jessie came to the front of the studio, where a few people had gathered. She pushed her way past them. Lilly was in the crowd.

Jessie gasped.

Mr. Bauer had framed the print of his double exposure and placed it in the window. Jessie told herself there was nothing to be alarmed about. She was simply a model, an employee. But she hadn't cleared it with her mother, and her mother didn't like surprises. Worse, here in this setting, away from the technicalities of the developing room, she could see the portrait for its nuances. He'd once again made her look wistful, reflective, and even pretty. He'd taken a photograph that showed her to be more than what she was. And very likely, Mrs. Bauer too would see things in the print that were better left unexposed. She never should have agreed. But it was too late now.

>—·—◆>—O—<◆—·—<

Mrs. Bauer had heard about the Taft photograph by reading the paper. But it was the dressmaker, Lilly Gaebele, who mentioned to her that her sister's photograph was in the window beside the president's. "It's a double exposure or something like that," Lilly had said. "I don't really understand it."

"Two images on one print," Mrs. Bauer explained as Lilly fit the dress. She had not lost all the weight she'd gained with Robert, but she'd decided to ask the elder Gaebele girl to take in at least a little from the dresses made for her while she carried the boy. "Were both images clear?"

"As far as I could tell, but there were several people staring and I couldn't really get too close."

Her dressmaker continued to work, circling her, pins plucked from an oval cushion attached to her bodice. Mrs. Bauer anticipated pricks at her waistline. They never came. The girl was good at what she did, and she could be silent too if Mrs. Bauer didn't pursue conversation. Was the girl bragging on her sister's portrait by mentioning the crowd gathered around? Maybe she ought to take a look at it.

Mrs. Bauer had known of the double exposure's success, of course, but not who the model was. She hadn't asked, nor had she requested to see it. She just hoped he hadn't had to pay the girl more for the modeling. The Bauer Studio wasn't made of gold. It might have been if her husband had put as much money into new cameras and promotions as he'd put into that ranch. Even getting a better market for that salve of his would help. Times were difficult right now. People were nervous about the economy, and the Bauers had three children to care for.

She never should have agreed to another child. The baby was easy to care for, but she was more tired now than she'd ever been. She dragged herself from bed each morning only to bring the child back to nurse him. Sometimes she fell back asleep before he did, and she worried she might roll onto him. She'd sent Winnie to her mother's, begging her to look after the girl for a few days each week even though Mr. Bauer had agreed to take Winnie to the studio. He made subtle comments about the distraction, having children's toys in the reception room, and she knew he was hoping to increase the portrait sittings what with the good news of the double exposure and Taft's photograph.

Winnie's absence helped, but she still felt herself going up and down the hills of exhaustion that always bottomed out in a lost temper with her husband, and even with Russell sometimes, though the boy rarely did a thing out of line.

If only they had enough money to hire a live-in girl, one of those Polish immigrants who populated the city. They were clean and tidy and said to be fine cooks. She didn't know how they might be with children, but she could ask.

Except what was the point? They couldn't afford it. Just as they couldn't afford Mr. Bauer's trips to the congress either, but he'd gone. Or his club memberships, but he continued to rejoin. And who knew how many hours and dollars he'd spent perfecting that double exposure? How many glass plates? How many tins of developing solutions had he gone through? However would they recover such frivolous losses? She felt her face grow warm, almost hot. She looked up into the mirror. *That flush again.* Sometimes she felt as though a thousand bees were stinging her, and this awful flush moved up through her body to her neck and face. She couldn't get her breath.

Her dressmaker spoke to her. What had she said? "I'm sorry, I didn't hear you," Mrs. Bauer said.

"Would you like to do something different?"

Lilly was talking about the retailoring of the dress, but when Mrs. Bauer answered yes, she referred to more than the shape of her gown.

⋗┼⬥⋗─O─⬥⋖┼⋘

Jessie's parents called her into the parlor. Her father began by telling her that both of them felt it would be better if she left the employ of Mr. Bauer.

Nothing made Jessie more likely to click a shutter shut than being told what to do. It was true she had considered leaving the Bauer Studio a while back, but her lack of success at finding work and the changes at the studio made her feel she had things under control. There'd been a realignment of the border between her and Mr. Bauer, and neither she nor he had crossed it. She believed she could have a life as a photographer, maybe one day independently. Why her parents would choose now to have her leave made no sense to her, but she was ready for this argument. She'd outlined several points in her mind about why she ought to remain. She started in, but her mother held her hand up for her to stop.

"Just keep in mind," her mother said,

"that with Ralph Carleton's evangelistic work, you might get to travel. You've always said you'd like to do that."

"He's the one who travels. I doubt he'd take a young female assistant along with him. And you wouldn't approve of that anyway, would you?"

"Hush now. He'd send you ahead," her mother said.

"I suspect he has a male secretary to handle the advance preparations, Mama. Arranging the site, getting the proper authorities to permit him to be there, all of that. And really, any man can do that. And any woman can write his letters for him. But how many women can make a photograph that other people look at and smile? Or even cry because it's so beautiful?"

"At least with Mr. Carleton you'd be exposed every day to rightful behavior," her mother said. She turned to her husband, who watched Jessie with kind eyes.

Jessie lowered her eyes. "I'm sorry you think I need that."

"The photograph," her father said. "Lilly says it is quite provocative."

So that was it. Somehow Lilly's scandalous and erroneous view of her relationship with Mr. Bauer had been conveyed to her parents by Lilly's tragic review of a simple photographic success.

"Have you seen it? It's nothing to be alarmed about. Just a technical photograph."

"We urged August to get you the camera because you were so sad after Roy's fall. We hoped it would help you, and it did. But now it's taking you places you ought not to go, Jessie."

"Don't you see? I have a *profession* because of it. Not like Lilly. She doesn't get to spend all her time doing what she'd like, making dresses. She's wrong about the portrait. She's just jealous!"

"She has a beginning," her mother said.

"This is my beginning."

"We'd like to see you happily married one day," her mother said. "And that isn't likely to happen while you hold on to these dreams that can't ever be achieved. We want you to be wise, Jessie, and not hold unnatural affections for an art or for a forbidden person." She folded her hands in her lap and looked like she'd just eaten some of her mother's vinegar pickles.

Jessie looked aghast.

"Unnatural affections?" She whispered the words. "I . . . I . . . admire his work. I think he's a good man. He has taught us well. There's nothing unnatural in that."

"He is putting thoughts in your head that you may never be able to secure. A studio of your own." This from her father. "We wanted you to have something to distract you from the hard times. But—"

"Papa, he doesn't know about my desire to have my own studio one day. He doesn't! I just don't see why I have to leave doing something I love. I only told Lilly and Selma and Roy!" She didn't want to cry, but she could feel the tears of frustration nibbling at the edge of her eyes. Her parents looked at each other.

Her father spoke then. "Sometimes people who love you can see what you can't."

"I have to see through my own eyes,"

Jessie said. "When I'm eighteen, Papa, I'll have to make my own choices."

"You have a few months to go until then. And while you're here with us, it's our responsibility to help you. You know our wishes and what we think is best for you." *Yes, and I considered leaving myself. But not now.* "Ralph Carleton has an opening. We trust that you'll make the best choice."

Jessie left the parlor, grabbed her hat, and stomped out into the autumn evening. She needed to walk. She looked up to see the streetcar making one last run across the Lake Winona bridge. She stepped on. She watched people as she moved by, the *click click* of the car on the tracks a steady rhythm to match her heart. Her timing was always wrong. Just when she felt she could work beside someone she cared for deeply without violating her own emotions or challenging his, her parents decide she isn't deciding well at all.

They couldn't know how much she enjoyed the little moments in the studio when Voe danced around mimicking someone they all knew—the telephone operator or the postman. Her parents couldn't grasp how much pleasure she derived from watching Winnie play with her dolls at the small table Mr. Bauer had brought in for her, listening to the child's words soar and sing, unlike Roy's. They couldn't know—she hadn't ever told them—of the small pleasure she felt as she worked her way past the bricks of regret she carried because she found pleasure in the normal chattering of the child. Working for Ralph Carleton would be a constant reminder of those parts of her that were neglectful, fearful, and self-centered, evidence of her bankrupt soul. She'd face daily reminders of the inevitability of human error. She'd always wonder when she'd err again.

Jessie rode the streetcar to the end of the line, then rode it back. She did say prayers as she put her hands against the cool window. She'd have leaned her head there, but her hat wouldn't allow it. She didn't hear anything neat and tidy, no voice of God telling her just what to do. She'd planned to leave anyway, before the double exposure, so maybe it was time. Maybe she was being held back by being a mere assistant. She could have a studio of her own one day if she took a few risks, like photographing the president herself instead of convincing Mr. Bauer to do it. If she could buy a Graflex camera, it would be so much easier to make photographs for postcards. She could take wedding photographs too, she thought. Photograph happy occasions. It was getting out of the studio that would make a photographer's career. Just like those photographs from Pikes Peak, which made her want to go there. Advertisers like Ivory soap or Keen Kutters scissors and shears would buy prints of their products. Models didn't have to be . . . people.

She had to look up to the bank as the river flowed along and reach for those fruits and healing leaves. There would be another way. There had to be.

>—+—◆—○—◆—+—<

At the studio the next morning, silence greeted her. She remembered that Voe was going to meet the train and pick up the latest order of glass plates so they could save the drayage charge. Mr. Bauer had been hoping to make cuts, he'd told them earlier in the year, and that was one way of doing so. Jessie liked to get the orders, as she enjoyed the walk, and pulling the little cart behind her created extra effort that kept her legs strong and her arms slim. But today they had several portrait sittings scheduled, and Jessie assisted better than Voe did, or so Mr. Bauer had said.

It was just as well that the two of them would be alone for a time. She'd be better able to tell Mr. Bauer of her decision to leave his employ whether he could replace her or not, then tell Voe when she came in later.

She sighed and opened the door, coming in the front instead of the back, hesitating for a moment to look at the window display from the inside. There was nothing wrong with that photograph, not really. Just a simple working girl, exposed twice on one piece of paper. He'd placed both shots in the window: the one where she sat beside herself and the one where it appeared her own conscience looked over her shoulder. If she took a photograph of herself, she wondered if she couldn't get the same effect—not the double exposure but just a portrait shot. She'd do that one day and show her sister and her mother that it was the lens, not the person behind it, which brought the subject into artistic focus.

But that would have to wait. For a long time, now that she was leaving.

Not unlike the day they'd come in and found Mr. Bauer so absorbed in his double exposing that he'd forgotten Winnie, Jessie entered into silence. She walked to the back, hung up her coat and hat, adjusted the hairpins holding her hair roll and bun at the top of it. She put her purse into the desk, then called out, "Mr. Bauer? Winnie?" He'd been bringing the girl often, so Jessie half expected to see her. "It's Miss Gaebele. I'm here."

Jessie wandered back through the reception room and checked the door to the darkroom. He wasn't there. He wasn't in the operating room either. Yet he had to be there. The studio wasn't locked. She kept calling as she walked back through the kitchen to the back door. Perhaps he'd stopped to pull some weeds from the garden area. Jessie often tended the garden between appointments, just to clear her mind and inhale the scent of sweet outdoors. She loved perennials. Once begun, they could be counted on to come up every year: columbines, tulips, lilies of the valley.

She stepped out on the porch, scanning the garden. Then she saw him, sitting below her on the step, his back to her.

"Here you are."

He didn't turn around.

"Mr. Bauer? Are you all right?"

He turned to look at her then. He was as pale as Minnesota limestone, and when he raised his hands to her as if offering up his palms, they shook. His face wore the same agony her father's did when his side hurt so much that the pain propelled him to the floor. He brought his hands to stare at them, close. He hung his head. Jessie sat down beside him. Fear flooded his eyes. He whispered something.

She leaned to him. "I couldn't hear you."

"It's come back," he said. "The mercury poisoning, it's come back."

He stared at the back of his hands, and Jessie could see the reddish spots there now. She wanted to hold him the way she did her father when her mother would call the doctor. She wanted to take the discomfort onto herself, keep him free of it if she could. She'd want to do that for anyone.

But she didn't.

"I'll call the doctor," Jessie said and started to stand.

He grabbed her hand. "No. Call Mrs. Bauer. Tell her what's happened. Ask her to send a cab and have the doctor meet me at the house. You'll, you and Voe, you'll have to run the studio. Take the appointments. Can you do that?"

"All right," Jessie said, standing.

She made the phone call to Mrs. Bauer, telling her exactly what Mr. Bauer had said.

"The poisoning? Again? No, no, no, not that. Not now. It's all that developing, all that exposure to chemicals. He should have taught you girls how to do that so he wouldn't have to!"

Her voice rose, and Jessie tried to calm her. "He did teach us, Mrs. Bauer. It wasn't—"

"All those double exposures, that's what it is. All that time in the chemicals. Gracious, gracious, gracious me! What was he thinking? I'm so ill myself, so very ill. This is—"

"Can you send the cab, Mrs. Bauer? And call the doctor, or would you like me to do that?"

"He doesn't tell me half of what's going on, but he wants me to drop everything while he once again has this, this *poisoning* that barrels into our lives like one of his North Dakota bulls!"

"I'll go ahead and call," Jessie said. She hung up while Mrs. Bauer was still talking. She knew it might be considered rude, but she didn't think her staying on the line would help.

She clicked back on to get the operator, who said she'd call the doctor. Jessie waited for the cab and helped place Mr. Bauer in the horse-drawn vehicle, handed him his cane, noted the smudges on his spectacles. She watched the cab drive away. She waited for Voe to arrive, heard the squirrels chatter in the elm tree, and all the while wondered at this thing called timing.

Setting

The descent of the sun below the horizon is a setting, of course, as is any other celestial body making its way in the decline of our immediate vision. Music arranged around text is considered a setting too, I'm told by my sister Selma. Even amethysts, my birthstone, placed perfectly in gold, have a setting. It is the context in which events unfold that sets off the jewel.

The setting of this photograph is one I've come to love. It looks west over Lake Winona, taken from the streetcar bridge, with a fog bank at the edge that never lifted through the day, transforming it into a vista where nothing breaks the eye beyond but sea. The lake really isn't a lake, just a portion of alluvial plain formed by the Mississippi and fed by cold streams below the bluffs. I often walked along the lake on weekend mornings.

I took this photo as an evening view.

It's a landscape piece. One has less control over the elements in a landscape setting. The context is created by the seasons or the time of day, the entrance of canoes that slide like slender fingers across a frosted cake. In this photograph, taken with my Graflex, the sun has played its part in shining through a cloud opening and then reflecting on the water. The clouds hang low, making it look as though one could see across the lake into forever. I guess I like it most because it reminds me of my hopeful dreams.

Outdoor settings have special challenges, and FJ always questioned my ability to manage them. He preferred the studio, where he was master over the elements. I liked the excitement of not always knowing the results until the plate was developed.

Results are all about circumstances. In another setting, the outcome might have been different, but this was Winona in 1909. I decided that I couldn't leave him while he suffered the reoccurrence of his mercury poisoning, this scourge of a photographer's life.

Circumstances ruled us those many months of his poisoning. I wondered how Mrs. Bauer endured with his illness, the toddler, and two other children to care for. How was the ranch managed? He'd been unable to travel west to handle the harvest. I wondered what the setting of his ranch was. The paper said it was not too far from Bismarck, south in Emmons County near a little town called Hazelton. I'd seen landscape paintings of the Black Hills and a painting of former president Roosevelt's cabin there. It seemed a comely place, lush with trees and tall grasses. I especially liked the Russian olives that bloomed so full beside the president's hunting lodge. I imagined their sweet scent and restful setting for FJ's farm, wishing for his sake that he could have gone there to recuperate.

He told me once while we leaned over the printer in the darkroom that his ranch had once been grassland. He'd grazed eight hundred head of cattle there, but an accidental fire started by a neighbor burned the prairie. He lost most of the cattle, the home, and was even injured. So he became a farmer rather than a rancher, as those with cattle called themselves. But that was before my time.

It must have challenged him to allow others to do his work for him.

When Voe and I ran the studio while he suffered with pneumonia, we did it with very little help from Mrs. Bauer. She served as our liaison for maintaining the business. This time she preferred not to be a part of things at all. She had so much on her mind. She said she was too busy with his care and the baby's, and she didn't feel well.

We didn't have much to discuss. We needed her signature for our pay statements. I collected that twice a month, and beyond that we seldom saw her.

If we couldn't run the studio well for him, for the Bauers, maybe they'd sell out here in Winona and head west. The demand for wheat across the country lured hundreds, who purchased railroad-owned properties to populate the West or took advantage of the new government programs that offered one hundred sixty acres free to those who *proved it up. "Big Horn Basin Excursions" were offered by Burlington on the first and third Tuesdays of each month. People could travel with a land agent to Yellowstone and Big Horn Basin, Wyoming, look at potential property, walk through all the steps to make their claim, then come back to tell their families they'd be ranchers in the West.*

I'd actually thought about doing that, but I didn't want to make my life in the hard labor of farming. I still had my own dream.

I didn't see Winnie or Russell during those months we ran the studio, and I found I missed them. Their absence marked the end of something I couldn't quite name.

I asked FJ to help me print this shot when he returned. My efforts had yielded too much white in the clouds, which somehow phased out the brightness of the warming sun. Or I'd get the cloud part of the setting perfect but instead have no shine on the water. I'm not sure how he did it, but in the area around the cloud opening, he brought a brightness that sparkled as though tipped with sequins from a woman's fancy dress. When I commented about that, he told me to look closer. It wasn't the edge of the opening that sparkled but rather smaller clouds that the sun had picked up in its descent. I hadn't noticed. He'd brought out something in the photograph that I'd not seen when I happened to snap the shot. He'd also brought out something in me that wasn't a part of the setting I'd arranged for my life. But that's another part of the story.

The sunset photograph always reminds me of the ends of things. The end of winter, the end of girlhood. But its setting also suggested beginnings. No sun sets without rising somewhere else. No river flows without taking in new rains. Lake Winona, an example of beginnings and ends, was once deserted by the Mississippi River. But it found new life in those spring-giving bluffs.

Thirteen

Making Amends

In some ways, taking responsibility for the studio was different for Jessie than it had been before. Previously, Mr. Bauer had recovered in three months; the girls hadn't yet finished their training, so they'd listened carefully to Mrs. Bauer's messages from Mr. Bauer. Jessie no longer believed Mrs. Bauer had been accurate in her representation of his concerns, and she couldn't understand why the woman would say he'd complained when he hadn't. But this time, in the fall of 1909, Mr. Bauer's absence from the studio was likely to be six months at a minimum and possibly a year and a half. The girls would have to deal with every aspect of the business, unable to put something aside or defer to Mrs. Bauer, as she'd made it quite clear she was too occupied to assist them. They were on their own.

Jessie felt a bit anxious about doing well, lest the studio go under; at the same time, the independence tingled her skin like the icy winds when she walked beside the river. She felt invigorated and alive, ready for the new challenges that began shortly after they assumed their new responsibilities.

A Mr. D. Henderson sent a postcard to the Bauer Studio. It bore a picture of the Sugar Loaf drive and had been beautifully tinted. Jessie turned it over and read that it was printed exclusively for S. H. Knox & Co. Then she read the message. *Mr. Bauer, I have called at your office several times to see you about the framed picture, as it is unsatisfactory. Will call tomorrow, Wednesday, about 2 p.m.* It was signed "D. Henderson" and was addressed to "Mr. Bauer. Studio. City."

Jessie looked up D. Henderson in the city directory but didn't find him. Of course the directory wasn't published every year, so he might have moved in recently. She couldn't remember anyone coming by with that name, though a couple of people who asked for Mr. Bauer wouldn't tell her what they wanted to discuss with him. She imagined dealing with a woman wasn't always a comfort to a gentleman, so she hadn't pushed them, even though she'd stated clearly that Mr. Bauer was indisposed and it was uncertain when he'd be able to return.

Jessie called Mrs. Bauer about Mr. Henderson, one of the few calls initiated to her.

"Handle it as you must," she told Jessie. "I can't be bothered."

"How is Mr. Bauer feeling? Is he—"

"It's the usual. He's ill. He needs care. I have a baby. Winnie needs lessons. Russell is doing his best to take care of things here. I'm not well myself. Not well at all." She hung up.

Jessie felt bad for the Bauers. She wondered if she should talk to her parents about finding some way to assist them. It couldn't be easy. But the

Bauers had resources others didn't have, to hire a nurse perhaps, get someone to shovel snow when it came. The best Jessie could do was to keep the business solvent and hope Mr. Bauer recovered soon.

She felt sorry for Mr. Bauer because of the postcard too. People would have read that postcard coming through the mail, and gossip had its own system in Winona. If you wanted to know who was visiting whom or where they were, you could just ask the postman. It was expected. The phone system modeled that as well. The phone operator knew when the doctor left one person's home and just how long it would take for him to get to the next, and she could convey that when people tried to catch him between appointments, or she could cause everyone to wonder what he'd been doing if he didn't arrive in a timely manner.

The postcard about an unhappy client might mushroom into a terrible mess. It must have been a portrait Mr. Bauer had done months before, as neither girl recognized the name nor remembered any-

one complaining about a framed portrait. Mr. Henderson sounded upset on
the postcard. Jessie took a deep breath,
looked at the large wall clock as it approached two o'clock. She would learn
to handle it. It was part of the setting
she'd accepted.

As she waited, she thought about
Mrs. Bauer's reaction to her call. Mrs.
Bauer didn't dismiss her concern and
hadn't told them how Mr. Bauer was
feeling either. Not that she was required
to, but just the same, it would be nice to
know if Mr. Bauer had made progress
and might return in six months or if this
time he'd have to be away for much
longer. Sometimes Jessie didn't understand people.

Her sister Lilly, for example. Her parents had agreed with Jessie's decision
to remain at the studio after she told
them what had happened. "It's the
Christian thing to do," her father had
said.

"Jessie will be fine," her mother had
reassured Lilly over the supper table.

"It's even worse," Lilly complained.
"Now there'll be two girls there, alone.

Any number of people can come by, and who knows what might happen. She should work for Ralph Carleton."

Jessie bristled. "First you tell me I'm not safe with Mr. Bauer around; now you tell me I'm not safe without him."

"Not him. But some man. Security is very important for a woman, Jessie. You'll understand that one day; I only hope it doesn't happen in a difficult way."

Lilly hadn't been concerned when Jessie worked all by herself at the cycle shop, where Selma labored alone now. She thought to say something about it but decided to let the rancor go. Uncertainty came with a working woman's territory; she'd have to learn to handle it—and her sister's reaction—when or if trouble came around.

Jessie hoped it wouldn't present itself in the name of one D. Henderson.

Mr. Henderson arrived on time and turned out to be a gruff young man unhappy with everything, from the distance he'd had to walk to get to the studio to the framed photograph Mr. Bauer had taken of him some time before.

When he stomped in, Jessie realized she had seen him when he'd come by the studio a few weeks earlier. But he'd insisted on speaking with Mr. Bauer and wouldn't leave his name or tell her what he was concerned about. Even when she'd told him that Mr. Bauer wasn't available and had offered to help him, he wouldn't say what he needed. Jessie wondered if the postcard was a deliberate attempt to smear Mr. Bauer's name, or perhaps he just couldn't believe that two young women were managing a photo studio on their own. His belligerent stance made Jessie step behind the desk as she dealt with him.

There had been problems in other studios. Just this past September, someone had broken into Van Vranken's. The thief had been arrested and sent to the reform school in Red Wing. The incident was a reminder to Jessie to keep the shop locked at night and take any cash she had immediately to the bank at the end of each day. Remembering Lilly's concerns, Jessie changed her routine, as sometimes she had more than twenty dollars in the satchel. That would be a goodly catch for a desperate someone who might pay attention to predictability.

Jessie and Voe faced this man with blond hair and blue eyes and shoulders nearly as wide as the door. He held the framed portrait in his hand and lifted it up like a battle shield. From his accent and the addition of *then* at the end of some of his sentences, she knew he was Scandinavian.

"I need it changed, then. I can't spend hard-earned money on a picture that looks more like my father than me."

Jessie pointed out the advantages of the portrait and how well it had been rendered. The lighting and exposure were perfect. She didn't say that the portrait actually improved upon his looks, though it did. It was a perfect likeness when he stopped his snarling and took another breath before complaining again, which stilled his face. She tried not so much arguing as being clear and firm, something she'd read was important for a professional woman. She stood as tall as her five feet two inches allowed.

But her protests agitated him further. It was Voe who calmed him.

"It's the proportions that aren't right," Voe said. "Isn't that so, Mr. Henderson?"

"*Ja,*" he barked. He turned the picture around and jabbed his stubby finger at it. "*Ja.* That just might be what's wrong, then."

Jessie didn't agree that the proportions were wrong, but it was the first time he'd agreed with anything. The tone of his voice was less outraged than when Jessie had tried to convince him that he'd gotten value for his money. She needed to accept that he didn't like it and try to discover what might make it right for him so he wouldn't go sending bad postcards through the mail or telling his friends to go elsewhere.

"What if we put a mat around the picture?" Jessie proposed. "It would require a larger frame that way, but it would set off your face rather nicely, don't you think?"

"I'm not likely to pay for the larger frame," he said.

"I think we can work that out," Voe told him. "Can't we, Miss Gaebele?"

"Of course, Miss Kopp." She turned to Mr. Henderson and smiled. "We'd offer you the larger frame and mat and the labor for it at no additional charge."

It meant a cost to the studio, but it would save the loss of the total fee and give them a happy customer if he accepted the solution.

Voe took the man to the area where the frames were stored while Jessie considered possible mat colors that might complement the photograph. Voe spent quite a long time showing him frames with gold trim and others with smooth wood. *He'll probably pick the most expensive one,* Jessie thought, but it would still be better than losing the sale. Jessie heard laughter from him while she worked on the invoices for the week until finally they settled on the frame he wanted. Most of the cabinet portraits didn't have mats around them, so what Jessie had proposed was inventive.

But it was Voe who had named the man's discomfort, Voe who had listened to the words behind his concerns. He didn't want to look bad; he didn't want to pay for something that he thought did; he wanted a way to accept the portrait while being able to say to anyone who might question the "proportion" that he'd made a fine bargain by receiving such a handsome frame and matting with it as well.

With the chosen frame, Jessie shared her choices of matting, and Mr. Henderson was mollified. Voe had charmed him. She could learn from her friend. Voe's curling-ironed hair bore a wave up over her forehead, and she had high color on her cheeks when she brought Mr. Henderson back to the front. He said he'd return the following week to pick up his newly matted and framed portrait.

"We'll have it ready," Jessie said. "Just come by on Friday. You needn't send a postcard. We'll be expecting you."

Voe gave Jessie a frown, and Mr. Henderson dropped his eyes. "*Ja,* I was very upset. I should have just called, to say I was coming."

Jessie could have bitten her tongue for having brought up the postcard. He'd been ready to leave a happy customer, and now she'd mentioned something that might remind him of his earlier grievance. She sought a way to put him back on top.

"Was it having to talk to a . . . woman?" Jessie asked. "I can see where that might have been troubling."

"Ja." He had a sheepish grin. "A man doesn't like to show his bad side to a woman."

"But you don't have a bad side," Voe corrected. "It was just the proportion, remember?"

"A man's bad side of being taken advantage of, then," he said. "I didn't want that to be seen that way by anyone, but especially a woman."

"You're very helpful," Jessie told him. "Thank you. We'll attend better to others who might have concerns—not that we have many. Most really are pleased with our work."

"Next time maybe I'll have Miss Kopp take my picture," he said.

Voe smiled. "I don't do the portraits. I

just help Mr. Bauer and now Miss Gaebele, so you'd have to sit for her. But I'd
help choose the setting and the props
and pose you," she said.

Jessie hoped he wouldn't decide that
he wanted a totally new portrait now.
They'd worked out a solution. She'd recovered from her own stumble, and she
hoped to move him out the door.

"I'm pleased we found an agreeable
solution for *this* portrait," Jessie said.

"*Ja.* Agreeable," Mr. Henderson said.

"So we'll see you next week," Jessie
said and opened the door.

"You'll see me at five o'clock," he told
her. Jessie started to protest. There was
no way they could prepare the portrait
by then, but he continued, "I'll be escorting Miss Kopp home, if she allows
it."

"Then or anytime," Voe told him. She
curtsied and dropped her eyes. He
tipped his cap to her and left.

Voe had already turned eighteen and
was considered a legal woman by Minnesota law. She could do what she
wanted without asking her mother's approval and without tongues wagging if

she was to be seen alone with a beau. Even Jessie could see the spark between them.

"That was fast," Jessie said.

"We did get it worked out in record time, didn't we?"

"That wasn't the fast I was speaking of."

"The walk home? That'll be right smart," she said. "Maybe on the weekend we'll hike up Bluffside Park's new trail. I hear the views are worthy of a picture."

"Won't your other beaus be jealous?"

"Oh, Jessie, you're the only girl I know who doesn't have at least one beau. Having a dozen keeps a girl in motion. It's better than your long walks for exercising."

Jessie laughed.

"Truly. You have to be out there swimming or all the fish will pass you right by."

"I'm not interested in fishing," Jessie said.

"Me neither. It's the catching I like."

"Beaus interfere with my path."

"You want to know what I think?" Voe said.

Jessie pushed her glasses up on her nose. "Not really."

"I'll tell you anyway." She followed Jessie, who carried the frame into the back room. "You think getting Mr. B. to pay attention to you is enough. He'll help you with your career, teach you what he knows, keep you employed all right, but he'll keep you from finding the right man."

Jessie scoffed. "I'm not looking for a right man. I just want to learn more about photography, and this is a great chance for any girl interested in how a photograph comes together to form beauty."

"He might just keep you from learning more about photography too," Voe said.

Jessie turned to face her. "I don't see how."

Voe sighed. "What will you do when he returns? I bet you'll stay working for him for the rest of your life, claiming you're learning, but really you're playing it safe. You'll be independent and lonely, all because you wouldn't find a real beau. Small, bird-boned girls like you are always treated sweet as ice cream. You're used to pampering, Jessie. Your uncle August and even Mr. B. have kept you from—"

"I just like being in control," Jessie said.

"You like standing back, looking through a lens. You stay out of the picture that way."

"So you say," Jessie said and turned away.

She wasn't sure if she was more annoyed by the closeness of Voe's predictions to Lilly's or the possibility that they could both be right.

>→+◆→─O─◄+→─◄

FJ watched the spots on the back of his hands. They didn't waver. Same size. Same dark pink color, darker than the scars on his arms where he'd been burned in the prairie fire the year that Donald died. Eventually those scars on his forearms had faded, though they still reminded him of ridges, like the barbed wires that surrounded the ranch. But the backs of his hands and blotches over his chest and on his feet were bright as the Christmas berries he'd watched Russell and Winnie string around the tree.

He wanted to call the studio, just to see how things were going there, but he knew if he did, and if he sensed turmoil or problems, he'd want to pay a visit, help settle things, and he couldn't. He just couldn't.

He had other worries. He'd gotten a letter from his North Dakota partner, Herman Reinke, who said he planned to invest in some Canadian land. Everyone wanted to expand, but his partner's suggestion that they join a group of other businessmen to purchase more cropland disturbed him. They could manage what they had, or rather Herman could, with FJ's help. Herman was a day-to-day detail partner; FJ understood the bigger picture. The market for wheat was good now, but with the expansion of the Homestead Act, more and more people would be putting land into production across the plains, and there could well be a market glut if people weren't careful. He had planted flax too. Maybe he should have insisted on more flax, but Herman was closer to the soil and FJ held back his concern.

FJ intended to write to Herman about his objections, but he had no energy. It was the worst part about this illness, having to lie for hours doing nothing because he didn't have the strength to even sit up in bed and read. Not that he could read. The disease affected his eyes as well, and he'd been told to protect them. What good was a photographer, named a diplomat in the National Photographic Association, who couldn't use his eyes?

He couldn't ask Mrs. Bauer to transcribe a letter he might dictate. She could barely sustain caring for the baby. Some days Robert seemed to cry a very long time before Mrs. Bauer went to the child and picked him up. Or maybe he was colicky and nothing seemed to comfort. Sometimes she brought the boy in and laid him next to FJ, saying, "I just need a moment alone."

He nodded. She didn't have to scream. He welcomed the infant even if he cried. He would caress the boy's head, feel the velvet of his tiny ears, let the boy's fingers wrap around his own. Robert sat up by himself now, and FJ had to be careful that the boy didn't roll or crawl too close to the side of the narrow bed and fall off. When Russell came home from school, FJ would have him line up pillows around the side to keep Robert from crawling too far out of range. Winnie sometimes joined them too. She looked at books, rolled balls to the boy, and then when Robert tired, Winnie seemed to as well, and they would lie haphazard on the blankets beside him and sleep.

If he felt up to it, he and his oldest son would talk about the boy's day. He even thought of asking Russell to write the letter to Reinke for him, but he could not. Somehow he had to protect his children from the worries of adults, at least for a time. Russell had already assumed more responsibility than FJ wanted for a ten-year-old, and both of his older children were having to deal with sickly and often irritable parents.

Parents. Yes. They were both ill. He didn't know what to make of Mrs.

Bauer's present lack of personal care. Her hair looked as ratted as a hawk's nest, and she'd worn the same apron for several days now, stained with the meals she and Russell prepared. FJ couldn't understand what was happening. He'd been ill before, but she'd managed that. Maybe with three children it was just too much. Had she ever really recovered from the birth of Robert? She'd lost weight, as expected, but now that he thought of it, she looked thinner than she'd ever been, her arms like chicken legs. Her eyes sometimes looked out at him with a vacant raccoon gaze.

If he had the energy, he would call the doctor for her.

It would be something he should do to border and protect. He could still do that much. He made his way to the phone.

>─┤◆▷─O─◁◆┤─<

What had she forgotten? Something . . . To take the diapers from the pail where they soaked in bleach. She'd put Robert's Ruben shirts in there too, hadn't she? The strings that tied at the front were easier to manage than buttoned shirts. He was probably outgrowing them, but she couldn't do anything about that. She couldn't even order clothing from the catalog, and she certainly couldn't sew things. Her hands didn't want to move the way they were supposed to. Maybe she'd become afflicted by Mr. Bauer's disease. Or maybe during those years of holding the brushes of ink in her mouth while she retouched, she'd taken on some sort of chemical illness too. She looked at her hands. No blotches. What had she done with her ring? She'd taken it off when she brushed her teeth this morning. Had she brushed her teeth?

Mrs. Bauer's thoughts raced like rats around a basement post. In the water closet, she looked at the Rubifoam bottle. The cap was off. She must have brushed her teeth, but her tongue felt thick as woolen socks on a hot summer day, and her teeth—she ran her tongue around them—were coated with sawdust. She knew it couldn't be sawdust, but it felt grainy like that. She saw her wedding ring lying on the stand beside the sink. She shook her head. She was so forgetful. She hoped she hadn't forgotten to feed Robert. She no longer nursed him; she'd become so thin. But she had fixed his cereal this morning, hadn't she?

"Mrs. Bauer." It was her husband calling her yet again to bring him something, do something, fix something. She wasn't capable. On the day they met, she'd told him that she wasn't a strong woman. She'd never lied to him about it. But now he made demands she couldn't possibly meet. Thank goodness for Russell. Thank goodness for Donald.

No, there was no more Donald. He'd died on that terrible ranch that her husband refused to sell. How could he return there each year? How could he go back to the place where he'd failed their son, failed him as sure as if the child had been forgotten? At least his illness prevented that betrayal.

What had she forgotten?

The baby. She had to get the baby

from her husband. He was crying, a strange sort of wail that sounded like a shrill bell almost. No, that was the bell she'd given to her husband to ring if he needed her. Was that what she'd forgotten? The sound of the bell? If only she could get a good night's sleep. That would help. Otherwise she was simply no good, had nothing to offer, nothing to give. It would be better if she just sank into the ground. But she'd probably forget that's what she intended and make extra work for someone finding her frozen in place.

>--+>-O-<+--<

Jessie's eye caught the barren branches of the elm as she turned the corner near the Bauer home. Snow formed drifts at the stone walls and hedges that lined the street. She and Mrs. Bauer had worked out an arrangement for the girls to receive their checks: Jessie would send a kind of invoice noting the girls' hours for pay. Mrs. Bauer would sign the checks kept at their home and send them back. It had worked for several months, but it was now almost the tenth of January 1910, and they had yet to receive their pay.

"I could go over there," Voe told her. "Or I'll have Daniel do it." She and Mr. Henderson were on a first-name basis now. "Daniel would like to help. What's the good of having a beau if he can't protect a girl in distress?" Voe said.

"Mrs. Bauer has a lot to think about," Jessie said. "I doubt she'd welcome Daniel's visit."

"Could it have been lost in the mail, then?" Voe wondered.

Voe must be spending a lot of time with Mr. Henderson, more than his just coming by to walk her home. She'd started to sound like him.

"No one answered the phone when I called. Maybe it's off the hook so they can rest. After our last sitting today, I'll walk over to see what I can find out."

The afternoon photo session finished early, so Jessie donned her hat and scarf, struggled with the rubber boots that fit over her high-top shoes, pulled the hooks on her warm coat, and headed out. The sky reflected the white world she stepped into. Her breath fogged before her; freezing air bit at her throat. Despite the cold day, people dotted the street, shopping, picking up supplies for the week. Jessie liked the bustle of Winona's life. It reminded her of the street carnivals Uncle August took them to each September. The festivals brought color and movement to a city that otherwise could seem ordinary and plain. Uncle August. He'd intervene for her, if he were around. It would be nice to have a champion. She clucked her tongue. She sounded like Selma and her romance novels.

This day, dirty snowdrifts crowded the street gutters and blocked the wind and view from across the street as Jessie walked. Looking right, she was flanked by a corridor of crystal white; looking left, drifts reflected in the store windows behind dresses and draperies, powders and pins. A white eyelet dress caught Jessie's eye in Choate's window. She hesitated, then stepped inside.

The clerk took her coat, and Jessie held the dress up to herself, spinning around as she did. It was beautiful. If she could just squeeze twenty-five cents a week, it would be hers in time for summer. The idea of it made her feel happy and independent. She tried it on. It fit like one of Lilly's tailored dresses. Impulsively, she gave the clerk fifty cents and told her to set the dress aside. She'd pay on the first of each month. It was a risky commitment considering she hadn't been paid yet this month.

Back on the street, she silenced the twinge of guilt that nudged at her stomach. She dragged her mittened hand along the snowbanks, making a horizontal trail with her fingers. Though this weather bit at her skin, Jessie liked knowing there were seasons. A dreary, biting-cold time would be followed by long days of summer and canoe rides on the lake. Shadows slipped along behind her hand. She stopped. It would make an interesting picture. If she only had a decent camera, something even further from her grasp with the purchase she'd just made. Maybe she'd go back and get her money. That nubbin of regret gnawed deeper for having indulged an impulse. But the dress did look lovely on her.

She stopped walking. Here she was without a paycheck, hoping to assist with Roy's trip and one day have a decent camera, and she'd just bought an elegant dress she really had no place to wear.

She'd go back later, get the money back.

Still, she'd be eighteen in a month, and it might be a present to give herself. Roy's trip was scheduled for March if the weather cooperated, and after that she'd be free to save for the 3A Graflex. Even Lilly had said every person deserved to achieve her desires.

She picked up her pace, then climbed the icy stone steps to the Bauer home. A low stone wall defined the porch across the front, and Jessie removed her mittens and struck them against the porch stones, knocking off loose little balls of snow that had accumulated on the wool. She laid her mittens on the wide railing to dry out, then pushed the doorbell.

She heard the bleating sound of the

bell. Nothing happened. She pushed it again. She turned around. Someone had shoveled a path through the snow, but the walkway hadn't been salted and there weren't any snowmen sitting in the yard, no evidence that children had been out playing beneath an opaque sky. She stepped closer and put her ear to the door. No sounds. Russell would be in school, but she ought to hear Winnie and the baby making noises. No footsteps approached. Maybe they had all gone to the doctor, though it was more likely the doctor made home visits to the Bauers'. She walked around to the back of the house, hoping someone was in the kitchen. She knocked. No answer. As she turned to go back to the front, she saw that the door to a shed was open, and there sat one of those new automobiles! *They must have had a good harvest in the fall in North Dakota,* she thought.

Back at the front, she rang the bell once again, knocked, tried the latch. The door was unlocked. She stepped inside. "Mrs. Bauer? Are you here? Mr. Bauer?" She'd never been any farther into the house than the foyer, but now she looked into the living room on the right, a dining area on the left. She expected she'd find the kitchen beyond that and two bedrooms downstairs, other bedrooms upstairs. She wouldn't go any farther than the hall. That would be intrusive. She called out once again, and this time she heard a bell sounding from upstairs. It maintained a frantic clang.

"Mrs. Bauer?"

The bell rang out again. She followed the sound up the stairs.

>−·−◆−○−◇−·−≺

FJ sat at his desk in the bedroom wearing pants and a striped shirt that really needed washing. His wife had taken the children to her mother's at his request. He could see she was deteriorating. She wasn't sleeping, wasn't eating well, and taking care of all of them had taken its toll on her. He needed to hire a helper, someone who could stay here and look after the children at least. It would make things tight—but then he'd bought Henry Ford's car for eight hundred dollars as a Christmas gift, had it delivered. He didn't yet know how to drive it himself, but he'd learn. Something to look forward to. It would make life easier on them all. Still, a hired girl was what they needed now.

He heard the doorbell and knew he should go down, but the fatigue still captured him, pulled at his throat when he tried to catch his breath. It must be a girl answering the ad he'd run. He'd been dressed and ready and started to go downstairs but tired with the effort. He was sitting, working up the courage to stand again, when he heard the door open and someone call out his name. He choked at trying to shout back a hello, started ringing his bell instead. Then he heard the footsteps on the stairs. "Mrs. Bauer?" It was Jessie! Surely she wasn't planning to apply.

"Miss Gaebele," he croaked out as he took a full breath. "Wait."

She stepped into the doorway.

He could tell by the look on her face that he must look terrible. A tired old man. He stood and leaned one hand on the desk. She'd changed since he saw her last. Confidence was a woman's finest perfume, he thought. She pushed her glasses up on her nose.

"If you'll . . . I'll meet you downstairs," he said.

"Oh. Of course. I just . . . I heard the bell and no one said anything, so I—"

"Please," he said, motioning her out into the hallway. She retreated and he followed, closed the door behind them. "I think. If you'll assist me. The banister . . ."

"Take my arm," she told him. "Do you have your cane?"

"Down . . . stairs," he said.

The girl took his arm, and her hand felt firm and warm despite the fact that she wore no gloves or mittens. He'd have to ask her about that, but right now it took too much for him to speak. She smelled of the snow, refreshing after months of stale house air. They made their way back down the stairs, and she chattered on about the weather. It was too hard to listen. Putting one foot in front of the other required all his concentration. They reached the entry hall, and he took the chair by the small fireplace. She immediately went to start the fire, giving him a chance to collect himself, he supposed. She was chattering. "What did you say . . . about . . . your wages?"

"I stopped by to see if something had happened because Mrs. Bauer didn't send us our pay at the end of December. I tried to call but couldn't reach anyone. You're all busy, I know. And you"— she unbuttoned her coat, removed it, and laid it across the chair—"don't look well at all. Would you like tea? I'll just fix us some."

"I'll . . . sign the checks. Upstairs, I'll get . . ." He tried to stand. He looked for his cane.

"Nonsense. Tell me where they are, and I'll get them for you. After I make the tea."

She helped him move toward the kitchen, finished putting water in the teakettle, lit the fire under the gas stove, and set the kettle on to heat. He watched her while she worked, his cane now in his hand. Such smooth movements she had, yet busy and efficient. "There," she said. "Now if you'll direct me. I assume that your family will be home soon to look after you."

"Russell," he said. "He's helping."

"But where are Mrs. Bauer and the baby? Oh," she said, dropping her eyes. "It's none of my affair. I'll get what I came for and leave you in peace."

"I . . . like having you here," he said.

"No trouble."

"Good." *She's waiting for something.* "Oh, the checks . . . In the bedroom desk. Third drawer down. Left. Bring an ink pen too."

The girl—the young woman—pushed past him, and he smelled her lavender scent, wasn't sure but that the air she pushed as she walked by him wasn't the most refreshing breeze he'd felt in months.

⤳⟶◯⟵⤝

Jessie took the steps quickly and decided that was why she stood breathless at the door of his room. The covers on his bed were crumpled, and she could almost see the indentation of where his body had been. She felt her face grow warm with that awareness. A cigar leaned into a china plate on the chamber stand next to the bed, and beyond that, a small table held a bowl and pitcher. His interest in Indian artifacts showed in the small rug colored with triangular designs. Prints of birds and hunting dogs lined the wall. A photograph of Mrs. Bauer hung alone near the bay window, the dark frame accented against the yellow wall. It had been taken when she was younger. She was beautiful. Across from it was a portrait with Russell and Winnie. Robert was yet too young to hold still for his addition to the family sittings.

She wanted to walk nearer to the bed, just to see what book he'd been reading. But she didn't. Still, from where she stood she noticed that the pillow didn't show an indentation. It wasn't one of the expensive feather-filled ones. He didn't splurge on his own comfort. She turned to the desk centered in the bay window and sat down on the chair, bent to the drawer. She found the ledger book and checks. She paused at the page, curious about what sort of expenses a family like his might have, but she'd intruded enough; she picked up the checks as planned.

She saw herself framed in the oval mirror as she closed the drawer and stood. Her face was flushed. *From the stairs.* She looked behind her toward the bed. It was a single bed. He slept alone.

>–+–‹›–O–‹›–+–‹

FJ wrote the checks as Miss Gaebele sat and sipped her tea. She chattered on about studio activities and that her father was talking about the Sixteenth Amendment and wondered how congress's levying taxes would affect the business. "I know you can't talk right now. But when you're better, it'll be interesting to see what you think."

"Not. Much," he said.

"Have you seen the Hine books?" He shook his head. "They're almost all photographs, and they tell the stories of the terrible child labor activities in the Carolinas. There's another that's called *Day Laborers Before Their Time.* It's all about the injustices of children working so young. But the books are full of photographs and very few words! The library

just got them even though they were
published last year. Imagine, using photography to teach and help people understand problems."

"You think it will change things?" he
asked, surprised he'd gotten it out in
one breath. Maybe all he needed was a
good cup of tea.

"Once we know something, it's pretty
difficult to keep going on in the same
old way, don't you think?"

She was probably right.

"I really should be going. Thanks for
the tea and for writing the checks. I
hope Mrs. Bauer won't be upset that I
came and asked for them."

"Every right to," he told her. He was
aware as she stood that he hated to see
her leave. *I'd probably wish the gar-
bageman to stay awhile if he made hot
tea and talked.*

"It looks like it will be some time yet
before you're back at the studio," she
said.

He turned his hands over. The spots
had lessened, but they weren't gone.
And he was exceptionally tired. He'd
had a spurt in the fall of feeling im-

proved and imagined himself taking the train to the Dakota ranch to draw in the healthful fresh air there. He dreamed of sitting with his back against the white wall of the house, basking in the sun, staring out at the unbroken line of fields for as far as he could see. Herman had taken a portion of his share to invest in that Canadian land. But not FJ. It was enough responsibility to turn the earth as it had never been turned before, under a plow, and hope that growing food for the masses justified the drastic changes they'd made to the landscape. But he knew the trip would have exhausted him, and he'd come down with pneumonia anyway and was only now getting beyond it.

She had her coat on now. Must have been speaking, but he didn't hear what she said; he was daydreaming. He didn't want her to leave. She brought such pleasure into his life.

That was unacceptable. He knew it wasn't what he should be thinking.

"I didn't hear," he said.

"There's someone at the door," she said. "Shall I see who it is?"

He nodded and she swished past him. He heard the door open.

"Mama! Selma!"

"I thought those looked like mittens I had knitted. Child, what are you doing here, answering the Bauers' door?"

FOURTEEN

Roy's Ride

Jessie's explanation continued over the supper table with all her family in attendance. "I simply went there to get our paychecks when Mrs. Bauer forgot to send them. I expected her to be there. When she wasn't, Mr. Bauer wrote them. That's all."

"You were alone with Mr. Bauer in his house," Lilly said.

Not only alone with her employer in his house but nearly alone with him in his bedroom. Nothing had happened, she wanted to say to Lilly, but didn't.

"Selma will be alone sometimes too," Jessie said, "if he hires her to work for them. It was just a complication of the day, nothing more. You're making much of nothing, Lilly. Mama's settled with it, aren't you, Mama?"

Roy burped. Jessie wondered how he could do that at will. "I guess *you're* not settled, are you, Frog?" Roy grinned.

"I certainly did not expect to see my own daughter answering the doorbell," her mother said. "And when he showed us the house, I noticed two cups of tea on the table."

"Maybe leftover from before his wife left to visit her mother?" This from Selma. Jessie smiled. Her younger sister was trying to be helpful.

Jessie debated, then said, "The second cup was mine. I had to get the checks for him and he was so weak, so I just fixed a pot of tea. It's a really nice teapot, didn't you think, Selma? Not heavy like our cast-iron one but made of—"

"Porcelain," her mother finished.

"If I get the job, maybe he'll come pick me up in their new car. I saw it parked in the back," Selma said. "The shed door was open. I wasn't prying, Papa."

Jessie turned the discussion to Lilly. "Maybe you'll be making new clothes now for women who ride in cars. I saw a picture in the *Companion* magazine of special veils for hats worn in autos. And they suggested one always travel with a cucumber for wrinkles."

Jessie hoped she'd directed the conversation away from her tea with Mr. Bauer. But no.

"You had tea with him," Lilly said, shaking her finger at her. "A woman alone in the kitchen of her employer, a man. He ought to have known better than to do that. He doesn't have your best interests at heart, Jessie. What if word gets out? What will Mrs. Bauer say?"

"I might slip and tell her," Selma said, some alarm in her voice.

Jessie didn't want Selma to worry about anything. Everyone was stoking a fire that had no heat. "It wouldn't be a slip. There's no reason you couldn't tell Mrs. Bauer that I sat in the kitchen on a day when I came to pick up my wages. I simply did a kindness for an ill man and took the burden from her, getting our wages. Now she won't have to worry about that."

"Are you going to pick them up every week?" Lilly asked.

"If we don't receive them, I might."

Lilly folded her linen napkin ever so carefully, placed it beside her plate. "Sister, I think you're fluffing goose feathers in a pillow that isn't yours."

"Mr. Bauer doesn't use goose-down pillows on his bed," Jessie snapped. "They weren't crumpled enough."

Her mother choked on the piece of rutabaga she'd just placed in her mouth. "Jessie Ann Gaebele, I will see you in the parlor. You too, Mr. Gaebele."

"M-m-me?" Roy asked. He started to stand.

"Your father," Jessie's mother corrected.

Jessie and her father followed meekly after. Whatever had her loose tongue done now?

>-+<>-O-<+-+-<

Mrs. Bauer had just finished putting Robert to bed. Both of the other children were in their rooms, and she could hear nothing from them. That was good. She was too tired to deal with any of it. Her mother had her own aches and pains, and Mrs. Bauer ended up looking after yet one more person in need. She'd insisted that her mother bring her home, and they'd ridden in one of those cars belonging to a friend of her mother's. Now they even had an automobile and there it sat, with Mr. Bauer too ill to run it and her not knowing how.

She did admit that the ride had been pleasant—except for the way the wind blew at her face and the smelly smoke the automobile burped out and the way that horses startled on the street and the incredible jerking that occurred when they crossed over the streetcar tracks. She might get used to it, but she wasn't sure when. Russell had been delighted. They'd been dropped off just as he came home from school, and her mother's friend had agreed to drive him around the block. The boy chattered at her ears when he came inside until she pressed her hands to them and shouted for him to stop. He'd bowed his head and she hated herself for that, but she didn't mend what she'd done. She had no glue for that.

Now the two of them, she and Mr. Bauer, were in a discussion, though her mind wandered. "I thought it would be helpful." Her husband spoke. *Oh yes, about the girl he's hired and my worry over the finances of that.*

"I should be grateful you were thinking of me, is that it? How old is she?"

"Thirteen or so," he said. "She's been working. At Steffes's, for two years already."

"Surely not full-time. Isn't she still in school?"

"Finished. Isn't going on to the high school. Family. Needs money. Good people. You know that."

"I guess that will be fine, not that I have much say in things. I worry about the money. I hope she's strong. Is she a big girl?"

He shook his head. "But sturdy. I imagine like her sisters. Responsible." Mr. Bauer took a deep breath. "I wanted to be helpful. I can pay the wages. Write the weekly—"

"I didn't pay your shop girls!" Her hands flew to her face. "I forgot. I'm so sorry. I can't do anything right." She felt herself in that swamp of unworthiness, though the moment before she'd been irritated, frustrated that it had taken him so long to hire a girl. Why did she always argue, raise financial issues? They could obviously afford a hired girl since he had that splurge of a Ford vehicle in the shed. She supposed he'd start calling it his "garage" now and want one built on the property in St. Charles, where he'd invested in yet another cottage after the successful fall harvest. Last year someone had flown one of those aeroplanes across the English Channel. She supposed Mr. Bauer would want one of those next! She inhaled. Sometimes that stopped the racing of her mind, the fear that grabbed at her throat and threatened to suffocate her.

"I took care of it," he told her. "The wages."

"Did you mail them? I could take them tomorrow." She turned to see if she could find envelopes on the foyer table where he placed outgoing mail that he took with him to work. There was nothing there. *Of course not. He hasn't gone to work for months.*

"Miss Gaebele took them," he said.

"Oh. Well, that was clever thinking then, to give them to her when she came to interview. I'm sure she'll pass them along to her sister."

He nodded. "I'm sure they'll arrive safely."

She thought it an odd characterization but let it go at that. "When will you have her start?"

"In a week. Plenty of time to help plan Winnie's birthday next month."

Winnie's party. All the women at church were doing such things now. "I haven't planned—"

"Selma will help. It will be. One less thing. To worry over."

He motioned to her to help him stand. She assisted her husband up the stairs, settled him into bed. "I imagine Russell will be chattering to you yet tomorrow about his auto ride."

Mr. Bauer nodded. "I'll hope to learn. When spring comes."

"He sits in that thing. In the shed. Is that safe?"

Mr. Bauer nodded. He held her hand. "Not to worry, Mrs. Bauer," he said. He looked at her then, held her gaze. "Thank you, Mrs. Bauer. I so appreciate. Your help."

She grunted. She knew he might have liked a "You're entirely welcome," but she couldn't muster it. She pulled away and patted his hand instead. She checked the chamber pot to be sure Russell had remembered to empty it earlier, then left her husband alone. Only later in her room did she think to wonder how her husband had managed to make it downstairs for the interview. No matter. Things were looking up. She'd have help, and soon it would be spring, and Mr. Bauer would be better. She could look forward to that.

⇒·┤◆⟩·◦·⟨◆├·⇐

Jessie wasn't expecting to see Voe and Daniel Henderson at the studio before she arrived.

"Never you mind, then," Voe told Jessie. "Daniel and I will tend to this. You're not to be involved."

Jessie put her hat, coat, and mittens on the hook in the kitchen. As wet as she got walking to work in this snow-blowing weather, they'd decided to let things drip there rather than form pools beneath the oak coat tree in the hall. She came back in, annoyed that Daniel Henderson was there at all. And they were boxing something up that she was not privileged to know about. Everyone seemed to be doing things to her, affecting her life. Did it even matter to the others that she was turning eighteen in a week and would be responsible for herself? Apparently not. Her mother continued to harangue her (a word she put into her list of memorable words) and tell her how disappointed she was that Jessie had taken such liberties at the Bauer home. How could they trust her? How could she make such decisions as to be in a man's bedroom long enough to see the condition of his pillows? Could they ever count on her to be the young woman they'd raised her

to be? Her morals were being questioned—and theirs too if she continued
to do such risqué things.

"But if I had done anything wrong, I
wouldn't have told you," Jessie said.

"What?"

"I mean, it was so innocent, my seeing his bedroom. I was just getting
checks. If it had been something, you
know, wrong, would I have mentioned it
to you?"

That had silenced them, for the moment.

Jessie thought they were right about
one thing: she'd made a terrible slip in
commenting on the pillow. It was almost
as if she wanted them to know about it,
but what would be the point of that? It
was an innocent moment of seeing,
that's all. Being a photographer, an artist, made her aware of things that most
people weren't. But her mouth had gotten her into trouble. She never should
have described the pillow because to
them it suggested something that
slanted the truth when all the truth was
there wide open for anyone to see.
Nothing was happening that ought not

to. Her parents had finished their ha-rangue, and Jessie had gratefully gone up to bed.

Now, this next morning, here she was with Voe challenging her too.

"Mr. B. asked us to do this," Voe de-fended when Jessie stood with pursed lips, refusing to leave so they couldn't continue whatever secretive thing they were doing.

"I don't see how," Jessie said. "He's ill and can barely speak. It was all I could do to get the wages taken care of with-out him collapsing. Why would he tell you to box up a portrait and keep me from knowing about it?

"Well, he did."

"It's a kindness, Miss Gaebele," Mr. Henderson said. "Don't spoil the sur-prise, then. Maybe you can fix us coffee. Do you do that?"

Jessie bristled. "I do whatever has to be done." She turned and headed to the kitchen. Maybe he was going to give her the double exposure, but why wouldn't he tell her to just take it with her when she went home? There didn't have to be all this secrecy.

After her parents' remonstrating her (another word she'd read in a *Woman's Home Companion* story) she had made up her mind: she would go with Roy for his appointment, and then she would begin saving, not for a camera but for enough money to leave. She'd get a room, like the girls who worked at the hospital or who came in from the country to serve at the restaurants and cafés did. They had all kinds of free time when they finished their work, and they didn't have to account to anyone but themselves. She'd get by with her little old camera. She would.

She'd miss Roy and Selma and even Lilly. And yes, she'd miss her parents too. But the time had come. She needed to make a change, and she would do that even it meant sacrificing her own camera. She'd work for Mr. Bauer forever if she had to, but she wouldn't have everything she did be constantly held against her as though she had barely turned ten.

She scanned the red lines of the ledger page to pick up from where she'd left off the day before. She decided maybe she should go down to the train station and pick up the supplies. It would keep her from feeling excluded by the goings-on in the other room.

"I'm going to the train station," she shouted as she pulled her hat on. "The shipment is due, and our first sitting isn't until eleven. I'll be back by then." She added to herself, *And maybe Mr. Henderson will be gone by then.* It simply wasn't right that Voe had her beau right beside her while she was supposed to be working.

Voe hurried back into the room. "Not necessary, Jessie. Daniel picked it up early this morning and brought it along. It's ready to be put into the darkroom if you want to do that."

Now Jessie straightened her small shoulders to stand to her full height. Daniel had no right to do work that she and Voe were responsible for. Not that she minded tending to the shipments. She always checked off what was there against the invoice to be sure nothing was shorted. That happened sometimes. But to have someone not even associated with the studio signing for things, well, she'd have to speak to the railroad about that. Besides, how did Daniel even know there was a shipment? Voe rarely paid attention to things like that.

"How did you know to pick it up?" Jessie asked Voe.

"Mr. B. told me. And he said he'd call the station to be sure Daniel could do it."

So Mr. Bauer had strength enough for that. If people were going to keep surprising her, she'd just become all the more determined to make her own way. After all she did to make this studio work too. She might have to continue working until Mr. Bauer returned, but if she moved out of her parents' home, at least she wouldn't be surprised there.

⊱—⊱—◦—⊰—⊰

The visit to Rochester a few days before Jessie's eighteenth birthday took all of them from Winona. The appointment had been moved up from the original March date. The night before, Jessie had wondered out loud why the girls couldn't remain at home. She would take Roy to Rochester on her own if they'd like. All three girls and her father would be losing wages for the overnight journey, and it just seemed a waste of finances. But her mother said it was important for them all to go. The doctors had said so. It was one of the things the Mayo brothers did, involving everyone who might have information to help them decide what to do about a patient.

"That's different," Jessie conceded. "We can all help Roy. We're not taking up space on the train."

Old-timers said there was only one drift that winter, but it was twenty miles long and twenty feet high. Men earned extra money keeping the tracks of the Chicago and Northwestern Railway clear. Daniel Henderson had been doing such work, hoping to get into the good graces of the freight company so he could hire on a permanent railroad crew. He cut ice on the off days, and Voe proudly talked about how he always kept busy. Jessie supposed he'd be "helping" her at the studio while the Gaebeles made their way to Rochester.

She was a little worried about Voe's

taking care of things alone at the studio, but she'd have to trust that Voe could do the job. They'd not scheduled any sittings, so Voe would be making prints most of the time Jessie was gone.

Roy, though, acted delighted to have everyone together and going on what he called an a-a-advent-t-t-ture, when he could get the whole word out. Jessie decided to make it so. She'd con-tributed to this journey and prayed that they would find a way to help Roy speak better. Her mother had noted that what-ever the outcome, it wasn't in their hands. Maybe the wisdom of the Mayo brothers would do what Jessie's family could not. Maybe there'd be a way to transform Jessie's regret.

Jessie put the final hatpin into the felt to hold it tight against her hair. She lis-tened carefully to sounds down the hall coming from her brother's room. He hadn't left yet to go down the stairs. She could hear him making drum sounds with his hands on the footboard of the bed. Jessie swirled out of the door, pushing her hat onto her head, her car-petbag in her other hand. She knocked on Roy's door to see if he was ready to go. Her sisters were already downstairs.

"B-b-better g-g-go?" he asked, putting his hat on.

Jessie hugged him and then held him at arm's length and straightened his cap. "We're ready for your adventure."

They descended, his feet taking one step at a time, her being careful not to rush him. She had a moment of insight. Maybe their mother finished his words for him because she couldn't bear the pain of loss that waiting carried with it. Maybe Jessie endured the ache of his effort and waited for the very same reason.

⊳━◆◇━○━◇◆━◁

The morning air crisped their noses as the Gaebele family stepped up into the streetcar, rode it to within a few blocks of the train station, then walked the rest of the way, serenaded by the crunch of their boots on the packed snow. Jessie's face felt frozen by the time they boarded the cars and found two rows of leather seats facing each other near the back, by the stove. Mrs. Gaebele and

Lilly took one side; Selma and Jessie faced them. Across the aisle sat Roy and his father, facing strangers. They moved their bags into various places beneath their feet, and Jessie thought they looked liked hens settling into nests. Selma put the lunch basket beneath her feet. Jessie set her Kodak in a bag beneath hers. She'd grabbed it at the last minute, hoping she could catch some shots of the snows. She didn't think there were any lakes around Rochester, but if there were, she might get some interesting views of the wind-swept snow rippling on the frozen surface or catch some of the Scandinavians fishing through holes in the ice.

Roy leaned out from the other side of her father when the train began its rumble forward, his face filled with a dimpled grin. He must have belched because his cheeks puffed, but Jessie couldn't hear it, for the whistle blew and steam billowed down around the car like fog and then lifted as the wind brushed it away. Roy grinned and waved. Whatever else happened, he would enjoy the journey. She'd do her best to do the same. She took out her Kodak and snapped a picture of him. It would be a good way to remember the day.

Settled in and bundled up, they headed west to Rochester. The fifty-mile trip would consume several hours.

Jessie snapped a few other pictures but realized that the train's movement would make them fuzzy. The cold would affect the camera too, so she stuffed it in her tapestry bag and just took pictures with her eyes. On either side of the tracks, snow piled up like the creamy clay bricks of the Winona library.

"I think it's nice," Selma told her, moving closer so they could talk more easily without shouting.

"Looking up the valleys as we pass, seeing the trees covered with snow? I think you're right, Selma."

"No," Selma said. She eyed Lilly and their mother across the way. Both had nodded off, stitching in their laps. "Working for the Bauers is nice. Oh, there's lots to do, but the house is a fine place, Jessie. It's a lot cleaner than Mr. Steffes's shop."

Jessie hadn't asked Selma about her

work for the Bauer family. She wanted nothing to fuel "unnatural affections," as her mother might call them. But Selma's conversation drew her like the Ouija board game Voe had brought into the studio. Jessie had played it only once. She felt a kind of anticipation that she liked but then dreaded the outcome too. If her mother knew she'd indulged even once in such a thing, she'd have kept her from work for a week and made her read the Bible for hours just to remind her that the future wasn't in some Gypsy's board.

"They have English dishes with roses on them all along the plate rail, and Mrs. Bauer has paper on her bedroom walls, but just around the top, not all over. And—" Jessie interrupted her by putting her hand on Selma's knee. "What?" Selma asked, but when Jessie couldn't tell her why she shouldn't talk of her work at the Bauers, Selma continued. "They have enough rooms for everyone to have their own and a day nursery too. Winnie and I can play in there. Well, I'm there cleaning the checkered floor, but she shows me her toys. I see why you like her," Selma said.

"I do like the children." Jessie looked out the window, then turned back. "What about . . . Mrs. Bauer?"

"Oh, she's all right. She's all nervous about Winnie's party, but I told her that cake and a few games will be enough to make a five-year-old happy. I offered to sing if she wished."

"Did she want you to do that?"

Selma shook her head. "No. I think she worries so much about Mr. Bauer and the children. She's always asking if Russell is home yet or if Robert awoke and maybe she didn't hear him. I think she must sleep really sound. Maybe that worries her. She does forget things, and she naps a lot."

Jessie wanted to ask if the Bauers argued or what sort of things they talked about. A part of her didn't want to hear that Mrs. Bauer was worried about Mr. Bauer. She hadn't been so worried that she'd refused to leave him alone, sick as he was, that day Jessie was there. She must have forgotten about Selma's interview too, for it would have been more seemly for the woman of the house to make those arrangements. Why didn't her mother consider that? Mrs. Bauer was as much to blame for Jessie's being alone with Mr. Bauer as anyone. If only Mrs. Bauer had remembered to pay their wages, it wouldn't have happened at all.

Selma went on to talk of other things she liked about the Bauer home, but Jessie's thoughts moved back to the day she'd been there herself, to the gentleness of Mr. Bauer. After he gave her their wages, they finished their tea and he spoke to her like her uncle August might, though in his illness-halted way. She felt like an adult sitting with him, hearing him speak of what he'd read in the paper, of Bugatti, an Italian who had founded a company to compete with Ford, only Bugatti's cars were for racing. He was a man who noticed the world and wasn't just stuck on Winona, like the boys she encountered at the sleigh ride last week, the one sponsored by the Ladies of Foresters.

She shook her head. These thoughts weren't good for her.

"You're not interested, are you?" Selma said. She crossed her arms in a pout.

"Maybe later," Jessie told her. Selma shrugged her shoulders, took a book from her satchel, and was soon sound asleep, leaning onto Jessie's shoulder, a soft snore lifting a tendril of her curls. Jessie didn't need to hear about the Bauers. She wouldn't think of anything but Roy now. The scenery zipped by the window so quickly she could just make out the white world broken by dark tree trunks and branches, an occasional red barn and log house. She'd see what they could do for Roy, go home, and before the year was out, she'd save enough to move on. She'd be an adult and on her own, working somewhere besides the Bauer Studio, away from temptations of shadow and light.

FIFTEEN

Balance

St. Mary's Hospital, where the Mayo brothers and their father practiced medicine, was held in high regard. By 1904, the team of physicians had already performed more than three thousand specialized surgeries and now employed other physicians in all sorts of new medical studies. The men traveled around the world and learned the techniques of doctors in other places, bringing in new ideas to Minnesota.

It was toward this promise that the Gaebeles took a horse-drawn cab from the train station to the hospital, where the building's tall spires made Jessie think it looked like a church. She said that, and her mother told her she was sure there'd be a chapel inside.

Once there, Roy and their parents were taken into a room while the girls remained behind in a cavernous waiting area. "I thought they needed us all," Selma said.

"Someone will come out later," Lilly said. "I'm sure. Don't be impatient."

Selma stuck her tongue out at her older sister.

Jessie looked around. Many other families waited, and off to the side a group of Gypsies literally camped: colorful scarves hung across the backs of chairs, making an awning for the many small children who played on a thick rug placed over the cool marble floor.

Mr. Bauer had once told Jessie that he'd trained as a physician in the military and had only one more year of study to complete before he would have been a doctor. Maybe he could have diagnosed his conditions earlier. He certainly wouldn't have had to suffer the mercury poisonings if he'd been a doctor. He also told her that it was a mistake he'd made, leaving something he enjoyed doing that would have given him a livelihood and helped others too. He wished he had found another way to deal with the horrors of war.

"I was impatient," he'd said. "Young people often are. And I didn't realize that I was wounded too, like the men I treated. Their pain infected me, but I didn't know I carried that disease long years after their wounds healed. I imagine they hid wounds as well," he'd mused. "You'll find yourself compulsive like that sometimes too, Miss Gaebele. You must guard your heart and do what you most love, and don't get pulled away into something . . . less settling."

She wasn't being pulled away into anything she didn't wish. She guarded her heart. It belonged to her family first and attended to what they needed, as with Roy. She looked to her faith to help guard her heart too, though she had more questions than answers. Photography was next, and that did fill her up and make her heart sing. Photography gave her a plan and a path to pursue. Mr. Bauer had given her that path. *Mr. Bauer.*

She felt agitated, wasn't sure why.

"I'm going to walk around," Jessie said. "I could use the exercise after that bumpity ride."

"Mama told us to wait." This from Lilly.

"There's no reason to just sit. I'll be close enough that when they come out to get us, I can be here in a flash. I'll take some pictures." It would keep her from always thinking of Mr. Bauer.

Lilly stitched a blouse she'd brought with her, and Selma had her book. As Jessie walked past the Gypsies, she made eye contact with an old woman, who motioned her to come over. Jessie shook her head. Mama wouldn't like that. But a child crawled onto the woman's lap and put a finger in the old woman's mouth. Neither had teeth, and the old woman laughed. The baby cooed as the woman motioned for Jessie to join them. There was a photograph here. What could be the harm?

"I tell your fortune for you," the woman cackled.

"No one can do that," Jessie said.

"Ah, the soul speaks in mysterious ways. Give me your hand."

"I don't think so," Jessie said. She was glad she still had gloves on.

"It hurts nothing. Come. Enjoy. You're a pretty young girl. It is for fun. To entertain the children and an old woman."

Jessie turned back to look at her sisters. They hadn't noticed that she'd paused. "May I take your pictures?"

"First, your fortune."

She set the camera down, removed her glove, put her palm out for the woman.

"Ah . . . you will live a long time for such a little person."

"Where do you see that?"

The woman pointed to a line bisecting Jessie's palm.

She sniffed. "It doesn't say old age to me," she said. "But I do see a few grains of lint in there from my glove." She brushed at it. The woman held tight.

"And five children. Five. All healthy, all living long lives too. You're a fortunate woman."

"Five? I should get started then."

Jessie laughed. *This is ridiculous.* She pulled her hand free, or tried to.

"No. I see eight. Yes, eight."

Jessie shook her head and laughed again.

"Your time will come. And here, here I see that you will travel far. There will be many hills to climb and many valleys, but you will keep going and arrive back to where you began."

"With my eight children," Jessie said.

The woman folded Jessie's fingers into her palm and smiled. "It is a pleasure to meet so enduring a young woman."

Enduring? That was a strange word to use with her in mind, Jessie thought. It was a silly thing. Her mother wouldn't like that she'd indulged in it even in jest. But then, hadn't she read that God uses many people to fulfill each person's purpose? Even a Gypsy might be a prophet of some sort. At least she hadn't asked her for money or threatened to put a curse on her if she'd didn't give it.

"Now your picture." Jessie said. She removed her Kodak and took the photo, the baby still cooing with his finger in the woman's mouth. Maybe she'd take a series of baby photographs, Jessie thought, of people who could afford to pay her with more than strange fortunes.

A few people stared as Jessie walked the halls, swinging her camera. She stopped to photograph a statue of Mary and the baby Jesus in the lobby. A skylight gave the artwork depth, and Jessie thought she had enough light for a closeup of the Virgin's hands. She'd have to wait to find out. Large paintings of landscapes and the sea hung on the walls, but Jessie saw no photographs until she took a side hall, carpeted and not quite so wide but with high-back chairs pressed every few feet against the plaster. There she found framed oil portraits of the famous Dr. William Worrall Mayo and his two doctor sons, Dr. Will and Dr. Charlie. She evaluated the posing and thought the backgrounds were a little dark and somber for men who had such generous smiles on their faces and brought joy to so many. She thought she'd take a photograph of one of the portraits, held the Kodak up, but the light wasn't good. And besides, she hadn't had much luck in retaking pictures. She still owed Mr. Bauer money for the plates used to make prints of the baptized girls. Her only hope was to have a camera that allowed her to develop her own plates and prints.

She'd save the pictures she had left for the ride home tomorrow. Maybe someone interesting on the train would pose, but if not, she'd be more selective about what she photographed, truly frame the picture before she ever took it. If she couldn't see what she wanted to see, she'd wait. She'd be more patient. She could do that. She felt tears well up. She felt so grateful to have discovered this love of capturing a moment in time and sometimes making it even more perfect than it might otherwise be—a fragile moment retained as it really happened.

A side hall beckoned her, and she turned into it. A series of statues cast fascinating shadows on a carpeted floor that led to an office. She pretended to frame a practice shot of a statue of a large bird when the door opened. A man

wearing a suit and a shiny tie held se-
curely by a gold pin stepped out. "What
are you doing?" he asked her just as
Jessie heard her name called.

She looked toward Selma's voice,
looked back at him. "I was just . . . I'm
not really photographing." She realized
how ridiculous that response must
seem with a camera pointed his way
and a bag slung over her shoulder.

"Jessie!"

"We don't allow pictures here," he
said. He sounded angry, upset. "It's to
protect the patients."

"I didn't . . . No patients, just interesting things." She pointed the camera at
the bird statue. She remembered the
Gypsy and the child, but they had
agreed to pose.

She stepped away from him, her
glasses slipping down her nose. She
turned and saw Selma waving her arms
at the end of the corridor. "They want us
now," her sister shouted.

"I have to go," she said. "I'm so sorry.
I didn't mean to . . . I didn't think anyone
would mind. I was just—" She walked
backward. He took a step toward her.

She turned, moving quickly around the corner.

"What were you doing?" Selma asked when she caught up with her. "Who is that man?"

"Is he following us?"

He'd stopped, any threat she posed apparently diluted, and Jessie breathed relief that she'd escaped without consequence. As they hurried, she told Selma about the pictures while attempting to put her camera into the bag she'd taken from her shoulder, then at the intersection where the carpet met the smooth surface of the marble, Jessie stumbled. She should have secured the Kodak. That thought fleeted through her mind just as Jessie lost her grip on the camera. Like a ball, her precious Kodak bounced from one hand to the other, catching on the bag and forcing her off balance further, until, like a bad dream she ran from slowly, Jessie watched her camera crash to the stone floor. Behind it, Jessie sprawled out like a cat on an ice pond, watching her spectacles fly.

It's what I deserve, Jessie thought. *It's what I've deserved all along.*

Selma helped her sit, then retrieved her glasses. Jessie hooked the wire rims around each ear, feeling foolish and sad all at once.

⊱┈◈┈○┈◈┈⊰

Jessie listened carefully to Miss Jones, as the woman sitting across from them had introduced herself. Jessie's glasses were smudged, but she didn't remove them to clean them. Her knees were sore from her fall, but she put that discomfort from her thoughts. Miss Jones had been gathering information from their parents and talking with Roy, she told them. The sunlit room held all sorts of things a child would like: wooden horses and wagons, iron train engines, dolls, and books, lots of books. Roy held a book of buildings with rounded domes and spires and elephants wearing colorful strings of beads draped across their foreheads. He looked up and waved when the girls came in and then returned to his story. Jessie ached for him.

"The doctors will see him before long," Miss Jones said. She wasn't a nurse, because she wasn't wearing a blue-striped dress with a white apron and white hat as so many others wore as they fast-walked through the high-ceiling halls. She looked like a working woman, dressed as Jessie and Voe did when they met the public, except her linen suit molded to her slender frame more perfectly. She looked chic.

"They like me to talk first with every-one, to see how each of you sees your little brother," Miss Jones explained to the girls. "We've had a nice chat already, haven't we, Roy?" He nodded and smiled, those dimples sinking into his round cheeks like toe tracks in wet sand. "What do you notice about Roy's speech?" She looked at Lilly first. "You're Lilly, correct?"

Lilly had the same olive skin as Roy did, and really, those two looked more alike than either she or Selma, Lilly's thick dark hair doing what she wanted it to do. "He talked a lot as a baby," Lilly remembered. "Sometimes too much." She laughed and fussed with her perfect hair. "Not that we minded. He asked lots of questions, little ones like, 'What's that?' and, 'Why?' He still asks, but the questions take a long time for him to get out. It's like a motor getting started in one of those new cars," Lilly said. "Yes, that's what it's like. Only he never gets going any faster." She laughed again and touched her hair.

"Does he get frustrated when people don't understand him? Lose his temper?"

"Oh, we can always understand him," Lilly said. "We just have to wait for him to finish."

"Y-y-you d-d-don't," Roy said.

Lilly turned to him. Jessie thought Lilly would disagree, but she didn't. She nodded. "I guess that's true enough," she said. "I don't wait."

"J-J-Jessie w-w-waits." He finally got those words out.

Lilly frowned.

"Which of you is Jessie?" Jessie raised a gloved hand. "What do you notice?"

Could she tell them that what she noticed every time she looked at him was the lost opportunity of his life? Could she say that because of her, Jessie, her brother wouldn't have what he deserved? Could she say that it was Jessie who had gotten in the way of what Roy's talents would have given to the world? Could she?

"That he wants to say so much more," Jessie said as she gained her voice. "But it tires him, to get his mind and mouth to work together. It's as though they're out of tempo with each other."

"Temper?" Miss Jones asked.

"No, tempo. He's out of rhythm. He's very good-natured about it though. I suppose maybe Lilly's right that I wait for him because . . ." She looked at her parents, then dropped her eyes. She may as well confess it. She had dozens of times in her prayers, to no avail. She still felt that terrible ache each time she saw him try to speak and knew that any great joy in her life was undeserved because she'd stolen Roy's joy from him. "Because I feel so bad that it happened, that I wasn't watching him. I feel sad that he . . . that I didn't . . . well, that the door . . . I don't know. I guess I wait for him to speak because each time I do I feel like I'm rubbing away a brick of blame."

"Such bricks can build up quite a wall," Miss Jones said, not unkindly at all.

Jessie blinked back tears. She looked away, noticed a painting of a nurse holding a baby protectively against her chest, stared at it until her eyes no longer compromised her composure.

"You always blamed yourself more than anyone else did, Jessie," her mother said. Jessie heard both confusion and annoyance in her tone. "Which I never understood. We were all there in the backyard, saying good-bye to your grandparents. No one was to blame, not really. No one." Her mother had said this often, and Jessie wondered if she had explained this to Miss Jones. Maybe she repeated it to assure herself.

"Why, I don't even remember where you were in the backyard. Had you gone into the house for something? We told Miss Jones that Roy had been asleep on the quilt in the shade of the maple tree and, well, there was all that commotion of people saying good-bye. If anything, it was my fault for leaving the door to the basement open after I brought up jars of applesauce to give my mother."

"The boy woke up and waddled away while we weren't aware," her father said. "No one's fault. The girls were young."

"Not me," Lilly said. "I was nearly nineteen."

"I just think of you all as being young and innocent," her father said. "All of you." He nodded toward Jessie, who dropped her eyes.

"We didn't even know he'd fallen down the basement steps until we started looking for him," Selma said. "Jessie found him."

"Maybe that's why you took it so hard," Jessie's mother said.

She knew they expected a response.

"Afterward we thought we might have lost two children, what with Jessie being so sad all the time," her mother said.

They must have told Miss Jones about the doctor being called, about Roy's eyes rolling back and showing nothing but white before he closed them. Then there were the hours of waiting, followed by days of visits to the hospital and eventually the muted joy of Roy opening his eyes and smiling up at them. Then his slow return to speech, but only with words that stumbled and stuck to his tongue. Maybe they'd told of Jessie's sobbing as she carried the boy up the stairs. But they couldn't tell Jessie's real part in it because they didn't know. They'd never know.

"My brother suggested the camera for Jessie because she'd so enjoyed it at the fair." Her mother nodded toward Jessie's camera bag. "And it helped, though now she's become almost obsessed with those photographs and the studio she works in."

Selma mercifully changed the subject. "Roy sang with me once," Selma said. "He didn't do that word skipping at all then."

They all turned to her.

"That's the first time I've ever heard that," Jessie's mother said. "When did you sing with your sister?" her mother's words demanded as she stared at Roy.

Roy opened his mouth to speak, but Selma continued. "He came along for rehearsals at church." She brightened. "Maybe he could sing now."

"Would you?" Lilly asked. Roy nodded agreement.

"He can just sing out when he wants?" their mother asked. "And he hasn't done it? Why wouldn't you do that, Roy?"

Roy started to answer, but instead Selma opened her mouth and out came "Just as I Am," with that husky tone that made her sound like a woman much older than she was. Roy's dimples widened, and he opened his mouth to join her.

They all leaned forward.

But only Selma's haunting alto filled the room.

Jessie felt her chest tighten, and tears pooled in her eyes as she watched Roy's face take on the look of a trapped rabbit who couldn't even squeal about its struggle. She clasped her stomach and rocked the way her father sometimes did when his pains first began. She stopped herself.

"I didn't think he could," her mother said, turning away.

"Maybe it was the organ playing along with you, Selma, that let him do it," Jessie said. *I should take piano lessons and play for him, forget about my camera life.* "Sometimes when I ask him to talk smooth and tell him to think of it like wind coming down a narrow tunnel or water flowing lazily over a smooth rock, sometimes then he can speak without taking so long." She wanted to move past the blend of disappointment and relief she could see in her mother's face. And in Roy's eyes too.

"You can sing without the stutter," their mother said. She crossed her arms over her chest. Jessie's father touched their mother's hand gently. She looked startled, shook her head as her shoulders sagged, and she yielded her open palms to her lap.

"We have seen this before," Miss Jones said. "It may be the rhythm that helps him sing those words, though your voice is lovely"—she looked at her notes—"Selma, is it? Yes, well, it may just be the circumstances today."

"The complication of the day," Jessie

said. Her mother looked quizzically at her.

"A banjo was what assisted one young girl," Miss Jones reported. "She learned to play it, and it helped her speech immensely."

"They cost a lot," Selma said.

"We can save up for it," Jessie said. Here was something she could do to partially redeem what she hadn't done. "That's what we can all do. Save up our pennies."

"I'm not saying it would work in this instance," Miss Jones said. "Why don't you wait to see what the doctors advise before you invest in something like that? But it is a possible next step."

Jessie looked longingly at the carpet-bag that held her shattered camera. It would be a long time before she had another, a long time before she would be on her own, but the delay, the disappointment, was what she should expect. Roy looked over at her and grinned wide, his unwarranted absolution a trigger for her grief.

She would never tell them. She could never find the courage to say that on that day she *had* seen Roy awake and begin to wander. A thought *had* crossed her mind of how she ought to protect him, go get him while everyone else clustered at her grandparents' buggy and the steps to the basement beckoned a curious child. But it was only a fleeting thought. She told herself he'd waddle toward the family, or someone else would notice he'd awakened. Instead, she followed a butterfly more beautiful than any she'd ever seen. She hoped to capture it and show it to her relatives before they left. The fluttering wings took her moment by moment away from what might have changed everything for Roy, took her deeper into the peonies and roses and her own garden of regret.

>—◦—◦—◦—◦—<

FJ found his strength returning. He looked in the mirror. The dark circles beneath his eyes had faded. Some of the spots had become lighter. He'd taken to walking around the block despite the cold weather. He wasn't shoveling snow. Russell, the dear boy, had taken care of that. He straightened himself to parade position. He'd put some flesh back on. Selma, their hired girl, cooked well, and her presence had lessened some of Mrs. Bauer's volatility, or so he'd thought. All in all, he was feeling better. He might even be able to go into the studio in a month or so. Not full-time, but perhaps to assume a few photo sittings.

He needed to speak with Miss Gaebele anyway about the increased tariffs being charged to ship printed postcards back into the United States. He wondered if he should contract with Kroeger's Printers in Winona or V. O. Hamman in Minneapolis. He'd like her opinion, though the Germans truly did have the very finest printing equipment in the world. His postcards always returned with the photographs he'd taken looking precise and with the colors he'd ordered tinted to perfection. If the tariffs continued to rise, he'd have to find some other means of producing the cards. Or just let that part of the business go. But it was booming. Everyone seemed to love postcards since the postal service had authorized the divided card. A few words, the address, and the stamp on one side, a piece of art on the other. People liked having cards of themselves, but more and more, there was interest in, well, hometowns, buildings, tramplike street scenes.

Miss Gaebele would remind him of that. Miss Gaebele had recommended the parade when President Taft came through town. Though FJ was grateful he'd captured a good likeness of the man, unposed scenes bothered him. There was enough unpredictability in his life without adding street scenes. One couldn't afford to waste the paper, what with increased costs of the emulsions. There was always risk in business, yet one had to keep branching out, trying new things. Balance was what it took to be successful.

Miss Gaebele once said that a studio either had to be the best at one thing, such as serving their customers, or do the most or be the biggest at something. Anything less would be futile. How she had become so wise at such a young age amazed him. His portraits

were the best of any in Winona. Miss
Gaebele seemed to think that taking unposed shots, at weddings and such,
could be the studio's mark. That was
before she ran the studio on a winter's
day. She might think differently now,
working inside in the warmth instead of
racing a windstorm for a scenic shot.

She was someone with whom he
could really discuss these business
things. He didn't want to alarm Mrs.
Bauer with talk of tariffs or trends. And
for months he hadn't been able to visit
his lodge or the YMCA, nor attend
chamber of commerce meetings, where
he could have conferred with others. If
any other photographers were present,
though, he didn't want to have them
think he wasn't on top of things or that
his studio was in any way in trouble.
Neither did he wish them to think him ar-
rogant, as though he knew too much
and didn't need their advice. Balance,
always balance.

In fact, the studio appeared to be doing well, judging by the ledger accounts
Miss Gaebele provided to Mrs. Bauer
once a month. Miss Gaebele's visit, now

a few weeks past, had been pleasant. He thought he might invite her to come back and bring the books to discuss them here, with Mrs. Bauer present, of course. He sighed, sat down. Standing took its toll. No, it would be best if he waited until he was feeling better, fully up to going to the studio to assess things. No sense in alarming Mrs. Bauer with talk of rising tariffs. After all, she was getting ready for Winnie's party now that Selma had returned from her trip to Rochester.

"Mrs. Bauer wonders if you'd like to hold Robert for a time," Selma said, interrupting his reverie before the mirror. He shouldn't have left the door open, though she hadn't entered, just stood outside holding his son.

"I'd like that," he said. He reached for the child, who squirmed out of Selma's hands. He caught him just as he chose to stand beside her, wobbling, then clinging to Selma's skirt, then holding himself upright and as stiff as a military pose. "Are you going to walk for us, Robert, before you're even a year old?" The boy grinned, with drool hanging like a string of melted cheese from his mouth. "Well, good for you." FJ held his arms out. "Come along." The boy let loose of Selma, took two steps toward him. FJ bent down and reached out for him and barely caught him as he fell into FJ's arms.

He lifted Robert with effort, heard his heart start pounding. He turned to face the mirror with the boy. "There you are! A big boy," he told him. FJ considered the child. He would be their last. Mrs. Bauer had made that clear. She wanted no part of FJ, not even a gentle touch after he finished reading his evening paper and passed by his wife as she stitched. She had banished him from her bedroom and said she would only enter his to clean it. But with Selma here to work now, she needn't ever enter at all.

Robert laughed and pointed. "Baby." He wiggled to be let down again. FJ complied, bending down to settle the child close to Selma again. As he stood up, he felt his head go light. He was weaker than he'd thought. "Perhaps you can walk him to the nursery," he said.

"Oh no, Mr. Bauer. The party is about to start, and Robert will likely put his fist in the cake first thing. I think Mrs. Bauer was hoping you'd look after him, if you could."

"I'll do my best," he said. He reached for the boy's pudgy hand. "Come, Bob, we'll sit on the floor together and I'll show you my army buttons. Your big brother always liked to play with those."

"Bob. Bob," the boy said. He swung around as his father held his hand and nearly lost his balance. FJ settled him on the carpet. He took one last look in the mirror before he sat beside his son. The face he saw now frightened him; it was an old and aging face. He couldn't see much future there at all.

>–⤏⟶•〇•⟵⤎–⤜

Mrs. Bauer wanted the party to be perfect. Several other mothers were bringing their daughters to her home for the first time. She scanned the nursery. Could five little girls and their mothers be comfortable here? She should have held it somewhere else. She thought about asking her older sister, Eva, to host it, but Eva could be so . . . unpredictable at times. One never knew what mood she'd be in, so it was better to let her be. Eva had a birthday in this same month, and Mrs. Bauer had sent her a lovely card. She'd heard nothing back. Typical. Mrs. Bauer expected a little recognition for making that effort, but it rarely happened from her sister. Sometimes she even forgot she had a sibling.

This nursery room would be too confining. She wouldn't be able to stand the noise.

No. It was settled. The invitational card had been sent.

Why had she agreed to have this party? She did things she didn't really want to do because it seemed the right thing to do for her child, but maybe not. She found herself snapping at Winnie, poor soul. She could see the child's lower lip tremble before Mrs. Bauer even realized she'd raised her voice. Pressure throbbed against her head. She held her palms to her temples.

Scrapes of Winnie's chalk grated on her nerves as the child created pictures on her slate. Mr. Bauer just had to buy the dustless chalk introduced at the world's fair exposition in St. Louis. It was the newest rage. It was nice to have no dust in the nursery, yes, but the noise . . . she preferred the quiet Binney and Smith product, Crayola crayons, they called them. But their bright yellows, black, and reds filled a page that couldn't be reused the way the chalkboard could. Paper was expensive, Mr. Bauer told her. Of course, whatever he needed for his studio proved no obstacle. He could get paper shipped in for that at a much greater expense than Winnie's picture paper. Why, he'd even said he allowed Miss Gaebele to print photos of her liking. She hoped the girl would pay for that. It was only right.

"Are you all right, Mrs. Bauer? I could get you some tea."

"What?" Selma. The girl was so soft and secretive. "No. I'm fine. What time did they say they would come?"

"We told them three o'clock," Selma said. "From three to five."

Two hours! What would she do with them for two hours? "Do we have enough sandwiches made up? I wouldn't want to run out. Maybe I should fix more."

"No. That is, I think the two platters are enough," Selma said.

"You never know. You never know." She clasped her hands, looked at them. They were so red! Was she getting the same sickness her husband had? She caught her image in the mirror as she rushed toward the kitchen. Her face blotched as red as her tongue and felt bumpy as well. She needed to keep busy, that was all, not think of things. Avoid mirrors. She'd be fine.

"Yes, I'll fix more sandwiches. Is the knife sharp? I don't want to pressure the bread."

><+>-O-<+><

It was a family gathering and nothing more for Jessie's birthday. No Jerome this time, thank goodness. Uncle August couldn't make it in either; the roads from Cream were drifted shut. Darkness arrived before people even left their workplaces, so her other grandparents would remain home as well. Jessie would see them Sunday.

Jessie didn't expect any presents. They'd all been saving for Roy's needs. The doctor had told them about a book written by a Dr. Samuel Potter and that Roy likely would be found to have a condition called dyslalia. "It will mean hours each day of retraining Roy," one of the Mayo brothers had told them.

When Jessie asked, the Mayo brothers said the banjo was a fine idea, but they warned against anyone who might suggest using "mechanical contrivances and tyrannical practices prescribed by fools." Jessie fully intended to get Dr. Potter's book from the library and read more so she could work with Roy.

Lilly gave Jessie a stitched shirtwaist with a separate ruffle that hung over the bodice. She'd tatted the edges so it looked almost like eyelet, something expensive that the Gaebeles couldn't afford.

"It's beautiful, Lilly. Thank you."

"I just appreciate you going with me on the city sleigh ride."

"It was fine," Jessie said.

"So you'll do it again?"

"I might." She held the blouse up to her bodice, then showed it to her mother, commenting on the tiny stitches. The sleigh ride hadn't been as much fun as Lilly seemed to think it was. The cold air numbed her mouth and made it hard to talk to people. If she pulled her wool muffler up over her mouth and nose, just under her eyes, the moisture fogged her glasses and made her mouth all wet, so when she lowered the muffler to speak, her lips froze instantly. Jessie was a good sport about it and didn't complain, not even when the boys got to throwing handfuls of hay at one another over the heads of the girls. Just like boys.

"I wanted you to see that you can enjoy yourself with young men your own age," Lilly said.

"You worry over much, sister," Jessie said. "I get along fine with young men. Really, I do. I like them in a group like that."

"That's how I like them best too," Lilly admitted.

"Open my gift." Selma handed her a

paper envelope that she'd decorated with pictures of birds and lilacs. "To remind you of spring," she said. "I know you like flowers and everything."

"M-m-me t-t-too," Roy said.

"You sure do take good care of Mama's herbs and my lily of the valley," Jessie told him.

"No, he means he helped make the envelope, decorating on it when I brought it home."

"Thank you. You too, Selma," Jessie said. She brushed Roy's hair from his eyes.

"He needs a haircut, I know," her mother said. Jessie started to say that she hadn't meant any fault but realized her mother often chose offense where none was intended.

"I got the paper from Mrs. Bauer."

Jessie felt a little freezing with the mention of Mrs. Bauer.

"I wrote it myself," Selma said.

You are more to me than sister,
Taking pictures that you love;
Yet I know no other word to use
Than Sister, whom I love.

"It's really nice, Selma. It really is. I feel the same about you too. And Lilly. And . . . well, not you, Roy. You're a boy. But I love you just the same!"

Roy laughed.

"I can sing the words," Selma said. "I thought of music for them."

"Oh, that's all right," Jessie told her. She wasn't anxious to hear about "the pictures you love," as she wouldn't be able to take any for some time to come. The ones she'd taken on the train, the Gypsy grandma and baby, the other outdoor pictures of snow—those were all gone too.

But Selma began, and after the first words they all tried not to look at Roy, who opened his mouth. They hoped he'd sing, smooth as an ice skater on a newly brushed pond. But he didn't.

The doctors had told them that no surgery would help Roy speak more smoothly, but they had good news too. With a special kind of person who taught speech, someone Roy would have to visit in Rochester once a month, and with hard practice at home, he might be able to speak on his own with less hesitation. They would take turns working with Roy every day, and Jessie wondered as she watched him dig into her cake if he would tire of the activity or see it as valued attention. She could do it while she remained at home, which would be for quite a while now.

If he had a banjo to go with the exercises, it might lighten the drudge. Sears, Roebuck and Company catalog listed the Imperial Banjo at twenty-five dollars, but they could buy a cheaper model for seven. Both amounts stretched the family budget. The special language person was the higher priority, but even that expense would have to wait until spring. Jessie hoped the book would give them additional suggestions.

Her mother brought out her present then. It was a quilt, one she'd been working on for months, maybe even years. "I gave your sister Lilly a quilt on her eighteenth birthday, for her trousseau if she ever uses it, and this is yours. I hope you like it, Jessie."

The quilt was pieced with squares of material made up of an anchor print against an indigo blue. The alternating blocks were prints of horse heads on a lighter sky blue. Jessie wasn't familiar with the quilt pattern.

"What's the pattern called, Mama?"

"Contrary Wife," her father said. But he had a grin on his face.

"It is not," her mother corrected. "It's Road to California. I know you like to travel, and these pieces of shirtings were what I had available."

Jessie had seen the prints before, worn by Roy and her father. "They do have a transportation theme," Jessie said. "By land or by sea. All we need is a bicycle or a train." Jessie laughed as she said it, but her mother's eyes showed disappointment.

"I should have thought of that," her mother said.

"No, no, it's wonderful. I love it." Jessie stood up and hugged her mother with the quilt pressed between them. "It took hours and hours, and the stitching is beautiful. I'm so pleased. I'm just not good with a needle and thread myself."

"See to it that you don't just put it in your trunk and keep it there forever," her mother said, mollified. "Your sister's quilt will be gaining moth holes if she doesn't find herself a beau soon."

"Perhaps we'll always be shop girls," Jessie teased. "With our mama looking after us."

"Hush now," Jessie's mother said, but she smiled.

"I nearly forgot," her father said then, standing and stepping out onto the porch. He returned with a large box. "Voe brought this by. Or rather Daniel Henderson did. That pair might need one of your wedding quilts before long, Mother," he added.

"Daniel does seem sweet on her," Jessie said.

"Does he have a brother?" Selma asked.

Jessie stared at the box. She knew this had to be the surprise that Mr. Bauer had asked Voe and Daniel to pack up. Maybe it was the framed double-exposure portrait. Had it been removed from the window? It had caused such a row with her parents. Why would he do that? Well, he didn't know. She'd never told him. Her heart started to pound. Her parents would not like a gift coming from Mr. Bauer. It was one thing to drop by on his way home, as he had two years before, but to make a concerted effort to give a gift . . . She could only hope that he'd put no card inside.

"Voe is very generous," Jessie said, preparing the setting for her parents to see this gift as nothing to be wary of. "But let's everyone dig into the cake or Roy will have it all consumed, won't you, Frog?" she said. "Besides, we need to be turning the handle on the ice-cream maker or we'll never have ice cream tonight. Papa, it's your turn."

"Oops, I'm back on it," her father said.

"I'll get the plates and cut the cake," her mother said, rising.

Selma said, "I can't believe you can wait for such a big present to be opened!"

"I'm a patient one," Jessie said. "Ice cream and cake first." She forced a smile.

She looked across at Lilly, who wore a knowing look.

SIXTEEN

Affectionately

After ice cream, Jessie's father, without asking, took a screwdriver and opened up the box. Roy and Selma hovered over him.

"Wh-wh-what is it?"

"Well, I don't know," her father said. Selma began pulling out newspapers that settled across the top. "You'll have to ask our Jessie. Her name's on it, and it's from the Bauer Studio."

Jessie moved to the box then, dread caping her small shoulders. Her skirts brushed the newspapers piled on the floor. She'd tell her mother that the double exposure could just stay in the box until she had her own place to live in;

then she could hang it on her own wall. That's what an eighteen-year-old did, make these choices.

Jessie took a deep breath. "I think it's that double exposure that upset you, Mama. Mr. Bauer probably wanted it out of his studio display window and didn't know where to store it so he sent it here. As a little birthday surprise. You might just leave it in there," Jessie told them. "Is there any more cake?"

"It isn't a picture," Selma said. "It's too big to be a picture. It's a big black satchel."

He'd sent her a suitcase? Why would he give her something so personal as a satchel? Maybe he wanted her to leave, and this was his way of sending her off.

Roy and Selma stepped aside, and Jessie leaned over to look at the black handle that faced her. She started to pull, then saw the label: "Folmer & Schwing Division, Eastman Kodak Company, Rochester, New York."

Mr. Bauer had given her a camera? He couldn't have known about the broken Kodak . . . Well, maybe he could have, if Selma told him in the last few days. But Voe and Daniel had been working on the surprise package long before that.

She continued to pull up on the heavy object, which arrived in her hands as a rectangle. She knew immediately what it was without taking it out of the bag: a Graflex, one of the finest. She ran her fingers over the smooth leather, imagining what was inside. The lens was made by Goerz in Germany, and it would take five-by-seven plates, a perfect size for her work. The shutter speed was as fast as a thousandth of a second. Yet it was easy to carry, simple to operate, and so much more versatile than the little 3A Graflex she'd seen in the photo magazine that made postcard-size photographs. She'd seen this one in the photographic catalog, but it was much too expensive for her to even dream of. With this camera, she could take more photos that told bigger stories, like the man who'd done the exposé on the children laboring in the Carolinas. Jessie had never forgotten those pictures of emaciated children with the haunting eyes.

Mr. Bauer understood how much she

wished to take photographs out in the world, and he'd given her a gift to honor that desire.

Roy pulled on her sleeve. "O-o-open—"

"Open it up," her mother finished.

"I already know. It's a camera. A very nice one."

"Did you tell him you'd broken yours in Rochester?" Selma asked.

"Yours is broken?" This from her mother.

"It's a long story," Jessie said. "And no, I certainly did not tell Mr. Bauer."

"It was delivered a while ago, but Daniel Henderson asked that we keep it until your birthday."

"From Mr. Bauer," Lilly admonished.

"I'm sure it's a gift from the Bauer *family*," Jessie said. "They remember my birthday because it's the same day as Winnie's."

"Let me see it," her father said. Jessie opened the bag and passed the camera to her father as though she passed steaming water over the head of a baby.

"I'll look for a note. I'm sure it's from all of them." Jessie pawed through the packing that had been under the camera bag and felt a note there but decided to let it be.

"Voe must have forgotten to put it in," Jessie said, making her voice light. "I'll check with her tomorrow. Meanwhile, let me get this packaging out of here." She put the newspapers written in German back into the box and shoved it toward the door. Roy bent to help her and she let him. Anticipating her plan, he opened the door, and she pushed the box over the threshold and onto the back porch. "You go back in," she said. "It's cold out here. I'll just get it off to the side so no one trips over it in the morning." Roy complied. Jessie reached into the packing, felt for the slender card, pulled it from the box, and tucked it beneath her skirt supporter before going back inside.

"The Bauers must really like your work," Lilly said.

"I've done well for them." She pushed by Lilly into the kitchen. "And I haven't had a vacation since I began working there. Even you get a vacation now and then."

"When the shop closes to maintain the sewing machine," Lilly said.

"Photo assistants usually do get time away, but with Mr. Bauer's illnesses, that just hasn't been possible. So this is their way of saying thank you, I'm sure."

Her mother appeared to be fascinated by the camera her father still held. He turned it this way and that. Jessie took it from them and showed them the way the top handle lifted up and formed an opening that looked like those goggles men wore when they drove automobiles. She pulled on the lens, and the bellows behind it stretched like a small concertina. "You look down through here at your subject, and there's a mirror that reflects what you're looking at, only backward. Images used to be upside down, but not with this camera. You put film in here." She pointed. "And then you take the picture."

"Can you take mine?" Selma swirled around like a dancer.

"It has no film," Jessie said. "I'll have to get some, and then I can. But you'll have to sit still or I'll put you into one of those head clamps photographers used to use when it took so long to expose a picture." Jessie held her hands on either side of Selma's ears and pressed gently.

Selma laughed and then with Roy took turns looking into the camera while her father held it. Her mother said how nice it was that just when she needed it, God had provided by giving her a camera even better than the one she'd broken. "You're a very blessed girl."

>—+—<>—○—<>—+—<

"You have to stop it," Lilly said. She brushed Selma's hair while Jessie stood to the side.

"I'm going to try on your shirtwaist," Jessie said. "It's really lovely. Thank you."

"What should I stop?" Selma asked.

"Not you. Jessie. She knows what I mean." To Jessie she said, "It's going to hurt you in the end."

"What are you talking about? You need to tell me. Ouch! Don't pull so hard," Selma complained.

"Such an expensive gift." Lilly shook her head, starting to brush Selma's hair again.

"The Bauers can afford nice gifts," Selma said.

Lilly frowned. "That is none of your business, Selma. People's finances are their own personal affairs."

"And so their giving me an expensive thank-you gift is none of your affair either," Jessie said. She'd moved away from the girls and slipped off her blouse, unhooking the skirt supporter. The small card she laid on the dresser with the supporter over it. She put Lilly's gift on, let it fall over her chemise. It was a lovely blouse. "This fits perfectly, Lilly. Thank you. I'll wear it tomorrow."

"Jessie . . ."

"Better to be the darling of an old man than the slave of a young one," Jessie told her. She kept her voice light.

"You don't have to be either. You aren't allowing yourself to really—"

"It isn't your affair, Lilly. It's mine."

"That's just what I'm worried about."

><+>-O-<+><

Jessie felt guilty over letting the family think there'd been no card, but she didn't want the embarrassment of having to share it in case Mr. Bauer had written something personal. She'd wanted to get up in the night to read it, but her sisters were there, always there. One more reason to be out on her own. She slipped the card into her drawer and in the morning carried it with her to work while she imagined him writing it, ordering the camera, arranging for its delivery. A block or so from home, with the air so cold she could see her breath, she pulled the note from her muff and stopped beneath one of the big walnut trees, where the snow was beginning to melt in a circle out from the trunk. She pulled the card from the envelope before lifting the cream-colored paper with a bird stamped on the front.

Her heart hesitated. She admitted to herself that she hoped his words were more than comforting, maybe words of his fondness for her, something to indicate that she truly was special in his eyes. A wave of shame flushed through her. "I've done nothing wrong," she said out loud.

She imagined Mr. Bauer telling her the same thing in person. Maybe they'd stand in the darkroom, the orange glow covering up every blemish on her face, on his, as they stared at each other. Perhaps he'd reach out his hand to her. Maybe they would—

She stopped herself.

She was as bad as Selma with her ideas of romance. The thought frightened her but also made her heart beat a little faster. She wasn't sure what she felt for Mr. Bauer, but it wasn't romantic love. It was just fondness. Yet her breath quickened at the thought of his coming back to the studio, of being able to work side by side with him every day. Except that she was planning to go out on her own. Soon. *Probably just this cold weather making my breath come fast.* She looked at the cream-colored card. It would tell the story, true. She opened it and read: *Happy birthday wishes to you. We hope this camera will bring you many days of good shooting. Thank you for your association with us. Sincerely, the Bauer Studio.*

Sincerely, the Bauer Studio!

She turned it over to see if he'd written anything personal on it at all. Noth-

ing! Why, it was practically a formed letter that might be sent to a client or
maybe to one of their suppliers whose
birthday Mr. Bauer happened to remember. Tears pressed behind her nose,
pooled in her eyes, froze on her cheeks.

She was so foolish. She'd been defending his feelings to Lilly as though
they were nothing but good intentions
from a kindly older man, and so it was,
the truth laid out. It was simply a well-in-
tentioned gift from an employer. She'd
completely misread his intentions.

She thought about tearing the card up
but decided she could show it to Lilly,
reassure them all that there was nothing
unseemly happening. She wiped her
eyes, then put her gloved hands back
into the muff. She straightened her small
shoulders and stepped over a pile of
snow to return to the sidewalk and
started to walk. Frozen tears tightened
her face. She passed the studio, wanting a little more time to gather herself.
What had she expected? He was just
being kind to her. She had misread
everything: his helpfulness, his comments on her retouching skill, the silver

photo case, even the meaning of the day they'd had tea together.

Had tea together. Jessie scoffed at her naiveté. She was no different to him than Voe was, or Selma. She was nothing special. The camera was a generosity from both of the Bauers, Mrs. Bauer and the children too. The thought of the children brought a twinge to her heart.

She looked through her mind for the leaves that healed, Ezekiel's leaves. With the camera, she no longer had to wait to take her own photographs. She'd be able to develop at the studio, but eventually she could arrange a space in the basement of the family home for that. And if not, in the home of wherever she moved to when she branched out on her own.

><del>+</del>><del>O</del>><del>+</del><

Spring arrived in Winona with pussy willows soft and furry blooming along the river's slough. Lilac perfume filled the air, making Jessie's spirits rise. Not that she'd been discouraged, really. Jessie and her sisters rotated their exercises with Roy when he came home from school, and it did seem to Jessie that he slowly improved. Her father hoped to purchase a banjo for Roy's seventh birthday in the fall, and the trips to Rochester were now scheduled for four times a year. Miss Jones provided them with written instructions to follow when they worked with Roy at home. Jessie found satisfaction in the tasks.

In her spare moments, Jessie daydreamed of that studio of her own, but Mr. Bauer was always in it. She dreamed of having a family one day, of tending children of her own. But Mr. Bauer appeared in that daydream too, and the very idea of it made her face grow warm. If her parents knew, if Lilly knew what she thought of, how she went over the moments they'd shared, they'd be worried for her soul. She was worried about it herself, and yet she couldn't seem to help it. She had created a world that wasn't real; she knew that. And yet when she was in it, she felt loved and complete and forgiven in some strange way. Here she was, eighteen years old, and as Lilly said, she kept herself closed off from young men her age who could disappoint because they were real and not a romantic fantasy.

The salary envelopes arrived on schedule without comment or notation. She and Voe handled sittings. They even photographed a wedding party at the couple's home some miles outside of Winona, following the marriage. She'd borrowed her family's buggy and horse, and with Voe to help her (Daniel was off on a train crew, working), Jessie had used the Graflex to shoot them all standing in front of a mostly log home. The photograph had turned out well, she thought. She'd posed the wedding party and a few guests on the porch, looking casual, the parents on either side of the bride and groom. She found a place for the dog, the children, the aunts and uncles, and a dozen friends. In the future she intended to take the photographs before the revelers found the punch, for some had trouble standing still for the exposure. But she found she liked joking and laughing with people she didn't know who couldn't look too deep inside her. She was in charge, but at the same time, they treated her as though she was a part of the gathering, offering food and drinks to both her and Voe. The girls declined the latter, of course, but it was pleasant to think she had their attention, at least for the moments of the posing and exposure of the plates.

Jessie even handled a difficult guest. She'd gone around the house toward the barn and found there what she thought would make a lovely shot of puppies puddled on top of one another and curled up as though they were nearly one. She hadn't brought her tripod so held the camera steady, looking down into the lens.

She felt a heavy arm on her shoulder, accompanied by a strong whiskey smell.

"Are you takin' pitchers?" the man said. Jessie recognized the voice as one of the groom's attendants. Maybe a cousin.

Jessie laughed. "No, I'm washing dishes." She ducked her head under his arm and started back toward the house. A pickup band played now, and the laughter seemed to get louder.

"Aw, don't be shy," he said, stumbling along behind her. "You can wash my dishes anytime."

"All that would get me would be chapped hands."

"I could smooth those palms," he drawled, stepping in front of her, grabbing for her fingers. She gripped the Graflex in the other hand.

"Mr. McKay, you've had far too many spirits to ask to hold my hand. I only allow that in a man who has finished his day's work, rubbed the calluses to cream smoothness, and then, only then, might I allow him to be so familiar."

He let go and looked at the calluses on his hands. "And what if I should touch your hand anyway? What's a little thing like you to do about it?" He grabbed again.

"Why, push your head into the wash water," she said. "What else could I do?" She pushed his thumb as far as she could toward his wrist as she spoke. It was a trick Lilly had told her worked. He let out a short howl as she turned sideways and fast-walked to where the group stood gathered, pushing her hair behind her ears where it had loosened in the effort. She vowed to be more careful in the future about going off alone.

"Where've you been, McKay?" one of the guests shouted, so Jessie knew he was behind her. "You didn't try to take on the professional lady, now did you? She's pretty tough to be doing what she does, carrying that pho-to-graphic thing around. She'll clean your clock for certain."

"Sure, and I've had my share of cleaning already," he said, rubbing his thumb. General laughter followed. He didn't bother her after that, and when they left, he came to offer his hand to help her step up into the buggy. "It ain't got smooth calluses," he told her, "but they're clean." He grinned and stepped back, sweeping his hand low as though bowing.

The incident had strengthened Jessie's resolve that she could do more of these events, perhaps on her own. She'd make a few adjustments. She might be competing with the Bauer Studio, but on the other hand, Mr. Bauer didn't like to take such appointments. She could. And if she did well enough, she might get referrals. Certainly handling unruly guests without significant embarrassment to the bride made her a valuable asset at any wedding party.

>─┤◆)──○──(◆┤─<

She had sent a thank-you card to the Bauers, saying she appreciated their generosity, and she had sent a second letter—so that personal etiquette was not confused with business—in which she proposed the purchase of plates and paper and how she might pay for them with a reduction in her salary. No one responded for a long time. Then she received a note from Mr. Bauer in his quite strong and sweeping penmanship. Jessie had stared at the address on the outside for some time, running her fingers over her name, written by his very hand.

She sighed, read on. He suggested that she keep a record of expenses for chemicals, paper, and the like, and when he returned to the studio, they would settle up. He added that he was certain to return by early summer. Nothing more. A perfectly businesslike correspondence.

Except that he signed it, *Affectionately, F. J. Bauer.*

Affectionately. Jessie didn't show Voe or anyone. She certainly couldn't talk to her parents, and Voe, well, Voe would dismiss her and tell her she needed to get out and meet men her own age before she found herself a spinster dreaming of what could never be. Voe could say those things because she and Daniel had become engaged.

Lilly would say the same thing, and Selma was too young to understand and spent too much time now with the Bauers. Jessie didn't want any information about her life being dropped like candle wax on the Bauers' table. No, there was no one, not really. She had spoken her prayers, but she was pretty certain that requests to sort out the confusing feelings she had for another woman's husband would go unanswered. The best place she had to express her feelings was through photographs. But even then her thoughts came back to Mr. Bauer.

At the library, she looked up the word *affection.* "A feeling of fondness for another." A different definition was "the act of influencing, affecting, or acting upon." Then she found *affectionate.* "Having or showing fond feelings or affection; loving; tender."

Loving. Tender.

F. J. Bauer wasn't trying to *influence* or *act upon* her at all. Her nonsense thinking was doing that to herself. He didn't even know what he was saying.

She had to change the way she thought and felt. It had to be possible to do that. Mr. Bauer expected to return in this summer of 1910. She'd get no closer to her own studio if she couldn't put aside additional funds somehow. Even before he returned, she would find a job that paid more and take it as soon as he was back, or she would secure a second one so she had less time to daydream. She'd wasted too much time imagining what could never be. She'd follow her mother's suggestion and contact the evangelist Ralph Carleton.

Maybe working for him part-time to begin with might set her mind on holy things instead of on her speculations about words like *affectionate, tender,* and *loving.* Yes, those were words better left to family, brothers and sisters, and affectionate older uncles.

SEVENTEEN

Playing Fields of Degradation

Those years when FJ spent weeks in the military hospital had at least prepared him for what it took to recover. As he had done then, he did now, trying not to excite himself. He drank tea, lots of tea. He cut back on chewing his cigars. He spent time on the back porch taking in deep breaths, which often got him stepping down into the garden, where he could pull a few weeds, trim the roses until he tired. Sometimes he took the car out for a spin. That's what they called it, "taking a spin," though he wasn't sure why. He'd heard that the manufacturer wouldn't be offering white tires in the future. The same company that made

Winnie's Crayolas had been asked to provide a black pigment to paint a few tires, and they'd discovered it made the rubber stronger. He liked stronger tires, but he preferred the white color. It provided greater contrast against the jet black of the car, something the eye admired.

Most of all, he kept his thoughts to positive ones. Last February, when Winnie had turned five and he'd looked at himself as an old man in the mirror, had been a low point for him. Since then he'd made himself seek the brighter things in his life: his children, good help, a profession that suited him. He had the side businesses of the rental cottages and the salves. While neither brought in much cash, he did find the salve helped heal his own family of scratches and scrapes, so it was worth something for all the time he'd put into it. One day it might just take off, and he'd give old Watkins a run.

The sweet note from Miss Gaebele thanking them for the camera had warmed his heart. It had been an extravagant gift, he knew that. But she had worked for him for nearly three years and only taken off the days she'd gone with her brother to Rochester. She was as faithful as his windup clock, ticking away. But every clock needed a rewinding to keep going. The new camera was just that. Her natural bent for photography kept her going more than his instruction did. Miss Kopp was a good worker too, but he knew by the salary envelopes that she had taken any number of days away, leaving Jessie—Miss Gaebele—alone at the studio. He didn't like that and had written to Miss Kopp of his concerns, noting with some satisfaction that she'd had perfect attendance the month after his mention.

He had intercepted Miss Gaebele's note to the family, however. He didn't want Mrs. Bauer to see it. He hadn't wanted to upset her with his purchase. She would have questioned him, and while he felt he had a defensible response, it could also lead to one of their rows. He didn't want that, not in front of the children, not in front of Selma.

Why should he worry that Selma

witness marital discord? Was he concerned that Jessie would think poorly of him if her sister shared such goings-on? Why should he care what the girl thought? No, he just didn't want to stain the child's view of marriage. He supposed the Gaebeles rarely argued. They seemed such a gregarious family whenever he'd seen them all together. William Gaebele probably never lost his temper the way FJ sometimes did.

He walked out onto the porch, took the steps down to the garden, and bent to pull a few weeds. He knelt. That would be more comfortable. He thought he should go get his gloves, but he didn't plan to stay long and he liked the feel of the warm earth on his hands, the grit of the dirt. Garden planting time. He'd have to talk with Selma about that. It was funny how he had no difficulty calling Selma by her given name but made a point of not calling Jessie by hers except in private. And then she'd said she wanted to be known as Miss Gaebele anyway. He supposed it set a distance for her, kept the boundaries of work and privacy clear, ones that ought not be leapt over. *Miss Gaebele. That's how I must think of her.*

He looked at his hands. Most of the spots had disappeared, and he opened his shirt to the May breeze. He hadn't worn a collar for months now. He found himself getting excited about wearing that collar again, every day, donning his tie, vest, and suit and heading back to the studio. He had ordered in some new equipment, and it ought to have arrived by now. A more modern camera, some different papers that were said to take less time to expose. He remembered his trials with the Karsak and Solio "printing-out paper" and how they'd promised exposure using artificial light, such as an electric bulb, for only a few seconds. The paper hadn't worked out well. Sunlight was more reliable for printing. Something as natural as sunlight outperformed all the technological advances. There really was, as the verse in Ecclesiastes said, nothing new under the sun.

He stood, finished his breathing

exercises, and went inside. FJ made his way to the nursery, where Selma, Robert, and Winnie sat at the corner table. Selma held Robert on her lap, and he scribbled with a bright yellow Crayola held with a death grip in his right hand.

"Oh, Mr. Bauer, I wasn't meaning to sit down on my job." Selma rushed to stand up, her apron catching on the table edge, Robert pulled from his design.

"You're fine, Selma. Just fine. Please, sit." She did. The boy resumed as though nothing had happened. "I thought I'd check on you before I tried to take a walk."

"Mrs. Bauer is here," Selma assured him. "We'll be fine. She's just resting."

"As she almost always is," he said, then hated himself for it. What kind of man complained to his children and their nursery attendant? A restless man, he decided. If he felt invigorated by the walk today, he would plan to return to work next week. He'd been separated from what he loved too long.

"Don't forget your cane, Papa. You walk lots better with your extra leg."

"I do, Winnie," he said. "Thank you for the reminder."

It was the kind of thing he wished his wife would take note of. But she didn't notice much these days. He wondered if she ever would again, or if she ever really had. Though she was years younger than he was, there were days when she seemed more the age of the mother he'd left behind in Germany than the wife who once shared his bed. He guessed that was fitting for an old man. She had been listless, never even cleaned the closets anymore, it seemed.

Robert wiggled off Selma's lap and waddled to him. "Daddy. Write. Now," he said. He shoved the crayon toward FJ.

"You've made a pun," FJ told him, swooping the boy up into his arms. "Right. Now."

That's what he needed to pay attention to, what was right now before him. "Let's all go for a walk, maybe a little run, and have a fine time doing it."

He hoped he was still young enough for that.

>─┼─◄►─○─◄►─┼─◄

When Jessie saw him, it was as though nothing had changed, despite her efforts to make sense of the confusion and put her daydreams away. He looked almost dapper. His mustache was trimmed to a fine ledge above his upper lip, and his skin looked, well, healthy. A little pink, but that was likely from being outside in the late spring air.

"You're looking good, Mr. B.," Voe said. "Doesn't he, then?" She elbowed Jessie. The two stood shoulder to shoulder at the front door as he came up the steps.

"Yes. He looks very healthy. Welcome back, Mr. Bauer. I hope we've done well by you."

He stared into Jessie's eyes, and she had that old feeling of having her heart leave her body and soar around as though it needed to see the world first before settling back into the dreariness of simply beating. Neither of them spoke.

"Mr. Bauer?" Voe asked. "Are you feeling all right?"

"Yes, what? Oh, yes." He dropped his eyes, turned to Voe, cleared his throat. "Best I take a stroll around the studio, see if things are up to snuff." He smiled at her, then back at Jessie, and she heard her heart beat so loud she was sure that he could hear it too. She sucked in her breath, and it caught in her throat. She coughed.

"Should I get you some water?" Voe asked. Jessie shook her head. "You both looked sort of flushed," Voe said. "Coming down with ague?"

"Nonsense," Jessie said. "I'll just, in the kitchen, I'll . . . I'll make some coffee for us while you give him the tour." Her hands shook as she touched the back of her hair. She walked past him to the kitchen as though she were alone in the room, simply primping her hair.

She felt ill. Maybe Voe was right and she was coming down with a summer cold. But no. Jessie knew what this was. Her body knew what this was, and it was dangerous, like a moth to light.

She collected herself by the time the two of them entered the kitchen, and she heard him say, "Yes, yes, everything is quite fine. I'm impressed and grateful to you both." He took Voe's hand in his and patted it. "You did well." He dropped her hand and went to Jessie and reached for hers as well. "You exceeded my expectations, Miss Gaebele. You both have the gratitude of the entire Bauer family." Those were the words he spoke, but his eyes said something more.

Jessie pulled her hands out from his and fluttered around to pour their coffees. "I'm not supposed to have coffee," he said. "Just teas. But this is a special occasion, my coming back."

"Now we can take real vacations," Voe said. "Because there'll always be two of us here."

"That's right. You haven't had much time away, have you, Jessie? You've certainly deserved it. Perhaps you should take this next week. Voe and I can manage."

"Miss Gaebele," Jessie corrected. It

was all she could think to say to the conflict in her heart.

>-+-+>-0-<+-+-<

In her dreams that night, strong hands held Jessie back from a ledge, the hands of a faceless being. She awoke to an ache of longing for what could never be. She vowed she'd take the week off and talk with that evangelist. She was sure he'd filled the position that had opened last year, but he might have another. Taking it would be the safest thing she could do.

>-+-+>-0-<+-+-<

Ralph Carleton, Winona's own evangelist, said he'd heard of Jessie's fine ledger-keeping skills from her mother and understood she'd also managed to run a photo studio on more than one occasion all by herself. If she accepted this job, Ralph Carleton assured her, her life would be markedly improved.

Yes, Jessie thought to herself. No more having fuel for her daydreams, no more waiting for Mr. Bauer's step to come in through the door and pretending it could be more than it was: the tired steps of a married man tending to the needs of his family. No more imagining that the two of them were working for similar goals when they worked side by side to pose a portrait.

"My mother exaggerates my talents, Mr. Carleton," Jessie said. "I had an associate who helped me at the studio while Mr. Bauer, the owner, took the cure for mercury poisoning."

"She said you were just the person I needed—call me Ralph while we're here and Reverend Carleton in the correspondence—because what I need is someone who can organize this office and make sure that people get the right information for my tent gatherings. This year I branch out into Chicago, little towns around the outside, give Billy Sunday a run for his money. I'm called to take my message to places Mr. Sunday won't give the time of day to."

"The baseball player?" Jessie asked. She'd heard of a Billy Sunday, but he was a Chicago White Stockings player. Her father had mentioned him.

"Indeed. He became saved and

changed his ways, left the halls of degradation where he lounged after games drinking hard liquor, chewing tobacco, and wining wild women." Ralph Carleton appeared to take his own degradation in sweet cookies and cakes, judging from his size and the crumbs that littered the doily beneath a bowl of walnuts on the corner of his massive oak desk. He wore a white suit with the coat open and a bright blue vest stretched down his middle. The coat buttons were so far from the opposite holes he might have been trying to pull Wisconsin across the Mississippi into Minnesota. He had a wide face, black hair that he combed all to one side instead of in the middle as so many men did, and carried in his broad paw a crumpled handkerchief that he used to wipe his forehead of perspiration. Jessie wondered how much he perspired when he stood in the hot, stuffy summer tents and brought people to their knees. "He left the lure of fame and fortune, the hours afterward in the halls of degradation," Ralph repeated, wiped at his head and face.

"Don't you mean 'playing fields of degradation'?" Jessie asked.

He squinted. Jessie wondered if she'd offended him by making a correction or suggestion. Some men did not like women to even respond, let alone shape a thought. "Why, that's right. It has a better ring to it," Ralph said. " 'The playing fields of degradation' could apply to lots of men lost and needing the Lord's direction. Women too," he said. "Women need cleansing too, now, don't they, Miss Gaebele?" She squirmed in her chair. Her corset didn't fit right. "St. Augustine once claimed that women had no souls, that only men were made in God's image. Preached that women couldn't be saved from the pits of hell, without souls, you know. Or did you know that, Miss Gaebele? Or may I call you Jessie? Just here, of course. Yes, yes, women were believed to be lost except through marriage or the convent." He shook his head. "Times have changed." Jessie couldn't tell if it was a gesture of sadness for a lost way or one of hopefulness, for it doubled his potential to redeem the population.

Ralph wiped a drop of sweat sliding down his stubbled cheek below his ear, then directed her, "Take that down, Miss Gaebele. Write that down."

"About women and our lack of souls?"

"No, no, the 'playing fields of degradation' line. I'll put that in my notes. Playing fields of degradation. Good ring to it."

Jessie did as asked, seeing the inkwell and pen on his desk. She reached across, kept her gloves on, wrote, then put the pen down, grateful she hadn't spilled ink as she wrote the words. She looked at her penmanship. It wasn't as lovely as Mr. Bauer's.

"If you decide you want me, I can start next week. I'm sure that Mr. Bauer is well enough to resume responsibility for his business."

"I imagine your leaving will be a great loss to him."

It will be so much a greater loss to me. "Oh, I don't know about that." She looked at the stitching on her gloves, thought of Lilly, who might have made them though they were a gift from him. From the Bauers.

"Now, now, God wants no false humility. It is within Scripture to seek abundance in life and in spirit, for women too. God made you lovely, which we can all see, and made you capable too, Miss Gaebele. So your mother tells me. No cause to deny such based on your performance here."

Performance?

"We are all of us sinners, Miss Gaebele, and all of us still children in God's eyes, loved beyond measure. You must remember that. It is not arrogance to recognize gifts God has given. To do otherwise strikes on that."

Jessie wondered what else her mother might have conveyed to him about her, but the bit of praise, posed as it might be, felt warm against her cheek.

"I only meant that I did my job and Mr. Bauer trained me for it. The experience has enabled me to find something I love, a career in photographic work. I'd like to work for you so that I can earn money to help my family help my brother, but also because one day, I want my own photo-graphic studio."

He sat back on his wide haunches and stared. "That's a grand plan, Miss Gaebele. Though I must say the roles in this world are changing quickly, what with women in the labor force as they are. Most women wouldn't hope to have their own business. They'd be content to be attached to family, help their hus-bands in their work, allow themselves to be protected from the larger evils of the world." He hesitated as though another thought had entered his hummingbird mind, flitting here and there. His next sentence assured Jessie he had trav-eled far from a woman's hopes for a business of her own. "The state even has laws now to protect women from being transferred across state lines. Mann Act. You've heard of it?" Jessie nodded. "For immoral purposes, men take women to other states, and the government had to get involved. Got to protect them, our legislature says. Not capable, most of them, of protecting themselves, but the government isn't necessary. God is enough. He will protect.

"This is a special year, Miss Gaebele," Ralph continued. "Halley's Comet caused a near panic in Chicago last month on a dark day over that city. The comet will be a springboard to my ministries this year, warning people about getting their souls right before the end times come. The end could be near, very near. People will come to my tents to find answers to their fears."

Jessie hoped he wasn't the type to create fears and then offer no solutions. There'd been other disasters already that year. Mine explosions across the Atlantic, and in the Cascade Range of Washington State, 118 people had died in a terrible spring avalanche that buried three trains.

"Do you worry about the end, Jessie?" Ralph asked. She lowered her eyes. "You ought to."

She looked boldly at him then. "But the earth moved through the tail of the comet, and we did not burn up. Doesn't that mean humans have been given another chance to do right in this world?"

"We have time to confess our sins, but at any moment, *poof.*" He snapped his fingers. "You must think of that, Jessie. Women especially must remember these things and tell them to their children." He lifted his fist to the air as though announcing a new thought. "I believe I'll hold a special gathering just for women. Yes, that would be a wonderful thing. If women cleanse their souls, they'll lead their families to the purity necessary to be at peace, regardless of when the world ends. Write that down, Jessie." He smiled when she looked back up at him. "You'll be doing the Lord's work helping me," he said. "How fortunate you are."

Jessie knew she ought to think of her soul and what it needed for purity, because she'd had thoughts, some that, if she didn't ignore them, would take her to an unforgivable place. Lust in one's heart was the same as knowing someone in the biblical sense, wasn't it? Though she had not known Mr. Bauer that way, she had longed for what wasn't hers to have. And this emptiness she carried with her on her journey made her almost wish the tail of the comet had done what some had predicted and ended it all.

Ralph came around to the side of the desk where Jessie sat, her hands clasped now in her lap. "We can mutually benefit each other, Miss Gaebele. You provide good secretarial skills for my ministry, and I will ensure that you have the best working environment you could ever hope for. Only other women work here. No temptations."

What had her mother told him? He paused to put down the glob of limp cotton that was his hanky and pulled out a leather book. "Of course, a lot of my singers who travel with me are men. We urge local churches to provide the chorus, but we bring our own director. You'll have to deal with men but only at a distance. These are my past traveling schedules, contacts in various cities and whatnot; these are my current plans for the year." He pointed to stacks of folders on a side table. The pile of papers jutted out like the bad teeth of a neglected child. "And this will be our daily schedule. We'll begin with Bible reading each and every day. Your mother said that would be something you'd particularly want."

"I'm sure she did," Jessie said.

She'd have to speak with her mother about what led the reverend to think she couldn't work around men! But then she remembered how she'd felt the day Mr. Bauer returned to the studio, wishing she were all alone with him and feeling relief that while Voe was there she was protected from her own emotions. It certainly was worth a try to listen to her mother this once.

Ralph Carleton talked so much she wouldn't have time to daydream. And he promised to pay her more than what she'd been making at the studio.

Ralph stared into her eyes. "You will find your true direction here. We will keep you safe from temptation, Miss Gaebele."

"Isn't it the Lord Himself who keeps us from temptation?" Jessie said.

"Indeed," Ralph said. He sat back then, on the edge of his desk, one leg on the floor, his thick thigh squeezing the linen of his bent pant leg. He crossed one arm over his large chest to hold the opposite elbow. He looked at her through newly approving eyes. "I believe your mother underestimates you."

"My mother loves me dearly." *And she fears I'll say the right thing but not always do it.* Maybe working here would keep her feet from slipping. Jessie reached her hand out to shake Ralph Carleton's and set the date she'd begin to work for him.

><+>-O-<+>-<

For Jessie, knowing she would tell Mr. Bauer she was leaving made her think of the women who said good-bye to their men before they sent them off to the Philippine-American War. They had to put aside the future, think of how they'd live knowing that their husband or fiancé wouldn't be there to hold them when they needed it.

Jessie had never been held by the one she was leaving. The days before she told him of her departure were like the songs she never wanted to end, even knowing that when they did the melody would continue in her mind long after the music had stopped. It would never again ring in her ears as it had or be as transforming.

When could she tell him? Her eyes scanned the appointment book. His first appointment arrived. She listened to customers welcome FJ back, commenting that he looked well and that they hoped to see him at their lodge or at church before long. Jessie kept her face from expressing the jab of pain when someone mentioned church.

Jessie witnessed no knowing looks suggesting that she was anything other than a professional assisting him with a request for prints while he and Voe finished up. She kept the lines of professionalism as tightly tuned as a violin string. She answered, "Yes, Mr. Bauer," when he asked her to get him something, always by calling her Miss Gaebele. She made suggestions discreetly, never acted as though she had authority over his thoughts and actions, though she knew she did. Oh yes, she knew she did, which was the very reason she had to leave, had to work somewhere else. It was the only way.

She waited until the day ended. It was a Thursday. She was nervous. Then Voe said, just before she left, that she and Daniel had set the date for their wedding. "Saturday next," she told her. "You'll be my witness, won't you?"

"Of course. I didn't realize things had moved along so quickly."

"I think I'm ready," Voe said. Her face beamed, and Jessie felt her joy and let it wash over her, if only for a moment.

"Could I speak with you, Mr. Bauer?" Jessie said after Voe left and all the windows had been closed, the drapery drawn. They were in the office area.

"Mr. Bauer. FJ," she began.

"You sound so serious, Miss Gaebele. Shall I fix us tea?"

"No! Please. Just let me say this."

He looked suddenly alarmed, adjusted his glasses. "Is something wrong?"

"I've taken another position," she blurted. She'd planned to say how much she had liked working for him, how grateful she was for his instruction and the camera and for his supporting Lilly's seamstress work and for Selma's having fine employment. She'd rehearsed it all, but when she sat before him, watched his eyes as he sat behind the desk, the words flew out before she could think to control their exit.

"Are you ill? The mercury." He stood so quickly his chair nearly fell back. He walked around the desk. "Let me see your hands."

She let him hold them, knew she ought not to.

"I don't understand, Jessie," he said.

"I'm not ill. I . . . My mother thinks I ought to try another profession." She was such a coward!

"I have put much responsibility on you these past months, I know that. But you seemed to thrive on it. The studio is doing well. I know you haven't had time away, that you allowed Voe to have a vacation while you kept the studio open, and I'm grateful. But to leave? Surely I could relieve your mother's concerns. Unless they are your concerns too."

"It's . . . I think I should separate myself. I mean, don't you?"

She looked for some recognition on his face, some understanding that they shared feelings that had not been openly expressed, perhaps never should be. She longed to see that he too knew that to remain in close contact would only cause suffering, inflict a wound that would never heal, would just keep hurting, weeping.

He looked away. *Maybe I've read into his looks and movements. Lilly and my mother are wrong, and I half believed they weren't!* She swallowed, her throat thickening.

He began, "Was it that day in the retouching studio with the baby—?"

"Ralph Carleton has offered me a position that will earn me a little more money. So one day I can have my own studio," she said. She said it firmly, taking the attention from how she felt to the business at hand.

He stepped back, sat on the desk. His shoulders dropped, in relief, she thought. "Oh. Well. We could talk about an increase in pay then. Yes, we must."

"Eventually I'll be your competition," she said. "And it wouldn't be fair to have you train me further and be the source of an improved salary, then have me spin around and buy a studio that might take business from you."

He stared at her. *He's upset.* "Miss Gaebele. The chance that a young woman barely eighteen years old could purchase a business, compete with a diplomat in the photographic congress, and take clients from an established studio is quite a fantasy on your part. An indulgent fantasy, I'd say." He smiled as though she were fifteen and had just walked through his studio door.

Jessie felt her face grow warm and her breath shorten. She wasn't sure if it was his condescension of her talents and capability that riled her passion or that he failed to see that she was leaving because to stay would break her heart.

"Good, then. We won't have discussions anymore about portraits versus more candid shots. The world is moving faster, Mr. Bauer. My interests in the profession may well overtake stuffy studio artist's poses." He winced. "I'm sorry," she said, overcome with remorse for her sharp tongue. "You've done so much for me. I shouldn't have said that." She heard her heart pounding like raindrops on the rooftop. She fought back tears.

He said nothing for a time. She heard squirrels chatter outside the window.

"No, I'm the one to apologize, Miss Gaebele." His voice was as smooth as a finger brushed against her brow. "I had no call to poke holes in your dreams. No cause at all. You're very talented. You'll go far. I've no right to hold you back. I . . . A salary increase can certainly be considered, if I haven't insulted you to the extent that you'd refuse to consider it. I've become . . . fond of you, your presence."

"And I yours," she said. "Perhaps too much so."

"No, no," he told her. "I never should have . . . The presents, did they offend you? I sometimes felt so . . . different with you, so alive again. Young." He sat on the edge of the desk just as Ralph Carleton had, only he clasped his hands together as though in prayer, his elbows resting on his thighs. "I never meant to hurt you. I . . . Jessie, perhaps I ought not say this, but—"

He did feel as she did, at least a little. She had to be the stronger of the two. She had to keep the words from being spoken. It was up to her, before he began to see the depth of what she felt or acknowledged anything more of his own.

She stood, put out her hand. "I know Voe will be good for you, and you can find another assistant to train. You're very good at that. And I am truly grateful for all you've done for me, for my family too. Good-bye, Mr. Bauer," she said.

He tried to hold on to her hand after shaking it, but she pulled away.

He stood then, clasped his hands behind him as though a military man standing at ease. "Very well. But Voe, Miss Kopp, has just told me she'll be getting married at the end of next week. I'm sure you knew." Jessie nodded. "At least remain until after the wedding and her week of honeymooning. Please, don't leave me before that."

She'd be fine, she told herself. *Only*

two weeks and a day. "Very well. After their honeymoon, I'll be replaced."

She turned toward the door before he could say anything more. She ached for him to reach out to stop her, breathed a prayer of gratitude that he didn't. The last thing she saw clearly before her tears sent spirals of light shattering through her world was the portrait of his wife and his two sons hanging on the studio wall as Jessie rushed past.

EIGHTEEN

The Long Good-Bye

"My sister's found a new job," Selma told Mrs. Bauer. The two sat at the table shelling peas that Selma had picked from beneath the window hothouse Mr. Bauer had made. "Early peas are just the best, don't you think? So tiny and yet so tasty." She popped one into her mouth.

"Oh? Yes. I guess they're good."

"I like them in greens with a few carrots cut up on them. Mama likes to put onions in the greens, but I don't like the taste they leave in my mouth. Do you?"

"I don't notice much," Mrs. Bauer said. Something the girl had spoken of earlier made her want to ask a question, but she couldn't remember what it was. She was just so tired. All the time now. She'd thought after Robert was born this would all end, be different, and somehow she'd feel that life was worth living rather than just going through the motions. But even the laughter of her children failed to ignite some sort of spark in her. She was a weight on her husband and her children with her malaise.

She had left the Ladies Aid Society leadership more than a year ago and said it was because of her carrying Robert, but really, she hated being up front, hated the bickering that went on about such inane things as whether tulips or peonies should be the centerpieces for the spring luncheon. The real issue was about *whose* tulips or peonies would appear, whether Mrs. Jeffs or Mrs. Kursa would gain the upper hand by which flowers were placed. There'd been a time when that sort of thing mattered, but not anymore.

Even Mr. Bauer's leaving her alone, not scratching on her bedroom door anymore, even that had not relieved the pressure she felt in her head in the morning or the terrible weight she felt when she looked at him at the end of the day, wearing his own fatigue from his illnesses and the studio work now that he'd gone back. *Studio work.*

"Did you say your sister has taken another job, Selma?"

"Yes ma'am. She's going to work for the evangelist."

"Taking photographs?"

"Oh, no ma'am. She's going to be his secretary, write his letters and that sort of thing. It seems silly to me. She never liked school all that much, and my older sister, Lilly, makes fun of her wording when she writes notes. She writes *except* when she means *accept.* Even I know the difference!"

"That surprises me," Mrs. Bauer said. "My husband hasn't mentioned it. Maybe he feels now that he's back full-time he only needs one helper. But I would have thought he'd keep Miss Gaebele rather than that coarse girl, Voe Kopp."

"What's a coarse girl?" Selma asked.

"Forgive me. It's isn't a word I should have used to describe her. She's just . . .

I find her sharp in her words and not particularly faithful to our profession."

"Are you a photographer, Mrs. Bauer? I guess I didn't know that." Selma bit into a pea, and it squirted a tiny bit of juice onto the table. Selma didn't seem to notice.

"I did retouching for a time. Quite a long time, actually. But I never liked it. For my father. He was a photographer. And then for Mr. Bauer."

"I guess I thought that closet with the paintbrushes set up on a table belonged to Mr. Bauer. What does retouching do exactly?"

She needs to wipe up that wet spot from the pea.

"I'm sorry, did you say something?"

"I just wondered what retouching was for."

"It's to take out blemishes from a person's face. Or sometimes the extra lines around eyes or a mouth. The wrinkles formed when a person smiles a lot—some people don't like to see them held static forever, the way they are in a photograph."

"Did you retouch the picture of Russell and your other son, the one in the hall?"

She felt her stomach tighten. "No, I did not." She sounded upset even to her own ears. She took a deep breath. "He was a perfect child. As is Russell. And Robert. They're all perfect. They don't need retouching."

"And Winnie, she's perfect too?"

"Did I leave her out? How could I?" *How could a mother forget one of her children? What kind of mother is that?* She'd been having dreams where she left one or all of the children behind in Cosgrove's when she went there to buy a hat or gloves and left with packages filled with brushes and paints that weighed her down, and it wasn't until she got home that she discovered she had no children. They were all gone and she couldn't remember where to find them. *That pea juice will stain the oil-cloth if the girl doesn't wipe it up.*

"Selma, do you see the pea juice there, on the tablecloth? Wipe that up before it stains."

The girl squinted. "I can't see where it is, Mrs. Bauer. Can you point it out?"

"It's as large as the bottom of a pan," Mrs. Bauer snapped. "Are you blind? Right there!" She pointed.

Selma's face took on a frightened look. The girl rose and got a rag and wiped it around, but she obviously wasn't paying attention. She missed it. "Here, give me that." Mrs. Bauer grabbed the cloth and scrubbed at the table. She moved the rag, stared. It was still there. It had already stained! They'd have to throw it out. A perfectly good tablecloth ruined. The girl stood with her back jammed against the dry sink.

Mrs. Bauer yanked at the cloth, spilling the peas they'd shelled into the bowl. "It can't be repaired," she said. "Take it out, take it out." *Why am I so distressed? Where has my mind gone? They're only peas.*

"Mama?" It was Russell. He'd come in from outdoors. "Mama?"

"Would you take the tablecloth outside? It's been ruined by pea juice. Perhaps your father can use it to lie on when he does what he does with the car."

"Change the oil."

"Yes. When he does that. It will keep him from getting his coat dirty." The boy took the oilcloth from Selma. The two exchanged looks. *Is he mocking me?*

"Thanks for taking care of the cloth for me," Selma said. "I'm sure sorry."

Russell held the oilcloth up. He looked at Selma with a question on his face. "Mama? Are you sure you want to throw this out? I can't see the stain."

"You're both blind," she wailed. "Just do as I say. Get it out of here."

She shooed them out of the kitchen.

She thought her head would burst.

⊱─┄◆─○─◆┄─⊰

"You have to take the wedding pictures," Voe told FJ. Jessie had offered to pick up the order at the train station and hadn't yet arrived. These were her last days. *Last days.* FJ chided himself for using such terms. It wasn't like the girl was dying. She was simply moving on, and he'd managed to keep her here much longer than she'd intended. Or rather Voe had, repeatedly postponing the dates of her wedding—for more time to prepare the food, to bring the relatives from Wisconsin to sew a dress—until now it was June, and all was at last settled and this Saturday the girl was actually marrying.

He did wonder about the position Jessie had taken. She'd said she would wait until Voe's marriage, and she had, despite Voe's having moved the date back twice. Jessie had faithfully come to work as she'd agreed to, yet this Ralph Carleton job was still available, supposedly. Maybe she didn't really have a position at all. Maybe she just gave that as an excuse to move away from this studio, from him. At least she might have chosen a job that would utilize her photographic talents. It saddened him that she hadn't at least done that. Maybe locating a position for her at one of the other studios would be something good he could give her. He'd look into that.

"Mr. B.? You will take the photographs, won't you?" The girl spoke with that long vowel sound so typical to Scandinavians in the city.

"I'm not much good at those kinds of spontaneous poses," he said. He remembered Jessie had urged him to photograph wedding parties, but it smacked too much of that tramping work.

"It can be your wedding gift to Daniel and me," she said. "Jessie will help."

He sighed. "What kind of studio would we be if we didn't immortalize our favorite girl?" FJ said.

Once Voe married, there'd be but one more week with Jessie's brightening up his days, and then what?

"You'll let Jessie assist? She's done it before. Did we ever tell you how we took a reunion photograph at the normal school while you were ill? It was all posed of course, but we used the natural light and everyone bought a copy of the print."

"Quite resourceful, you girls," FJ said.

"Jessie was the one who set that up."

"I don't doubt that. She has a way of making things happen," he said, naming yet another quality of hers he'd miss.

><+>-O-<+><

The three of them sat in the kitchen, Voe, Mr. Bauer, and Jessie. Mr. Bauer twisted his mustache, which now had a fine upward point at both ends. He rolled the tips. Jessie looked away, not wanting to see these little endearing habits of his that she'd be reminded of each time she saw a man with a slender mustache. Her heart had begun that thumping, a rhythm beating *beware, beware, beware.* It was what Jessie had chanted to herself these past weeks, the words keeping her at a distance. Voe's marriage marked the next tow wrenching her from the Bauer Studio forever. She inhaled. It had to be. *I'm still here, I'm still here, I'm still here.* She vowed to maintain a professional stance.

"Just remember," Voe said, "I can't assist you this time, Jessie. I mean, I'll be in the pose, not handling people who spent too much time near the brew."

"Will your mother allow you to be at an event that serves spirits?" Mr. Bauer said. He turned to Jessie again.

"I'm not serving spirits," Voe corrected. "At least not until Daniel says, 'I do.'" She laughed.

Before Jessie could answer, Mr.

Bauer offered, "We can take my car. I'll come by and pick you up, Miss Gaebele, and we can—"

"No, no. We'll need to load the camera and plates. I'll just meet you at the studio at nine."

"That won't work," Voe said. "You're my maid of honor, Jessie. Remember? You'll have to come out earlier than that, to help me dress."

Mr. Bauer said. "Let's say we meet at seven, Miss Gaebele."

Voe beamed. "I never would have met Daniel if it hadn't been for the two of you."

>─┤─♦─○─♦─┤─<

There were problems Jessie hadn't considered.

First, she was certain her parents had been invited to the wedding. While they might not attend, they'd know that beer would be served and might try to keep her home even without knowing that she and Mr. Bauer would be riding out together. Just the two of them, alone.

On the other hand, Jessie was eighteen and her presence honored a friend.

Jessie *had* to be there, and she would assure her parents that she was wise enough not to do anything so foolish as to take a taste of liquor. She'd worked hard to defer to them these past weeks, as they were mollified that she had turned a corner and was on what her mother called "the straight and narrow" road. Ralph Carleton had even saved that job just for her. They'd allowed her to keep her commitment to the Bauer Studio until Voe's marriage, never knowing how difficult the past weeks had been for Jessie, saying good-bye over and over in her mind. She'd remember from this that it's always better to rip off the bandage rather than slowly pull it back from the wound.

"Besides," Jessie reminded them that evening when she brought up the subject of her Saturday plans, "there are always beer tents at the street fairs and carnivals, so temptation's often present and I've survived those well."

"But," her mother cautioned, "you always have a chaperone with you at such events—your uncle August or your family."

Jessie had never told them about the wedding she and Voe photographed, where more than ale had presented problems.

"I have to take pictures," Jessie urged. "For Voe's sake. It's my present to her."

"Well . . . how will you get out there, go the night before? There could be carousing then too, you know. She's marrying a Swede."

"Oh, Mama. No, I won't go the night before. And he's Norwegian. They're different, you know. Someone will come pick me up . . . at the studio, early, so I can get the plates and film holders I need and whatnot. Maybe Daniel himself so I can talk sense into him and make sure he knows what he's doing." She made light of her comments and saw her mother easing into the decision.

"He just might need a little talking to about marrying Voe, though I think that's a little late, don't you? Maybe it wasn't Voe setting the dates back, but Daniel," her mother said.

Jessie smiled. "It's never too late to think marriage through, is it?"

Her father lowered the paper he'd been reading. "I never had second thoughts," he said.

"You wouldn't have lived to tell of it if you had," her mother told him, and they laughed together. That camaraderie was what Jessie wanted one day, being as comfortable together as shoulder to shawl.

"So it's decided, then?"

"May as well let her go, Ida," her father said. "It's going to happen anyway, knowing Jessie."

Her mother had sighed and said, "I guess."

Their acceptance of her remaining at the studio until after Voe's marriage had surprised her. But then they had no objection to Selma's working for the Bauer family, so it wasn't Mr. Bauer they had issues with; it was her, Jessie, and how they felt their own daughter had compromised herself by wanting to be an independent woman.

The second problem presented while she stood before the mirror, holding dresses up in front of her. If she wore the white eyelet dress she'd bought on the spur of the moment and finally paid for, it would look sweet and secondary to the bride, which a bridesmaid ought to be. But perhaps it was too sweet, too much like a bridal gown itself. Her mother had told her when she brought it home that it looked like a "kept-woman dress" and acted as though she didn't believe that Jessie had paid for it herself. She held up the simple suit she usually wore when she wanted to look professional. Perhaps she could wear the dress for the wedding and change into the suit for her professional duties as a photographer. She'd change at Voe's. But no, that wouldn't make any sense if she wanted to quickly move into the photographer's role right after the vows. She'd wear the suit with matching blue hat, forgo the hat once she arrived at Voe's grandparents' farmhouse where the wedding would be held, and put it back on when she stood behind the camera. The hat with the tiny row of white flowers around the rim would mark the transition between her roles that day. Bridesmaid to professional woman.

And what role will you play with Mr. Bauer?

Jessie might well be asked to be *in* the picture as part of the wedding party. She didn't want to be there that way; she wanted to attend as the photographer. Maybe she could pose the shots and use a long cable return to her place so she was actually taking the shot and not Mr. Bauer. She wondered at why she felt a rise of competition with him, especially now.

Jessie poked the pin into the felt and the roll of her hair on the top of her head. She imagined herself posing people and moving them in the way her eye wanted them to appear on paper. Mr. Bauer would want the role of exposing the film. Jessie would be relegated to *his* apprentice, running to the car to pick up plates and whatnot, even though she had been the one to urge him to do the outdoor shots. But they'd be using her camera. *That he gave me.* It would be especially difficult to convince him otherwise if she was there more as a member of the wedding party than as the photographer. She'd have to balance that.

When she'd agreed to do the wedding photos together, she'd been interested in delaying the pain she knew would come when she finally left his employ. She could hear Lilly saying to her, "Be careful or you'll poke your finger with the very needle you bought to sew things up."

It was the complication of the day.

She'd work it out. What mattered was that she would have the time driving out with him and the time driving back. She'd allow herself to enjoy Voe's wedding, being with him to photograph this celebration. Affection. That's all it was he felt for her, and that's what she'd reduce her feelings to as well. Eventually.

Maybe these weren't logistics problems. Maybe they were signs of her life maturing.

>─+─<→>─O─<+>─+─<

FJ combed his mustache, put the paste on the tips, found his fedora hat. He took one last look at himself in the mirror by the umbrella stand. Collar starched. Tie in place. Coat brushed. Then quietly he made his way out the door to the garage in the back. Selma had stayed over the previous night. She'd assist with the children in the morning, when Mrs. Bauer was feeling especially out of sorts, as he'd taken to thinking of it. Selma sometimes helped Mrs. Bauer begin her day, even on Saturday, if he had appointments. The request was nothing out of the ordinary. He told himself that.

He bent to brush at his pants and smelled the scent of his cologne. He hadn't worn it for months and wasn't at all sure why he'd put it on this morning. But he had. Perhaps it would cover that "old" smell he sometimes noticed on his wool. *Old.* He would be forty-five in August. That certainly wasn't old, but his life had that gasping feel to it: his heart, his struggles with the poisonings, his emptiness of love from Jessie—Mrs. Bauer. He couldn't say his wife's name even to himself without thinking of Miss Gaebele.

His emptiness of spirit.

At least he had his children. They soothed his wounded heart, made him find gladness in being home, made him grateful that he'd met their mother all those years before. Despite what had happened between their parents, the children had been the treasure of their marriage and always would be.

He stepped outside into the June morning. Clouds skipped across the bluffs, big puffy ones that would offer good shade for the photographs but enough sun for exposure. The air smelled of sawdust, the wind carrying the scent from the construction going on down the street and the mills in operation. Rain had fallen in the night and cleaned away the burnt-coal smell of trains and steamboats and their companions.

He opened one half of the shed door—he'd start calling it his garage when the word felt less pretentious. It creaked on the hinge, especially loud this morning. Then he opened the other door and placed rocks to keep them from closing while he drove out. He hadn't purchased Ford's model the first year. He waited to see if it was a sticking thing or not. Then he'd bought the Touring Car, a 1908 model. It wasn't really as practical as the first models produced at the Piquette Avenue plant in Detroit. This one had all forward speeds operating by a foot pedal and backward by a stick. He checked the cylindrical gas tank mounted on the frame by the running boards. Not that he needed to. He hadn't been anywhere except the few blocks to church since he'd filled the tank the previous Saturday. The side lamps had enough oil, though he wasn't expecting to be out at night. He walked around the car, checked the tail lamp. He wouldn't try the tube horn; no need to wake the neighbors. But once in the country, he'd use it. He'd enjoy using it then. He decided to lower the top, folding it back like an accordion. The day was perfect for a country drive, and why not see the birds and the clouds as they drove along, let the sunlight scrub their faces?

At the front he pulled the crank, twisted it. It took nothing before the magnetos did their work, and he stepped into the vehicle and put his hands on the wheel and started his drive out. All would have been perfect except that as he pulled beside the house he caught movement at the side of his eye.

Russell!

The boy waved at him in the window, then ran through the house to the front porch.

"Wait! I want to go too!" he shouted. "Can't I?"

And why can't he? The thought flitted through FJ's head. He was a well-mannered boy, curious. He'd be good help and surely would offer no trouble. He'd enjoy the day, the drive, wind blowing his hair about. FJ could stop. Give the boy time to dress. He had time. There was no hurry, not really. It had been only six thirty when he pulled at his pocket watch just before starting the car. Why not spend the day with the boy?

"It's work, Son," FJ shouted back to him. "I'll come back early and we'll take a spin then. Go back to bed now. Get some rest."

He shouted all that in a rush as he drove on by and rattled over the railroad

tracks. He didn't want to see the disappointment in Russell's face. He didn't
want to feel the ache in his own old foolish heart.

>─┤◆├──○──◇┤─<

Jessie arrived early. She put the camera
into its case, selected the glass plates,
loaded several into holders. She decided to take three boxes. She couldn't
imagine taking more than thirty-six wedding shots, but then it might happen
that way. Perhaps other guests would
want individual photographs made.
Maybe on the way back they'd shoot
pictures of the bluffs, the river, or the ar-
row grass that bordered the edges of
streams, luring ducks and geese. Scenic shots. There'd be ample opportunity
for those kinds of pictures on the way
toward the village of Cream in Wisconsin, where Voe's grandparents worked
as dairymen. That's where the wedding
would take place, nestled in the green
valley where Holsteins ripped at grass
and woods dotted the heights. Maybe
they'd stop and pick mushrooms.
There'd be other flowers in bloom: large

lavender wildflowers and the pasques that speared up through last year's grasses. Jacob's ladder, lady slippers, shooting stars, and phlox would dot the bluff slopes. She grabbed a fourth box.

As she gathered her supplies, she thought it probably would have been better if she'd gone out to Voe's the evening before. There'd be no pressure then to arrive on time. It might take a good hour for them to reach the farm and no telling how the roads might be. Streams ran high; they'd have to cross a creek before arriving at the wedding site. She looked at the Seth Thomas clock. Six forty-five. Plenty of time. If they didn't arrive until eight it would still be well before the vows, scheduled for eleven. She could help Voe dress and set up the camera the way she wanted. Besides, leaving the night before meant not having this morning with FJ, alone.

Guard your heart.

She felt warm. She removed her suit jacket and was hanging it on the back of the chair, looking for any smudges she might rub away, when the puttering sounds of a car engine rolled past the studio. She looked out the window. He'd arrived. "Stop it," she chided her heart out loud. "Just stop."

He drove his touring car. The top was pulled back! Her hair would be a mess, an absolute crow's-nest by the time they arrived. She didn't have one of those veils either. She hadn't wanted to tell her mother specifics of her plans to arrive and depart, but Jessie certainly should have secreted a way to keep the dust from her face or keep her hat on. She needed a wrapper over her dress too. She looked around. She'd take one of the props, a colorful blanket, and put it across her lap to protect her pale blue skirt. That silk scarf she sometimes draped over a woman's shoulder might also work as her veil of the moment, tied over her hat and around her chin.

She watched him get out, remove his fedora, and lean over the open side to lay it in the seat. He ran his hands through his hair, pulled at his vest, twisted his mustache. Wiped at his face. He looked nervous. *He isn't accustomed to driving his car.* He started up the steps.

She wasn't sure what moment of bright and brilliant light seared into her soul, telling her for certain that he shared feelings he'd tried to secret away. Maybe it was the way he hesitated when he looked up at her as she opened the back door to the kitchen, the way he stood on the stone step and inhaled, head cocked as if to say, *Are we doing this?* before he made his way inside. Maybe it happened when she stepped back to let him pass but he turned instead, so close to her she could see the hair of his mustache lift as he exhaled with his lower lip slightly out to send the air upward, cooling his red face. His face looked warm. Hers was.

It was as though he saw her for the first time, not as an apprentice, not as someone he could talk to about cameras and lenses and poses, but as a singular woman. She saw her own desire reflected in his eyes.

A sound escaped from his mouth. He pulled her to him then and she yielded, let the door slam shut. He pressed her head into his chest, tendered his fingers on the back of her neck, making her aware of each tendril of hair loosened. He held her as though she were fragile glass. His hands burned through her cotton blouse until she could feel the pads of his flesh moving slowly down her back and settling at her waist. She had not worn her corset. Her heart raced. She trembled.

"I'm not a good man, Jessie," he whispered. She didn't know how long they'd stood in silence, listening to the breathing of their bodies. "I've left my son standing on the porch, begging me to take him. I refused him. To be alone with you. I'm old enough to be—"

"Shh." She stepped back and put a finger to his lips. Strange feelings screamed through her body like a spring freshet strong enough to tumble rocks and send them over the precipice into the Mississippi. He had acted first. He, too, felt whatever it was that had driven her from him and now threatened to pull her back. "It doesn't mat—"

He kissed her then, his lips sweet and soft enough to make her heart fold like a feather pillow, sinking into comfort. He would never know that this was her first kiss, the first time she'd felt lips on hers of someone who was not her mother or father, touching her with love. This was more than affection. So much more.

"I'm not good either," she whispered, breaking away but keeping her cheek to his. She whispered in his ear. "I know that ending this will hurt more than I can ever imagine. And it will have to stop. I know that. But somehow . . . somehow, Mr. Bauer—"

"Fred," he said, his voice hoarse. "You must call me Fred."

"I can't . . . I want . . . We shouldn't talk as though we—"

"Anybody in there?" A man's voice followed by a loud pounding on the back door separated them like the Red Sea parting. *Has the man been pounding long? Did we not hear it? Has he seen us?*

Fred—she would ever after think of him as Fred—opened the door as Jessie moved back into the kitchen shadows.

"All right if I look at your touring car?" the man said. "I was walking by and saw you pass me and pull in here. Quite a machine. Runs well, does it?" He tapped his fingers to his hat when he noticed Jessie. "Missus," he said, nodding.

Fred stepped out to show him the touring car. She heard their voices as from a well, echoing and far away. Her limbs felt weak. Her heart slowed. *Who is he?* She could hear Lilly's voice saying to her, *Are you mad?*

Maybe she was.

NINETEEN

Too Much Exposure

"We'd best load the car," FJ said after the man had had his fill of specifications, patted the fuel tank, looked under the hood, and even sat in the leather seat as though he planned to drive away. Finally, the man tipped his hat and went on down the walk. FJ didn't look at Jessie when he came back inside, couldn't let himself look at her. He would apologize, but he feared desperately his own weakness, that he would be unable to finish his apology when he faced her again and would instead sweep her to him, clinging to the softness and strength he knew was there, the fire of passion so long missing from his life.

Thank goodness the man had come by when he did! Inner voices argued with him, told him to drive by and pick up Russell before they headed out. Russell's presence would protect them. But he was deaf now. Deaf. He made his voice gruff. Cleared his throat. She spoke first.

"I'm not going to let anything happen, Mr. Bauer. FJ." He smiled at her. "Fred," she croaked, then stiffened her spine. "Mr. Bauer." She kept a safe distance from him. "I understand. I really do. I'm going to work for Ralph. I'll be gone by next week, once Voe returns. So this, whatever this is, is nothing. Nothing to worry over."

She would keep this professional and be in control. *Good.*

"I'll need to leave," Jessie said. "We won't see each other except in passing on the street." She didn't pose it as a question. "Nothing will come of that kiss, I know. You have commitments. I won't come between them. I won't let that happen. I'm not that kind of woman."

"I know you're not." He felt disappointed, though he didn't know why.

"It's just that I have longed to kiss you, to comfort, to feel your face against mine."

"Jessie—"

"In a week it will be over. I'll be out of your life and you out of mine."

He moaned and reached for her again, but she stepped back into the shadow. She put her palms up to ward him off. "Working for Ralph will keep me, keep us, safe. I'll pile up rocks there, enough to build a wall against the path to you."

"The path is already there."

"After this week, we won't walk on it," she said.

"But let's have this week. Please." She looked in pain. He was giving someone else he loved pain too. His wife, his children—he had to think of them.

"We can pretend that—"

"No pretending, not anymore, Jessie. What is, is."

"But we don't have to act on it. So we'll be all right."

"We'll be all right," he said. He wondered if she believed him.

"We need to go," she said then. "Voe . . ." She pointed to the kitchen clock.

"Right."

She straightened her narrow shoulders, and he thought he saw something shift inside her, tense her face and make her blue gray eyes widen. *She is so beautiful.*

"I have several ideas for poses I think you might like. I'm quite good at posing."

"Jessie, I didn't mean to hurt you. Not ever, not with what I said about you having a studio of your own. If those were words that made you want to leave here, then—"

"I take good care of my feelings. They haven't been wounded in the least. Let's go get Voe married."

She sounded as though she really meant it. He would cling to that.

>─┼─◄►─Ο─◄►┼─◄

Jessie wondered if he was frightened of her, not sure she'd be strong enough to prevent this rush of feeling from moving too far. She was frightened herself as she stepped up into the car. Fred closed the door behind her. He smiled and she made herself turn away. She had to assure him that this euphoria would fade. She'd be safe from the strength of her feelings. She wanted to imagine that they might last longer, that she and Fred had a future, but the truth was, they did not. They had only one week where they could just be comfortable with each other, sate the longing that each felt for the other—not by doing anything either would ever regret but by sharing time together, proving to themselves that they could care deeply without ever threatening a marriage vow or the safety of their souls. It would be a harmless caring, a careful affection, nothing more. She wouldn't let it be anything more.

It wasn't easy to talk as they drove. The wind rushed across their faces, and she was glad for that. The day sang of joy. Even the weather celebrated a new bride and groom's love. She felt . . . envy for Voe, who wouldn't have a mere week of bliss with Daniel but instead

had the promise that it could go on forever.

Timing. It was all about timing.

At one point, when the tires slipped
into the ruts they'd been straddling on
the dirt road and back out again, she
was thrown against him as a cloud of
dust *whoosh*ed up into her face. She
straightened, coughed, then shouted as
she could, "Can we stop and put the top
up? It might help a little."

He'd done so immediately, apologiz-
ing through nervous movements as he
did. "I should have considered. Good
thing the camera's in a case. Is your
skirt ruined? The ruts tend to pull the
wheels toward them whether the wheels
planned to go that way or not."

She'd stepped out of the car to
stretch her legs and shake the blanket
of the dust. "Not unlike life." Jessie
laughed. Her laughter calmed him, and
he smiled.

"Not unlike one's life exactly," he said.
"We get on the road and just keep going, thinking we can avoid the ruts, but
of course we can't."

"No. There are always challenges of

some kind. But we have time," Jessie said.

"What do you mean?" He looked alarmed again.

"I meant we don't have to try to go full speed in your car. We have time to reach the farm and still set things up." She lifted her locket watch. "It's not even nine, and we can't be that far. Voe said their farm was right off the road and they'd tie long scarves to the gatepost so we'd be sure not to pass it."

"Right. Of course that's what you meant."

Jessie unwound the scarf she had around her hat, tossed the hat into the back. She used the ends of her fingers to push up her hair. She was glad she'd worn the smaller-brimmed hat because otherwise she might have taken flight like a bird with the wind rushing through the auto. He tied the scarf for her to protect her jacket, touching her neck, letting his fingers linger along her jaw. He bent to kiss her, but she moved away. It took all the strength she had.

They got back into the car, which had sat idling. Now they were out of the sunshine, but it did seem to Jessie that the wind was less swirling as they drove. And he'd slowed, reducing the dust that had started to shroud her. Eight hundred dollars could be better spent on a good horse, a buggy, and extra glass plates rather than on a touring car, she thought.

The creek lay at the bottom of a slope of the driveway, and he sped up to plunge through it, the speed propelling them up the bank. Jessie squealed and laughed out loud, and he took one hand off the wheel and pulled her scarf to him, stealing a kiss on her check as they lifted over the rise and rolled into the yard, scattering chickens as they approached the house. *He's a risk-taker too.*

They arrived with plenty of time to spare. Jessie told Fred she'd go in to help Voe and that it would be useful if he walked around the house seeking possible settings for the wedding party photographs.

He had a grin on his face. "I think I can manage that much. Should I wait until you return before I open the camera case?" He clicked his heels and saluted her as though a commander had just given him an order. He meant it to be funny, she was certain, but it cut her.

She had started into the house, turned, and didn't speak the sentence loudly but enough so he could hear. "Don't . . . don't treat me like a child," she said. He scratched at his mustache in that way he had but kept his tongue.

Voe's mother wrapped her in a hug when Jessie entered. She introduced people sitting at a large round table. "Now we've got to get you off to Voe. She's a bucket of bees this morning, and I don't think they're the honey-making kind. At least we're this far. I don't know why that girl has gone up and down with the dates."

"She said it was to have time for relatives to arrive and to make enough food."

"Oh, pawh. I fix meals four times a day for ten threshers. It wasn't for me she delayed."

"I'll see what I can do," Jessie said.

"Who's the gentleman casing the

house?" someone asked. Jessie thought he was probably one of Daniel's cousins from the looks of him, with the big blond head and blue eyes. He stared out through the kitchen window.

"That's Voe's boss," someone else answered, a tallish man with a long mustache that draped down either side of his wide mouth. "Voe's a photographer. Or was until Daniel up and took her away."

"I'm only going away for a week," Voe said, coming out of the bedroom.

"Daniel certainly won't let you work after that." This from yet another young man. "Women belong in one place and one place only and that's—"

"The kitchen," her mother interrupted.

"Well, that's what I intended to say, Auntie. What was you thinkin' I was gonna say?"

Mrs. Kopp blushed. "Oh, pawh," she said, swatting a towel at him. "Take this apple pie and put it outside on the table."

He raised his hands in protest. "Women's work!" he said. "You wouldn't want to be sissifying your own nephew, now, would you?"

"No one would ever mistake your size-twelve feet for a sissy's," Mrs. Kopp told him. "Do as you're told."

"Come on, Jessie," Voe told her. "The rest of the girls are waiting in here."

"You are coming back after the honeymoon, aren't you?" Jessie asked her as the girls padded down the hall.

"Oh sure. I wouldn't dare leave you and Mr. B. alone for more than a week," she said. She elbowed Jessie to show she was teasing. "And I know you're anxious to start your new job."

Jessie wished she were.

"How come, I mean, why have you postponed the date so often, Voe? Are you having second thoughts?"

Voe stopped. "Maybe I was," she said. "To be with the same man forever and ever? After having two and three beaus at one time? I wasn't sure I was up to the promises I'll be making, you know? But my ma said it was a treasure to find someone who makes you laugh on your down days and can cry with you in joy. Dan does that. I'd be a fool to let him get away, then. Wouldn't I?"

⤐ ⟡ O ⟡ ⤏

Jessie stood near Voe on the women's side of the parlor when the wedding vows were spoken. Daniel looked scared as a fox caught with his paw in the chicken house just as the lights came on. Only this was a fox who knew he was in the right place at the right time. His eyes warmed as he looked at his soon-to-be wife. Jessie could see his face more easily than Voe's. She could see the men's side if she looked at an angle, noticed Voe's grandfather seated in a high-back chair. She kept her eyes forward for the most part and listened to what the minister had to say. She pushed back thoughts about Fred and the morning kiss that was as much hello as good-bye; she pushed down the ache at seeing Voe and Daniel's happiness.

Voe's minister spoke to the crowd about the holy state of marriage and how these two people could keep those vows to be faithful and obedient to God *and* to each other. He emphasized "to each other." Some had kept the vows for seventy-five years, he assured them. "Let your goal be that you two will be together until death parts you from this earth."

Jessie felt her face grow warm with shame. She *was* one of those fallen women that Ralph Carleton talked about, someone needing her soul cleansed. She was a woman who ignored a man trying to keep his vows to another. *What kind of woman am I?*

The minister kept the message short because people stood in the parlor, and the aroma of Mrs. Kopp's cooking and the neighbors' contributions, all of which filled the table outside the open window, wafted over them like a silk scarf blowing gently in the wind, luring them to sustenance.

Daniel boomed out his vows and Voe hers, and when the minister said Daniel could kiss his young bride, he lifted Voe off her feet at the waist and held her to him as though she might fly away if he let her down. People applauded and cheered, and Jessie clapped along with them, though tears pooled in her eyes. She was happy for Voe, glad she could feel that. She looked for Fred, tried to catch his eye to see if he might be thinking the same thoughts as she. What she found instead was the face of Voe's brother, Jerome, staring back.

When the pastor sent the couple out, Jessie followed close behind, along with a blond-haired man who was Daniel's older brother. His wife had been introduced to Jessie in the bedroom where the women had congregated to help Voe dress, and she'd learned there that it was Thomas whom she'd be standing up with. She took Thomas's arm, and he led her outside. "For pitures, then?" Jessie nodded, resisted the urge to correct his pronunciation.

Fred already waited outside. He'd set the camera up just beyond the porch. "Everyone stand up there, as many as you can. Thank you," he directed. "Voe and Daniel, on the second step, and Jessie and—Thomas, is it? Yes, you stand just behind them, in the middle of the crowd there. That's good. Thank you."

People muddled around, moving into position, laughing. Jessie grabbed Thomas's hand. "Let's take the second step, and Voe and Daniel, you cuddle on the first step. We'll be off to the side on the step above you but still look as though we're flanking you both."

Jessie could see Fred frown when he looked up from the camera. "Just take one this way," she shouted. "Don't you think this will work well, Voe?"

"You're the poser," Voe told her. "Any way you want it is all right with us, isn't it, Danny Man?"

Daniel's face burned red up through his ears. His brother clapped him on the back and said it was every man's wish to be called a man by his bride. "Not in public," Daniel said.

"Oh, especially in public," Thomas told him to general laughter.

Fred signaled he was ready and asked people to look toward the camera and at the count of four he would take the shot. He took it at three, to everyone's groan.

"Now let's get some family photos." Jessie elbowed her way past Voe and stood in front of the wedding party, her back to Fred. She began directing the immediate Kopp-Henderson family members to the table, where women of the Herold church had been fanning flies from the food. "Just settle down like you were going to eat," Jessie said. "Then every other one lean forward or out so that I can see each of your faces. Go ahead and pick up a fork or something. A biscuit about to go into your mouth. Make it natural."

"Don't you start eating," Voe's mother warned. "There's more to come, and it hasn't been prayed over yet."

Jostling and joking continued until all were settled enough, and Jessie walked behind them as though playing Duck, Duck, Goose, tapping shoulders, saying, "In, out, in, out," indicating which way to lean. When she got to Jerome and said, "Out," he reached behind his neck and grabbed her wrist. "I'm in," he said. "Aren't I in with you?"

"You'll always be in my heart, Jerome Kopp," Jessie joked.

"I will?"

"My artichoke heart." The guests

laughed. "But never in my dreams." Those sitting next to Jerome elbowed him. "Now keep your head back out so we can catch you in the camera."

"What else do you catch with that camera, Miss Jessie?" he said. "Your very own photographer?" Jessie felt her face burn as she wiggled her hand free of his and kept herself from looking at Fred.

"Why, I catch the faces of strong, handsome men like . . . Daniel here." More kudos and applause. "Didn't you see his portrait hanging in the parlor? Voe and I did the matting and the frame for that."

"I don't think you can get them all in that way," Fred said, coming up behind her.

"It'll be fine. I've done this before."

"There's too much in the photograph for the eye to accept," Fred argued. He kept his voice low. "The food becomes the focus instead of the people. There's too much chance of movement, Jessie. Miss Gaebele."

"Just do it as I've set it up, or move

aside so I can, Mr. Bauer," she told him, her voice a slightly louder whisper.

"The sun hits in the wrong place. There'll be shadows. No one will stand out. It's the bride and groom who should draw the viewer's eye."

"They will. People will know. Just do it, please, before they tire."

"Lover's spat or professional squabble?" Jerome called out.

Jessie felt like someone had struck her with a chunk of ice.

Fred stood still as a post, so Jessie pushed past him, stuck her head under the cloth so she could see the image, pulled the shutter open, counted, then closed it.

"Now the wedding party alone," Voe said. "You and me and Daniel and Thomas. Come on, Jessie."

"All right," Jessie said. "But let's set it up over there in the garden. The two of you sitting with Thomas and me behind you." She picked up the camera before Fred could protest, set it up again as she wanted.

The shot was taken among the rows of new greens sprouting up. "New life,"

Jessie said. "It's the perfect place." A yellow butterfly fluttered at the camera.

"I think a nice portrait shot of the bride and groom in the parlor would be good," Fred suggested then. Voe agreed, and so once again the camera was carried back inside while Daniel commented on the growl in his stomach.

Jerome walked beside Jessie, carrying some plates he'd gotten from Fred, who had gone on ahead with the camera to arrange chairs and pull the drapes.

"Still giving directions, are you?" Jerome said.

"It's what I do," she told him. She smiled.

"I take directions well."

"Maybe that's your problem," she said.

"It's a lost cause, Jess. It is. You're ruining your future hoping for what can't be." He nodded his head toward the parlor.

"Don't be small, Jerome," Jessie said. "Or foolish. I like you. You're Voe's brother. But I have a career to pursue. That's all."

"It's him, isn't it? I can tell."

"Did you see the way I directed him? Do you think anyone would want to spend time with a woman like that if he didn't have to? If the woman wasn't his mere associate? Better think twice, Jerome."

"Aw, you're not so tough," he said. His eyes sparkled.

"As tough as I have to be," she told him, then started giving orders to Voe and Daniel.

"Hurry up, Mr. B.," Voe said after several minutes of his arranging and rearranging. "We don't have all day."

"Yes, you do," he told them. "You have a lifetime. Stay there. Don't try to smile. It freezes in the frame and makes you look pasted." Jessie wiggled rabbit ears behind Fred, making Voe and Daniel both laugh just as Fred snapped the shutter. Everyone applauded. It was as it should be. It was a wedding day.

>-+-+-O-+-+-<

The afternoon waned. The meal had been blessed and the food consumed (before the ale, at the direction of Mrs.

Kopp), and the pickup band that played afterward took a break. "I think we ought to leave," FJ said. "I'm going to be late getting you back, and I promised a ride to Russell yet before the day is over."

"I suppose so," Jessie said. She sat on one of the dining room chairs brought under the shade tree. She fanned herself. She looked incredibly young and vulnerable, and he hated himself for his loss of control that morning. It was a momentary lapse. It couldn't happen again. It must not happen again.

Yet her presence comforted him. Even her pointing and prodding about how to do this or that, while annoying, also demonstrated her vitality, her amazing fire as she flitted like a bee around the honey of the wedding crowd.

"Oh, look," Jessie said. "There's a mourning butterfly. Don't you just love the way they have that little white edge around the gray, as though they're wearing a little cloak?" One settled on the back of her hand. "They always have the proper clothes to wear."

"It mourns the loss of sweetness when it leaves your hand," FJ said.

She turned to him. "You're poetic," she said. "I didn't know."

"The band's starting up again," Jerome Kopp said, motioning as he approached the two of them. "Wouldn't you like to dance once, Jess?"

"Jessie," she corrected. "It's bad enough my mother gave me a boy's name, so please don't shorten it any more than it is. And no. You know I don't dance. Our church doesn't allow it."

Jerome cocked his head, looked at her and at FJ. "Doesn't allow dancing, your church. I bet it doesn't allow a number of things that you *are* indulging in."

FJ watched Jessie's face turn pink before she said, "You're right, Mr. Bauer. We ought to be getting back so you can give your son a ride in the touring car. I'll say my good-byes to Voe and Daniel." She stood then and smoothed her skirt before striding off with as much stature as her short legs allowed.

"She's quite a woman, wouldn't you

say?" Jerome said. Both men stood staring after her.

"She has a bright future ahead of her as a photographer," FJ told him. "Your sister too, if she applies herself a little more."

"Oh, Voe won't last long at your studio. Daniel will have her waiting on a babe before a year is out. Then he'll want her home at the end of the day when his train crew's in town, now that he's certain she'll be there waiting. A man likes to have a wife waiting for him, wouldn't you say?"

"It seems to be the way of things, yes."

"You've got a wife counting on you, don't you? I'm sure Voe said you were married with children."

"Indeed," FJ said. The collar of his shirt felt tight. *The heat of the day.*

"A man has to appreciate what he's got or he'll forget and start looking for what isn't his to have."

"You're a wise young man," FJ said, "but you don't have all your facts straight, Mr. Kopp. So perhaps you ought to forestall any more advice."

He walked to the car then. They'd long ago loaded the camera and plates. He busied himself with his back to Jerome, hoping the boy had gone back to the crowd. He could hear his heart pounding a little louder than it should. He opened his shirt and the collar. If a bumpkin like Jerome Kopp saw what he thought he saw, how many others might see it as well?

>─┼─◆>─○─<◆┼─<

"I'll drop you off at your home," Fred said. "No sense in you having to carry the camera back. I'll bring the plates in on Monday, and we can develop them together."

"Oh, just let me off at the studio now," Jessie told him. "I may as well get started on some of them. I don't have anything better to do. Besides, my parents don't know that you drove me. They think Daniel or his brother came and picked me up here this morning."

"Why would they think that?"

"Because I told the truth slant."

The drive back had been a silent one, but Jessie assumed that the warm wind breathing on their faces and the tight goggles Fred had remembered he could wear to keep his eyes clear were the cause of the stillness between them. Maybe he was upset about her pushiness with the camera at the wedding or Jerome's guessing at something improper. But she'd wanted him to see that she was fully capable of managing herself and that she didn't need his protection or guidance in matters of the lens or her heart. She hadn't liked Jerome's comment about what her church didn't allow. She'd wanted to look at Fred when he said that but didn't dare. Jerome was seeing things, but she could handle him. He wouldn't tell anyone that mattered, and what did he have to tell, after all? They'd shared a moment of intimacy, of *affection.* The world needed people to be more affectionate toward one another, more tender. That's all this had been. Jerome saw things that weren't there.

She just wanted to get back to the safety of the studio, where they could be themselves and talk if they wanted to, or work together as a couple who cared about the same things. Her grandparents had worked together on the farm, and her parents too, until her father's illness had forced the move to town. They were a team, raising children, though it wasn't the same as when her mother had been out with him milking the cows or pitching hay beside him. How many people had the privilege of working beside someone they loved?

She startled herself with that statement. She wasn't in love with Fred. She wasn't. She could not be. She simply wanted his company, his companionship, his . . . tenderness for one more week.

"Jessie," Fred said when he pulled up next to the studio. He turned the engine off, removed his goggles. "We're in dangerous water here. At the moment, it's just been a splash, nothing too harmful. But it could be. And I'd be terribly remiss if I let this continue. Even to say how wonderful it was to hold you. Even if I told you that I have never in my life been unfaithful to my wife, never. And I don't consider that one kiss an act of unfaithfulness. Maybe some would."

She stared at him. "It is." He covered that last with a cough. "It was a moment of loveliness that I will cherish. I—"

"Let's just carry the camera inside, and you can go on your way. We have all next week to discuss this. Just next week and then I'm gone. *Poof!*" She snapped her fingers the way Lilly sometimes did to make her points. "Out of your life forever. So let's not ruin what was a lovely, tender thing. Let's not."

He nodded, opened his door, and came around to open hers. He took her hand to help her step on the running board, and through her gloves she felt the electricity of his touch. It sparked a tingling in her throat and, like a long ellipsis, moved through her body to her toes. She saw by the look on his face that he had felt it too, and she pulled her hand from his.

"Can you reach the camera all right?" she asked. "I can take the plates. Oh, and where's my hat? I was going to wear it to make my transition from bridal party participant to professional wedding photographer." She looked over the side into the back. "I forgot I even had it."

"It must have flown out," Fred said. "Though I didn't see it. Or maybe you left it at Voe's."

"I probably did," Jessie said. "It was just a small-brimmed one I thought would keep the wind from lifting me up and carrying me away if it got beneath the felt."

"You were quite professional without it," Fred said. He bowed his head to her.

"We did well, didn't we? I can hardly wait to see how the pictures come out. We can always take out the background in the shot we took of them eating. I know you didn't like that one."

"An unpainted house isn't the best backdrop," he noted. "Not to mention all the distractions on the table."

"Good backdrops are hard to find in the unposed world," Jessie said. "At least in photography we can dismantle them, make it into just the picture we want."

"A benefit of our profession."

Jessie sighed.

He carried the camera into the studio,

set it on the table in the kitchen. She walked past him and took the plates into the darkroom area. She hoped he'd follow her, willed him to be curious about the photographs, hoping it would overcome his reticence of being too close to her.

She waited to hear his footsteps. Instead she heard the engine of the touring car start up, and she stepped out in the lobby of the studio just in time to see him pulling away.

TWENTY

Lessons of a Night Sky

"Hey, look what I found." Russell came running in from the touring car as they readied themselves for church Sunday morning. Mrs. Bauer frowned.

"You left it in the car, Mama," Winnie said.

"It was under a rug like the one Papa has at the studio," Russell said.

"What?"

He handed her a small-brimmed blue hat with tiny white flowers dotting the brim. The felt was soft. Holding something firm made Mrs. Bauer feel steady. The color was a deep blue, not a color she liked at all. She didn't think it was her hat, but it must have been. Whose hat would it otherwise be?

"Thank you, Russell. I must have left it there on Sunday last."

She sat then, staring at the hat that she was certain wasn't hers, but maybe she saw stains others couldn't see and maybe she wore hats that looked better on a lovely young woman who was working with her husband. Could that be? Voe Kopp didn't wear such hats as that. Had she seen it on . . . ? She tried to remember. Maybe Lilly wore it and had left it. Or Selma. But how would it have gotten into the car?

It must be her hat, and she couldn't even recall it. She felt a pang of—she searched for the word—envy. Envy of young women who remembered things. Envy of young women who felt something for their lovers, their husbands, something she never had and never would. That Kopp girl had married, hadn't she? Hadn't Mr. Bauer said something about the wedding dates being set up and changed? And the other one, Jessie, her name was, she'd found another job. Had her husband hired a new girl? Why hadn't he told her? Maybe he had. She didn't know. She couldn't remember. She had become more like her sister Eva than she wanted to admit.

At least Eva was better now. Not so scattered, her husband said. The doctors in Rochester had helped her. *Maybe they could help me. But I'm all right.*

It's my hat. It must be.

She was so tired she could hardly lift a hand to shell a pea, and yet she could feel envy. For a young woman getting married? Why envy her? For the new beginning, perhaps. It would be nice to begin again. There had been a time with Mr. Bauer when the children had brought them both such joy. Until Donald . . . She felt tears slip down her cheeks.

"Are you all right, Mama?" Russell again, touching her. She jerked back.

"I'm fine. Fine." She shook her head. At least she could feel something.

><+>+O+<+><

Jessie had a plan for how this was going to be. She ignored Lilly's looks as she readied herself for work at the studio. "My last week," she told her.

"I'm sorry it's worked out this way, Jessie. Really, I am. Maybe you can photograph things on the side, get Papa to help put up a darkroom in the basement and develop your pictures here. You can still pursue your dream . . . in a good way." Jessie stiffened. Lilly reacted to it. "I only meant that you won't be giving up what you want for something you can never have. That's all I meant. That you are being good to yourself."

"Not that I deserve it," Jessie said.

"We do. It's just that if we pray for things that will hurt us, we won't get them."

"So if we get them, and they still hurt, then it was all right with God? Our suffering wipes away what we shouldn't have wanted in the first place?" She was being obstinate, she knew.

Lilly hesitated. "You have a fresh start with Mr. Carleton waiting for you. Don't do anything to risk that."

She thought of Fred as she walked to the studio the Monday after Voe's wed-

ding. Fred waited for her. She held resolve like a fan against her face. The
fabric proved too slender a separation.
All the promises they'd made to themselves and to each other when last
they'd met disappeared like snowmelt in
the spring.

Each day became a treasured ritual
for Jessie. When they first arrived, they
allowed their passion to set free the desire of the nights, to hold, caress—nothing more, nothing more, and only for a
moment. *I am a good girl.* She was.
People would be coming in; knowing
that set the boundaries. There could be
no flushed faces greeting clients, no
fluttering at an interruption. Professionalism. Her mother might come by or
even Lilly, knowing Voe was on her honeymoon and here was their precious
daughter and sister alone with a man.
They could come in anytime at all,
though Jessie was quite certain they
wouldn't. She wasn't sure why. Her parents trusted her. She pushed at her
glasses.

Jessie and Fred stole a moment for

themselves, each tasting of the morning, and then went to work.

When people left, when Jessie held the door open for them to leave, she'd watch Fred shake the man's hand and graciously assist the woman with her purse, offer a few chatted words, exchange thank-yous as he watched them, hand to elbow, walk down the street. Then Fred would step back inside. Jessie organized the props of scarves or watered the plants set on the stands for the previous pose. She would sense his movement toward her as though the very air he stirred reached out with tentacles of longing. He'd trace her chin with his fingers or frame her shoulders, his face against her cheek, the stubble rough. He'd wrap his arms around her so she could sink into him and sigh. It was enough then to know that he carried in his heart the same vibrancy that shuddered in her own. It wasn't what she'd intended; it wasn't. They kept the boundaries, together ignored that they'd already stretched beyond forgiveness.

After the last client left, Jessie took the plates into the developing room. They allowed themselves but one embrace, in the entryway between the darkroom and the light, where they'd taken refuge from the storm those years before. Jessie waited for this moment every day that week, predictable as a heartbeat. Just one enfolding of two lives, one clasp in the darkness, where loving was allowed but sating not.

Jessie always broke the embrace. To reassure him she still controlled her heart.

Until they neared the end of the magical week.

They'd been in the entryway, and Fred held her so tight that she understood why dancing was forbidden—such closeness: self-control and linens all that separated them.

They hadn't heard the bell announcing visitors, Jessie realized later. Instead, Winnie, with Selma in tow, rushed into the darkroom entry, startling Jessie and Fred.

Jessie turned. "Selma." She rubbed

her finger over her lip, quickly dropped her hand.

Winnie ran to her father. "I don't see you. It's all dark, Papa."

"You mustn't rush in like that, Winnie. The room must be dark, remember?" He sounded gruff.

"I'm sorry, Papa."

"Yes, yes, I know you are."

Winnie hugged Jessie's legs then. "Mama!"

Jessie patted Winnie's head. The child was frazzled by her father's sharpness. "It's been a while, hasn't it?"

"I didn't mean Mama," Winnie said, her lower lip rolled into a pout. "Jessie. I know."

Selma said nothing, but she held a question on her face.

"You walked a long way to get here. Or did you take the streetcar?" Her heart was slowing.

"Mrs. Bauer has a terrible headache, so I thought I'd leave the house quiet for a time until Russell gets home from school. Winnie wanted to walk home with her father, and I thought I'd walk back with you."

"Time to go, Papa." Winnie pulled on her father's hand.

He pulled his watch out. "In a while," he said. "We have a few more things to finish up." His voice quivered a bit. "Go ahead, Misses Gaebeles. I can manage here with Winnie. You walk home with your sister. It's the right thing to do."

Jessie moved into the reception area, secured her gloves, and told him she'd lock the front door so they might exit through the kitchen. She said good-bye to Winnie, talking a little too loudly, she knew. As they walked, Selma said nothing as Jessie sorted out just what it was she was doing. How easily the mind is capable of slanting truth. What they'd done would have no long-term impact, would it?

>—+◆>—O—<◆—+—<

Mrs. Bauer noted with calmness that her husband came home right after work, on time, this entire week, and this pleased her. He was especially attentive, not even reading the paper before he came in to nod to her and ask about her day. He sorted through the mail while she talked, commenting on what she shared. He didn't raise his voice. Mostly she spoke of the children or of Selma. The girl was faultless except for those occasions when she failed to see necessary cleanup, but then Russell seemed to have the same problem these days. She had intended to bring that up with Mr. Bauer but told him instead of some school event they ought to attend on behalf of the children. He'd have to come home early. It was on Friday.

"Is something wrong?" he asked. "With the children's schoolwork?"

"You can read the letter," she told him.

"The children are doing well, aren't they? No problems?"

"Read the letter," she repeated, hearing annoyance in her voice. "It's Friday. It's the last day of school for the term. The ice-cream social happens then, you remember. Winnie can come. Her kindergarten schooling ends too."

"Yes," he said. "Of course. Friday."

She thought his mind went somewhere as he stopped sorting but then returned as he looked for the letter. He still had not told her anything about Selma's sister leaving the studio, and she wondered why. Wouldn't he have to train another? Were their finances so short that he had let her go in order to save money and no one would replace her? Maybe Mrs. Bauer should return to retouching, to help him out. No. She'd done that while he was ill, before the Gaebele girl was trained. A wife ought not have to do such work. She had enough demands with the children. She hoped he wasn't waiting to replace the girl in order to force *her* back into the studio.

Too many problems to deal with. Her mother counted on her more because of Eva, her sister. She sometimes forgot she had a brother and sister, she saw them so little. Why was that? Something had happened years ago, maybe when their father died, that had separated the three of them. But now her mother wanted her to "help with Eva." She'd have to ask Mr. Bauer to assist. It wasn't something she could handle on her own. Was that part of what the estrangement was about, that her sister didn't like Mr. Bauer? Was that it? Something like that, something having to do with what happened with the studio. Yes, but she couldn't remember what. Funny how memory played tricks on her. She'd have to ask him. If she could remember to do it.

"I thought we could ride in the touring car," FJ said as they finished supper.

"Isn't that a waste of petroleum?" Mrs. Bauer asked. It was an unusual suggestion. She didn't like changes in their evening routine.

"We could go to the park if you'd like. Or tour up to Sugar Loaf. Take all the children."

"I suppose you could drive slowly. The children will enjoy that. The wind won't tug at my hair so much if you drive slowly."

He'd been different of late. More attentive, she thought. More conversational with the children and kindly toward her. She detected something different.

"Maybe we could see Mama. It's been a while."

"If that's what you'd like."

Russell groaned. "Can't we go up Sugar Loaf, Mama? Grandma's house is dull." How old was he now? Eleven. What interested eleven-year-old boys?

"Russell," Mr. Bauer cautioned. "No need to complain."

"He's right. It would be more pleasant to see the view from Sugar Loaf and watch the sunset. Let's keep that top up so it doesn't muss my hair. Mr. Bauer, are you all right?"

Again it seemed her husband's mind went somewhere else, and then she remembered, speaking of the wind, what it was she wanted to ask him about. "Russell found one of my hats out there in the car," she said. "I've never worn one like it, I don't think. Did you buy that one for me some time ago and forget to give it to me?"

"A hat?" His voice seemed to catch and he frowned. "I didn't buy you a hat, no."

"How did it get there then, in the back of your car? It's a Lottie Fort hat, I know it is, and she doesn't make the same hat for more than one woman."

"It must be yours," he said now, firmness in his voice. "You and your mother sometimes shop and forget what you've bought."

"I haven't been shopping with Mama for months. Months! She doesn't even call me to see how I am, what with all the demands I have here, the children, your illness, my own tiredness, Robert's stomach complaints. Yes, he complains, holds his side." She had to tell him everything! He didn't notice!

"Robert's ill? You've called the doctor? I had no idea."

"Oh, he's fine," she snapped. Why did he always act more concerned about the children than about her? Maybe because he sometimes snapped at them too.

"Your sister, then. Might it be her hat? Maybe when we went to visit her that time."

She hadn't thought of that.

"We drove your mother to church last Sunday, remember? I got back late from work Saturday and couldn't take Russell for his promised ride, so we took the car to church and picked up your mother."

She couldn't remember just when it was Russell had brought the hat in, whether it was before the Sunday drive . . . yes . . . no . . .

"Jessie Gaebele has one like it," Mrs. Bauer said. "I'm sure I saw her wear it once when she came to pick up the girls' wages."

"Must be two, then," he said.

Mr. Bauer sounded so certain. "That must be it," she said. "I'll have to return it to my mother."

"Let me," he said. "No sense having one more thing for you to fret over."

"You'd take care of that for me?"

"Whatever I can do to make things a little easier for you, Mrs. Bauer."

"I thank you for that, Mr. Bauer."

"You'll get it for me, Russell?"

"Where did you put it, Mama?"

She tried to remember exactly where she'd placed the hat and what that feeling was she'd had when she held it . . . that felt. "I'll be sure to tell my mother that her milliner isn't keeping her originals all that original since I'm sure Miss Gaebele has the very same hat."

>−⊢◆>−O−<◆⊢<

He'd take the hat and return it to Jessie. Why didn't he just say it was hers? Why not be open about her having worked with him on the Kopp wedding? It would be so much easier.

But no. He couldn't say that because he didn't want anything to interfere with what was happening in his life at this moment. He was tumbling through space, spinning out of control, and he didn't want a life preserver. He didn't want this to stop. He looked forward to his day; he felt alive, fully, fully alive. He deliberately tried to be more attentive to Mrs. Bauer in order to absolve his own guilt for what he was doing, allowing himself to feel again. But it was so futile, so very futile! Why had he chosen to punish himself this way? And punish everyone . . . unless he could do extra things for them, make their lives better despite his behavior, which threatened who he was and would be forever, if he did not make this stop.

Jessie had the strength. He needed to be strong too.

Russell got the hat for his mother, and FJ put it near the cane stand. "I'll return it next week," he said. "Will that be all right?"

"Of course," his wife told him. "Unless we stop by Mama's on our way—"

Russell's groan interrupted her.

"Yes, well, let's get the car started so we can have that little ride you promised us."

He and Jessie had stood between the darkroom and the light—a perfect metaphor for how his feelings raged these days.

"We only have this week," she'd said, and then it would be over.

Temptation would be thumped.

She was so certain that each of them would be able to go separate ways after tomorrow. Her clarity silenced the inner voices shouting at him at night when he put his head down on the pillow and willed her into his dreams.

On Sunday he'd awake with newness. He'd thank God for keeping him from doing anything worse than holding a

young woman like a flower in his hands.
For holding him back from doing anything more than savoring a moment of
beauty and fresh fragrance in his
heart—all he really needed to fill the
emptiness that had become his life.
When Sunday came, he vowed, he
would renew his devotion to his children
and his wife, whether she accepted it or
not. He must be there for her. It was
what he'd committed to those years before.

But he had not met Jessie then. And
his wife had not become the distant
woman she was. No matter. He had obligations, and soon he'd do a better job
of meeting them.

Just one more day, and Jessie Gaebele would be out of his temptation.
He'd bought a gift for her to mark her
leaving. Tonight he would not sleep.

>—<>—O—<>—<

Jessie deserved the pain she felt that
kept her from sleep.

She had thought that posing Fred into
this scenario would take any responsibility from him so he wouldn't feel bad

about taking the time from his children and wife. He hadn't really; he'd just been working as always, except for Voe's wedding day, which had gone on longer than either of them thought it would. She was actually making him *more* attentive to his family, from what he said. He'd not gone to his lodge but walked right straight home after work. Because of her. And from what he'd told her, that Mrs. Bauer wanted no part of any . . . intimacy anymore, then she was really helping Mrs. Bauer too, so she didn't have to feel guilty about not meeting all her obligations as a wife. Not that Jessie had! No, she had not done that which belongs to married people only. She had not.

But she had reveled in the softness of his whispers, the closeness of his face to hers, the press of her body to his for just those few moments they allowed themselves. It was a troubling dance that pulled two halves that did not belong together into one.

Yes, she had given both the Bauers a gift in a way. That was the truth, wasn't it? Without slant?

The dreams that caused her to toss and turn this week just happened because of the hot summer weather. The girls had even moved the feather mattress out onto the enclosed porch because it had become so hot. That was the cause of those night sweats and strange dreams of flying things that startled her awake with a pounding heart.

"Can't you sleep quieter?" Lilly had chastised. "What's wrong with you, anyway?"

"It's the heat," Jessie said.

Jessie picked up her pillow and went back upstairs to their room. She could at least sit outside on the roof to cool off. A breeze blew through the window, already open, and she slipped out to stare at the stars.

"Please let me be able to end this well with Fred," Jessie said out loud. "You know I have to, and I need Your help now even if I didn't ask for Your advice before I started. I know it's going to be difficult. I know that. And I deserve it all. Just help us make the end a knot that won't come unraveled."

"Who's Fred?"

Jessie jumped. "You scared me half to death." She choked the words out. Selma's use of his name made her throat tighten.

Her sister had padded up the stairs behind her. Jessie didn't know how long she'd been standing there. *One more reason not to pray out loud.* "If you fall asleep on the roof, you could tumble off," Selma said. "Papa always says, remember? You better come in off of there."

"Sometimes I think that wouldn't be so bad," Jessie said. She moved over as Selma crawled out onto the shingled roof, ignoring her own advice.

"What are you trying to do well, anyway? What needs a knot? And who is Fred? A new beau?"

"It's none of your affair, Selma. Go back downstairs and go to sleep."

"I'll make sure you don't fall off the roof."

Jessie put her arm around Selma to keep her from sliding on the pitch of the roof. Through the thin cotton nightdress, the shingles felt warm against her legs.

"Why can't you sleep?"

"I have this project at the studio, and I want it to go well. That's all. Mr. Bauer has a lot on his mind, and I want to clear some of that from him."

"I think Mr. Bauer is your Fred and that it's terribly romantic. Just like those stories in the magazines."

Jessie felt a chunk of ice pierce her heart.

"No. Fred is not Mr. Bauer." *I have to lie, to protect him, myself, even Selma.* "You're imagining things. Too much hot sun this week." Jessie's heart pounded, and she felt her face grow hot with shame. "You weren't wearing your hat when you came to the studio."

"Mrs. Bauer has a hat just like yours," Selma said. "That surprised me because Lottie doesn't do that usually. I mean, it wasn't that interesting of a design, all blue with those little white flowers bordering the brim. I'd like to design something with big flaring feathers and little dried berries and maybe put a stuffed bird in there, one that has fallen from a tree. I'd never kill one just for the hat. I think I could work for Lottie, don't you?"

"My blue hat?"

Selma nodded. "Mrs. Bauer said she had one just like it at home. Then she said she couldn't remember if it was hers or not. I told her to look to see if it had Lottie's label in it. Maybe Lottie made it for her mother, but I didn't think she'd do that sort of thing. One of a kind and all, that's her motto."

"Did you tell Mrs. Bauer that?"

"Where is yours, anyway?" Selma asked. She moved as if to crawl back in through the window, but Jessie held her. "I just want to see if Lottie did something special to it to make it different from the hat Mrs. Bauer described."

"I . . . I must have left it at work." Jessie said.

"She wasn't having a good day. She sees stuff that isn't there sometimes, gets all upset over it, remember? Some days she complains about Mr. Bauer, his cigars and his spending on the car. Did you know he sold a big chunk of the North Dakota land?"

"Those land transactions were in the paper," Jessie said. "Several months ago."

"Well, Mrs. Bauer wasn't very happy about it."

"I thought she didn't like the ranch," Jessie said.

"She doesn't, but it makes money and she was worried about the lost income, and then he bought the car. They had a row once. I saw this hole in the water closet door, and Mrs. Bauer said he'd kicked it in!"

"Maybe Winnie locked herself inside."

"I don't think so," Selma said. "My being there keeps them from arguing, I think."

"I'm sure your being there is important," Jessie said. She couldn't imagine that he had a temper.

"But he's sweet on you. I could see that when Winnie and I stopped by."

"He isn't! Don't, don't think things like that, Selma. Your imagination—"

"I didn't imagine him holding you in that little room," Selma said.

"Oh, Selma, don't, don't say anything about what you thought you saw, please? Not to Mrs. Bauer or the children. Please don't. It meant nothing. He was . . . I tripped and fell into him as he was coming out of the darkroom."

The lies now wrap Selma into them. Jessie's chest tightened. "Don't say anything to anyone."

"I won't," Selma protested. "I think it's . . . romantic."

"It isn't. It's wrong. It's nothing."

"I just think it would be nice if Mr. and Mrs. Bauer were in love."

"Yes, it would."

"He wouldn't be in love with you if he was still in love with Mrs. Bauer."

"No, Selma," Jessie whispered to her. "No, no, no." Jessie held herself against the pain. She rocked. It was bad enough that she'd threatened her own future, but she couldn't let Selma ever believe that what she'd seen was somehow romantic and safe and agreeable just because she'd also seen tenderness pass between her and Fred.

Jessie stopped rocking and brushed the hair back from Selma's eyes.

"I need a little more time," she said, her lips quivering. *Thinking. Praying.* She was grateful the stars gave out only pale light so Selma couldn't see the tears leaving tracks on her hot face or look into Jessie's eyes and find the darkness of her soul. "Why don't you go back down before Lilly wakes up and finds us? You know how cranky she is when she doesn't get enough sleep."

Selma giggled, a sound like a baby being tickled. Free and without pretense.

"This is nice, Jessie. I like sitting and talking with you."

Selma leaned into Jessie; the scent of lavender wafted through the night. Jessie stroked her sister's hair. "This is nice," Jessie said. "I've had this photography project this week, but I'll be putting my treasured camera aside for a time."

"Mama says to be wary of where your treasure is because there lays your heart also. I'd hate to think your heart belongs more to that camera than to us."

"I'd hate to think that too," Jessie said. "And it doesn't. After tomorrow I'll have a lot more time to be with you."

"What's happening on Saturday?" Selma asked.

"My project will be finished."

TWENTY-ONE

Too Much Exposure

Selma returned to their bed. Jessie heard her deep in slumber behind her, as she sat on the roof. She imagined Lilly wearing her sleeping cap, a waste on this hot night as far as Jessie was concerned. She'd read that heat left the body through one's head, so why keep it contained on a June night? Habit, she supposed.

Maybe habit had led Jessie astray, her habit of stepping ahead when others might have heeded their hesitating heart. If she didn't face the truth, Selma might be led astray too. She'd have to get the strength from somewhere else to "truly finish the project," because relying on her own determination had gotten her lying to her sister. She wouldn't even let herself think about how far she'd fallen from God's grace. First Roy and now this.

Jessie remained awake, ruminating on what she had to do. She still hadn't slept when she heard the stirrings of her father in the kitchen, then her mother talking quietly about their day. The smell of bacon lifted through the room. Soft laughter arose. She heard Roy rustling about in his room. This was what a relationship between a man and woman was meant to be.

Why had she let herself fall in love with the wrong person? She'd been distracted from who she really was. She wasn't "the other woman." Jessie wasn't a part of what happened between Mrs. Bauer and her husband. And Mrs. Bauer had no place in what had happened between Jessie and Fred. It was just the two of them. No one else need be affected.

And yet Selma was entangled in it now. And perhaps Winnie, depending on what the five-year-old really understood. Their witness was the greatest shame of all.

The truth was that she'd tarnished what love was meant to be by giving it to someone who could never return it in the way she wanted. Maybe she *was* just a conniving woman who lacked any kind of soul. Maybe those early church fathers who argued over whether women have souls were right to wonder.

No, she did have a soul, and she had tried to make it whole. But love without integrity failed to make anything complete; it could only rub the soul raw, leave a sore behind. Her pain was her own doing, and she deserved what she got. But not Selma. She couldn't bring Selma down, hoped that she could reverse her younger sister's romantic views. She had to. She planned to leave the house without her mother's asking why she was going in so early. She needed all the time she could get to do what must be done.

>-•-›-•-O-‹-•-‹

The door stood open, inviting the morning breeze to clear the air of chemical smells and that stuffy feel of a studio with doors and windows locked all night. FJ lifted the window in the operating room, hoping no flies planned to make their home on the sill. The black dots they caused had to be watched for on the studio's white backdrops. One wouldn't think such a little thing as a fly spot would show up in a photo, but it did. Even worse was having a fly or some moth flit around and bother people in their poses. Just as he'd be ready to snap the shutter, a man might wave his hand at the insect and they'd have a ruined plate. Now that he thought of it, he hadn't noticed many flies of late. He wondered if Voe put something out to discourage them. Or maybe Jessie had. He'd have to ask.

He expected Jessie to be early, as she said she'd prepared a surprise for him. He awaited yet dreaded her appearance. Their last morning. He, a foolish man, felt alive in her presence as he never had before, but the aching life force was terminal, and he knew it. He cheated his own family by drawing on her instead of on them, instead of on his own vows, for sustenance. He was hurting his children. Who knew how Winnie interpreted their encounter? And Russell's eyes the day of Voe's wedding would haunt him forever. He'd kept his imagination in check, carefully in check. He'd brought her hat in. He'd stuffed it with his shirt collars and meant to keep it, but then he saw it this morning and he knew. He had to return it. There could be no hanging on.

He had something else he wanted her to have too.

But she was late. He checked the clock. He went about trying to concentrate on what had to be done. He scanned the appointment book. The Wobitz family of four was scheduled for ten. He didn't know them. But it didn't matter. He set about moving the cabinet to the position usually used for a four-person portrait that included children and at least one person sitting. He hoped the children were well behaved. He heard the back door open.

"Jessie?" he asked. His clients would use the front door, surely. "Miss Gaebele?" He left the operating room, walked through the lobby area and the office area back toward the kitchen.

"We know we're early, but it took us less time to get here than we woulda thought. Wobitz." The man removed his hat, reached out his hand. "We came in the back way. What we're used to. Hope you can arrange us now. We'll get our chores done here in town and then get an early start back home."

"My assistant is due anytime," FJ said. "I'm sure we can work you in right away." He kept annoyance from his voice.

He took the woman's purse and was introduced to the children, a bright-looking girl and glowering boy, who plopped crossly on the bench and said, "Why do we have to do this?" He must have been around ten. Where was Jessie?

He'd done this alone long before Jessie came into his life. He'd have to do it again. "Let's begin," he said, "so we can get young William here taken care of and on his way. Here, will you hold this prop for me?" He handed the boy a wooden ship he removed from the closet.

William brightened and began to co-operate, so FJ was able to pose them all quickly. He thanked the child several times, and the lad paid close attention. FJ took three shots, then had to stop and put more plates into the frame before sliding it into the camera. Jessie or Voe usually anticipated this and had it done for him. The boy fidgeted. The girl sneezed. A fly buzzed by. Just one, but he thought he ought to close the windows. Was that a box elder bug crawling on the backdrop? It was late for a box elder bug. He didn't want to take the time. Jessie could retouch it. He reset the pose, moved the window drape to change the light, all the while growing worried that Jessie wasn't there.

The hour passed. The family gave him their deposit, and he told them the photographs would be ready in a week or so for them to look at and decide which they might want to keep and how many prints they might want to purchase. Voe would have to do some of the developing. He wanted to limit his exposure to the chemicals as much as he could. The girl would one day have to stop working with chemicals, but it had taken him years, nearly fifteen, before he'd had his first episode, and that after developing thousands of photographs for himself and his father-in-law.

The girl. Voe was the girl, but Jessie was Jessie. Hopefully Jessie would find a young man to marry before exposure to the chemicals ever took its toll on her. Working for Ralph Carleton would keep her safe for a time. But she loved her art . . . more than he did, he suspected.

FJ's mind went to Carleton as he removed the last plates from the frames. He'd never heard the man preach, but Mrs. Bauer and her mother and sister had gone once to his tent meeting. A Reverend Moody had spoken too, and the women praised him more highly than the local man. A prophet in his own home is never appreciated, FJ thought, or maybe the man wasn't as good as Moody. Or Billy Sunday, the baseball player turned evangelist. He didn't want to think about these men now, nor of the messages they preached. Oh, he knew they talked about redemption, but not first and foremost. Sin and shame took top billing with them. He swallowed. Jessie was a good girl. It was he who had violated the order of things, as the poet had said, he who'd failed to "protect and border and salute," acts which were the marks of love.

Maybe Jessie hadn't intended to come in until the scheduled appointment. FJ couldn't remember if they'd discussed that. Maybe something had happened to her. She'd been hit by a train or sprained an ankle while walking as fast as she always did. Could she have been injured? Was she simply going to walk out of his life? Was that the surprise? He'd wait until noon, and if she wasn't there by then, he would call her house, just to be sure that something hadn't gone wrong. He couldn't live if something had happened to her.

His hands shook at the outrageous thought he'd just had. He would be living without her the rest of his days.

>—+‹›—O—‹•›+‹<

Jessie opened her eyes with a start. The house reeked of quiet. She heard voices outside in the yard. A light breeze moved the fringe on the lamp. She had just curled up in the window seat for a minute, hoping her late prayers might give her direction, if she took a few moments to listen when her pleading finished, if she could follow the Spirit's leading before leaving the house. If she could do what she must. But she'd fallen asleep! What time was it? Her neck ached.

She untwisted her legs while folding the flannel sheet. She grabbed for her glasses and found her necklace watch. Eleven o'clock! She'd slept four hours? Why hadn't they awakened her, her brother and sisters?

Selma! She'd probably told them Jessie hadn't slept all night, and when they came in to dress and saw her sound asleep, they had simply left her there. But how could they have dressed and carried on without her hearing anything? She'd missed the appointment that was scheduled at the studio! He'd had to do it alone.

It wasn't like her to sleep through something so important. Her fingers trembled as she sponged herself off, then buttoned her shirtwaist. Her body had made the decision without her head's even knowing about it. She rushed around now, grabbed the small box she'd buried beneath the winter quilts in the hall chest, looked for the Formalin tablet. Found it. She located her Graflex satchel, ran down the narrow stairs, shouted out the back door that she was off to work and would be home for supper.

She turned and ran into her mother.

Her mother stood like an oak, unmoving. Behind her, Jessie's father waited with torment in his eyes. He looked worse than when he writhed on the floor, holding his side. *And I've done this to him.* Jessie shrank in shame.

"Are you all right, Papa?" Jessie asked. He had his hand on his side. "Do I need to help you—"

"I am not well," he said.

"Have you called the doc—"

"We are profoundly troubled to have raised a daughter who would choose to corrupt another's marriage bed." This from her mother, who trembled as she spoke.

Jessie stepped back from both of them, the force like wind sucking the breath from her. Her heart pounded; her eyes darted this way and that seeking escape, knowing there was none. "I . . . I haven't . . . We, no—"

"Such shame!" Her mother's words stabbed through lips quivering, eyes blazing. Screaming violins raged inside Jessie's head. She felt hot and cold at once, her heart at breakneck speed, her palms wet. She couldn't look at their faces. This must be how a rabbit caught in a trap felt, knowing all would change now. Life as she'd known it was over.

Selma had told them. But how much? *Enough.* Whatever Selma told them would be enough. The disappointment on her parents' faces hurt her like a burn.

"He gave you a career, and you threw it all away and seared your soul as well," her father said. He shook his head.

"He should have known better, but so should you," her mother said. "Why? How could you?"

She didn't know what to say, how to

say anything with her heart racing and her breath choking in her throat.

Deny it! It wasn't his fault.

"Selma has it wrong," Jessie croaked. "I don't know what she told you, but we haven't, that is, I haven't. Nothing's passed between us. Nothing about a marriage bed, Mama. Truly. If there had been, do you think I'd dare work for Ralph Carleton, who sees into people's souls?"

Her mother reached for a handkerchief and dabbed at her eyes. Jessie took the reprieve as a time to leave. "I need to go on to work, to finish my last day. That's all it's been. A professional relationship. Selma misunderstood. I've been planning to quit. You know I have. I'll be working for Ralph."

"You're not going anywhere until you speak the truth!"

Jessie had never in her life heard her father shout, not at troubling mules, not at his pain, not at any family member, not ever. The redness of his face frightened Jessie, and she stumbled backward, farther from her parents.

In that moment, she knew, truly accepted what she'd done.

"Papa . . . I . . . tried. I truly did. I just couldn't avoid it. It was as though I was drawn to him, like needing to breathe." She was crying now, her nose running as she wiped at her eyes, reached for a hanky embroidered with lilies of the valley. "All I ever wanted was to take the photographs, but then . . ." She trembled. "I'm so sorry, Papa, so sorry." She stood with heaving shoulders. "I didn't know how to stop. I kept doing what I didn't want to do, and what I wanted to do, I just couldn't."

He'd dropped his hands to his sides and shook his head. He might have looked calmer, but Jessie couldn't tell through her tear-swollen eyes.

"We always fall short, Daughter. It's a human thing that only unwarranted love can bring us through."

"I only wanted to help him, Papa."

"The truth, Jessie. Only the truth will set you free."

She wouldn't have to pretend anymore, wouldn't have to lie to herself or mislead Lilly or Selma or Voe or anyone else. But oh, to admit this truth, to admit that she had acted so unwisely, had compromised her future and her heart. She shivered now as though a cold breeze had moved into her chest, and she ached so profoundly she thought she'd never gain her breath. Deep sobs wracked up through her from the darkness of who she'd been. Long shards of yearning pierced her side. Not unlike her father's rolling pain, she doubled over, holding herself, bleeding inside. She rocked. "I am so sorry. So sorry."

Her father reached out, then took steps toward her, and she fell into his arms. Hot tears ran from her eyes, pushed out through her nose, and made her stomach ache with the waves of her shame.

"I am too, Daughter," he said. He held her. "We'll send a letter to him explaining why you didn't go today."

"A letter?" She stepped back to look at him. "No, Papa. I have to go in. I have to. I have this present I got for him, as a thank-you for all the years of his teaching me, and I need to give it to him, to keep my commitment to help him during this week with Voe gone."

"A gift? For that man? No." Her mother crossed her arms over her chest. "He's done enough damage."

"Please, Mama. It's my fault, not his."

"Gifts." She snorted. "When we're saving every penny to help Roy and you said you were too. That dress was one thing, but a gift for him? You must take it back."

"I can't, Mama. But it will be the last of things with him, I promise. I'll be strong enough." She wasn't sure that was true, but she had to make it so.

"Not on your own, Daughter," her father said. "You must lean on us and the Source of your faith. You've been given so much. I'm so sorry you didn't know how to receive it."

><-+>-O-<+>-<

She forced herself up the studio's back steps. He must have been waiting, seen her dragging down the street with her blotchy face and puffy eyes, because as soon as she opened the door, he pulled her into the kitchen and into his arms. She sank like a flower to a bee.

"Where have you been? I worried over you, worried!"

His arms felt so safe, so warm . . . *I do the things I do not want to do.*

She pushed him away. She had to be strong. This had to end. If she didn't do it right, her father would come here or her mother, and oh, the humiliation of that! Or worse, she'd fail again.

"Your eyes," he said, holding her at arm's length. "You've been crying. You did get hurt. What happened? Who? I'll—"

She moved as far from him in the kitchen as she could without leaving the room, crossed her arms over her chest, held herself together with her fingers pinching. *Feel this pain so you will know what you have to do.* "They know," she whispered. "My parents know. Selma . . . Whatever she thought she saw was enough to convince them, and I . . . I confessed, told them it was all me, not you."

"But we've done nothing—"

"Yes. We. Have. That's the truth of

it. We have." She dropped her arms, leaned into the oak door frame; the rounded edges pushed against her back, and she gained strength from the oak. She pushed at her hair, tucked the tendrils behind her glasses, lenses no longer steamed by the tears and his closeness.

He paced, his hands gripping into fists and releasing. "I am so sorry, so very sorry. What a confounded fool I am. I should have—"

"I'm responsible for my part in this, and I have to get myself out of it," she said. "I've come to say good-bye, to give you this small gift as a thank-you for all you've taught me." She moved like a wary cat in a room full of dogs, around the table to her camera bag. She took the small box from it, put it out to him. He stared at her, not understanding. She shoved it toward him. "Here, take it."

He could hold it in his palm, and he did that now, lifting the cover. She had eked out five cents a week from her paycheck to pay for it, ever since he'd purchased that camera for her. As her mother had noted, she'd deprived her family of that five cents, put money into trespass.

"I won't be around to give it to you in August, when you turn forty-five. It's the last gift I'll ever give you, except for my going away."

It was at that moment she made the decision. She *would* go away. She'd push him away, farther than Ralph Carleton's tents. She wasn't sure where or how, but she had to. Just being in the same room with him, the same city, compromised every hope she had to regain her footing.

He set the box down on the kitchen table, opened it. "It's quite remarkable," he said. "I don't have a brass match holder."

"It has a cigar tip cutter on this end." She stepped forward and pulled the tiny peg and swung out the small knife. When she did, she touched him. She hadn't meant to do that, only to give him the gift. Her will weakened. She heard it in her voice. "It's from the world's fair. See the different pavilions on each side?" Tears pressed against her nose, her eyes.

"This was costly, Jessie."

"You deserve it," she said. "For teaching me."

"I don't deserve anything. Everything I have in my life is a gift. Including you."

He reached for her then. "Don't," she whispered, backing up. "Don't, please. I have to do what I came to do, and that's to thank you for what you've done for me. The camera, the training. And then I have to leave." She eased her way toward the front so she wouldn't have to pass by him.

"Wait. I have something for you as well." He pulled a package from his pocket. "It's an extravagance, but then . . ." For a moment Jessie thought he'd cry too. He bore pain in his eyes not unlike what she'd seen in her father's face less than an hour before.

Should she take it? Would that just prolong what was wrong? She opened the box, then rubbed her fingers over the pearl inlay on the gold locket. "I can't accept it." She handed it back.

"It's not a chain attached to me," he said. "Please. Let me put it on you."

She hesitated. She'd been so firm when she left her parents, so certain she could end this now. But maybe the necklace would be all right. It wasn't a tie to him; it wasn't. She turned and let him put it on her neck, so aware of his breath, the fleck of his fingers against her neck. Once he was finished, she felt his hands rest on her shoulders, but she slipped away, stood to face him at a distance.

"Now we're finished. And I'm on my own. I tried to quit here two times. Did you know that? Two times." It was the truth, but she had chosen to make a hammer of it, not give it any slant. "I just didn't want to do all these stuffy studio shots. That's why I didn't show up for the one today. I guess it went all right."

"What are you doing?"

"Telling the truth," Jessie said. "I've just had a grand time at your expense. You didn't think a young girl would really be interested in someone as old as—"

He stepped across the distance and shook her shoulders. "I know what you're doing. I know. And it will make no difference. I have come to love you, Jessie Gaebele, but there is nothing I can do about it."

"You don't love me," she charged. "You—"

He silenced her with his mouth. *No, no, no!* Not even ten minutes with him and her resolve was gone. However would she make it for the rest of her life? She pushed him away, but he wouldn't let go.

TWENTY-TWO

For a Reason

Instead of being strong, she'd collapsed, made a perfect mess of herself in front of him, when what she'd wanted was for him to detest her because that was what she deserved.

Instead, he'd held her like a child, rocking her in comfort, the necklace like a hot stone between them. *I'm so weak, so weak. Please, please, please,* the only prayer she could muster.

"You have to hate me," she said, "so you can go back to your family and never think of me again."

"Nothing you could do would make me hate you, and the guilt and shame is mine to deal with. I've added to yours by letting this happen instead of taking care of you, doing things to make your life easier. People who love each other don't do that, Jessie. Or at least they ought not to."

"You're thinking of your wife."

"I've hurt her too. All of them. Donald especially . . ."

"What will we do?" Jessie asked. The ache inside her was worse than her fear that Roy would never speak as smooth as cream. Nothing had ever felt as terrible as this.

"You'll work for Mr. Carleton and pursue your hobby," he said.

She stiffened in his arms. "My hobby?" She pushed back from him. "You think that all this time of working with cameras and lights I've been doing it as a hobby?"

"I didn't mean to say that. You're a professional photographer, Jessie. You could go to work as an assistant in any studio you wanted. I'd be pleased to help you do that. But maybe Ralph Carleton's position is best. Something not so demanding."

The tone of his voice set Jessie on the path she needed. She hadn't planned to tell him, but now she would. "I'm not going to work for Ralph," she said. "I'm going away. I'll find a studio that needs an assistant, somewhere far from here, somewhere where your influence can't pave the way for me. I'll do it on my own, which was what I always intended, and one day I'll have my own studio. I will."

"Don't, Jessie. You don't have to—"

"I do! I didn't think I needed to, but I do. I couldn't even keep my resolve for a few minutes, to just come here, hand you that gift, tell you good-bye, and leave. That's all I had to do and I couldn't do it. My parents think Seattle will be far enough, but even there we have relatives and I don't deserve anyone's help. I have to do this on my own. I can't trust what I might do here with the possibility of chance encounters with you. You're like an . . . obsession. I say I won't think of you or come near, and then here I am. I don't want to know anything about you or what's going on in your life. I don't. There has to be distance. And I have to pay the price of separation from those I love."

"Distance," he said.

"Like the chamber outside the dark-room, I need a safe and separate place to recover. You must never think of me again. Not ever, ever again." She was being dramatic, but she had to exagger-ate what she felt in order to break the pull.

"Ah, Jessie. When you care for some-one very much, they come unbidden to your mind. I don't think of Donald all day long as I did when he first died. But mo-ments sneak up on me. I think of him while I'm here even though his death occurred in North Dakota. Distance doesn't stop the sting."

She began crying again, embarrassed by the sounds, but she could not stop. It was as though she grieved a death. Perhaps she did. She refused to let him hold her now; the pain kept her resolve. She adjusted her glasses, gave her hands something to do.

"We'll both come to the other's mind without wishing it so; in fact, with our trying to prevent it, it's likely to get worse."

He spoke of her as though she was dying too, and perhaps she was. Dying to the promise, dying to the fanciful girl who had dreamed too much, the girl who liked going up on Mr. Ferris's wheel with her uncle, flirting and laughing without consequence. She had convinced this father and husband that they could have a pleasure together and not have it affect them later. She'd deceived him and herself.

"Let me help you find a position," he said.

I must make myself think of him as Mr. Bauer yet again. "No, Mr. Bauer. No. No help."

Pain flickered across his face.

Passions did burn out; they had to. She hadn't considered how wrenching it would be before they did. That her parents knew would make this easier in the end, give her a fresh chance. By leaving she'd save Selma from thinking that what she and Mr. Bauer had done was anything but wrong. She'd save him from acting when he ought not to. The separation would be fair punishment for what she'd done. She could seek forgiveness if she went away.

Would her passion for photography go away one day too?

She supposed it might if she couldn't find a way to sustain it. She must not feed this love between the two of them but feed only what could truly nurture her: a gift she'd been given. She'd use it for good. She had to.

Ralph Carleton had told her once that sin was something each human had to deal with and that in Hebrew the word meant "to have missed the mark" or "to have taken the wrong road." She had done both of those; she only hoped she could plead her way back onto a good and proper path.

The bell rang over the studio door. They both jumped toward the sound. Jessie stepped back into the kitchen shadow. "You'll have to do this sitting on your own." He took one last stare at her, then moved out of the kitchen, greeted the couple, and left her alone.

>⋅⟨⧫⟩⋅O⋅⟨⧫⟩⋅<

He wondered if she'd be there when he finished, or would she do as she'd proposed, just disappear, go where he had no way of imagining her being? She was right, of course, so right. And yet . . . it was as though a knife had slipped between his ribs. He was bleeding internally and didn't know if it would stop.

He pasted a smile onto his face, bowed slightly, and lifted his hand to direct the clients to the operating room. "This way," he said to the couple. "I hope you'll enjoy your portraits."

>⋅⟨⧫⟩⋅O⋅⟨⧫⟩⋅<

She had planned to leave before he finished. But she'd found the latest issue of *Camera World* and, inside, what she was seeking. By the time Mr. Bauer finished, Jessie was more composed. She took the plates to the darkroom and mixed the solutions. He did not follow her there. But he seemed to know when she was finished. He waited for her, paused a moment before she stepped out into the natural light. Jessie looked into desiring eyes but slipped past him, her heart pounding. What had been was over.

She'd gone around the studio then, closing windows, pulling drapes shut. She asked him to do likewise. She refused his efforts to keep talking about *them.* Instead, she took the Formalin tablet from her satchel and set it on a tin tray in the lobby area. He'd helped with the windows but frowned at the tablet. "It will keep the flies and insects out," she said. "I used to set it once a month in the summer. We'll fire it just before we leave, then close the doors. We'll have to stuff the keyholes. Do the back door from the inside." She handed him small pieces of cloth she'd used before. "When you come in on Monday, Voe can sweep up any dead moths or flies lying about, and you'll not have pests to upset your sittings."

"No pests," he said.

"It's a way to clean the slate of them, start fresh."

She picked up a match from the box and set the tablet aflame. The smoke began to rise like incense. It would cover everything, seep into the lampshades, the wreath of silk flowers on the inside door, the photographs that hung on the walls, and then burn out. They didn't need to be there to see that it would happen; in fact, it was best if they weren't there at all. Everything would be different in the morning.

They left together out the front door. Jessie nodded her head to him as she straightened her hat, fingered the heart-shaped locket at her neck. "I need to go to the library. Good-bye, Mr. Bauer. You've changed my life, and I will be forever grateful."

He held her matchbox gift in his hand, rubbed his thumb over the embossing. "I love you, Jessie Gaebele."

"No, you don't," she said as she turned from him. "No, you surely don't."

She didn't look behind her to see if he'd stayed watching or had turned himself and walked away. She didn't need to know what he did; what mattered was what she did next.

>─┤─◆>─0─<◆─┤─<

She didn't want to go home, not yet. The summer evening proved long, and she knew her parents would be wondering about her. Yet she needed time alone. One day, maybe, she'd ask forgiveness of Mrs. Bauer and the children, but that would only absolve a portion of her guilt. And it would add to their misery. If they didn't know now, then placing her burden on their shoulders could only add to her list of faults. No, she wouldn't indulge in the luxury of purging on the backs of those she'd betrayed.

Certain he'd continued on—she could imagine his cane tapping as his image became smaller in the distance—she returned to the studio, sat on the back steps. The fumigant would be doing its work inside, and she preferred looking out over the garden with the restored fountain, the leggy purple cosmos, his rosebushes bearing faded blooms. Here she let her sorrow overtake her. She tried to find the words, couldn't. She rocked with her arms around her and choked on the air, her throat tight and raw, her eyes swelling from the burning tears. It wasn't his love that had protected her in the end but the love of her parents, her family, who had forced her to face the truth. A breeze worked its way through the oak leaves, and Jessie remembered that comforting verse. She prayed for mending from the sanctuary, longed for healing leaves beside the river. Jessie wasn't sure she had the strength to stay above the water, at least not by herself, but she would learn to trust that the river would indeed carry her along.

Her body, mind, and soul spent, she stood, and at the little fountain she splashed cold water on her face, her swollen eyes. She felt shaky but walked to the library, grateful it was still open. Behind a large book, she forced herself to repeat the word she read over and over. *Disconsolate. Disconsolate.* That's what she was. The word gave boundaries to her feelings, helped keep them in check. Nothing would make this better except time, and even then . . . She found it hard to take a breath.

She knew what she had to do, so she wrote the letter, making several drafts. She'd make a terrible secretary. Why had she ever thought she could write letters for Ralph Carleton? Because her mother thought she should; because it would be safe. She walked to the postal office, purchased an envelope, and wrote the address on the outside. She'd begun to change her path.

Wind gusted and pushed her skirts against her legs as she headed home. She held her hat. She missed the blue one, knew she'd left it in Mr. Bauer's touring car. It belonged to Mrs. Bauer now. As did the man Jessie had come to love and left.

>—○—<

Jessie spent the Fourth of July with her family. The parade came down Broadway, and Jessie held her camera at the ready. Selma acted as her helper, and Roy hung on to a box of rolls of film as though it were gold. Even Lilly seemed to enjoy the day and offered to pose. Jessie chuckled to herself when she saw the background of that photograph: one of the parade horses had taken that moment to relieve itself. It would be a blur, but Jessie thought she might make a print with that background as a reminder to herself that nothing can be controlled, not one thing except how one thinks and how one acts on those thoughts—and even then one often needs help. She'd take the background out in the print she gave to Lilly. No sense in stirring any more flames with her older sister. Things were settling down after her confession.

Jessie had told Lilly the following week as they dressed in their room. Selma had already gone downstairs. "Your dour predictions and knowing looks were the truth," Jessie said. "Except that Mr. Bauer and I did not . . . We never . . . The marriage bed . . ."

"You let that man take all you loved, and you gave it up, for him. I knew it! What an evil, evil man."

"He isn't evil, Lilly. I don't think I am

either. We all make mistakes; we all do. Part of the tragedy of this is that until recently I didn't experience any real pain. I imagined myself into another world when I was with him. I didn't expect you and Selma and Mama and Papa would ever intersect it. He didn't make me give up anything."

"Except your integrity and good name. Oh, Jess, I just can't believe you did that! Why? Why couldn't you just appreciate that you'd found something you loved to do and were being paid for it, and carried on without undermining it?"

"I took photographs. I learned how to run a studio. It wasn't all bad, which is part of what let me convince myself I wasn't hurting anyone."

She shook her finger at Jessie, more angry than her father had been, matching her mother's wrath. Jessie stepped back. Jessie's mother hadn't spoken directly to her since the revelation. She spoke through her sisters to "tell Jessie to set the table" or whatnot.

"How can you ever think that your life

can be anything now except burdened with shame and guilt? Such a waste," Lilly said. She turned her back. Jessie thought her shoulders shook. *Is she crying?*

"There's no reason for you to be so angry, Lilly. It was my wrongdoing, not yours."

"But you had happiness with your camera. Joy, and you tossed it away. I don't understand it."

It occurred to Jessie that Lilly might have been speaking of herself, and she wondered what joy Lilly had let pass by. "Papa has forgiven me, I think, and I hope Mama will in time. I really do believe what they teach, Lilly, and that we get second chances. Maybe many chances. We may not deserve it, but I'm going to take it if it comes my way."

"You ought to suffer," Lilly said. "Now I'll have to be extra careful when I do Mrs. Bauer's fittings to not let anything slip. I'll *know* things I shouldn't know."

"I guess I shouldn't have told you, but you'd find out before long anyway. Selma would tell. Or Mama. And I didn't want Selma to slip sometime and you feel you'd been excluded."

"Selma knows?"

"She was the one who really made me face up to . . . well, what I'd done. I couldn't let her think that what she'd seen—a chaste embrace, Lilly, that's all it was—was somehow 'romantic,' as she put it. I couldn't let that stand. I intended to break it off with him that very next morning, and then she said something that told Mama and Papa they had to intervene. But I think I would have cut it off without them. I think I would have."

"How long has everyone else known?" Lilly pouted.

"Only a little while." She took a deep breath. "I wanted to tell you myself and to tell you too that I'm going to be leaving town. So you won't have to look at your sinful sister every day."

Lilly's shoulders slumped. "I just don't understand why some people shoot themselves in the foot and then wonder why they can't step forward."

"I am sorry," Jessie said and wondered if Lilly was speaking to herself as well, but she didn't pursue it. It would be a while, if ever, before Lilly opened her arms to Jessie as her father had.

At the parade, Jessie clasped her own hands, opening and closing them in nervous action until she found another photo opportunity. She caught herself looking for the Bauer family at the parade, but only once, when she glimpsed a woman in a blue hat riding in a touring car. It wasn't her hat or his car. Her mother caught the direction of her gaze and frowned at her. Jessie dropped her eyes. Shame came as easily as breath.

She didn't see the Bauer children anywhere along the parade route or in the gardens where other children rushed about. She was sad about that. She would have liked to say good-bye to the children.

The children. She hoped those moments of stolen care she'd had with their father wouldn't tarnish any shine in their lives. It was one more fervent prayer she would remember to offer up.

As the night blackened, a boom announced the beginning of the fireworks. It was a wet spring, so there'd be more fireworks and less fear of the sparks falling onto dry grassy bluffs and starting fires. Jessie thought of the irony of that: some flames were set to burn the bluffs and be put out by the snowmelt; other flames would do damage falling hither and yon from the explosions. Set fires could have value; playing with fire did not.

Roy shouted and came closer to her. "Y-y-you should stay here," he said. "D-d-don't go. I-I-I n-n-need you."

"Oh, Frog." She pulled him to her. Could she learn to live with the surprise of seeing Mr. Bauer, his wife, and his children around every corner? Maybe that was exactly what she needed. Maybe seeing them, knowing they would be there on the streets of Winona every now and then, would be a good reminder to her of what she'd done, flesh out her character on the bones of remorse. Roy needed her. She wasn't one to run away when someone needed something.

But this time she had to go.

"I'll see you now and then," she assured him. He leaned into her shoulder, and she held him.

Leaving Roy behind was part of her penance.

>-I-‹›-O-‹›-I-‹

The Bauers drove to Bluffside Park to watch the Fourth of July celebration. Robert sat on FJ's lap in the touring car once they had parked. FJ had a momentary flash of memory sear him with Robert so close. He'd been holding Donald just so when the horse had kicked up past the wagon board in a bizarre way that caught Donald in the head. *While I held him.* The horse's hoof had lifted high enough just as Donald had leaned forward. Timing. The boy had died instantly.

He pulled Robert to him. He'd keep this child safe. It was what he had to do now. Think of the children. Winnie and Russell argued over who got to sit on the hood of the car so they could see better. "Russell, you're so tall that if you sit there we'll all miss the fireworks. Get in the back. Winnie, you can stand beside him. Look up when you hear the

boom. It's really not a good idea for anyone to sit on the hood."

After a few groans, they complied.

"How are you doing, Mrs. Bauer?"
he'd asked then. She sat bundled up
beside him as though it were winter, a
shawl wrapped as tight as a boa around
her arms. "Aren't you too warm?"

"Why do you ask?" she'd snapped,
then calmed. "I'm fine."

"Good. Very good."

His mind roamed to Jessie and the
weeks past. He would stop the memories eventually, but he wanted to savor
them for a time. He rehearsed in his
mind how he'd act if he encountered
her: nonchalant, as though he were only
a former employer meeting with his student. She might come in to visit with
Voe, or he might meet her walking in
Levee Park. He should write a letter of
recommendation for her, even locate a
studio if that's what she planned to do.
He knew no one in Seattle. That's the
city she'd mentioned. In the end, he
hoped she wouldn't leave Winona and
the support of her family. She was a
good girl, and the Gaebeles good peo-

ple. Making major changes as she proposed required the support of those
who loved you.

"I think you should take me to Rochester next week," Mrs. Bauer said.

"Oh? Some shopping you'd like to
do?"

"No. The hospital. The one my sister
went to. I want to talk to those doctors there. Maybe something would . . .
change."

"What brings this on?" He twisted so
he was sitting nearly facing her, Robert
still between them.

"Aren't I allowed to improve myself?
Find out why I'm so . . . why I have so
little stamina. Why I'm so forgetful." She
stared ahead.

Winnie leaned down from the back of
the car to pat her mother's shoulder.

"Of course. Whatever I can do." He
turned back, looked out the side into the
growing darkness.

"Come with me. You could come with
me."

He turned back to her. "You think that
would be helpful?" She nodded. He was

trying to lose memories, and she was hoping to regain some.

"Is that girl back, Miss Kopp?" Mrs. Bauer asked.

"It's Mrs. Henderson now," he told her. "And yes. She's been back for a week already."

"She'll become . . . well, you know. You'll lose her. Have to train another. What about that Gaebele girl?"

"She's going to work for Ralph Carleton."

"Such a loss of your good training, having her end up there."

"Would you consider doing some retouching again?" he asked. "I could use the help with Miss Gaebele gone. I have a couple of wedding pictures, Mrs. Henderson's, in fact, that could use a little work."

"I don't think so. Train Mrs. Henderson."

"Yes, there's that." He sighed.

"It's always good to have a back-up person, especially with your illnesses sneaking up on us. Winnie, stop kicking the back of the seat."

"They have affected all of us, my illnesses, haven't they?" FJ said.

"Not as much as Donald's death," she said. He believed it was the first time she'd said such a thing out loud.

"I am so sorry," he said. He leaned his head back, closed his eyes. He patted Robert's knees. "So very sorry." He had said it so often to himself, but perhaps he'd never said it out loud to her before. He couldn't remember. He reached to pat her hand. She withdrew it from beneath his. "We'll go to Rochester and see what we can find. We'll all go," he said, opening his eyes. "Make a day of it." Make something good to come from all this.

"It's not going to be an outing," Mrs. Bauer corrected. "Did I say I wanted an outing?"

"No. You said you wanted to see what Eva's doctors might have to say. But we all have an interest. So all of us can go, and all of us can enjoy the ride at least. A little thing to make the children smile. Even you, Mrs. Bauer." He tipped his hat to her. She looked shy for a moment, flashed a quick smile that came, then left, as fleeting as a happy thought. It was the best he could hope for today.

>―·‹•›·―O―‹•›·‹―

Jessie helped her mother and sisters with the laundry. She and Lilly wrung out the sheet too large to go through the wringer.

"But where will you stay?" her mother asked Jessie. At least Mama was talking to her. They hung wash in the backyard while the hot July wind whipped their skirts and sometimes plastered the wet sheets against their faces as they clipped the wooden pins over the cloth and wash line. A few mallards lifted from the river, sweeping low across the sky, quacking as they rose.

Roy sat on the back porch steps and plucked away on his banjo. They'd all saved enough to get him the instrument, but the speech hesitations continued when he tried to ask that the potatoes be passed or if he wanted to alert his father to a spill on the floor. He hadn't tried to sing with Selma again. In spite of everyone's focus on Roy's speech, and even Jessie's extra time with Roy now that she wasn't out taking photographs or staying extra long at the studio to develop them, it hadn't advanced his initial progress. But with the banjo, he was happier at least.

Jessie felt guilty about that too, because getting it had taken longer in part because she'd put her money into an eyelet dress and that brass cigar cutter and match holder for Mr. Bauer. She had to keep admitting her ways and allow forgiveness to sift through her. At least now Roy could soothe away the sad memories of taunting at school. Music could do that. So could art. Her kind of art, through the lens. Music and photography were beautiful, and beauty healed. It was what she needed now. Healing. Somewhere far from here.

She'd written several more letters to studios across the West, and then she'd written one to Ralph Carleton, telling him she would be leaving town. It would save him the embarrassment of having employed her if her shame ever became public. She supposed she was a coward not to face him directly, but Jessie sometimes remembered Jerome's remarks at Voe's wedding, in particular how knowing looks like his could spike her guilt. She prayed that for now only her family knew. They had not turned her out. Neither had they resisted her decision to leave.

Then the letter from Milwaukee had arrived, and she allowed herself a moment of joy. She'd been hired to help run a studio with a new widow. *Newly widowed. Fine studio. Broadway district of Milwaukee. Need female assistant.* She hadn't told Mr. Bauer she'd found this ad that day, and wouldn't. She'd take her disgrace with her, along with the camera and the memories he'd given her, and she'd begin again.

"Is there an apartment attached to the studio? There are so many immigrants in Milwaukee."

"Mama," Jessie said. "Grandma and Grandpa came from Germany. More than half of Winona is immigrant!"

"Hush now. But women involved in suffrage live there too. They could lead you astray, Jessie. Milwaukee is known for such goings-on."

"We know you're impressionable," Lilly added, but she smiled too.

"Why not look for an opening in Eau Claire or—"

"No matter where I go there will be temptations, Mama. Chances asking for caution just because they're unfamiliar, regardless of their true danger. Mrs. Johnson has need of me now, and if I stay here . . ."

"There are temptations right here at home, aren't there, Jessie?" Lilly again.

Maybe she ought to stay to pay penance by listening to Lilly, but she would also suffer by leaving the safety of this family—who did love her despite the rules she'd violated, despite the disappointment she'd brought to their doorstep. That she *had* to leave such comfort would be the highest price to pay.

"But we're told in Scripture that we never face too great a temptation for God to help us through, isn't that right, Mama?" Jessie said.

"You're one to be quoting Scripture," Lilly said.

Jessie held a clothespin in her hand.

"Lilly, you don't need to do this. Maybe you need to give your sorrow words too."

Lilly gasped and ducked behind the hanging sheet.

"You could sew clothes full time," Jessie offered.

"It's never been that," Lilly said, muffled by the sheet. The wind lifted it and it brushed Jessie's cheek, the scent of bleach carried with it.

"My heart's fine," Lilly said. Jessie didn't say that Lilly protested a charge she hadn't made.

"I'll miss you," Selma said. "I finally get a beau interested in me and—"

"What?" This from their mother, who had just put a wooden clothespin in her mouth and had to take it out to exclaim. "You're just turning fourteen. Having a beau is not something you should be considering at your age. Goodness."

"Yes, Mama," Selma said. She winked at Jessie when her mother turned back.

Jessie's mother pushed the wooden pin over the shirttail.

"Your sister is a bad influence on you," Lilly said, but some of the sting had faded from her words. She handed Jessie the end of another sheet.

"Why? She hasn't had any beaus," Selma said. She cast a quick glance at Jessie. "Not really."

"She taught you to take too long for your morning toilet."

"Then my going to Milwaukee will be a good thing," Jessie said. "Allow Lilly more time at the mirror, not that you need it, Sister, and offer more time for you to influence Selma without my interference."

Lilly appeared settled with that response, and the discussion turned to where Jessie would stay in Milwaukee. There was an apartment attached to the Johnson Studio, but Jessie didn't know if there'd be room for her there or not. She planned to get a room nearby. That's how she'd begin.

"Where will you take your meals? How far will it be from the studio? How will we reach you? What kind of neighborhood it?" Her mother wiped her hands on her apron in that way she had. "I don't know. You may not be safe there."

Jessie took her interest as a sign of love.

"I'll have to learn that I can do what I say I will and not get, well, sidetracked."

Could she do the right thing in Milwaukee? She had to believe that she could. Maybe one day she'd feel happy again. Experiencing joy wasn't sinful, was it? It was how one got to those joyful moments and kept them close that mattered.

"And besides, with me gone," Jessie said, "Selma will have a more . . . mature influence around her. And I'll be safe from whatever evil influences live in Lilly's head." Jessie grinned.

"Mama," Lilly complained.

"Wh-wh-what lives in Lil-Lil-Lilly's head?"

"Her imagination, Frog," Jessie said. Roy burped as she ran her fingers across his banjo strings.

"Hush now, Roy," her mother chastened.

"Play me a tune," Jessie said. "One from your imagination."

He did, and the music made Jessie

forget for a moment the struggles that still lived within her.

⊱┈◈┈○┈◈┈⊰

FJ sat at his studio desk and looked out through the window toward the library. He found himself doing that often, hoping he might see Jessie on the streets or in the Gaebeles' yard when he walked by, but he hadn't. So earlier that day he had sent the letter of recommendation by post, though he'd have preferred to deliver it himself. But that was out of the question. He'd listened to the inner voice that told him no, that doing so wasn't necessary and would offer no assistance to Jessie. He'd written the first letter with his flowing hand, something he admired in himself, his learning English and writing it with German precision. It would have been a selfish act on his part to hand it to her, to look into her eyes and again be comforted by the scent of her perfume, the blush on her face, the way her hair frizzed around her ears even when she tugged at it out of nervousness.

She had not crossed the threshold of

the studio since the day she left. He'd heard through his photographic friends that she was headed to Milwaukee. She had to be taking the position at the Johnson Studio. It would be a good place for her, the timing perfect, though it came on the heels of a loss for Mrs. Johnson.

He hoped Jessie would never learn about the other letter he'd posted.

He'd been making changes these past three weeks himself. He'd made the appointment at Rochester. He'd increased his time at the lodge, volunteering to assist with various civic projects. The veterans met weekly and he started attending, surprising himself that he could tell stories about his service and exchange compassion with soldiers who'd had it much harder. He felt rested after he left those meetings and slept then without the dreams that for so long had haunted him in the night.

He'd made more effort with his wife too. He brought flowers to her; she looked at them, said thank you, then turned back to whatever it was she'd

been doing. So he arranged them himself in the slender glass vases, and he
even took a bloom for his studio. He
looked at the rose that lowered its head
to him. He turned the glass vase and felt
the cut crystal beneath his fingertips.
Good German precision. Beautiful. The
flowers, too, were lovely, and he found
he liked seeing them when he arrived
home, where a new girl now helped out.
Selma had decided to work for Lottie
Fort, the milliner. It had seemed to him a
sudden decision but perhaps for the
better. He wouldn't be seeing Jessie's
moves inside her sister's. He tried to remember the new girl's name . . . Melba.
Yes. She walked with heavy footsteps
through the house, and the children had
accepted her. That latter was the only
similarity between her and the Gaebele
girls.

Sunlight through the window struck
the glass vase, sending a shattering of
light across the room. The china and
glassware for their home had mostly
come from Mrs. Bauer's side of the family, except for what they'd purchased

over the years. He had no family heir-looms. What his parents had sent with him had been lost on the docks. Nothing more had arrived from the Old Country. All but one of his brothers and sisters were still in Germany. His sister, Luise, had followed him to New York, married there and had two sons. She lost them all to typhoid before a second marriage brought her to Wisconsin. Losses were a part of his life, he decided, that and saying good-bye. His family wrote to him.

One sister had surprised him by writing that she'd become a Catholic nun. That must have set the family's German Lutheran tongues to wagging. She wrote that they felt she had sinned grievously and that they would no longer speak or write to her. She hoped that wouldn't be so of "my Gottlieb." It wasn't.

He wrote her immediately, telling her it was right for her to follow her heart despite the family's protests. If the family knew of his heart's journey, they wouldn't speak to him either, though he didn't say this in the letter. He'd keep the door open to his Catholic sister. There was too much dissension in life to put one's family in a silent cage because of how they chose to follow their faith.

He checked his watch as the phone rang. He had a sitting soon, and Voe was busy in the darkroom. He really did need another apprentice. He might even consider hiring that young man who had stopped by and indicated his interest in photography. FJ wasn't sure why he hadn't thought about a male assistant before. It would be less complicated, and he wouldn't lose the lad to a family as he assumed he'd lose Voe before too long. But right now he lacked enthusiasm for the search.

He folded the copy of Jessie's recommendation just in case something should happen and he be asked to send another. He put it in the safe with a copy of the other letter he'd sent on ahead. He didn't allow himself to think about how Jessie would come to his mind every time he opened that door or how he'd wonder if he ought to have done

what he did. He'd only tried to be helpful. It was how he hoped to redeem himself.

>-┼-◆>-○-<◆┼-<

The train trip was nothing like the one
Jessie had taken with her family to
Rochester. It was a much longer ride to
Milwaukee, Wisconsin, a different state
altogether from Minnesota. But the
countryside shimmered its prodigal
growth, corn and wheat spreading
sheets of green across the rolling hills.
When she thought of what she'd face in
Milwaukee, all the uncertainty, her heart
beat faster and her palms sweated. All
the doubts came roaring back: Maybe
she wasn't as good a photographer as
she thought herself to be. Maybe Mr.
Bauer had indulged her all this time,
hadn't really told her the truth about her
work so she'd keep learning from him.
Maybe she couldn't make it on her own
without her family to protect and salute
her efforts.

She'd have to take one step at a time
and trust that she wasn't alone on the
journey. *The Lord knows my lot. He*

makes my boundaries fall on pleasant places. She'd cling to that psalm, those boundaries.

The train lumbered its way across the Mississippi, heading east and leaving behind the bluffs she'd known all her life. It traveled through areas where geese and ducks clustered like thick flies on reedy waters. Maples and oaks stretched in long arcs of woods. In the fall, as their foliage changed, they'd look like an artist had cleaned her brush on their leaves, but now they boasted green. A dog splashed into a pond, followed by children, as the train chugged by. Jessie strained her neck looking back at them. *Children.* She thought of Roy. He never even knew that she'd deprived him of time and resources too, just to have her own way. He'd forgive her, though. There never was a soul as generous as Roy's. Still, she felt her face grow warm with shame again.

The land flattened out the farther south and east she went, but she could see smaller hills and valleys rolling away from the tracks.

She remembered the Gypsy at the

Rochester hospital who had said Jessie would travel far. In one of the library books, Jessie had read about glaciers, ice pushing earth eons ago, and that Wisconsin's western rolling landscape was what remained. She wondered if Milwaukee had a library. She allowed herself a moment of anticipation. She was going somewhere new. She could pose a new picture of who Jessie Gaebele was.

Mrs. Johnson had sent the fare for her to come. As the fields and lakes and trees whispered into her consciousness and then whisked out again, Jessie felt encouraged. Strong. This was the best next step, and sometimes that's all one had. The end of the journey was just too far away, and as the Gypsy said, there'd be many valleys and hills in between.

For I know the plans I have for you, says the Lord, Jessie remembered. *Plans to give you a future and a hope.* The verse from Jeremiah had come to her as she'd thought of the Gypsy. She wasn't sure she had it memorized correctly, but the sentiment was true. Her mother must be praying for her, or someone was.

What was similar to the ride to Rochester was the burping and belching of the engine smoke and the array of people. She was traveling, all right, far away from the home she'd known. She would let her art lift her above her fear and sadness. She took her camera out and invited a hovering child or two to examine it. Their interest, looking into the lens, passed the time, and the photographs she took she thought might be the beginning of her own study in everyday faces in everyday places. A couple of businessmen nodded their heads when she passed to the dining car, careful not to let her large camera bag bump them. She put it on the chair next to the window and sat on the outside seat at the table so no one would pick it up and whisk away the spoon that fed her dream. The moon rose, and it was full enough to shadow the trees they rumbled by. She could see cows standing in fields, it was so bright. Her thoughts turned to her uncle August, her home, and her parting.

Lilly had directed Jessie to talk to no one, not a single person, while on the train. Her mother told her that speaking to another woman or the conductor, if she needed help, would be fine. Roy's dimples disappeared when he looked at Jessie, and he acted as though someone had stepped on his banjo and he would never play it again. Tears pooled in Selma's eyes as she watched Jessie pack her trunk.

"It's my fault," Selma said. "That's why you're leaving."

"I'm the one who acted improperly. You are innocent, Selma. You are."

"I just let it slip out that you'd hugged Mr. Bauer and called him Fred and—"

"Selma." Jessie held her sister's shoulders. "You did nothing wrong. See, I get to leave Winona and travel to Milwaukee. It's something I always wanted to do."

"Maybe," Selma said, not convinced.

Jessie hugged them all. She held her mother longer than she had in years but still felt the stiffness of her judgment. Jessie told them she'd write as soon as she had an address. Then Roy and

Selma said they had a song, and so they had, the very hymn Roy had tried to sing at the hospital, "Just as I Am." Jessie savored the sentiment. She was accepted just as she was. Again though, Selma sang alone, her voice as smooth as their grandmother's pancake batter. Jessie hugged Selma, lifted Roy's chin. "You keep at it," she told him. "You'll sing smooth again one day; I just know it. You're powerful!"

"P-p-power is wh-wh-when you w-w-want to quit but y-y-you k-k-keep going," Roy said.

"So it is," Jessie said and held him close.

"Y-y-you're p-p-powerful too."

Disgraced, yes. But powerful. Now she was strong enough to walk away.

Her father drove Jessie to the station, just the two of them. Daniel was there working, and he helped unload the trunk. "Taking a trip?" Jessie nodded. "Does Voe know?"

"I haven't told many people. I'm going to help run a photo studio in—" She stopped herself. He might tell Voe, who might tell Mr. Bauer. "Out of town," she finished, keeping her voice light. "I'll write to Voe when I get there and find a place to stay."

"She'll be unsettled that I saw you off and she didn't. She said you were going to work for that evangelist."

"Things change," her father interjected.

"Just tell Voe I'm thinking of her. If Voe had come along to say good-bye, I would have blubbered the entire way. I'll write."

"I guess that makes sense, then," Daniel said.

Jessie reached over to hug him. She didn't care what her father thought of that. And then she hugged her father, the man who had always been there, perceptive and strong.

"I'll miss you, Jess," her father said. "You keep your mother from becoming too certain of herself." He grinned as he held her narrow shoulders and looked into her eyes.

"That's something you'll have to do on your own now," Jessie told him.

"A father ought to give his daughter good advice when she leaves home," he said, clearing his throat. "Usually that happens when she's off to marry and he knows she'll be in the hands of a good man, or at least he hopes. But you, you were always more of a fireball that even spring snowmelt couldn't put out."

"I'm sorry I've been a trial to you, Papa. I never intended—"

"You feel deeply, Jess, and there's nothing wrong with that. But our loves can burn us up if we're not careful. Your photography—it's a good thing for you, even though your mother worries over your being an unmarried career woman your entire life."

Jessie smiled.

"I don't worry about that. You're a lovely young woman with much to give. But for now, give it to your art. Let some time pass before you share your heart, *Liebchen. Ja?*"

His use of the German endearment, which she'd only heard him say to her mother, made her want to weep. She hugged him again, pressing her face against his cotton shirt. "Thank you, Papa," she whispered, breathing in the scent of his dray horses. "I'll do my best to make you proud of me, I will."

He held her, then spoke softly. "I'd ask a blessing over you, if you'd let me. I know I haven't done much out-loud praying over you children. I let your mother do most of that. Maybe that's my error, my part in your downfall."

She stepped back to stare. "Oh, Papa, you couldn't be a better father. You couldn't. It wasn't you, the cause of this. It was me."

He nodded, then pulled her back to him and spoke low, his chin resting on the top of her head. "So I say it now. I ask the Lord to bless your journey, to keep you ever safe and strong. Let Him be the One to light your path and bring you back to us one day."

She was so moved she couldn't speak. She kissed him on the cheek, then stepped aboard the train, wiping her tears with her gloved hands and waving as the train left the station.

She remembered now, in the dining car of the train, the rough of his weathered face. He'd had tears too, Jessie thought. That's why his cheek tasted of salt.

She blinked back her own tears as the train's porter came by to ask what she'd like to eat.

Memories, she thought but didn't say. *I'd like to eat the memories until they fill me up and I'm no longer aching alone.*

TWENTY-THREE

Lakeshore Lighting

It was dark when Jessie arrived in Mil-waukee, and she decided to simply stay in the well-lit train station until morning. Then she'd get a horse cab and make her way to the Broadway Street address of the Johnson Studio. She should have thought about some arrangement for this first night. Well, she would adjust. Cool air greeted her as she stepped into the stone building. It felt like fall here, though it was July. She could remain in the terminal with its oak benches and marble tiles. It was an elegant place to spend a night.

Jessie put her camera on the var-nished bench, sat beside it, pulled her knees up, turned, then used the camera bag as a pillow. She had shoved her trunk under the bench as far as it would go but assumed if anyone tried to move it or the camera, she would certainly wake up. She hadn't realized how tired she'd be after just sitting all that time on the train, thinking, entertaining children. She fell asleep when her head touched the tapestry bag.

She woke to someone shaking her shoulder.

"Miss Gaebele? I'm so sorry. I had the cab waiting at the far side. And I ran a little late, so I hope you haven't been here too long."

Jessie's mouth felt dry as the chicken pen and just as foul, she thought to herself, then smiled at her terrible pun. "What time is it?" Jessie asked.

"Midnight. The bewitching hour, my husband always used to call it. I'm Suzanne Johnson."

She was a tall, stately woman, and her hat feathers brushed Jessie's face as the woman leaned over her. Jessie sat up.

"I hate to waken you, but I'm sure

you'll rest more comfortably at the Harmses' home."

"Is that where my room is?"

"Well, you might call it a room, but I'd say it's more like an apartment. You're quite a fortunate young woman with all your connections."

>─┤─◆⟩─O─⟨◆─┤─≺

The Harmses, Mary and Henry C. and their daughter, Marie, embraced Jessie from the moment she arrived. They were in their nightclothes but still gracious and kind and all three standing by the door when the doorman let her in. She was given a room on the third floor large enough to house a family of four. She imagined the letters she'd write to her sisters telling them about her night of lovely accommodations in a fine German home. She wouldn't be able to remain, that was certain. It was simply too elegant for a single working woman. She wrote a brief postcard to her mother that Mrs. Johnson was familiar with a family who had put her up for the night. Then she turned out the gaslight and fell immediately asleep.

In the morning, Jessie pulled open the window drape to gaze out onto Lake Michigan. The sun rose up behind it. Below the window, a rolling lawn of green eased toward a hedge that marked the cliff's edge. A winding path meandered along the edge of the bluff like icing trim on a layer cake.

It was beautiful. Lush. Her heart sank. She'd had a luxury for a night that she didn't deserve. She was grateful for that, but her final destination would pale in comparison.

She dressed quickly in a skirt, the blouse Lilly had made for her, and the cream-colored tailored jacket that had been her uniform at work. It was likely too warm to wear the jacket, but she wanted to look professional after all, especially on her first day. Her eye caught FJ's necklace. She left it in its box.

She made her way down the carpeted stairs, looking for the kitchen. She hoped to find Mary Harms, who insisted she use their Christian names. Instead, a white-capped maid stopped her and directed her into the dining area, where she'd bring "Miss, your tea if you'd care to tell whether cream and sugar are needed." Jessie sank into the chair when the tea arrived, with cream and sugar, an indulgence. Her hands shook as she lifted the porcelain cup. Everything here spoke of wealth. She surely didn't belong.

When the family appeared, minus Marie, who was sleeping in, her mother said, Jessie thanked them for their kind hospitality. "I'll have my trunk removed as soon as I find proper accommodations."

The couple looked at each other. "Is there something wrong with your room?"

"Oh no, Mrs. Harms, Mary. It's just that I can't possibly afford . . . I'm saving so I can buy my own studio one day, and your room is much too grand for my small allowance."

"But Gottlieb told us all about you and insisted you stay here."

"Gottlieb?"

"Mr. Bauer to you, I'm sure," Mary said.

Gottlieb?

"He goes by Frederick now, I think,"

Henry Harms offered. "FJ is how he signed the letter. A poached egg?"

"He did tell us of your plans to one day have your own studio. Yes, dear," Mary answered her husband. "And for you, Miss Gaebele?" Jessie nodded assent, her mouth open in surprise at what they knew of her.

"Mr. Bauer arranged this?"

"He's a cousin, dear. And spoke highly of you. We contacted Mrs. Johnson as soon as we knew you were coming and would need rooms."

"A fine business mind is worthy of welcome," Henry continued, and Jessie wasn't sure if he spoke of Mr. Bauer's business mind or of someone who had just entered the room. He couldn't mean her. She turned around. No one was there.

"Gottlieb," Mary said, "is a family name but one that is often difficult to pronounce here in America. And when what happens in the homeland makes people here uncomfortable, we don't like to bring attention to our German heritage. I'm sure that happens in Winona too, *ja*?"

Jessie nodded, though she wasn't at all sure. Her head spun, her thoughts in a swirl. *Gottlieb? Mr. Bauer knows I'm in Milwaukee?*

Her mouth went dry. She lifted the crystal glass of water.

"So, then. It is the Christian thing to do, to offer to others what one has to give. You'll stay with us. Perhaps you can show Marie how to use your camera in return. And there's always enough for breakfast and dinner, should you be present at those times. Nothing would be expected, of course."

"I should warn you," Henry said. "There are a number of galas that my wife and daughter attend each year, and a young woman of high repute is always a welcome addition." Jessie wasn't sure she met the criteria. She lowered her eyes. *Surely they cannot know.*

"You may find yourself quite busy in an evening if Marie and Mary have anything to say about it," he continued. "Good music. Fine food and dancing." Henry bit into a honey-draped biscuit, letting the crumbs litter the linen. The white-capped maid brought the silver crumb chaser and swept the area clean before stepping back into the shadows behind him.

"I . . . wouldn't have the proper clothes," Jessie said. It was such a lame excuse. *Dancing? A new temptation already?*

"You're Marie's size. I'm sure that won't be a problem," Henry said in the blithe way fathers had of expressing their ignorance about women and fashion. Marie was larger and rounder than Jessie and three inches taller at least. If Marie was like Lilly, she'd hate having to loan her clothing out to a total stranger, even with the best of recommendations. But more, the thought of attending events where she'd be asked to dance made her skin feel like ants had found her flesh. The Harmses were apparently not of the faith that frowned on dancing. Well, what did it matter? She couldn't possibly stay here.

"I can have the cook pack a lunch for you if you'd like each day," Mary said. "We always have extras."

"I . . . I couldn't accept it."

"The apartment was simply gathering

dust. We have plenty of room. It'll be lovely to have someone occupy that space who will appreciate it."

"It's arranged," Henry said before he finished his coffee and went off to the brewery, one of several businesses Mary Harms told her that they owned.

"I'll need to consider," Jessie said. "How far this is from the studio . . . I'm not sure that staying here would be wise. I . . ." Such luxury, such gifts. *I don't deserve this.* No, she had to change that inner voice. She'd been given healing leaves while she stayed on that river.

"You think about it, dear," Mary Harms said. "We can talk this evening when Marie's with us. That girl . . . She should have a little of your gumption, leaving home and starting on your own. Well, we'll just love to help. That's what family is for."

Mary gave Jessie directions to the Johnson Studio, which wasn't more than two miles away. Then Jessie picked up her things and headed out.

Jessie strode along the shore, her mind spinning with Mr. Bauer's reach. *He must not come here. Surely he wouldn't. No. He wouldn't.* Maybe he hoped to absolve some of his guilt by making this arrangement for her.

She couldn't stay there, not without the Harmses' allowing her to pay them. It wouldn't be right.

It might also be unwise, if she were to hear stories of "Gottlieb" every time she turned around. And then there'd be the dancing. Her mother would be appalled, and it would be another challenge that she didn't need, something else pressing against her fragile faith that she so desperately hoped to nurture. Sea gulls dipped above her, and she pulled her jacket tighter. This lake country was so much cooler than Winona. And here she walked on top of the bluffs rather than looking up at them. She thought of that morning when she'd wanted so much to take the photograph of the fires moving up the bluffs. Mr. Steffes's fall had intervened, but even so, she got the job that changed her life. It had been only three years ago.

She recalled the morning of restoration, which was how she'd come to think of the day her father demanded she speak the truth. She hadn't realized how weighted she had been by her forbidden actions. Now she felt the weight lift.

Grace. She'd been given grace, an unwarranted second chance.

Light reflected on the water, sparkling like diamonds. Above, puffy clouds filtered rays of sun. That photograph she'd taken over Lake Winona of the sunset breaking through the clouds came to mind. She saw the spears of light as signs that she was not alone.

Here she was, walking to work in a new city. She was making her own way. It would be a lovely path to work each day. But there'd be other trails to take too, in Milwaukee, paths that didn't have any connection to the life she'd left behind.

She had to do what was right; she had to do it on her own.

She stopped to watch two boys lift red and yellow kites into the air, watched them rise ever higher in the increasing warmth. She knew the Author of this plan, the One who deserved gratitude for allowing her to turn prohibited love into this: a new beginning.

She'd meet with Mrs. Johnson and propose actions she'd thought of on the train. Then she'd decide about her living arrangements. Everything didn't have to be done in a moment. She was strong enough to go slowly. She would hesitate before she leapt this time, be certain of her source, and so guard her heart. She waved at the boys with their kites. Better yet, she stopped. She took out her Graflex and was about to take a shot of the boys unraveling their kite strings when a mourning butterfly flitted by, then landed just a foot from her, moving its white-trimmed gray wings back and forth on a red rose. She heard a boy shout. She looked around. They played, nothing more. No one needed her attention. She turned back to the butterfly. The lighting was perfect. She felt her heart fill up with joy as she snapped the shutter.

Timing and Lighting

This photograph was my first taken in the Johnson Studio. I discovered while developing it what Mr. Bauer so appreciated about a studio portrait. The child became more than what she was, the way a great story can become greater than its writer or a magnificent statue overtake its humble sculptor. Certainly it wasn't I who made this child look like innocence. It was the light and shadow, the exposure, the setting, everything rolled into one. And the timing, of course. Maybe not perfect timing, but close enough to make me think of this subject as without guile.

Her mother had cut her hair because the girl had gotten into pitch and smeared it in her long locks, and it proved impossible to remove. They'd tried turpentine, butter—"good butter too," her mother had said—but nothing worked, and so they'd trimmed it out.

A natural wave formed. The mother

said her daughter's hair had always been straight as a clothespin and just as stiff. But after they cut it, soft curls capped her head without the use of the iron, a treasure appearing as the result of something otherwise unwanted.

The lighting, natural from the studio window, brought out the side of her face so one eye is seen clearly and the other is in shadow. The girl had an injury to her right eye, so I posed her with focus on the left side of her face. In developing it, I dodged the area behind her to bring more light where I wanted it. I like the effect, with the viewer's eye moving to where it should go. There's a smile on the child's face, a sweet smile that always makes me wistful when I look at her image.

The timing was perfect. Even though the portrait had been scheduled weeks before, when the girl's hair was long, they decided to take the picture anyway after the fracas. They'd been pleasantly surprised by the results and told me so. I was pleased. So was Mrs. Johnson.

I also made the background in the

portrait soft. And I asked the child, Pearl was her name, to look down. I placed a flower in her hand, but you can't see that. Her narrow little shoulders, bare as the day she was born, hold her steady and true. The pose reminded me of the one Mr. Bauer took of Winnie when she was three. There is blamelessness in the child's face. Purity. Innocence.

The poet Lord Byron calls innocence "the unbounded hope, and heavenly ignorance." I read that at the library. Milwaukee has more than one. I admit, I read dictionaries and little short pieces like poems because my mind otherwise seems to wander over words in long books. I'm more patient with pictures.

Byron's unbounded hope makes perfect sense to me, and I see that in the face of this child. Hope. But heavenly ignorance, no. We are closer to heaven when we are born, I believe, and walk away from it throughout life, even while we may confess to be walking toward it and wonder why we keep doing things that separate us from it. Distance. Perhaps that's what Byron meant: that when we are made new, when we are innocent once again, our trails of wrong turns point us back to what is good. Maybe we become ignorant of heaven's judgments. Or perhaps, as we begin again, take that second chance, we return to the hope of innocence no longer bound by fears of judgment. We act out of love instead of fear. I made such a turn and, with my family's help, hope to sustain it.

All things come in due time, my father says, or they were not meant to be.

I kept a copy of this print, and Mrs. Johnson placed it in the window, framed in smooth wood. A little piece ran in the Milwaukee Journal *about the photograph and my new association with the studio. I sent the article to my family.*

A letter arrived soon after from Mr. Bauer. I was afraid to open it at first, wondering why my family would have shared the article with him!

But I was strong enough now, and I opened the letter.

"Congratulations, Miss Gaebele," he

wrote. "Mary Harms sent me the article about your fine portrait. I'm pleased at the success of my student."

My portrait was nothing so grand as what he'd done recently. I'd read about his latest work in the photographic journal I subscribed to. He had made an enlargement of Bishop Cotter for the literary society in Winona. It must have been a fabulous portrait. Thirty by fifty inches. Practically life-size. He'd generously offered it to the society. It must have taken him hours in the darkroom. I worried about the poisoning, but perhaps Voe did that work now. And it wasn't my place to worry.

The remainder of the letter shared stories I might not have heard from my family. Robert grew well; Winnie enjoyed school. Russell had taken an interest in the camera. And J. R. Watkins had passed away. "Remarried last September and died in December. Life is fleeting."

He also said that Mrs. Bauer's health was much improved following a visit to Rochester. I was grateful he mentioned her and his family because it made the *letter platonic, simple words expressed to a colleague. Still, I debated about whether to write him back. He understood my dream to become the photographer I am, but he was also a part of my nearly destroying the joyous possibilities.*

I looked at this fine photograph—and I think this one of Pearl is that—and remembered something Mr. Bauer told me in my training: the source and understanding of light marks a portrait master. I held that thought close, ever grateful for the lesson, hoping always to reflect that learning in my life.

⊱—⊹—◦—⊹—⊰

A Flickering Light is the first book in the series Portrait of a Woman. Look for *Shimmering Grasses* from WaterBrook Multnomah Publishing Group in the spring of 2010 to learn more about what happens to Jessie and her family. The publisher and author thank you for making room in your heart for these stories.

AUTHOR'S NOTES AND ACKNOWLEDGMENTS

A Flickering Light was inspired by my grandmother, a photographer's assistant who traveled and worked as this novel portrays in Winona, Minnesota, and many other places in America's heartland. Winona is the city my mother was born in. I was named for my grandmother, Jessie, though it was said she didn't like her name because in the nineteenth century *jessy* was used as a swear word. So I was given the name Jane as a derivative; we share a middle name. I say this story is inspired by her because this is a work of biographical fiction, or as a writer friend of mine, Linda Crew, calls such novels, "a true story, imagined."

My aunt Fern Griffin, Jessie's oldest child, was a lover of stories and genealogy. Fern is the aunt who, when preparing to move, wrote on some boxes: "Books I have only read once." A true reader and a gifted writer, Fern wrote short stories and captured many of her mother's memories on paper that she later sent to me. It was her love of genealogy and self-publication of a family story that formed many of the details of this work of fiction. I am deeply indebted to her research and her writing. We often exchanged letters and phone calls about her mother, my grandmother. I wish she had lived to see my version of a family story.

In the 1980s, when Jessie was in her nineties, three of her children and their spouses interviewed Jessie and made copies of those audiotapes for family members. I treasure them and listened often to hear the cadence and lilt in her voice, which expressed her independent spirit. She had opinions. She also had talents, including photography, an unusual occupation for a woman at that time. Corinne Kronen, her youngest child, also answered tons of questions and let me speculate about what might have been. She shared family information, such as Roy's fall or Selma's singing. Corinne and her husband, Ron, also made copies of photographs and documents and written remembrances that added greatly to this novel and to the one to follow. I deeply appreciate her allowing me to speculate and explore. My aunt Helen, wife of Jessie's son, Stanley, also shared memories, photographs, glass negatives, and documents with me, for which I'm grateful.

I thank the staff of the Sherman County Library in Moro, Oregon, who located that 1913 copy of *The History of Winona County,* compiled by Franklyn Curtis-Wedge and others, and acquired it through the University of Minnesota. This reference book proved invaluable; I'm grateful for it and other materials they made available. My sister-in-law Normadine Kirkpatrick introduced me to the treasures of eBay and the items I collected from the St. Louis World's Fair of 1904, the July 1907 issue of *Woman's Home Companion,* and the 1910 *Home and Household* edition of *The Library of Knowledge* edited by Francis Neston Thorpe, PhD, LLD (which offered remedies for every kind of ailment, insect management, and home furnishing for the period). My paternal aunt, Idella

Rutschow, remembered hearing Selma sing and had a few other stories of the region as well. I'm grateful for her good memory at the age of ninety-two.

My brother and sister-in-law, Craig and Barb Rutschow of Red Wing, made trips with me to find our roots in the Cream valley, located photographs, and shared stories. Her sister and brother-in-law, Curt and Bev Youngbauer, made it possible for us to visit the original homestead in Cream and gave me a place for Voe's wedding to occur. At various times throughout the writing, Barb sent me "landscape images" of the season, reminding me of the nearly thirty years I lived in the Midwest, restoring my sense of the countryside and the small treasures that keep Minnesotans warm through long winters and grateful for spring. My family at home, Matt and Melissa, tended the homestead while Jerry and I researched and when I wrote; Kathleen and Joe Larsen and family in Florida sent words of encouragement; friends Blair and Kay, Judy, Gabby, Carol, Sandy, Loris, and Susan, and nieces Arlene and Michelle gave prayers and sustenance as needed. Carol Morrison, friend, psychotherapist, and writer extraordinaire, especially shared insights about passion, fear, and self-sabotage that offered possible motivation for Jessie's actions. I'm grateful to them all.

Despite the wonderful help of others, this is my version of my grandmother's life, and I'm responsible for any errors about it or any other mistakes related to photography, the everyday lives of people in Winona between 1907 and 1910, or other factual data presented. Often two people who attended the same event remember it differently, and so it is with family stories. These are my memories woven into Jessie's life and history, and I hope it brings alive the actions she took and the difficulties she had to deal with because of those choices.

I learned of the availability of digitized articles of the *Republican-Herald,* a Winona newspaper, from writer Dianne Gray. Compiled by Winona State University, the collection provided invaluable information about the rare tornado,

Mrs. Bauer's work with the Ladies Aid Society, Jessie's sleigh-ride parties with her sisters, F. J. Bauer's awards, his photograph of President Taft, the double exposure, activities on the North Dakota ranch, and best of all, an article revealing that Jessie did come to own her own studio—but those details come with the rest of the story. The mention of other studios and businesses in Winona, the baptism at Levee Park, as well as the Harms family and the Johnson Studio mentioned near the end of *A Flickering Light* are authentic parts of the historical record.

The Winona County Historical Society staff was wonderful! They provided me copies of city directories so I could see where people lived, who lived with them, their occupations, and just how close the library was to the Bauer Studio, among other things. They answered my strange questions about cycle liveries and streetcars, and archivist Marianne Mastenbrook even found an avid reader, Audrey Gorney, to review the manuscript. I am indebted to Audrey, the society, and especially Marianne.

The Buffalo County Historical Society of Wisconsin and the Buffalo County clerk helped us locate original farms and the Herold Cemetery where my great-grandparents are buried and made our journey to walk there an adventure.

The images that make up the sequence of photographs referred to as "Subjects," "The Pose," "Exposure," "Setting," and "Timing and Lighting" are from the family collection. It was always believed that these were photographs (glass negatives) taken by my grandfather, but that was before my discovery that Jessie owned her own studio. On the audio interview tapes, we learned that she did photographic work herself in addition to retouching and coloring, but she did not mention being an owner. Newspaper records report not only the purchase of the studio but also her work within it. In this novel, I've ascribed the photographs to Jessie and given them her voice of explanation.

Among Jessie's personal artifacts given me when she died was the red glass cup from the St. Louis World's

Fair with the Gaebele name inscribed on it, an elegant green glass vase, many glass photographic plates, ledger books, sheet music, a tied quilt, a list of coloring pigments she used in coloring photographs, and several postcards, including one from *D. Henderson* urging resolution of a complaint. Through these disparate objects, family stories, and my imagination, I hope I've told a true story worthy of her faithful life.

Jessie did grow up near Cream, Wisconsin, not far from the Mississippi River (and as it happens, not far from where my father grew up and where he met my mother). Jessie's parents were dairy farmers until, because of her father's health, they moved into Winona, where he ran a drayage business. Roy, her brother, did struggle with stuttering said to be related to a basement fall. He loved music and plants and as an adult supported himself as a jeweler and entertained us by playing his Hawaiian guitar. Lilly worked for the Stott Glove Company of Winona and later in the drapery section at a department store in

Minneapolis. She did have strong feelings about Jessie's employer. Selma was a milliner for Lottie Fort and with her beautiful voice sang duets at the Winona Immanuel Evangelical Church and, later, on the radio with "Cowboy Jim."

Jessie was trained by F. J. Bauer, who hired her and another young girl when Jessie was fifteen. He was married to Jessie Otis, and they had four children together, three of whom survived. Stories of Mrs. Bauer's fragile health were shared by her family members, and I'm indebted to Molly Bauer Livingston Hanson (one of Robert's daughters) and Patricia Bauer Butenhoff (Russell's daughter) for sharing their stories. Other events and stories were provided by my own memories and my brother (Craig Rutschow), my sister (Judy Hurtley, before her death in 1997), cousins Joanne Krejca and Barb Strand, especially. Having written fourteen novels based on other people's ancestors, I also gained immense appreciation for those in the past who have allowed me to write their stories. Exploring who I am through who

my grandmother was brought me personal insights and a degree of sadness I
could not have anticipated.

Jessie was an adventurer. My brother
took her up on a Ferris wheel at the Minnesota State Fair when she was in her
nineties, something she loved to do. I
remember her climbing the sand dunes
of Florence, Oregon, while on a trip to
Oregon. She even took off her whalebone corset to don Levi's jeans so we
could pick blackberries together on our
Wisconsin farm when I was in my teens.
She did like to go places, and her profession before she married was to manage photographic studios when the
principal photographer was waylaid by
mercury poisonings or other circumstances. She did this work throughout
Wisconsin and Minnesota and later
North Dakota, also part of the rest of
this story.

It appears from the record that she
made decisions that probably brought
her heartache, but she also kept finding
ways to redeem herself, to restore her
integrity, and make the best of things as

she learned the importance of forgiveness and starting again. Even as a widow later in life, her daughters remember her riding the streetcars and later buses to the end of the line and back. Traveling, even a short distance it seemed, allowed her to put her life into perspective and restored her hopeful outlook. Her involvement in the Joyce Memorial Methodist Church in Minneapolis strengthened her faith, and she transferred that love to many of her grandchildren, who have gone on to become pastors, missionaries, writers, musicians in service, and loving parents. In business and as family members, they reflect her abiding faith and commitment to community.

On the occasion of my second marriage, to a man sixteen years my senior, when some expressed that he was too old, it was my grandmother who advised me that age had nothing to do with love. "If you love each other and trust in God, you'll do just fine," she told me. And so Jerry and I have these thirty-two years. She was a kind and loving grandmother, and she is missed.

I express gratitude to a number of people who made the publication of this fifteenth novel possible, including editors Erin Healy and Shannon Hill of WaterBrook Multnomah Publishing Group / Random House. Their insights and gentle suggestions and their love of story contributed greatly to this book. The fine editorial and production staff there, especially Laura Wright, continue to serve these stories well. To sales and marketing and publicity, distributors and retailers, and everyone in between who brings these stories into readers' hands, I'm grateful. Thanks go to my agent, Joyce Hart of Hartline Literary Services in Pennsylvania, for sticking with me. I hope this story has the hopeful ending that, as I do, she so enjoys.

I'm forever grateful to have shared this part of my early life with Jerry. I'd be lost without his map making. His years as a naval photographer were invaluable as I tried to understand the profession my grandmother had chosen.

To my readers, who have willingly traveled with me through the Pacific

Northwest for years, some to Florida too, I thank you for journeying to the heartland of America and to the roots of who I am.

I've been writing this story forever and began by thinking it had contemporary application for women today, who work shoulder to shoulder with men, who have seen relationships fracture without necessarily being restored. I find relevance in exploring how the men and women who get caught up in poor choices make meaningful lives of the consequences. But as the story unfolded, I was led to also explore why a woman with such gifts and talents would make decisions that seemed to undermine her desires. The Norse word from which we receive *to read* means "to unveil a mystery." I hope I've unveiled a bit of Jessie's mystery (and my own) by showing a route Jessie took as she spiraled into sorrow. I hope I've suggested ways in which many of us who make such choices can begin to tell ourselves the truth. Most of all, I wanted to give readers a woman who was human, who made mistakes, and who found her way to grace.

Jane Kirkpatrick

⊱┈◈┈○┈◈┈⊰

Reader groups may request a phone visit with Jane through her Web site, www.jkbooks.com, or by contacting her at 99997 Starvation Lane, Moro, OR 97039.

DISCUSSION QUESTIONS

At prearranged times, the author makes herself available by speakerphone to answer questions and participate in book group gatherings. She's done this from the Netherlands to Nebraska, from Florida to the Pacific Northwest. Arrangements can be made through her Web site at www.jkbooks.com. The use of this guide is not a prerequisite for such phone gatherings.

1. In the author's own notes prior to writing this story, she described her attitude toward *A Flickering Light* this way: "This is a story about integrity, wholeness, the blend of soul and role in order to fulfill God's promise in our lives." Did she accomplish that goal? Why or why not?

2. What did Jessie Ann Gaebele think she wanted? What got in her way of achieving that? Or did she achieve her goal? What role

did her being a woman in a man's profession play in the arc of her story?

3. What does Emily Dickinson's poetic line "Tell all the Truth but tell it slant" have to say about this novel? How do the lines "The Truth must dazzle gradually / Or every man be blind—" apply?

4. How did a sense of unworthiness affect Jessie's decision making? What role did grief play? How did her sense of self affect the outcome of this story?

5. Who in this story deceived themselves the most: FJ? Mrs. Bauer? Jessie? What truths did they have to tell themselves in order to change the paths they were on? Did they? Why or why not?

6. Do you know gifted people who appear to sabotage or squander their talents? What kinds of actions by others can bring them back, or must one make such a journey alone?

7. Have you ever acted in ways that were contrary to your own self-

interest? What might have motivated you? What lessons did you learn from that experience?

8. People engaged in clandestine activities often justify their thinking. A common thread of thought is, *No one else is being injured by my actions.* In this story, who was adversely affected? Is there anything these people could have done to change their own destinies?

9. How can we offer compassion to people we love who make poor choices, without preventing them from discovering their own truths? Has there been a time in your life when someone spoke the truth with less dazzle so you could see it?

10. What role did artistry play in the lives of these characters? For whom did a particular art form (such as music, textile creation, and photography) provide direction? How?

11. What do you think of the definitions of faith, hope, and love of-

fered by Edward Everett Hale at the beginning of this novel? Did the characters portrayed act in ways that demonstrated those "three eternities"?

12. While most of the story was told in third person, through the eyes of Jessie, FJ, and Mrs. Bauer, what role did the first-person accounts and photographs play in your experience of this story? Did their presence distract, or did you look forward to what the next photograph would reveal about Jessie's life?

13. *A Flickering Light* is based on the story of the author's own grandmother. Does that knowledge in any way shape your reading of the book differently than a novel that is formed of fully imagined characters? Were you aware of this prior to reading *A Flickering Light*? Does the timing of that awareness change your perspective on this story?

Books by Jane Kirkpatrick

NOVELS

Change and Cherish Historical Series
A Clearing in the Wild
A Tendering in the Storm
A Mending at the Edge

A Land of Sheltered Promise

Tender Ties Historical Series
A Name of Her Own
Every Fixed Star
Hold Tight the Thread

Kinship and Courage Historical Series
All Together in One Place
No Eye Can See
What Once We Loved

Dreamcatcher Collection
A Sweetness to the Soul
(winner of the Western Heritage Wrangler Award
for Outstanding Western Novel and Literary Oregon
100, Best Books about Oregon published in the past
two hundred years)
Love to Water My Soul
A Gathering of Finches
Mystic Sweet Communion

NONFICTION

Aurora: An American Experience in Quilt and Craft
*Homestead: A Memoir of Modern Pioneers Pursuing the
Edge of Possibility*
A Simple Gift of Comfort (formerly *A Burden Shared*)

4/14